MW00768083

This book is dedicated to all parents who have lost a child to S.I.D.S. Sudden Infant Death Syndrome and is dedicated in memory of my older brother,

Richard Jonathan Earl

who died at nine weeks of age, March 3, 1944

ACKNOWLEDGEMENTS

My heartfelt thanks to all who labored so diligently with me in making this book possible. A big thank you to Karen Melton, Margie Simmons, Linda Engle, and Bonnie Turner for the countless hours you spent editing the book for me. I appreciate your hard work, and love you all very much.

Special thanks also to my husband, Ron, for his research efforts and his patience.

~~~
~~~

CHAPTER 1
A NIGHT TO REMEMBER

Lydia carefully set Grandma's delicate china back on the polished shelves of the old hutch and closed the glass doors.

"I'm glad that's finally done," she murmured to herself. She picked up the small can of fine furniture wax and snapped the lid on tightly. Standing back from the small dining room table, she admired her finished project. The old hutch gleamed under the new coat of wax. Someday, maybe they'd have enough money to buy a new hutch. She smiled, thinking about the growing list of new things she was going to buy for their little home ... someday when they could afford it. She sighed and collected the pile of dust rags that lay in a heap on the floor and stuffed them in her rag bag in the corner of the kitchen. She stood quietly for a few minutes, absentmindedly cleaning the wax from underneath her fingernails. My hands are a terrible mess, she thought, holding them up in front of her. It's all this cleaning I've been doing lately.

The small clock on the far wall in the living room chimed the hour and pulled Lydia from her daydreams. Doug would be home from the sawmill soon and she needed to check on supper. The chicken stew that was simmering on the wood cook stove filled the tiny house with a mouthwatering aroma, making her stomach growl. She laughed and patted her rounded waistline. "Just be patient," she said aloud, chuckling to herself. "I've never forgotten to feed you yet." Tomorrow she'd tackle washing all the windows and maybe scrubbing the floor if her strength held out. She wanted everything sparkling clean, or at least as clean as she could possibly get it before their first child came into the world. Her mother planned on coming to help her for a few days after the baby was born and she certainly didn't want her to think she never cleaned anything. She stirred the thick stew and replaced the heavy lid with a bang, thinking about how much their lives were going to change in the very near future. She suddenly could not resist the urge to sneak one more peek at the precious baby gift that arrived just this afternoon from Doug's mother. For the past few months, her mother-in-law had sent a colorful variety of knitted and crocheted booties, blankets and sweaters. Lydia hurried through the living room into her bedroom and picked up the tiny light blue sweater with matching cap and booties. She fingered the tiny booties and smiled to herself. Sitting on the edge of the bed, she sighed and pressed her nose into the folds of the soft sweater. Just two months more, she thought happily.

She stretched her long frame out across the bed and thought about all the names she and Doug had picked out and argued over the past few months. They had finally agreed on Aaron if the baby was a boy and Rebecca if a girl. Even though they had argued about what to name the baby, they had agreed early on that it should be a Bible name. She smiled, thinking about her husband. He was just as excited about becoming a parent as she was. They had been married a year and seven months, and she had never been happier in her life. He was a wonderful husband, a hard worker, loving and faithful, and she just knew he was going to be the world's best daddy as well. She closed her eyes and allowed her mind to picture life a few months from now. By Christmas, their baby would be three months old and wouldn't Doug be proud to hang a tiny stocking over the fireplace? She smiled, just imagining his happy, grinning face.

Thunder rumbled in the distance. It was hot and sticky this afternoon. The usual mountain breeze had failed to come up today and the air was heavy with the scent of rain. Lydia wiped the perspiration from her forehead and pushed herself back up into a sitting position. Mr. Lawson, the mailman, had predicted rain this afternoon, as he had every afternoon all week long. She hoped he was right today. They desperately needed the moisture. She placed the tiny baby clothes back in the box and headed back to the kitchen to set the table. She picked up her makeshift fan, a sturdy piece of cardboard, and fanned her sweat-streaked face. It was becoming increasingly dark outside. She looked nervously down the dusty road toward town, hoping to catch a glimpse of her husband walking home from work. It was oddly quiet this afternoon. She could usually hear some of the neighborhood children out playing this time of day, but the road meandering down the hill past their house was deserted. Lydia watched, fascinated, as a sudden gust of wind swirled dust into a mini tornado. It briefly followed the road, then abruptly switched direction and spun through an open field, snatching up grass and small weeds in its wake. She jumped and stifled a scream as lightning struck nearby, immediately followed by peals of deafening thunder. Standing in the middle of the room, Lydia watched with apprehension as the wind began to blow in earnest, raising clouds of dust that settled in fine rows on the windowsills. The willow tree outside the living room window began thrashing its lacy fingers wildly on the ground. Again, lightning struck close by. Lydia hurried to the kitchen and slammed the back door closed against the sudden storm. Poor Doug, she thought. He's going to be caught out in this. I hope he stays in town until it blows over.

Without further prelude, huge drops of rain began pelting the tin roof of their home. It was as if the thick, dark clouds had been stretched to their limit and could contain their contents no longer. Louder and louder the din became until she was forced to cover her ears. She ran to check all the windows when suddenly the roar overhead became deafening.

Marble-sized hailstones began bouncing wildly around in the yard. She stared wide-eyed as the hail began stripping the trees of their tender new leaves. The wind began to howl, smashing a torrent of rain and hail against the back door. Lydia stared dumbfounded at the pool of muddy water that rapidly began seeping under the door. Another crack of lightning jerked her back in motion and she snatched up the bag of cleaning rags and stuffed several tightly under to door. She glanced out the window just in time to see her clothesline poles snap like small twigs and disappear into the melee, dangling the wire in grotesque shapes around the base of the maple tree in front of their house. Large sections of tin blew by the window like so many sheets of paper. The windows rattled alarmingly in the gale and threatened to break as the hail pounded them unmercifully.

"God, please protect poor Doug," Lydia cried aloud, though she couldn't hear her own voice. "Watch over him and keep him safe." She stifled another scream and instinctively ducked as another bolt of lightning hit something with a deafening explosion.

Suddenly, she could smell smoke. Her eyes widened in terror as she looked wildly around the room. Something was on fire!

"Oh God, no!" she screamed. The violently blowing rain, mixed with hail, completely obscured her view outside. She huddled in the doorway between her small kitchen and living room. "Oh Doug," she moaned. "Doug, come home ... I need you. Oh God, please ... please...." She slowly rocked to and fro, hugging her body protectively with her arms.

The wind abruptly lessened somewhat, and she rose from her crouched position, looking fearfully around the room. Nothing seemed to be burning, yet she could still smell the pungent odor of smoke. Peering through the window, she was finally able to see some of the destruction outside. The willow tree was nearly stripped bare of its branches and leaves. Piles of muddy sleet were stacked several inches deep. Rivers of dark, rushing water flowed through the yard, down to the fields below the house. She watched, mesmerized, as a parade of strange, unidentifiable objects floated by the window, seemingly anxious to continue on their journey to some obscure, unknown place. Her clothesline was gone, as were the large galvanized washtubs she had hanging on the back porch. She went to the kitchen window and looked down the driveway at the old carriage house.

"Oh no!" she cried, her hand flying to her mouth. The old building was flat on the ground. The rising water was carrying huge sections of it across the driveway and on down the road to only God knew where. Lydia was thankful that the old buggy house had been empty except for a woodpile they kept stored there for the fireplace and cook stove. They didn't even own a buggy, much less a car. She turned to inspect the living room and, to her dismay, heard the unmistakable pitter-patter of water hitting the floor. Her shoulders slumped in defeat and exhaustion as she reached for her mop bucket. Where was Doug? Her anxiety grew with each passing minute.

So much for washing windows and scrubbing floors tomorrow, she thought dismally. I'll be lucky to keep a river of mud and water from washing my entire house away. She sat down with a thud and listened to the steady ping, ping, ping as the leak grew in size and intensity. The wind and hail had finally stopped, and the rain had lessened to a steady downpour and was now falling at a much calmer pace. Thunder rumbled again in the distance, warning folks in the next valley of what lay in store for them. Lydia had never seen a storm that fierce come up that fast. She sat lost in thought, watching the muddy water as it soaked through the roof and spattered into the bucket below.

She jumped up and nearly knocked her chair over as she heard a tremendous crash at the kitchen door. Running to the kitchen, she saw Doug's foot in the doorway as he pushed and shoved, trying to open the door against the pile of sodden rags on the floor.

"Wait a minute, honey!" she cried, as she dragged the soggy lump away from the door. The door swung open, and there stood her husband, drenched and bleeding. She sprang into his arms with a cry of alarm and relief. He was alive!

He folded his aching, cold arms around her and held her for a moment, breathing hard. He felt her body tremble before he released her.

"Hail nearly killed me," he muttered, wiping his bleeding forehead with his soggy handkerchief.

"Doug, oh Doug!" Lydia managed to gasp. "I was so afraid for you … I was…." She stopped short and stared wide-eyed at his bleeding forehead. "Honey, your head, what happened to your head … and you're soaked. Are you hurt bad?"

"Just a flesh wound … nothing serious," he assured her, wiping his head again. "Get me a towel, would you, sweetheart?" he asked, wincing in pain as he wiped his face. Lydia wrapped his head in a strip of clean, white cloth, handed her husband the towel, and then stooped to help him out of his muddy boots and dripping clothes.

"Road's washed out in several places," Doug finally managed to say after he had wiped his face and neck. "I've never in all my days seen it storm like that around here. If I hadn't just lived through it, I would never have believed it!"

Lydia shook her head, tears forming in spite of her efforts to keep them at bay. "The old buggy barn is gone," she said softly.

"Mmmm," Doug nodded. "I saw that, and so is part of our chimney. Looks like lightning might have hit that end of the house. Probably hit the chimney and…." He couldn't finish. His voice broke as he scooped his young wife up into his arms again.

"I was so afraid for you, honey," he said, as he pressed her tightly to his own body and felt the slight kick of his unborn child. "Thank God you're all right," he murmured, stroking her hair, "and the baby too."

The emotion that Lydia had been holding back burst forth at that moment. "I … I prayed … for you … too," she sobbed. "I was absolutely terrified … you'd be struck down … by a tree, or hit by lightning … or … or something." She began to cry uncontrollably. Doug pulled her close once again and held her until the storm within began to subside. He buried his face in her hair and breathed in her sweet fragrance. That's when he heard the steady drip, drip, drip in the living room. He groaned and looked up at the ceiling.

"Guess I'd better get up there and see if I can fix the roof," he said wearily. "No tellin' what I'll find up there."

"You get into some dry clothes first, and I'll fix you something to eat," his wife said, suddenly remembering the chicken stew on the stove. She dried her eyes and ladled up steaming bowls of stew while Doug struggled into a dry shirt and a clean pair of pants.

The gash on his forehead had stopped bleeding, so he pulled his makeshift bandage off and sat down to a hearty meal. He grinned at his pretty wife. "Don't worry honey," he said. "I'll have us fixed up in no time at all. The roof won't be hard to fix, and I'm sure I can repair the chimney, given a little time and a few new bricks. I'm glad it's summer … we don't have to use it right now." He winked at her and grinned. "We'll be good as new in a few days … I promise."

Lydia nodded and smiled back. "Guess I'll have to take some of the money I've been saving for the baby, and get a couple of new washtubs and more wire for the clothesline."

Doug nodded as he wolfed down his second piece of cornbread.

"Maybe we'll find your old ones. Got to have washtubs and a clothesline with a baby coming, that's for sure." He smiled at her, his dark brown eyes twinkling.

She watched him as he ravenously downed a second bowl of stew. That was just one reason why she loved this man so much. He always saw the bright side of every situation. No matter how black the world looked, Doug Wheeler managed to see hope just around the corner.

She had never seen him mad, or even upset a single day that she had known him. She fervently hoped and prayed their child would inherit his sunny disposition. What a wonderful father he was going to be for their children. Tears sprang into her eyes again and she quickly lowered her head so that Doug wouldn't see them.

"Thank you, Lord, for the best cook on the mountain," he said loudly when he had finished his meal. "And for making her so cute to boot," he added as he bent down to kiss her. Lydia laughed and rolled her eyes at him while he donned a clean pair of socks and jammed his feet into his Sunday shoes. He was whistling as he briskly walked outside to fully assess the damage to his home. She cleared the dishes from the table and put a pot of water on the stove to heat so she could wash them. She wiped the cornbread crumbs from the table and reached for the kerosene lamp, when a sharp, searing pain tore through her body.

"Oh!" she cried, grabbing her stomach. She leaned against the sink to catch her breath. Must have been the stew … didn't agree with me, she thought as the pain eased and finally dissipated altogether. She straightened up cautiously and decided it was probably nothing. She poured the steaming water on the dishes and let them soak for a minute. Lighting the lamp, she carried it to the table and glanced again at the hutch with pride. It sparkled, even in the dim lamp light.

Doug found his ladder beneath the pile of rubble of what, just three hours ago, had been the old carriage house that he and Lydia had nicknamed the buggy barn. He lugged it back up to the house and climbed up to see what damage had been done to the roof and chimney. Several pieces of tin had been blown loose, and a number were missing. The chimney was toppled over on one side. Red bricks, blackened with soot on the inside, lay scattered over the roof and down on the ground below. He made a mental note of the supplies that he would need to make the necessary repairs. All in all, it wasn't nearly as bad as he had suspected it might be, however, it would more than likely take most of what they had managed to save for the baby. Doug sighed and slowly descended the ladder. He drew a deep breath and surveyed the yard. Deep gullies had been gouged in the soft earth around the house itself. Thick mud was piled up in the strangest places. Hope I can find my shovel, he thought. He would also have to devote some of his time and join his neighbors in fixing the washed out road.

Most of the mountain people living near them had a horse and buggy for transportation, and a few of the older, wealthier folks had a car. Neither would be of any use for a few days until the road was made passable again.

Doug set the ladder on its side and kicked the thick mud off his good shoes.

"Sure is a mess outside," he said, as he came back inside the kitchen. "I'm going to need some money for supplies, but the good news is that everything is fixable. I just need the time to do it."

Lydia didn't comment but nodded her head. She hung her damp dishtowel up on the nail when the pain hit again, this time even harder. She gasped and grabbed the side of the sink for support. Doug stared at her, his mouth hanging open.

"What is it, honey … what's the matter?" he asked, his mouth suddenly as dry as cotton. He grabbed her arms to help support and steady her.

"I don't know," she gasped, her face turning white as the pain reached a peak and then slowly began to subside. "I feel rather sick."

The color drained from Doug's face. "Is it … is it the baby?" he stammered.

His wife nodded her head. "Maybe," she whispered, "but I'm not sure. I guess you'd better go get Doc Sorenson."

Doug licked his lips and swallowed hard. He turned her to face him. "He can't get up here unless he walks," he said, his voice sounding flat and strangely unfamiliar. He helped ease her into a chair at the table. "Maybe it's just something you ate, honey," he suggested hopefully. "It's too early to be the baby, isn't it?"

She smiled up at him and nodded. "You're probably right … just something I ate didn't agree with me."

The gravity of their situation hit both of them at that instant, and they stared wide-eyed at one another.

"Just the same, I'm going to run and get Mrs. Baker and see what she thinks."

"All right," she said, struggling to her feet. Doug helped her to the bed and pulled off her shoes.

"Don't do anything while I'm gone, babe," he said, beads of sweat forming on his worried brow. "Just stay right there, and I'll be back in about fifteen minutes."

Lydia giggled nervously. "I'm not going anywhere, honey."

Doug tore through the house, nearly tripping over a chair in the kitchen, the screen door slamming with a bang behind him. He ran his fastest, struggling through the deep mud that threatened to remove the shoes from his feet. He charged up the hill, sliding on the slimy, wet grass, and darted in and out of small stands of trees. When he reached the top, he could see smoke slowly rising from the Baker's kitchen chimney. Thank God they were home. He bolted down the hill, leaping over fallen logs, nearly falling headlong into a small ditch that still ran with water. He chided himself for his clumsiness and raced on. When he finally reached the Bakers' front door, he was completely out of breath. Pounding his fists on the heavy beams of the door, he made short, gasping sounds in a feeble attempt to call out the occupants of the home.

Somewhere at the back of the house, a dog began to bark excitedly. Mrs. Baker herself opened the door and stared at him.

"Why, Mr. Wheeler, do come in," she said with a smile and stood to one side. It was then that she took in the sight of his muddy shoes and mud-caked clothes. "Is … is everything all right? Something wrong?"

Doug chose that very minute to have a coughing fit and could do nothing more than helplessly shake his head and cough. Muddy water began to pool around his feet on the front porch.

"Barbara Ann, get Mr. Wheeler a glass of cold water," she yelled to her oldest daughter. Doug gulped down the water and squeaked his thanks to the young girl.

"It's my wife … can you come and take a look at her?" he finally managed to gasp. "I think the baby's coming."

"Oh dear!" Mrs. Baker exclaimed. "I've never birthed a baby before. You need to get Doc Sorenson up here for that."

"I can't right now. The road's washed out in several places, and he's nearly three miles away. Can't you please come and stay with Lydia for a bit and tell us what you think? Please Mrs. Baker … I beg you…." His voice trailed off into a near whimper. "Please, ma'am. We're wasting precious time," he said, wringing his hands.

The heavyset woman drew a deep breath and bit her lower lip.

"Max!" she yelled over her shoulder. She waited for a reply, and when none came, she blew out a loud sigh of resignation.

"Barbara Ann, go tell your father that I'm going over to the Wheelers' for a little while. You get the little ones ready for bed, you hear?"

"Yes, Mama," the young girl replied as she disappeared into the back of the house.

"Oh thank you, ma'am," Doug whispered and started coughing again.

Mrs. Baker yanked her apron off and tossed it over the back of a chair.

"Where's your buggy?" she asked, as she glanced around the front yard.

"I don't have a buggy ma'am," Doug replied apologetically. "I ran all the way here."

"In all this mud?"

"I'm afraid so." Doug looked embarrassed and worried at the same time. "I'm sorry…."

The older woman sighed again and gathered up her billowing skirt. "Lead the way, Mr. Wheeler," she said.

"Call me Doug," he said, once they were under way, walking at a brisk pace.

"Doug, it is," she said with a smile, offering her hand. "I'm Georgia. Guess when I was born, my Daddy wanted a boy so bad he would have named me George if Mama hadn't stopped him."

Doug chuckled. "Pleased to meet you, Georgia. I'm surely beholden to you for this."

The pair struggled up the muddy slope just as dusk was falling. A single dim light shone faintly through the small window of the Wheelers' home in the valley below. Doug had the sudden urge to pick Georgia up and run down the hillside to his house with her in his arms. He grabbed her hand to help support her. "Watch your step," he warned. "It's pretty treacherous going down." She slipped and slid all the way to the bottom of the hill.

"That was quite a ride!" she panted, wiping her muddy shoes on the soaked and matted grass outside the back door of the Wheeler home.

"Yes ma'am, it was," Doug agreed, impatience rising in his voice. He yanked the door open and stomped his feet hard.

"Lydia, honey! I brought Mrs. Baker … Georgia back with me." He quickly ushered the woman into the dimly lit bedroom.

"How are you doing, sweetheart?" he asked anxiously, grabbing his wife's hand. Lydia opened her eyes and smiled at them.

"All right," she said rather nervously. Doug introduced her to their neighbor.

"How far along are you, honey?" Georgia asked.

"About seven months … maybe seven and a half." Another sharp pain seized her body just then, and she arched her back, gasping at its strength. Doug turned deathly white and clung to the bedpost.

"How close are the pains coming?" Georgia asked the young woman when the pain had subsided.

"I think about five to seven minutes apart."

Georgia looked at Doug, pulled his hands free from the bedpost and nudged him toward the door.

"Go boil me some water … lots of water," she said. "I need to wash my hands and I also need soap and some fresh towels."

Lydia uttered a sharp cry of pain again and began twisting the bed covers in her hands. Doug wrenched himself free of Georgia's grasp and ran to the bed, hovering over his wife.

"Do something!" he hissed in Georgia's direction. "Please, for the love of God … *do* something!"

"I'm tryin', Mr. Wheeler," the woman said with a note of exasperation in her voice, "but like I told you at my place, I've never birthed a baby before in my life. I've had six of my own but never helped bring one into the world this way. Do you understand what I'm saying?"

Doug straightened up and looked frantically at her. "What are we gonna do?" he asked in a pitiful voice. "I'm begging you, ma'am…."

"What we're going to do is this," she said in a suddenly stern voice. "First of all, you're going to get me that hot water and some soap. Then you're going to gather up all the clean towels you can find. I've helped my husband bring lambs and calves into this world before and this can't be that much different," she said, more for her own benefit than for Doug's.

He numbly obeyed and hurried out of the room in search of towels. Georgia scrubbed her hands and put on a clean apron she found in the kitchen.

"Bring an extra lamp in here," she ordered as she hurried back to the bedroom. "We're going to need plenty of light."

Lydia moaned loudly again and resumed twisting the edge of the sheet in a futile attempt to ease the pain.

"Breathe deeply, honey," Georgia advised. "And try to relax between the pains."

Doug set the lamp and extra towels down on the table beside the bed. Georgia glanced at him as he fumbled with the matches. His hands were shaking, and his face was the same color as the bed sheets.

"You all right?" she asked, noting the good-sized gash on his forehead for the first time. "Maybe you'd better sit down out in the living room."

Doug mumbled something inaudible and backed out of the small, stuffy room and collapsed into his chair. He buried his head in his hands and moaned softly, rocking back and forth. Georgia didn't know which of these two young people needed her the most. They were both in a bad way. She closed the door quietly and went to check on her patient. The pains were coming hard and fast now. This baby was determined to make an appearance tonight. She felt sure of that.

Time and again, Doug started into the bedroom but changed his mind. He couldn't bear to see his wife in so much pain. He couldn't stand hearing her groans of agony. He flopped down into his big chair again and prayed. Finally the door flew open and Georgia stood there, looking hot and weary.

"Is it over?" Doug asked hopefully, half-rising from his chair.

Georgia shook her head. "No, it's not over yet," she said, "but she's progressing nicely. You should have a baby by morning."

"*By morning!*" Doug gasped. "It's only half-past twelve. How long do these things usually take?"

Georgia drew a deep breath and exhaled slowly. "I don't know exactly ... there's really no hard and fast rule, especially with first babies, but it could be somewhere between twenty-four and thirty-six hours."

"*Twenty-four hours!*" Doug whispered hoarsely. He looked as though he might faint.

Georgia smiled sympathetically and patted his hand. "Thought I'd fix us some coffee," she said, as she headed for the dark kitchen. "You look like you could use some."

Doug followed her into the kitchen and lit another lamp. He sat down at the table and watched the older woman bustling around in the kitchen. He felt numb and powerless to do anything to help her. She sat down across from him and placed her hands over his.

"It's hard the first time around," she said with a smile, "but you'll get used to it. Next time, it won't take this...."

"*Next time!*" Doug exploded, interrupting her. "There's never going to be a next time, I can promise you that right now!"

Georgia laughed heartily and patted his hand. "Believe me, Doug, you'll change your mind when you hold this baby for the first time. There's nothing like it in the world."

A loud, piercing cry from the bedroom shocked both of them to their feet. Georgia hurried in and closed the door behind her. Doug gulped his coffee and burned the inside of his mouth. He slammed the coffee cup down hard on the table, sloshing a fair portion of the hot liquid over his right, clenched fist.

"Agggh!" he cried in anguish, wiping his hand dry on his pants. Next time indeed! He couldn't imagine going through this again or putting Lydia through this much pain again for anything in the world. Gulping a glass of water down to soothe his burning mouth, he began pacing back and forth in the tiny living room and finally slumped back down in his chair in exhaustion. How had his mother gone through this four times? How had his dad managed? Matter of fact, he thought dismally, how does any couple survive something like this? He heard Lydia's continued loud moaning, and Georgia's muffled voice filtering through the closed door. Twenty-four to thirty-six hours!

"Oh Lord, have mercy," he prayed fervently, wiping his weary face with a sweaty palm. "I can't take another hour, much less twenty-four!"

Doug's eyes flew open and he leaped to his feet. What was that noise? He listened intently before taking a step forward. All was quiet in the room behind the closed door. Had he drifted off to sleep? His mind seemed fuzzy and refused to work properly. His heart was pounding so loud that he couldn't even hear the ticking of the clock. What was it that he thought he had heard? He must have fallen asleep and been dreaming. He glanced at the clock and was shocked to see that it was almost 5:00 a.m. He rubbed his tired eyes and strained to hear something … anything beyond the closed bedroom door. He decided that he had indeed been dreaming when the door opened suddenly, and there stood Georgia holding a tiny bundle wrapped in a soft blanket. Doug blinked stupidly at her.

"Mr. Wheeler," she said softly, "meet your new son."

"My son?" he said, bewilderment showing on his face. "*My son! I have a son?*"

Tears that had been threatening all night long now coursed unhindered down his tired face. "My son!" he exclaimed for the third time, a smile spreading across his handsome, unshaven face. He quickly wiped his eyes with the sleeve of his shirt.

Georgia smiled wearily at him. "Your wife is doing just fine … she's sleeping right now. Why don't you hold this little fellow, and I'll go clean things up a bit."

Doug dropped back down into his chair and reached for the baby. He pulled the soft blanket back and stared down into the most precious little face he had ever seen. He had a son!

Georgia patted his shoulder and ambled out to the kitchen to heat some water. "How 'bout a cup of coffee?" she asked over her shoulder. "Are you hungry? How does eggs and toast sound?" She was not surprised when he didn't answer.

Doug listened to the barely audible sucking sounds the baby was making and smiled through tears that were very near the surface again.

What a night this had been! The worst storm to hit these mountains in decades, and now … and now, a few short hours later, he had a son who arrived two months early! Funny, he thought. A few minutes ago, I felt like I hadn't been to bed in over a month, and now … now I couldn't sleep if my life depended on it. I'm on top of the world. He bent to kiss the baby's soft, velvety cheek.

"Welcome to the Wheeler family, little Aaron," he said softly. "Your Mama and I love you very much." He studied every detail of his son's tiny face. What a perfect round head he had. What a perfect little mouth ... just like Lydia's. His hair, what there was of it, was the color of spun gold, also just like Lydia's. Doug thought his heart would burst. God was so good.

"Georgia," he croaked, "how can I ever thank you?"

The good-natured woman laughed heartily. "I have to admit it, I was pretty nervous in there, but I'm actually pretty proud of the job I've done. Guess I could become the mountain midwife."

"Indeed you could," Doug agreed. "We're naming our son Aaron George ... the George is after you."

Georgia beamed her thanks at him as she handed him a cup of steaming coffee. The clock struck 5:00 a.m., but neither of them felt like sleeping. This had surely been a night for remembering.

CHAPTER 2
WINTER INTRUDERS

The summer days of 1923 were hot and sultry with evening showers, but nothing like the storm that swept through the town of Northridge, and the surrounding community the afternoon of July 16th. Lydia knew she would never forget that particular day in July as long as she lived. The terror of that one afternoon brought about the birth of her new son six weeks earlier than they had expected him. She gazed lovingly at the plump sleeping baby. He would soon be two months old.

Doug had joined forces with several of the community's able-bodied men and young boys and had done his share of the road repair. He had helped Max Baker, Georgia's husband, repair his fence and hen house, and Max in return had helped him with roofing repairs and the rebuilding of their chimney. All in all, things were getting back to normal.

Lydia's garden had grown nearly as fast as the weeds, and now only the late summer squash needed her attention. She hurriedly tied a bonnet on her head and headed outside to do some weeding while little Aaron took his nap. A blue jay scolded her noisily as she began her work. She and Doug had planted squash, green pole beans, sweet corn, onions, tomatoes and turnips. She was proud of her very first attempt at gardening. She glanced around at the puffy, white clouds that were steadily building in the west. Maybe they'd get some more rain today. She sighed contentedly and picked up her hoe.

"Lydiaaaaa!" someone called from the top of the hill. Lydia straightened up and shaded her eyes with her free hand. Who was that coming down through the trees? She leaned on her hoe and watched until she made out the plump figure of Georgia, her daughter, Barbara Ann, and the baby of the family, Peter, who was just six months old.

"Hi there!" Lydia called out happily when they were within hearing range.

"We thought we'd drop in and say hello," Georgia said, panting as she shifted the weight of her baby to her other hip. "How are you all doing?"

"Just great," Lydia said with a smile. "Hi, Barbara Ann."

The young girl smiled and looked bashful.

"Please, come in and have something to drink."

Georgia and Barbara Ann followed Lydia into the small kitchen and settled themselves at the table. Lydia pulled an extra chair up to the table and poured homemade lemonade for her guests.

"How's the baby?" Georgia asked.

Lydia smiled. "He's growing like a little weed. He's asleep right now, but he should be up soon."

"They do grow fast," Georgia said with a smile. She smoothed her baby's thick hair from his forehead. He grinned a sideways, toothless grin at Lydia and drooled, soaking the bib he was wearing.

"He's almost crawling," Barbara Ann said shyly.

"Really!" Lydia exclaimed. "Doesn't take long, does it?"

"No, it doesn't, and I for one hate to see him start crawling," Georgia said with a short laugh. "Seems like once they start crawling, then in nothing flat, they're walking and then running and getting into everything."

The chubby baby squealed with delight as Lydia ran her fingers quickly up his leg and tickled him.

"Ssshhh!" Barbara Ann warned him. "You'll wake up Mrs. Wheeler's baby."

The three of them laughed as Aaron, at that very moment, made his presence known from the back bedroom.

"Speaking of Aaron...." Lydia said over her shoulder as she disappeared into the bedroom and scooped up her infant son. "We have company, dumplin'," she murmured, kissing his warm, soft cheek.

"Lord have mercy!" Georgia exclaimed when she saw the baby. "Look how this youngin' has grown. Why, he's already nearly as big as my little Petey here." Little Peter stared at the baby and smiled. "One of these days, you boys can play together," Georgia said to her son.

"Wouldn't that be great if our little guys became best friends?"

Lydia nodded her head in agreement. "Would you like that, Aaron?"

Georgia handed Peter to his sister and stood to straighten her dress.

"Look at me!" she exclaimed. "I'm a perfect mess!" She smoothed out the wrinkles of her skirt and wiped her forehead with a hankie.

"Are you about to get back to normal at your place, what with school starting and all?" Lydia asked her neighbor. "How are the kids doing in school so far this year?"

"Terrible!" Barbara Ann offered. "It's not nearly as much fun this year as it was last ... and it's still too hot to go to school."

Lydia nodded in agreement. "I can just imagine how warm that small room must get when it's full of kids."

"We need a new school, that's for sure," Georgia added. "Too many kids this year for one room. Maybe by the time these two are ready to go, we'll have a new one with more room."

"Wouldn't that be nice?" Lydia agreed.

"Nice for them but too late for me." Barbara Ann wrinkled her nose and made a face, showing her disdain for the idea.

Both women laughed. "Poor baby!" Georgia teased.

Barbara Ann grinned and bounced her brother on her knee.

"Isn't it nice to have the road fixed again?" Lydia asked, changing the subject. "I didn't think they were ever going to get finished with it."

"I was afraid they might finish just in time for another flood and have all that work to do over again," Georgia said, her normally happy, smiling face pinched into a deep frown. "I guess this last storm did a lot more damage than we had first thought."

Lydia studied her friend as she sipped her lemonade. She decided that Georgia must have been quite beautiful when she was younger. She still had a pretty face, even when she was frowning. Even though she was heavier and had several strands of gray running throughout her short auburn hair, Lydia thought she was still quite attractive. She and Georgia had become fast friends since the birth of Aaron.

All too soon, the visit was over. Georgia is the sweetest person I know, she thought to herself as she collected the drinking glasses and carried them to the sink. She watched them as mother and daughter disappeared over the crest of the hill. I'm so lucky to have such a wonderful neighbor. What on earth would Doug and I have done without Georgia the night Aaron was born, she wondered. She stood lost in thought for a few minutes, recalling the events of that night. Aaron's fussing jolted her out of her reverie.

There was a definite change in the air, very subtle at first, but noticeable. A delicious crispness to the morning, and a mild pleasant balminess about the noonday heat. Lydia looked around her. The corn had been harvested, and she had canned dozens of jars of beans and tomatoes. This had been a good year. Their small cellar was full of potatoes and assorted vegetables, and if Doug got lucky during hunting season, no matter how harsh the winter, they'd be all right. Doug had been busy all summer and on weekends, cutting and stacking firewood for the coming winter.

Mother Wheeler was coming for a brief visit to see her new grandson. Lydia hummed a little tune to herself as she mopped and scoured the kitchen, making everything spotless. Doug's father had died of the dreaded influenza in 1918, leaving Louise Wheeler to raise her children on her own. Lydia had never had the chance to meet him, but Doug assured her she would have loved him. Max and Georgia had sent over an old army cot for Doug to sleep on while his mother was visiting. Lydia had done her best to make a comfortable bed of sorts over in the corner of the living room. Doug would be happy sleeping on the floor or even down in the cellar, she thought as she plumped the bed pillow for the hundredth time. What a wonderful guy I married.

Lydia washed the bedding, the curtains, scrubbed the windows and floor, and polished her good glasses and the few pieces of silver that her grandmother had given her when she and Doug were married. Everything was finally ready for the big day. Doug was going to fetch his mother at the train depot in Newton, seventeen miles away. Jack Doss, Doug's boss, had graciously offered to lend him his car for the trip.

"Do you know how to drive a car?" Lydia had asked, a worried frown on her face. "I've never even seen you in a car."

"Sure," Doug replied quickly. "There's really nothing to it. Just shifting and steering."

Saturday dawned bright and clear. A slight frost covered the ground and made the few green things that were left in the garden sparkle. Lydia kissed Doug good-bye and watched as he quickly strode down the road and out of sight. He said he'd be back by 11:00 this morning, she thought as she glanced at the clock. That will give me time to feed Aaron, give him a bath, and straighten up the house one last time. The morning passed quickly, and Lydia finished the chores she'd planned to complete before her mother-in-law and husband returned home. She sat nervously watching the clock and the road. It was after 11:00, and Aaron would need to be fed again pretty soon. She glanced out the window and thought she could see dust rising in the direction of town. Maybe that was them coming now. She waited. Little Aaron began to fuss. She picked him up and headed to the bedroom to change his diaper. He cooed and smiled at her, and she kissed him for the millionth time.

Where were Doug and his mother? The clock struck 12:00 noon. She fed Aaron and burped him. She didn't want him to be fast asleep when his grandmother saw him for the first time. The baby yawned and began to fuss. She had no choice but to rock him to sleep and tuck him back into the cradle beside her bed. She fixed herself a bite of lunch and decided she would try to read for a while. Curling up in Doug's big chair, she tried to focus her eyes long enough to read.

Suddenly, a car door slammed somewhere. She struggled out of the chair and picked up her book that had somehow fallen to the floor. She glanced in the mirror and discovered to her horror that her eyes were swollen with sleep and her hair was a mess. She quickly smoothed her hair and looked out the window. Doug was helping his mother out of Jack's shiny, black car. That's when she discovered that her left leg was numb. She frantically tried to beat some feeling back into it, to no avail. She limped and half-dragged her tingling leg across the kitchen floor and flung open the back door.

"Mother Wheeler!" she exclaimed loudly, too loudly, as she held the door open for them.

Frances Louise Wheeler, who preferred to be called by her middle name, was a tall, angular woman, with graying hair that she pulled tightly into a small knot at the nape of her neck. She had piercing blue eyes that seemed to look right through Lydia from time to time. Her mother-in-law was a no-nonsense woman who rarely smiled. Doug's sunny disposition must have come from his dad's side of the family, she thought.

"Hello Lydia. Where's my new grandson?" Mother Wheeler asked with just a hint of a smile.

Lydia smiled. "He's taking his afternoon nap." Her leg was beginning to throb. What if she fell down right in front of Doug's mother? She dismissed the thought and tried wiggling her toes. The pain was becoming unbearable. The senior Mrs. Wheeler was chattering about something as Doug clawed her bags out of the trunk.

"Come on in, Mother," he said, stopping to kiss his wife as he walked through the doorway. "Sorry to be so late, honey," he murmured. "Mother's train was late getting in to the Newton station, and then we had a flat tire on the way home." He carried her bags into the bedroom and dropped them on the bed. Aaron stirred in his cradle, lifted his head up and began to wail.

Louise Wheeler rushed into the bedroom. "Oh, you precious little angel," she crooned. "You couldn't wait to see your grandma, could you, sweetheart?"

Lydia rolled her eyes. "Mother, would you like something to drink?"

Doug's mother ignored the question and sat down with the baby in the rocking chair, the very one that she had rocked her own son in, and began to inspect her grandson. "You've got your mother's eyes and nose," she said, "but your daddy's feet. Land of Goshen … look at those big feet!" The baby smiled up at her and cooed. "Oh," she crooned again. "You precious little angel."

Lydia glanced at her husband, who was standing off to one side, a big grin plastered on his face. She smiled as she watched him, thankful that her leg was finally beginning to feel normal again.

"Have you and Mother had anything to eat?" she asked as she slipped her arm around his waist.

"No, we haven't," he replied, "and I'm hungry enough to eat a full-grown bear all by myself. How about you, Mother, are you hungry?"

"So-so," she replied and dismissed them both with a wave of her hand. "I'm just thankful I made it here alive."

The next few days were crowded and hectic in the tiny Wheeler household. The senior Mrs. Wheeler had fully briefed the junior Mrs. Wheeler on the do's and don't's of child rearing. On more than one occasion, Lydia had bitten her tongue hard to keep from saying what was on her mind. Finally, the last day of her visit came, and Doug had packed his mother into Jack's car again for the trip back to Newton.

"You kids simply must come for Christmas," she was saying as she kissed Lydia and the baby good-bye. "Honestly, Doug, please think about it. I could send you the train tickets and ... it's really not that far. Please promise me that you'll both think about it."

Lydia nodded her head and hugged Aaron tightly to her as a gust of cold air blew around the corner of the house.

"Better get my little angel in out of this cold air, Lydia," Louise called to her daughter-in-law as Doug started the car. "I sure don't want to hear that he's been sick."

Lydia stood defiantly rooted to the spot and watched as Doug drove slowly down the driveway and disappeared down the road in a cloud of dust.

"Her little angel!" Lydia said sarcastically under her breath. "I believe you're *my* little angel." She turned and walked back into the house. Thank the Lord that was over!

The blustery days of autumn passed quickly, and all too soon, the first snow came. Lydia was out hanging diapers on the clothesline when she heard Max and Georgia's kids with some of the other neighborhood children on their way to school. They were having the time of their lives throwing snowballs at one another as they raced down the hill toward town. Lydia smiled. It wasn't that long ago that she herself had been one of those kids, on her way to school, looking forward to Christmas and Christmas vacation. She pinned the last diaper on the line and noticed that the first few had frozen solid. Maybe the sun would thaw things out later.

Her days had been busy since Mother Wheeler's visit, getting her house back to normal and taking care of her husband and son. Doug had been busy the past three months as well, carefully rebuilding the old buggy barn to house their wood supply for the winter. She was proud of him. There was nothing that he couldn't do or couldn't fix. He had great plans for next year's garden. It was going to be bigger and better than last year's. He had built wooden boxes in which to store their vegetables down in the cellar, but the project she was most proud of was a new crib for Aaron. He had outgrown the tiny cradle weeks ago, and Doug had gone to work, lovingly fashioning "the pen" as he had referred to it.

She and Doug had decided … or rather Doug had decided that they would stay home for Christmas. He had given her some pretty phony reasons, but she knew that his pride wouldn't let him accept tickets from his mother. He had made the decision, but it was up to her to let Mother Wheeler know. Lydia sighed and picked up her wicker clothes basket and hurried into the warm kitchen. She'd better get busy and write her mother-in-law the bad news. She wouldn't like it, Lydia knew, but there really wasn't much she could do about it. She finished her laundry and decided today had to be the day that she'd compose the letter. First of all, she'd have to think up a believable excuse. Why did Doug leave all of that to her? She sat down at the table, pen and paper before her, and drew blank after blank. She started the letter with general news, still thinking about what she was going to say when her fountain pen decided to empty itself right in the middle of her stationery. Lydia groaned and wadded the paper into a ball. Stupid pen, she thought. Guess I'm going to have to get a new one. She started again. Dear Mother, she began, when again, the pen leaked ink, soaking through to the tablecloth.

"Oh no!" she cried, thoroughly disgusted now. "I'm throwing this thing in the garbage."

A sudden, rapid knocking on the back door startled her, and she jumped up to find Mr. Lawson, the mailman, who had trudged through shin-deep snow to deliver a letter to her with his usual flourish.

"Letter for you folks," he said with a smile, his breath puffing out little white clouds of mist. He pulled it out of his bag and presented it to her as though it was an award.

"Come in and thaw out, Mr. Lawson," she invited as she accepted the letter. She recognized the handwriting almost immediately. It was from Doug's mother.

"Can't today. Got lots more mail to deliver before my day is over," Mr. Lawson said, tipping the bill of his small cap in her direction.

Lydia quickly tore open the envelope and sat down to read the letter.

My Dear Ones,

My, how time flies. It seems like only yesterday I was visiting with you and now here we are staring Christmas in the face. Where does the time go? I hope my precious angel is in good health and growing. How I would dearly love to see all of you again. I know I invited you for Christmas, however, something has come up, and I'm afraid I'm going to have to withdraw my offer. I hope this doesn't interfere with your plans too much.

Carl, Peggy, and the children have invited me to come and stay for a month at their place, and well, after much thought, I've decided to take them up on their offer. They have plenty of room now, so I won't be in the way. The children are looking forward to spending Christmas with Grandma, and I'm sure it will be fun. I do hope this doesn't cause any problems for you. A Christmas package will arrive shortly.

My love to all, Mother

Well, that was certainly nervy, Lydia thought. She invites us to her home for Christmas but gets a better offer and withdraws her invitation. She reread the brief note, and then sighed with relief. She wouldn't have to write her letter after all.

"Thank you, Lord, for all your blessings," she said aloud, as she gathered up her stationery and put it away. Now she could relax and plan a simple family Christmas with just the three of them. She wondered briefly if Doug would be disappointed. She sat thinking about Christmas when she realized that it had started snowing again. She grabbed her basket, threw her shawl over her head, and dashed back outside to the clothesline. Her fingers were numb by the time she had pulled all the clothes and diapers off the line and jammed them into the basket. She would have to dry them as best she could by the fire. She glanced at the wood stacked on the back porch and decided she'd better get some more in. This storm might last longer than a day or two. Throwing her basket of frozen clothes on the kitchen floor, she stopped briefly to listen for Aaron. All was quiet, so she closed the door and drew her shawl tightly over her head and back. Filling the little wagon that Doug had made from salvaged junk, she pulled it to the back porch and unloaded it. This is going to be Aaron's job one of these days, she thought. On her way back down to the buggy barn, she noticed bright, red stains on the snow. Bending over, she examined it closely.

"Oh my goodness!" she exclaimed out loud. "That's blood!" Looking around, she saw nothing but snowflakes swirling in every direction. That's funny, she thought. I didn't hear any kind of struggle down here. Something must have been hurt or killed while I was unloading the wagon. She headed back to the barn for a second load. She had just begun tossing chunks of wood in the wagon when she heard a vicious snarl. Whirling around, she peered into the back of the barn. It was dark, and at first she could see nothing. Then, suddenly, the ugly, bloodstained head of a full-grown wolverine appeared, growling menacingly at her. Lydia stared at the advancing animal and froze. What should she do? She grabbed the small wagon and tipped it on its side. She wanted to keep something between her and this ferocious beast. The animal took several threatening steps toward her, snarling viciously. Slowly, she inched her way out of the barn, keeping her eyes fastened on the creature in front of her. She instinctively grabbed several good-sized sticks of wood as she left the entrance of the barn. Her breath was coming in short, painful gasps. The wolverine kept its eyes locked on her, advancing all the while.

"Scat!" she screamed, her voice sounding strange and oddly high-pitched. She threw a large chunk of wood in the direction of the animal. The sudden noise and movement temporarily confused it. The wolverine stopped and sniffed at the wood. It then turned, as if going back into the barn, when suddenly, without any warning at all, it turned again and charged her, running full speed straight for her. Lydia screamed and threw her armload of wood at the beast. She turned and fairly flew through the deep snow up to the back porch and into the house. She slammed the door and stood leaning against it, shaking from head to toe. Aaron was screaming at the top of his lungs. She dropped her shawl on the floor and pulled soaked shoes from her frozen feet. She cautiously looked out the window. The wolverine was nowhere in sight. She ran to the bedroom and snatched up her son.

The sudden movement startled him, and he redoubled his crying efforts. She hugged him tightly to her breast and sank down on the edge of the bed. Rocking back and forth, she burst into tears and sobbed with him. It was dark and cold in the house when she finally ventured out into the living room to stoke the fire and light the lamps. Why did nothing like this ever happen when Doug was home? Her thoughts turned to her husband, and she began to worry about him walking up on the hungry wolverine like she did. She was greatly relieved when she heard him stomping his boots off at the back door.

Doug listened white-faced as his wife recounted the day's events a few minutes later. "We're getting a dog … a hound," he said with finality. "A good hunting dog won't let anything like a wolverine on the property … guaranteed. I'll ask in town tomorrow and see if anyone has a dog they'd like to part with. Jack will probably know someone I should talk to. He knows everything and everybody in town."

Just to put Lydia's mind at ease, Doug took his rifle down to the buggy barn and gathered up the strewn wood. The wolverine was long gone, but he definitely saw evidence of it having had a meal there.

"A dog is just the ticket," he assured his wife over supper that night. "A dog will be good for Aaron too. Dogs and boys go together. In the meantime, young lady, I don't want you going any farther from the house than the clothesline. You let me get in all the wood from now on, do you hear? I don't want you going down to the buggy barn for anything. I'll make sure that you have plenty of wood on the back porch."

Lydia nodded her head and kissed her husband. "What would I ever do without you, honey?" she asked.

"Hopefully, you'll never have to find out, my dear," Doug said. "Incidentally sweetie pie, I'll bet that old wolverine was as scared as you were. Looks like you put up a pretty good fight yourself. I never saw so much wood laying around down there."

Lydia knew that he was teasing her, but despite all the willpower she could summon, her eyes filled with tears.

"Come here, babe," Doug said tenderly and pulled her down into his lap. "I'm real proud of you, sweetheart. You're real level-headed under fire." He kissed his wife tenderly and dried her tears with his handkerchief. "My brave little warrior," he whispered.

Lydia laughed and blew out the lamp.

CHAPTER 3
THE VISITOR

Christmas was over all too soon, and a parade of dark winter days stretched out ahead like an endless ribbon. Lydia was already tired of being cooped up in the house all day, and she longed to get outside, breathe some fresh mountain air, and start her garden. She tried her hand at crocheting but soon lost interest. There was, however, plenty of work to be done with feeding Aaron and dealing with the mounds of diapers and baby clothes that needed to be scrubbed and somehow dried.

She looked wistfully at the garden area, now covered with a fresh blanket of snow. She sighed and turned her attention again to the seed catalog that Doug had brought from town. Maybe she could have a small flower bed this spring. Even the thought of flowers brightened her mood. A sudden, frantic scratching at the kitchen door made her jump. She opened it a crack to admit Rusty, their seven-month-old red hound that Doug had brought home from town one day last week. Just as Doug suspected, his boss knew of an old farmer in Brighton who raised good hunting dogs on his farm. He suggested that Doug give him a call and see if he had any left from the last litter. The old man was happy to get rid of the runt of the litter and told Doug the dog was his if he could come and get it. Doug had gone the same day and happily brought the pup home.

"Poor little guy," Lydia said, bending down to scratch his cold head. "It's cold out there, isn't it, boy?" The small red hound looked up at her with doleful eyes. "Why don't you get in your doghouse … you crazy hound? You'd stay a lot warmer if you'd stay out of the snow."

In response, Rusty shook his red coat free of water and snow, showering Lydia and the kitchen.

"Rusty!" she scolded loudly, backing away from the dog. "Stop that right now!"

The dog began sniffing out the kitchen and living room, investigating every nook and cranny, pausing only once to sit and scratch behind his left ear. He raced into the bedroom, scattering small rugs in his wake. Jumping up on the side of the crib, he sniffed the air. Aaron sat up and looked sleepily at the busy nose that was thrust through the slats of his crib. He began to cry loudly. "Ooooooow!" Rusty howled, tipping his head straight back. The more the baby cried, the more the dog howled. Lydia rushed over to Aaron and lifted him up into her arms, his blanket trailing on the floor.

"It's okay, sweetheart," she soothed, trying her best to comfort her son. "Rusty, stop it right now!" she scolded.

He stopped and jumped up on her, nearly knocking her over backwards. She shoved the puppy down and scolded him again. Aaron stared at the dog and smiled. Spying the forgotten blanket on the floor, Rusty lunged for it and snatched it up in his mouth. Lydia grabbed for a corner, and a serious game of tug of war ensued.

"Rusty, let go!" Lydia demanded. However, the dog had other plans, shaking his head vigorously in an effort to loosen her grip. Aaron began to giggle ... until the blanket ripped nearly in half.

"Now look what you've done!" Lydia cried, releasing her hold on the soft blanket. "It's ruined. I hope you're happy, Rusty. You now have a new blanket to put in your doghouse."

The dog dropped his end of the blanket and looked at her with what Lydia later swore was a big grin on his face.

"You're sopping wet," she murmured to her son. "Time to change you." Laying the baby back down in the crib, she reached for a clean diaper and nearly tripped over Rusty who, once again, had his nose jammed between the slats of the little bed.

"Brother!" she cried. "Instead of having one baby, I now have two. Rusty, get down."

Suddenly, the dog turned and tore back out into the kitchen, scattering the rugs once again. He let out a mournful wail and then began baying. Aaron looked wildly at his mother and began screaming. What under the sun was wrong with that crazy dog? Lydia wondered. She picked the baby up and hurried to the kitchen to see what had triggered all the noise. That's when she heard the loud knocking at the kitchen door.

"Quiet, Rusty!" she yelled. Who on earth could that be on such a cold, windy day? She opened the door to Rodney and Bess Jamison, the local pastor and his wife. Rusty leaped up to give Mrs. Jamison a wet greeting on her face as she bent down to pet him.

"Oh my!" the stout woman sputtered, wiping her face with her gloved hand. "That was quite a hello."

Lydia yanked the young dog back into a sitting position and scolded him again. She then apologized to the older couple as she invited them into the living room. Rusty followed close behind, sniffing the ankles of the newcomers. Pastor Jamison laughed and scratched the dog's ears.

"Where on earth did you get this little fella?" he asked, rather amused.

Lydia sighed. "Doug thought we needed a dog around here and brought him home one day last week. I'm afraid he takes almost as much care as Aaron does," she said, smoothing down the baby's fine hair. "Please have a seat and don't mind the mess in the living room. Rusty just sailed through here and made a mess of things."

Bess pulled her gloves off and reached for Aaron. "May I?" she asked, holding out her hands.

Lydia handed her son over to the older woman, who cuddled and kissed him, while Lydia poured some coffee left over from breakfast.

"What on earth brings you two all the way up here on the mountain on such a cold day?" she asked as she set the wooden tray down on the small table in the living room. She handed Pastor Rod a steaming cup just as Rusty jumped up to investigate the interesting smells coming from the tray. His big feet tipped the tray and sent the other two mugs of coffee as well as a small plate of cookies crashing to the floor. Lydia whirled around as the terrified pup ran yelping to the back door.

"You'd better run!" she cried, staring at the mess scattered over the floor. "That dog is going to drive me crazy. What on earth am I going to do with him? Bad, bad boy!" she scolded, opening the back door. Rusty escaped outside and made a beeline to his doghouse.

"I'm so sorry," she murmured, rather embarrassed. The pastor and his wife burst out laughing. Baby Aaron smiled too and clapped his tiny hands.

"In answer to your first question," Rod began, when the mess was finally cleaned up and they were all seated again, "we wanted to get better acquainted with as many families up here on the mountain as time will allow and invite you all to church. I know you and Doug come whenever you can, so Bess and I thought we'd just drop in and see how you were doing."

Lydia nodded and smiled. "I'm glad you did. Not very many people come by to see us."

"I'm sure it must get lonely at times for you," Bess said.

"Aaron keeps me pretty busy nowadays, and of course, as you can tell, Rusty keeps things very interesting. At times, he's actually more work than Aaron is."

The Jamisons laughed and agreed that she did indeed have her hands full.

"Years ago, we had a dog … don't know what kind he was, but we can certainly sympathize with you. We know how much work they can be. I think I came closer to cussing in public when we had that dog than I ever had before or since," Rodney admitted with a grin. "He nearly drove Bess and me crazy for a few months, didn't he, honey?"

His wife nodded in agreement and then giggled. "There were times I wanted to shoot him," she said, still laughing.

"Same here," Lydia admitted.

"Getting back to church," Rodney said with a grin, "we certainly hope to see you folks soon. As you most likely know, we have a small nursery for the baby and we have a young adults' Sunday school class that you'd probably enjoy … so please … do come."

The Jamisons rose to say good-bye after visiting a few more minutes. Bess kissed Aaron and hugged him tight. "I could just squeeze you to pieces," she said before handing him back to his mother.

"See you in church Sunday?" Pastor Rod asked, when they got to the door. "I'm counting on seeing the three of you there."

Lydia smiled and nodded. "If the weather's decent, we'll do our best to be there."

They're such nice people, she thought as she finished straightening up the living room. Why did that stupid dog have to make such a scene while they were here? She added a log to the fire, and fixed lunch for herself and Aaron.

Winter reluctantly gave up its hold on the mountain, and spring finally took center stage. Lydia watched through the window as Rusty, now a full-grown dog, chased a butterfly down the grassy slope behind the house, baying every step of the way. It was hard to tell which had grown the fastest, Aaron or his dog.

They were inseparable these days. Doug had been right, of course. Boys and dogs did go together. Aaron had just started taking a few tentative steps on his own and Rusty, eager to help him practice, repeatedly knocked him down. Though Lydia scolded him, he never seemed to tire in his efforts to help Aaron master the art of ambulation. In just a matter of days, Aaron was literally running through the house with his ever-present companion bounding by his side.

Nearly every afternoon, Lydia worked in her garden while Aaron took his nap. She spaded up the soil, planted the seeds and watered diligently. Rusty, unable to leave those interesting scents of freshly turned earth unexplored, worked just as diligently digging up most of what she had just planted.

"Get out of here," she yelled angrily at him one afternoon. He had methodically "undone" her work for the day. "You stinkin' mutt!" she muttered loudly as he ran with his head down. He flopped down inside his doghouse and watched her intently.

"You're incorrigible … you worthless mutt. For two cents, I'd…." She turned and looked at Rusty who seemed to sense that he'd been forgiven. He raised his head and cocked it to one side, blinking at her with newborn innocence. Lydia laughed in spite of the aggravation she felt. She busied herself with replanting and had just finished her third row of sweet peas when Rusty let out a howl and streaked by her, yipping and howling as he ran.

"What on earth is wrong with that maniac dog?" she said, shading her eyes against the afternoon sun. "Has he completely lost his mind?"

The dog barked and yipped excitedly until he came to an abrupt halt about fifty yards from her. Lydia froze. Her heart began to hammer in her chest. There in the clearing, not far from the house, stood a young mountain lion. Rusty pranced in circles around the good-sized cat, dodging the huge paw that swiped the air in front of him. The lion backed away, arched its back and began hissing at the dog. Suddenly, the cat turned and fled back up the slope into the trees with Rusty just a few feet behind. From the frantic yelping and baying, Lydia knew that he had treed it. She ran to the porch still clutching her shovel.

"Rusty!" she yelled. "Come on, boy, come on home." The baying stopped abruptly and Lydia began to fear that something terrible had happened to him. She strained her eyes, scanning the wooded area where she had last seen him. All of a sudden, he burst through the trees and bounded down the hill with a most satisfied look on his face. He skidded to a stop at her feet and looked up at her as if to say, "Now what do you think of me?" Lydia dropped to one knee and threw her arms around his neck.

"Oh Rusty!" she exclaimed. "I'm so proud of you. Good boy! Good boy!" She patted him and checked him over for signs of injury. Seeing none, she hugged him again. "Good boy, Rusty," she said again. "I'll never call you stupid or worthless again, I promise."

The red hound looked up at her, clearly understanding the warm praise. He licked her hand and ran to get a drink of water. Lydia picked up the rest of her tools and glanced nervously back at the clearing. We need to put up a fence or something, she decided. She stomped the dust from her feet and patted Rusty on the head one more time. "Just stay out of my garden, Rusty, you hear me?"

"He understands exactly what I'm saying," she said to Doug as she relayed the incident to him that evening. "I'm so proud of him … he wasn't the least bit scared today."

Doug, however, was very alarmed when he heard the news of the big cat venturing so close to his home. "They're usually afraid to come close to people," he said with a worried expression on his face. "I'd better let the sheriff know about this … it might have been rabid."

Lydia bit her lower lip. "Do you think Rusty will be all right?"

"Oh yeah," Doug assured her. "I'm sure he'll be fine. I didn't see any signs of a bite or any broken skin anywhere, but just the same, I'm going to let the sheriff know about the cat … just in case." Doug sighed loudly. "Guess I'd better see if Max can help me put up some kind of fence around here.

Much to Lydia's amazement, the red hound did seem to understand. From that day on, he never again ventured into the garden area.

Aaron celebrated his first birthday with a big cake and homemade gifts from the Bakers and both sets of grandparents. He ate his cake while 'Ruffy,' as Aaron called his dog, appreciatively gobbled up the crumbs that fell from his plate. Doug and Max Baker fenced in a small area around the front of the house so that Aaron and Ruffy, as they had renamed him, could play outside during the long summer. The bond between boy and dog grew, and Lydia gradually relaxed and began trusting Ruffy to watch Aaron for her.

It was just after Aaron's birthday that she discovered she was expecting a baby again. She decided to wait for the perfect moment to tell Doug her news. She wasn't sure how he'd take it. Poor guy, she thought to herself with a smile. I think he suffered as much as I did before Aaron was born. At least this baby would be born in the spring, before it got so hot.

Lydia sat one morning at the kitchen table, reluctant to start her work for the day. Aaron was playing with his bowl of oatmeal, dribbling milk over the table, his chair, and the floor.

"Ruffy go?" he asked, looking out the kitchen window.

"He's outside somewhere. Watch what you're doing," she scolded, grabbing his spoon away from him. "What a mess!"

Aaron began to cry, big tears rolling down his cheeks.

"Oh stop it!" his mother said irritably.

"Oooooww!" Ruffy howled mournfully. He stopped and looked at them through the window.

"Look at Ruffy. You made him cry. He's sad when he hears you crying, and now he's crying too."

The little boy stopped crying and stared at the dog. "Ruffy cry."

"Can you make Ruffy laugh?" his mother asked suddenly. "See if you can make him laugh."

Aaron shook his spoon at the dog outside and smiled.

"Oooooww!" Ruffy howled again. Mother and son enjoyed a hearty laugh. Aaron began imitating the dog, and Lydia couldn't help but join in.

All three were howling at the top of their lungs when Lydia heard a loud knock at the front door. She stopped and stared at her son.

"Ssshhh!" she said, putting her finger to her lips. "Somebody's here."

The loud knocking resumed.

"Wonder who in the world that could be this early in the morning?" she said in a hushed tone as she hurried to the door. She smoothed her hair back in place and straightened her apron. Glancing quickly back at Aaron, she pulled the heavy door open.

"Why, Miss Potts! How nice to see you. Won't you please come in?" Lydia gushed, slightly embarrassed.

Ina Potts, one of their neighbors from farther up the hill came down for a visit from time to time. She made it her business to find out what was going on in the neighborhood, the church and the town. Lydia once jokingly told Doug that if not for Miss Ina, she'd never know what was going on around her. Ina never tired of sharing what she had heard or what she thought about people and their problems in the community. The tall, thin woman clutched her purse and ducked inside.

"Hrumph!" she said, glancing sideways at Lydia. "Some people have entirely too many dogs."

Lydia's face flushed a hot pink. "I ... that is, the baby and I ... aahh...." Lydia stammered, trying desperately to think of a sensible reason as to why she and her son had been howling with the dog, but Miss Ina had something better on her mind to talk about. She flopped down in the big chair in the living room while Lydia ran to get Aaron.

"Too many dogs, I say, and speaking of dogs, did you know that skinny school teacher ... oh, what's her name ... Miss Lender, got herself one of those ugly, curly-haired mutts? I don't remember what they call them, but they're sure ugly little brutes. And what in the name of heaven does she need with a dog, I ask you? Gone all day at school, leaving that nasty thing to bark and disturb law-abiding citizens. It'll probably get out one of these days and come up to my place and dig up all my flower beds." She paused to take a deep breath. "I declare, I'm sure I don't know what's gotten into people wantin' so many dogs. They're such filthy beasts. Now what would a schoolteacher want with one? It's beyond me. I don't understand what's the matter with people anymore."

Lydia sat down and pulled Aaron into her lap. "I'm sure I don't –"

"There's entirely too many dogs in this neighborhood," the older woman interrupted. "Used to be a nice, quiet place to live ... honestly, I've never heard such a racket as when I came up your driveway." She shook her head with disgust. "How many mongrels do you folks have now anyway?"

"Only one," Lydia said, her cheeks burning with embarrassment and indignation.

"Hrumph!" Miss Potts said again. "What a racket. Tsk, tsk, tsk," she clucked her tongue in obvious distaste. "I hear the Bakers are lookin' for a bigger place to live. I can't for the life of me figure out why folks aren't satisfied with what they have. Always got to have more an' bigger an' better. It's sinful ... that's what it is. Just plain sinful!" She looked at Lydia with disgust.

"Why do the Bakers want a bigger place?" Lydia asked, thankful that the subject of dogs had been dropped.

"Why, haven't you heard?" Ina asked in surprise. "They're going to have another child ... as if they didn't have enough already. There must be ten or fifteen kids runnin' all over the countryside down there around their place. If it isn't dogs, it's kids. I declare, I don't know what this world is comin' to."

"They have six children, I believe," Lydia said, wondering why Georgia hadn't mentioned this piece of news to her.

"Well, six is more than enough," snorted Miss Potts. "That oldest girl of theirs is nearly big enough to have a family of her own. What on earth are they thinkin' of producing more mouths to feed?" She clucked her tongue again and picked an imaginary piece of lint from her skirt.

"Would you like something to drink?" Lydia asked suddenly, anxious to change the subject. She set Aaron down and scurried to the kitchen to pour what was left of the morning coffee before her visitor could respond. When she returned to the living room, Ina was busy chattering about something else.

"And did you see that dress she wore? Why, you could see right through it! She ought to be ashamed of herself ... wearin' a flimsy thing like that ... and to church too! All the deacons up there a gawkin' at her. I don't know what this world is comin' to." She gulped her coffee and stared at Aaron. "If I was married to one of those no account deacons, believe you me, he wouldn't look more 'n once. What on earth is a woman thinkin' of dressing like that?"

"I'm sure I don't know," Lydia said, wishing she hadn't offered the coffee. She needed to get some work done sometime this morning.

"Ruffy go?" Aaron said, his big, blue eyes searching the window.

"What?" Miss Potts asked. "Did he call me a name?"

"Heavens no!" Lydia laughed. "He doesn't know enough to call anybody a name, Miss Ina. He's just a baby! He wants to know where our dog went."

"Oh! Speakin' of dogs ... you've got the noisiest dog I've ever heard in all my life," Ina said, fidgeting with her coffee cup. "It sounded more like fifteen to twenty dogs out back if you ask me. If you want my opinion, I say we've got entirely too many dogs in this neighborhood right now. They're absolutely takin' over the community. It's disgusting ... absolutely disgusting! It's gettin' to where decent folks can't go for a walk without some huge, smelly beast lunging at them, yapping their heads off. I don't know what this world is comin' to ... no sireeee, I don't."

Oh brother, Lydia sighed quietly to herself. I had to go and mention dogs again. "He's usually pretty quiet," she said, "and he's been great for Aaron."

"I wouldn't have one of the filthy beasts in my home," sniffed the old woman.

Lydia started to tell her about Ruffy chasing away the mountain lion but thought better of it. She would probably have a fit and fall in it if she heard that story. Aaron toddled over to the window searching for his constant companion.

"Have you put in a garden this year, Miss Ina?" Lydia asked, trying desperately to think of a benign subject to talk about.

"Oh yes, of course. I always have a good-sized garden and wind up givin' most of it away. That's my Christian service, you know ... giving to the less fortunate. Anyway, I loaned my brand new hoe to Mr. Hodgkiss ... you know Mr. Hodgkiss way up on the mountain above me, don't you?"

Lydia shook her head. "No, I don't think I've ever met him," she murmured, afraid Miss Ina would start another tirade.

"Well, I loaned him my brand new hoe three months back, and he's yet to bring it back to me. I'm glad you mentioned gardening. I'm just gonna march up there to his house this very morning and kindly get my hoe back. That's some Christian, isn't it? Just helps himself to whatever I have without so much as a thank you. I haven't seen him since." She rose suddenly and clutched her purse close to her side. "I'd best be going," she said. "Good morning, Mrs. Wheeler."

Poor Mr. Hodgkiss, thought Lydia. He's liable to get scalped. She yanked the door open for her guest, hoping that her eagerness to end the visit wasn't too apparent. Miss Potts threw her a sideways glance and muttered something about there being too many bugs in the air this time of year. Didn't know why God didn't do something about it ... after all, that was His department. Lydia closed the door and sighed with relief.

"I was afraid she might stay all day, Aaron," she said, picking up the toddler. "Maybe we could train Ruffy to warn us when she's coming."

"Ruffy go?" Aaron asked again, craning his neck to see outside. His mother laughed as she balanced him on one hip and grabbed up the coffee cups with her free hand.

"Come on, pumpkin," she said, kissing the top of his head. "Let's go outside and find that filthy, noisy beast."

CHAPTER 4
BOYS AND THEIR TOYS

It didn't take Lydia long to find out the truth regarding their neighbors, the Bakers. Georgia, along with her two daughters, Barbara Ann and Cynthia and little Peter came for a visit the very next week. Georgia, her face red from the exertion of hiking over the hill in the hot afternoon sun, gratefully accepted a tall glass of lemonade. She and Lydia sat in the shade out near the garden while the girls played with the two little boys.

"You didn't tell me that you were in the family way again," Lydia accused with a pretend hurt look on her face.

"What?" Georgia exclaimed. "Where'd you hear that?"

"Miss Potts paid me a visit last week and told me that you and Max were looking for a bigger place because you were expecting an addition to your family."

Georgia threw her head back and enjoyed a hearty laugh. "Oh, that's a good one!" she exclaimed, wiping her eyes. "I can't wait to tell Max. He'll die laughin' over that one. Boy oh boy, the stories that get started."

"You mean you're not?" Lydia asked, laughing with her friend, though she had a quizzical look on her face.

"No," Georgia said, "I'm not. However, we are expecting an addition to our family, but not like you think."

Lydia frowned, not understanding. "Would you please make sense, woman! What on earth are you talking about?"

Georgia laughed again. "I can't believe how things get twisted around. We're expecting Max's mother to come and live with us. She's alone now and really needs to be with family, so Max and I talked it over and decided that it would be good for the children as well as Grandma Baker to have her come and live with us. We're only planning to add a new bedroom to the house so that she can have a little privacy."

"Where on earth did Miss Ina get a story like that?" Lydia wondered aloud. "Makes me wonder what else she's been talking about … if you know what I mean."

"Who knows?" Georgia started laughing again. "It's probably all over town by now."

"You're not upset by such false gossip?"

"Naw!" Georgia said, wiping her eyes for the second time. "It's better than some of the stories I've heard in the past. Actually, I think it's pretty funny."

"By the way Georgia, do you and Max know Mr. Hodgkiss, Miss Ina's neighbor?"

"You mean Miss Ina's admirer?" Georgia said, rolling her eyes. "Now there's a story for you! Yes, we know him quite well as a matter of fact. Dear old Russell's been sweet on Miss Ina for years now ... just doesn't have the courage to let her know ... not that I can blame him for that. He's a real quiet man ... comes to church once in a great while. Next time he's there, I'll introduce you. Why do you ask?"

"I just wondered about him. Ina mentioned him the other day when she was here ... said something about him borrowing a hoe from her and never having returned it. She sounded quite angry about it. Said she was going to march right up there and get it back...."

Georgia's hearty laugh interrupted her train of thought. She stopped and looked at her friend. "That's what she'd *like* you to think. The fact is, she's mighty sweet on him too."

"No kidding!"

"I don't know if those two will ever get together, the way they carry on. They're like two scared rabbits. He's extremely shy, and she's everything but."

"Aren't people funny? The way she talked about him, I thought for sure she was going up there to club him good for stealing her hoe. In fact, I felt bad for him. I was wishing there was some way I could warn him that she was on her way. I had no idea they were secretly friends."

"Oh yes," Georgia said with a chuckle. "This has been goin' on for years now. I really doubt that they'll ever do anything about it, and it's really kind of sad ... they're not getting any younger." She shook her head and laughed again. "How 'bout that? Me in the family way again!"

"I wondered why you hadn't mentioned it to me," Lydia said. "I thought for sure I'd be the first to know something like that."

"And you shall, my dear, but hopefully and prayerfully, I'll never have to share that kind of news with anyone again." She folded her hands in mock prayer. "Speaking of additions, how is yours coming along?" she asked, leaning forward in her chair to take in the beginnings of another bedroom.

"Oh, slow but sure," Lydia said. "Doug's been working on it in the evenings after supper every night, and on the weekends when he has time. I hope it's closed in enough for us to use by the time the baby arrives," Lydia said, patting her stomach.

"Baby! What ba … why you little stinker!" Georgia exploded. "You haven't said a word about this … lettin' me go on and on about my false rumor when you have genuine news yourself. When's this one due?"

"Not until the end of March. Keep your calendar free in March, Georgia," she kidded her friend.

"Oh no, you don't!" Georgia said loudly, a big grin on her face. "No sirreee … not again. You get Doc Sorenson this time. Leave me out of your plans on this one. I don't think Doug and I could survive another night like that last one. By the way, how did Doug handle the good news?"

"He was really surprised at first, and looked rather alarmed, but I think he's had time to think about it, and, well … he's really pretty excited about being a daddy again. We're really hoping for a girl this time, and I'm keeping my fingers crossed and praying that this one won't come two months early like Aaron did."

"You an' me both," Georgia agreed. "Maybe Max and I can come over and help with the walls and roof when you get that far on the new room, but don't count on me for anything else beyond that. You'll like Doc Sorenson, Lydia. He's really a good family doctor. Have you been in to see him yet?"

Before Lydia could answer, Peter and Aaron toddled up to their mothers, sweat streaming down their dirt-streaked faces.

"Where's your sisters?" Georgia asked her son. He shrugged his shoulders and ran to the end of the porch.

"Barbie Ann … Cineee!" he yelled in the direction of the woods. "There are!" he exclaimed, pointing his chubby finger. He grinned up at his big sisters as they approached the house.

"Are you girls excited about your grandmother coming to stay with you?" Lydia asked.

"Oh yes!" Barbara Ann said. "We always have so much fun when Gram is with us. We get to help Daddy with the new room, and Mama said we could help her pick out material to make some curtains for the windows."

"I think that's so nice," Lydia said, smiling at the girls. "I never got to know my grandmother very well. She lived down south, and we never went to see her, and she rarely came to see us. She was really a stranger to me. You girls are really very fortunate."

"Gram makes super great pies too," Cynthia added, licking her lips. "Her best pie is apple, right, Mama?"

Georgia nodded her head.

"Daddy told us that Gram could have our room, and we get to move into the new bedroom when it's finished," Cynthia said, her dark eyes dancing. "It's even gonna have a fireplace in it."

"*Maybe* it will," their mother corrected. "We're not absolutely certain about that part of it yet. It depends on how much time your dad has this winter."

Fall was glorious the year of 1924. Old-timers had never seen the colors as brilliant and plentiful as they were that year. However, many of them predicted a long, hard winter. Lydia and Aaron took short walks through the woods surrounding their home to gather aspen, red maples, and golden oak leaves. She brought them inside and put them on display throughout her small house.

"I can hardly tell the inside from the outside," Doug teased her one morning. "I may have to use my hatchet just to get to the kitchen." He buttoned up his long-sleeved wool shirt and grabbed his lunch pail. "Hold down the fort, sweet thing," he said, grabbing his wife and kissing her hard. "Say," he added with a grin, "aren't you putting on a little weight there ma'am?" He ran to the door chuckling as Lydia threw a tin cup at him.

"No supper for you tonight," she yelled at him through the closed door. She watched him walk down the road until he was out of sight. What a wonderful husband and father he was. I'm so lucky, she thought, her eyes suddenly filling with tears.

"No supper night … Daddy," Aaron repeated.

Lydia laughed and scooped him up into her arms.

Autumn quickly turned into winter, and another Christmas was looming on the horizon. This year, Lydia's parents, Harry and Lillian Begg, were coming to spend a few days with them. Lydia worked long hours and finally finished her homemade gifts for everyone and then turned her attention to the food and house cleaning. Doug had finally finished the addition of the small bedroom, and her parents would be the first to use it. She opened the door and drank in the beauty of the new room with its big window to the west. She loved the smell of the newly peeled logs, all snugly fitted together to keep out the cold north wind. She placed her mother's big quilt on the old bed and stood back to admire it. This would be her and Doug's new bedroom after the baby was born. She straightened the ruffle on the curtains that she had starched and ironed just yesterday and admired the effect. She shivered against the chill of the room and quickly closed the door.

"Mama," Aaron called from their tiny bedroom. "Eat!" he said simply.

"Are you hungry?" she asked, picking up her growing son.

"Eat," he said again. Lydia laughed and carried him into the cozy, warm kitchen.

"Mama will fix you some hot oatmeal and toast," she said. Aaron scrambled up into his little chair at the table and picked up his spoon. "Eat!" he said rather impatiently.

"All right … all right!" his mother laughed.

With breakfast finally over, Lydia went over her list of things to do for the hundredth time. She had plenty of potatoes and vegetables from their garden that she had crammed into the cellar last summer. Doug and Max were going turkey hunting this weekend, and she was hopeful both would bag a big one, and they'd be all set as far as Christmas dinner was concerned. She ran through her box of recipes and finally decided on apple and pumpkin pies. She could get those out of the way this afternoon and devote tomorrow to cleaning. She peeled several apples for her pie and listened to the howl of the wind with growing anxiety. I'm sure glad Mom and Dad have a car now and can travel in this weather without too much discomfort, she thought, glancing outside at the bare trees. With her pies finally in the oven, she had just begun the arduous task of cleaning up, when Ruffy suddenly began howling to the top of his lungs. What on earth is wrong with that dog now? Lydia wondered, looking through the kitchen window. To her complete surprise, a shiny, black car had pulled quietly into the driveway. A loud knock at the back door made her jump. She dried her hands on her apron and ran to open the door.

"Oh!" she squealed with delight. "Mom … Dad … come in … come in! What a wonderful surprise! I didn't really expect you for a couple of days yet." She hugged each of them tight and ushered them into her tiny, warm kitchen. Glancing past them, she suddenly realized that she hadn't really cleaned the house yet. Aaron's toys and blankets were scattered everywhere in the living room.

"Well, honey, you know how your father is," her mother said with a smile. "If he can't get somewhere at least two if not three days early, he thinks he's late."

"Oh Daddy," Lydia said, hugging her father again.

"Your mother's crazy," he said with a wink. "I didn't know what this weather was going to be like in a few days, so we decided we'd surprise you and come a bit early."

"I'm glad you did, Daddy. I don't get to see you and Mom near enough as it is. Daddy, you can put your things in our new bedroom. Come and see it … Doug and I just finished it a few days ago." She grabbed his arm and pulled him toward the door.

"Saaaaay, this is nice!" Harry said with appreciation. "I just might decide to stay the winter."

"Hope so," Lydia said with a laugh.

"Honey, I hope you haven't been working too hard. That's another reason we came early. I wanted to help you with Christmas preparations and all," her mother said with a slightly worried expression on her face. She held her daughter at arm's length for a moment and studied her face. "You look tired, sweetheart. I hope you're not doing too much."

Lydia shook her head. "I'm not, Mom, believe me."

"Mama eat!" Aaron yelled from the bedroom. "Eat!"

The three adults laughed as Lydia made her way into the bedroom to collect her son. "Grandma and Grandpa are here, pumpkin," she said as she lifted him from his crib.

"My! Oh my! Has he grown!" Grandma exclaimed, as she reached for him. "Hi, sweetheart … come to Grandma."

Aaron buried his face in his mother's neck and began to cry.

"Leave him alone, Lil," Harry said. "He doesn't want women fussin' over him all the time, right, big fella?"

"He'll be all right in a minute or two," Lydia said. "He's a little shy at first. Daddy, can you add a log or two to the fire? It feels rather chilly in here since we opened up the bedroom door."

After stoking the fire, Harry unloaded the car and made friends with Ruffy, while the two women cleaned the small kitchen, chattering happily together while they worked.

"When did you and Dad get a new car?" Lydia asked, watching her father as he pulled a large suitcase from the backseat.

"Oh, he saw this one in town a few months ago and couldn't live without it. I'm telling you, honey, that's all I heard about for more than a week … he had to have this car or die. He scares me to death the way he takes corners in it," her mother confided. "I'm sure he'll insist you go for a drive with him, so be forewarned."

"I hate to think what one of those things cost," Lydia said. "We can't even afford a buggy yet, much less a car. You watch, Mom … mark my words … when Doug sees your car, he's going to want one too."

"Probably," the older woman replied. "Boys and their toys!"

"Mom, do you know how to drive, too?"

"Heavens no! And I'm not the least bit interested in learning how to either. Dad would have a fit and fall in it if I put a dent or even a scratch in his precious toy."

Lydia laughed. "You're right, Mom … boys and their toys!"

Harry was only too happy to take his son-in-law for a quick spin when

Doug got home from work late in the afternoon.

"She'll do around fifty miles per hour just cruising along, and about twice that fast when she's goin' downhill," he told Doug as he jumped behind the wheel. "I'll let you drive her home," he promised.

Doug grinned with eager anticipation. "She sure is a beauty," he said admiringly. "Boy, oh boy, what I wouldn't give to have something like this."

Lydia watched with a sinking feeling in her heart as she saw the two men climb from the car and lift the hood. Doug was so like a small boy sometimes. He was grinning from ear to ear when they tromped into the kitchen to wash up for supper a little while later.

"Honey, we've just got to have a car," he announced happily. "You wouldn't believe how comfortable they ride an' how fast they go."

"What'd I tell you, Mom?" Lydia said, laughing. "Do I know my husband or do I know my husband?" The two women enjoyed a hearty laugh while the two men looked at one another and shrugged.

"I can get you a real good deal on a used one, Doug," Harry said while they were eating supper.

"Harry! That's something he needs to discuss with Lydia first. Don't you be encouraging him."

"Mother, keep quiet!" Harry warned, with a twinkle in his eye.

Lydia's mother shook her head. "I'm sorry, honey," she said, as she passed the potatoes to her daughter. "You know how Dad is."

Lydia nodded. She did indeed know how her dad was. He could talk anyone into anything. A few minutes later, she watched the two men in her life walk back outside into the cold night air, completely oblivious to the cold, totally absorbed in their discussion of today's automobiles.

"I hope your dad doesn't try to talk Doug into buying a car," Lillian said, a worried frown settling over her pretty face.

"Don't worry, Mom. We can't afford anything like that right now … especially with the baby coming, and Doug knows that. He's not going to do anything foolish."

A cold, windy Christmas without snow, and without a turkey for Christmas dinner, came and went, and still Doug talked of little else but the possibility of buying a car. Lydia began to feel rather uneasy, and her mother began to feel quite irritated. And to make matters worse, Harry encouraged Doug to drive his car to work every day … to get the feel of her … as he put it. Doug burst into the kitchen late one afternoon, grinning from ear to ear a few days after Christmas.

"I made it home from work in just over six minutes!" he announced with joyful exuberance. "Do you realize that it would have taken me well over an hour to walk that distance in this wind? What a difference a car makes. And just think, honey ... you could learn to drive too and you could take it into town when we need groceries and stuff. Boy oh boy, would that ever come in handy." Lydia rolled her eyes at him. She was getting very tired of the subject. She wished Doug would just drop it, but with each passing day, he seemed more obsessed about it. Maybe when her parents were gone, he would finally forget about cars.

The night before her parents were due to leave, a light snow began falling. By morning, there was almost a foot on the ground when Lydia got up to cook breakfast.

"Wonder how she's gonna handle in this snow," Doug said at the breakfast table.

"Guess we'll find out in a bit here, but I'm certainly not worried," Harry said, reaching for another biscuit. He had loaded the car up the night before and though they had not counted on a foot of snow, they were eager to get an early start.

"Doug, we'll take you into town and drop you off at the mill if you'd like," he offered. "Sure beats plowin' through this stuff on foot ... unless you prefer walkin'."

"Not hardly!" Doug mumbled, his mouth full. "Thanks, I'll take you up on that."

Quite suddenly, the house that had been bustling with activity and been so full of people for the past two weeks was now empty, lonely and very quiet. Lydia sat at the table, her chin cupped in her hand, listening to the ticking of the clock while Aaron took a brief morning nap. I hate good-byes, she thought miserably. She and her mother had clung to one another while the men shook hands. Her mother had held Aaron close and cried unashamedly. Aaron pushed away from her, stared at Nana and Poppa, as he called his grandparents, and ran to his mother.

"He knows something's wrong this morning," Lydia said through her tears. "He can feel it too."

She watched a few minutes later as the car took her parents and her husband down the road through a swirling mass of snowflakes, and slowly disappeared from her sight. She sat alone in her darkened house, feeling so lonely she thought she might die. I really should go do the dishes, she thought miserably, and I need to get some clothes washed today. Still, she sat and gazed, trance-like, at the white world outside. Somewhere, deep inside, a part of her desperately wanted to go with her parents. She had a sudden longing to go back ... back to her childhood ... to a time when life was carefree and wonderful … to a time when a little girl had no problems or worries. Her mind drifted back to the Christmas when she had received Anna Belle, her favorite doll. She must have been six or seven at the time. Anna Belle had been her pride and joy. Oh, how she had loved that doll, with her beautiful hand-painted face and blonde curls tucked neatly under a trim little hat. Lydia sat lost in thought for several minutes, remembering how Snickers, the cat, had nearly destroyed Anna Belle one morning while she was at school. Her heart had been broken that day when she found Anna Belle abandoned and forgotten in a dark corner of the living room. Her mother … her dear, sweet mother had come to Anna Belle's rescue and lovingly restored her to near-pristine condition. What had ever become of Anna Belle? Lydia sat lost in thought, reaching back through the years when suddenly the back door banged open, jarring her out of her doldrums. She gasped when she saw Doug and her parents stomping their feet at the back door.

"What happened?" she nearly screamed, as she rushed through the kitchen. "Why are you back again?"

"Stinkin' worthless hunk of steel," her father muttered.

"Car slid off in the ditch, honey. We can't move it until the storm lets up some," Doug explained. "It's kind of lying to one side. We had a hard time getting out of it, but we're all fine," he added, when he saw the color drain from his wife's face. He put his arms around her to steady her.

"Are you sure you're all right?" Lydia asked fearfully. "Mom, are you and Dad all right?"

"Yes, darling, we're all fine. I'm sorry we're all so much trouble. You thought you were rid of us and now here we are back again."

"Stinkin' worthless piece of scrap iron … that's all it is," her dad muttered again. "Smashed to smithereens!"

"Boy, has he ever changed his tune!" Lydia laughed through her tears.

"Honey, you don't know that it's hurt at all," her mother soothed. "Wait until the storm's over and we'll see if it's bad."

"It's bad … real bad," he insisted. "Stupid, worthless car … just headed straight for the ditch. No matter what I did, it was determined to lay over on its side. A few little snowflakes on the road, and it's suddenly helpless. Why, I used to keep a wagon on the road with twice this amount of snow. Worthless junk!"

Lydia and her mother burst out laughing with Doug joining in and finally Harry grinned and shook his head.

"Boys and their toys," Lillian said again.

"This boy had better get himself off to work," Doug said suddenly, glancing at the clock. "Guess I'll be a little late, but late is better than not at all. At least my feet won't head for the ditch."

"You'd better hope they don't," Harry said with a laugh.

"Nana … Mama … eat!" Aaron called loudly from his crib, awakened by the loud commotion in the kitchen.

"You'd *better* get to work, Doug," Dad said. "You've got a couple more mouths to feed for the next few days thanks to that worthless machine out there in the ditch."

"Be very careful, honey," Lydia said as her husband hugged everyone good-bye again. "Don't slide off the road."

CHAPTER 5
A NEW ARRIVAL

"Doug, honey, wake up!" Lydia tugged at her sleeping husband's shoulder. Doug, wake up!"

"Huh? Whatsa matter?"

"Honey, wake up. It's time."

Doug shot straight out of bed, ran to jump into his pants, and promptly stubbed his big toe on the corner of the dresser.

"Owww!" he howled, jumping around the darkened bedroom on one foot. "Ohhhh! My toe!" he moaned loudly as he gingerly forced his foot down into his work boot.

Lydia moaned softly. "Honey, you'd better hurry," she warned, arching her back as she tried to ease the pain.

Doug quickly lit the kerosene lamp by the bed and glanced anxiously at his wife. "I'll be back in a jiffy," he promised. "Are you going to be all right?" he asked, a look of alarm written across his sleepy face. "Don't do anything while I'm gone."

Lydia managed a quick smile and nodded her head. "Tie your shoes, silly, or you're going to break your neck."

Doug bent forward and quickly tied his boots. "If only we had a car, honey," he said with a nervous grin. "It'd take only a few minutes, but I promise, I'll hurry," he added, noting the look of exasperation on her face. He forgot about his throbbing toe and covered the distance to the doctor's house in record time, the predawn air stinging his face as he ran.

"Doc Sorenson, Doc Sorenson!" he yelled, pounding his fist on the massive front door of the doctor's home a short time later. He saw a light come on in the back of the house, and within a few seconds, the good doctor himself was at the door, tying his robe about his thin waist.

"What's all the ruckus about?" he asked, peering at Doug through the darkness.

"It's my wife," he panted. "She's havin' a baby." Doug coughed to clear his throat and catch his breath.

"Nothin' to get upset about, son. Women do it all the time. Let me get dressed and grab my bag. Come on in and warm up for a minute."

Doug stood before the dying embers of the great, massive fireplace in the living room and warmed his face and hands. It was at that moment he realized his toe was throbbing. What on earth was taking that doctor so long anyway?

"All right son, lead the way." The doctor reappeared, fully dressed, his bag in his hand.

Doug clambered into the front seat of the doctor's shiny car and wished again that he had one of his own. Within a few short minutes, they were pulling into his own driveway. Doug yanked the car door open and ran to the house, leaving the doctor to find his own way inside.

Lydia smiled when she saw Doug standing over her. "That was quick," she murmured, her eyes dull with pain.

The doctor stood in the doorway, rolling up his sleeves. "Go boil me some water, young man," he said with a grin.

Doug left immediately to do his bidding.

"Why do you always need lots of hot water, doctor?" Lydia asked, when she could talk again.

"I don't," he said simply, "but it makes the husbands feel needed, and it keeps them out of my hair for a bit. Now, let's see how things are progressing here. He examined her and finally murmured, "Uh-huh. Mrs. Wheeler, you're going to have a new mouth to feed in about fifteen to twenty minutes would be my guess."

"She can't ... come ...quick enough to ... suit me," Lydia finally managed to grunt, biting her lower lip. She moaned loudly and gripped the bed sheet, twisting it in her hands.

One hour later, just as the sun was rising over the horizon, the doctor presented Doug with his second son. "Congratulations, Mr. Wheeler. Your new son is the first delivered this spring. It's now March 21st," he added, glancing at his pocket watch. "First baby of the new season."

Doug grinned and held the baby up in the dim light so that he could take a good look at him.

"My wife," he said suddenly, "is she...."

"She's just fine. Sleeping right now. She's to have plenty of rest for at least two weeks," the doctor said, making his way to the back door. "You can settle up with me later when you're in town," he added, glancing at Doug as he jammed his hat on his head.

"Thank you so much Doc," Doug said, a lump forming in his throat. "I can't thank you enough for coming up here this morning and taking...."

"Not like I had much choice in the matter," the doctor interrupted, a slow grin spreading across his tired face. "Just doin' my job. If the Mrs. or your little youngin' here should have any problems at all, you know where to find me." He tipped his hat and disappeared outside into the early March morning.

Doug sat down to examine his new son. "Benjamin Douglas Wheeler, welcome to our family. How 'bout that? I have two sons!" This baby is the exact opposite of Aaron, Doug thought. Benjamin was darker skinned, had lots of dark hair, and had a longer face than Aaron. "Guess you look more like your old man," Doug said with a happy grin. "Poor little guy. That's two strikes against you right there. Did you know you have a big brother who's going to be very excited when he sees you?" The lump returned to his throat.

Funny how quickly things can change, he thought. Just yesterday, he had thought of Aaron as the baby, and now he was a big brother. He wiggled out of his chair and hobbled over to the closed bedroom door. He opened it a crack and peeked at his wife.

She was sprawled in the middle of their bed, her eyes closed. She stirred, briefly opened her eyes, and gave him a tired smile.

"So glad that's over," she murmured groggily. "How is she? Is she beautiful?" She held up her arms to accept the baby.

"Beautiful … yes. She … no!" Doug said with a wide grin. "We have another beautiful son, sweetheart."

"A boy!" Lydia exclaimed, now fully awake. "But I wanted a little girl. I thought for sure this one was a girl. Everyone in town thought so too."

"Sorry, honey, but we can't take him back. Besides, he's cute as a button, and Aaron is going to love having a little brother to play with."

Lydia smiled and closed her eyes again. "Maybe next time, I'll get my little girl."

"Next time!" Doug exclaimed. What under the sun was the matter with women anyway? Going through all that pain and suffering only to smile and say, 'next time!' He shook his head in disbelief, and placed the warm little bundle next to his wife. Lydia opened her eyes and instantly fell in love with her new son.

"You're so right, Doug," she said softly. "He's absolutely beautiful." She closed her eyes and slipped once again into a peaceful sleep.

She awoke some time later to the aroma of breakfast and the sound of Georgia's voice.

"Come on, sugar pie," she heard Georgia coax. "Climb up here like a big boy and eat your breakfast for Auntie Georgia."

She looked around for her new son and saw him sleeping peacefully in the tiny cradle next to her bed. She sighed and turned on her side so that she could see him better. He really is a beautiful baby, she thought. He looks just like his daddy. What a handsome man he's going to be one of these days. He's certainly not going to be in that cradle very long, she thought, noting the length of her new son. He was definitely a lot bigger than Aaron had been. It seemed only yesterday that she had rocked Aaron in that very same cradle. Time was passing too quickly.

"Well, hi there, sleepy head," Georgia whispered when she saw Lydia was awake. "I thought you were gonna sleep all day. How 'bout some breakfast? Are you hungry after all that work?"

Lydia nodded and grinned at her friend. "I could eat some toast, and I'd love a cup of coffee."

"Comin' right up," Georgia said quietly, patting Lydia's hand. "You feel like a team of horses just ran you over?"

"Something like that," Lydia agreed. "What in the world would I ever do without you, Georgia? You're the most wonderful woman in the entire world," she added before her friend could respond.

Georgia rolled her eyes and snickered. "You're gonna swell my head up like a pumpkin talkin' like that. I'll go get that toast and coffee for you. By the way, you sure make beautiful little boys."

Lydia smiled, closed her eyes, and dozed for a few minutes. Georgia placed a tray on the bed and opened the curtains to allow the sunlight to stream in. "What a beautiful day for a birthday," she said happily. She stooped over the cradle for a minute and peeked at the baby, lifting the blanket away from his tiny face.

"Mm-mmm!" she murmured. "He's so precious. Lord sure blessed you and Doug with beautiful children. Prettiest I've seen in a long time." She lowered the blanket and glanced at Lydia. "Aaron would like to come in and see him when he's finished his breakfast."

Lydia smiled and nodded her approval, gratefully sipping the hot coffee. "Georgia, you make delicious coffee. Like I said before, what in the world would I ever do without you?"

"Oh fiddle sticks!" she said with a wave of her hand. "You'd do the same for me, but thank the good Lord above, my days for bringing more babies into the world are about behind me. That's your job for the next few years, and I might add, it appears as if you're off to a good start." She leaned over the bed and gave Lydia a bear hug, patting her shoulder hard. "Just doin' what I can to help out a little," she said. "You know, you're like the little sister I never had ... that's how I feel about you."

To Lydia's dismay, tears began to stream down her face. She grabbed the top sheet and buried her face in it, wiping her tears.

Georgia laughed lightly and kissed the top of her head. "Drink your coffee before it gets cold. I'll be back in just a few minutes."

The warm sun, the hot coffee, and the obvious love that Georgia had for her warmed Lydia's heart. She finished her breakfast and shoved the tray aside. The Lord certainly was good to her and she said a quick, silent prayer of thanks for all His blessings. A few minutes later, Georgia brought in a dressed, fed, and well-scrubbed Aaron to see his new brother.

"Mama!" Aaron squealed happily and scrambled up on the bed close to his mother.

"Look, Aaron … down here, next to Mama," she said, pointing to the cradle on the floor. Aaron peered over the side of the bed, studying the tiny face and hands without saying a word.

"What is that?" Lydia prompted. "What do you see in the cradle down there?"

"Ahhh … baaaaa-by!" he finally said and immediately lost interest. He snuggled down close to his mother's side. "Story, pease, Mama. Story?" he asked hopefully, looking up into his mother's tired face.

"Auntie Georgia will read you a story, sugar pie," Georgia offered. "Right now, your mama has to take a nap. Come on, sweetie, let's go find a good story to read."

"Where's Doug?" Lydia asked as Georgia lifted Aaron into her arms.

"He's out in the kitchen soaking his smashed toe. Poor guy. It's red and swollen, but I don't think he broke it."

Lydia sighed and smiled her thanks to Georgia. Poor Doug, she thought. Sometimes he was such a little boy himself. Was it just a few hours ago that he had stubbed his toe? She drifted off into a luxurious, dreamless sleep. The sun was gone from the window when she opened her eyes again. She glanced at the clock on the dresser. My stars! It was past noon. Have I been asleep that long? The baby began to stir. Lydia watched, mesmerized by his movements and sounds. Poor little thing, she thought. He must be starved by now. She cuddled her new son close and placed him at her breast, her heart swelling nearly to the bursting point as she stroked his soft little cheek, encouraging him to suckle. Through the closed door, she could hear Barbara Ann's voice, reading to Aaron. Georgia must have gone home and sent her daughter back in her place. A soft, rapid knock at the door confirmed it a few minutes later. The young girl stood in the doorway with Aaron in her arms.

"Mama sent me over to help you out for a few days," she explained. "I'll go home at night after I get the supper dishes done for you."

"What about school?" Lydia asked.

"Oh, Mama will come during the day, and then when school's out for the day, I'll stop by here, an' she can go home."

"Thank you both soooo much," Lydia said with feeling. "I'm so grateful to you and your sweet mother."

Barbara Ann smiled, suddenly embarrassed. She shrugged and shifted Aaron's weight to her other hip. "Let me know if you need anything," she said. "Mr. Wheeler went to work this afternoon. I'll stay and fix supper for him an' Aaron and get the dishes done. Oh yeah, he said to tell you that his toe was better."

"You're going to make a terrific wife for some lucky boy one of these days," Lydia said with a smile.

Barbara Ann blushed, lowered her eyes, and backed out of the room. "Come on Aaron, let's go feed Ruffy, and get something started for your supper."

"Feed Ruffy," Aaron repeated, anxious to get outside. "Me feed Ruffy."

The days of early spring flew by, and Lydia quickly regained her strength under the care of Georgia and Barbara Ann. When Benjamin was just two weeks old, she felt she was strong enough to take over again. Georgia was not quite so sure.

"I don't know about this," she said dubiously, a worried frown wrinkling her tired face. "You look awfully pale to me."

"Honestly, Georgia, you're spoiling me rotten," Lydia protested. "If I don't get up and start doing for myself again, I'm going to get so fat and lazy that I'll never be good for anything ever again."

Georgia sighed and finally agreed. "Okay, you win. Have it your way, but promise me that you won't overdo. That's so easy to do when you've got two hungry little mouths to feed. Just be careful and promise that you'll take it slow and easy ... and promise that you'll get a nap every day while the babies are asleep."

"I solemnly promise," Lydia said, her right hand held high. "Should I swear on a stack of Bibles?"

"It wouldn't hurt," Georgia said with a laugh. "Not that I'd believe you any more if you did though."

Lydia's soft blue eyes suddenly filled with tears that threatened to spill down her cheeks. "You've been so good to me, Georgia, and I love you so much...." The tears ran in rivulets and splashed down the front of her dress.

Georgia smiled and hugged her friend just as her own tears ran down her face. "Look at us!" she exclaimed suddenly. "Cryin' like we're the babies around here."

Lydia laughed and pulled her hankie from her apron pocket.

"Where Bubba Nan go?" Aaron asked, looking past Georgia.

Both women laughed. "Bubba Nan went to school, sweetie pie," she said, kissing the little boy's head. "Take care of Mama," she added and slipped out the door.

Baby Benjamin began crying lustily from the bedroom.

"Aw-oh, baby wake, Mama," Aaron said. He rushed ahead of his mother into the bedroom and bent over the small cradle and stared at his tiny brother. Lydia picked up the baby and kissed his warm cheek.

"Baby kiss," Aaron said, reaching his hands upward toward her. Lydia bent forward and kissed Aaron on his forehead. He frowned at her and shook his head.

"No, baby kiss," he said again, his frown drawing small lines across his forehead. "Baby kiss," he said again. Lydia held the baby down close to Aaron and he put his arms across his little brother's chest and hugged him. He then turned the baby's head and kissed the tiny cheek with a wet, warm, smacking kiss. Lydia was moved to tears to witness such a tender display of affection that her two-year-old had for his newborn sibling. Aaron stroked the baby's arm and put his face up close to Benjamin's.

"Do you love your baby?" Lydia asked him after she had mopped up her tears again.

Aaron nodded his head and kissed the baby again. "See eyes?" he asked suddenly, nearly sticking his finger in the baby's eye.

"Be careful of his eyes," Lydia said gently.

"See hair?"

Lydia smiled. "Yes, he has lots of hair, and his eyes are probably going to be brown, like Daddy's."

"See ears?" he asked. "Wike Daddy's."

Lydia laughed and hugged him, kissing his hair, eyes, ears, forehead and cheeks. "You monkey!"

"*You monkey!*" Aaron repeated and laughed at his own joke.

The days drifted by, warm and mild at first, and then into summer, hot and humid. Lydia did her best to plant a small garden but found that most of her time was spent changing and washing diapers. Baby Ben, as Aaron called him, was growing faster than the weeds in her little garden.

In July, Aaron celebrated his second birthday and was thrilled with a new wooden wagon full of colorful wooden blocks that Doug had made him. He played for hours at a time, dumping the blocks out and restacking them in the wagon. He pulled the wagon around in the front yard with Ruffy close at his heels. Lydia found great pleasure in watching the two of them as they interacted in play. It won't be any time at all before Baby Ben will be out there playing with them, she thought. She stared at the enormous stack of dirty clothes piled high in the corner of the kitchen waiting to be scrubbed and reluctantly forced herself away from the table and her daydreams. She had to get busy around here. She had just put her white things in the big galvanized tub full of hot, soapy water to soak for a few minutes when the back door flew open with a bang and Aaron ran into the kitchen, his eyes wide with excitement.

"What's the matter?" she asked, rather anxiously. "Where's Ruffy?"

"Ruffy gone," the little boy said simply, pointing out the open window.

"He's gone? Where'd he go?" She walked to the door and called the dog. Funny, she hadn't heard him barking at all. Usually when he was excited enough to jump the fence he was loud enough to wake the dead. Squinting in the bright sunlight, she walked around to the front of the house. The dog was nowhere in sight. Oh brother, just what I need this morning, she thought. I can't for the life of me figure out what gets into that hound every once in a while. She heard the commotion before she saw it. Looking up the dusty road past their driveway, she saw Ina Potts struggling valiantly to stay on her feet, swinging her purse with all the strength she could muster, in a desperate effort to keep the dog at bay. Ruffy was running circles around her, delightedly jumping up and licking her face in a warm and exuberant greeting.

CHAPTER 6
OF THINGS HOPED FOR

Doug howled with laughter when Lydia related to him the events of the day. She couldn't help laughing herself, but it had been anything but funny at the time. "I could have strangled Ruffy," she said when she could finally speak again. "I yelled my head off at him, but he never paid the slightest attention to me at all. I've never heard so much sputtering and fuming … it looked just like a hound dancing with a praying mantis out in the road … a mantis with a big purse."

"Poor Miss Ina," he said, wiping his eyes. "I'll betcha' she doesn't ever come visiting you again."

"Probably not," Lydia agreed. "She must have wiped her face with her hankie and muttered, 'Filthy beast!' a dozen times or more."

"She wasn't hurt, was she?" Doug asked suddenly, remembering how slight of build and frail-looking Ina was.

"No, she said she wasn't hurt, and I didn't see any evidence of anything other than dog slobber all over her."

"Poor woman! She'll probably tell everyone she meets that we have a vicious, filthy beast for a dog up here on the mountain," Doug said, suddenly serious. "She could have been hurt really bad. I guess we should count our blessings that he didn't knock her down out there in the driveway. I wonder why he didn't start barking when he saw her coming?"

"I've wondered that myself. That's the first time I know of that Ruffy hasn't yelped loud enough to wake the dead when someone came. To this day, he still barks at Mr. Lawson when he brings the mail."

"I would sure hate to do it, but we may have to start chaining him up so he doesn't dance a jig out in the driveway with any other visitors we may have." They looked at one another for a few seconds and burst into gales of laughter again. Only when Benjamin's cries rose above the din in the kitchen did Lydia hurry to the bedroom to retrieve her son.

"Let's go see your daddy," she said, smiling at his tiny, red face.

She picked him up and hurried back to the kitchen where Doug was engaged in an animated conversation with Aaron.

"Ruffy bad dog," Aaron said, rolling his eyes.

"Ruffy was a bad dog?" Doug asked.

The little boy nodded his head. "Bad dog."

Doug held the baby while Lydia bustled around the kitchen getting supper on the table.

"Go wash your hands, Aaron," she said. "Supper's almost ready." The little boy scurried over to the tub that his mother kept beside the stove and grabbed the big bar of soap and splashed his hands in the lukewarm water.

"Dere," he exclaimed. "See, Mama, all queen." He proudly held his hands up high over his head for his mother's inspection and then scrambled into his chair at the table, wiping his dripping hands on his pants.

"Honey, as soon as the boys are tucked in bed, I need to discuss something important with you," Doug said, just as they were finishing their meal.

"Oh?" Lydia looked questioningly at her husband. "What's going on? Anything change down at the sawmill?"

Doug shook his head and drained his glass of milk. "No, no, nothing like that," he managed to mumble between mouthfuls. "Just something that I want to get your opinion about."

Lydia studied her husband's face with growing suspicion. He looked perfectly calm and relaxed, yet she was instinctively uneasy. She frowned at him, chewing thoughtfully. Something was amiss, she could feel it. Doug continued eating his meal with his usual gusto and told her to quit worrying. It wasn't anything that important. She finally relaxed, finished the meal, and busied herself with the dishes, bedtime stories for Aaron, and feeding Benjamin one last time. Doug's request was totally forgotten by the time she finally finished the evening's chores and slumped down in her chair with a loud sigh. She hadn't even had time to settle herself comfortably when Doug called her outside on the porch. She rose with another loud sigh and joined him in the small porch swing that he had made last summer. He was enjoying the last rays of a beautiful sunset and the constant call of a whippoorwill somewhere in the woods below their house. He pulled her down into his lap and breathed in the fragrance of her hair and skin.

"Mmmm, sweetheart, you smell awfully good," he murmured, burying his face in her neck and hair.

"You mean I smell awful," his wife corrected him with a light laugh. She pulled back from him and leveled her gaze on him, suddenly remembering his earlier request. "What's this all about anyway? Why all the mystery?" Her anxiety had returned.

"No mystery, honey," he assured her, pulling her tight again. "I just wanted to get your opinion on something."

"I smell a rat!" Lydia said, eyeing him doubtfully. Again, she pushed back from him and sat up straight in his lap. "Doug what are you up to?"

Doug swallowed hard and inhaled deeply. "Nothing … really. You know honey, how much I've always wanted a car…."

"So that's it!" Lydia exploded, leaping to her feet. "I thought you had given that idea up a long time ago. Doug, you know we can't afford a car, and besides … they're so dangerous."

"Wait a minute, honey. Give me a chance to explain," he pleaded, turning her to face him. "You don't even give me a chance to explain the…."

"Explain away!" Lydia snapped, interrupting him. "By all means, Doug, please do explain it to me."

Doug tilted his face upward for a moment, seemingly studying the bare rafters of the porch, his jaw muscles working furiously. Even in the diminishing light, Lydia could see the determination on his face and in his stance. He seemed to have grown a foot or more just standing there in front of her.

Doug inhaled deeply and cleared his throat. "You remember meeting T.C. Murdock, the foreman at the mill … you met him at the last town council meeting … tall guy with graying hair … glasses?"

Lydia nodded. "I remember him. What about him?"

"Well, he called me into his office today and told me that he's giving me a raise in pay, starting with this next pay period."

"Oh honey!" Lydia gasped, grabbing his hands. "That's wonderful! Why didn't you tell me that right away?"

"Because I love to have you all to myself and watch your beautiful eyes light up when you hear good news." He kissed the top of her head and then her nose.

"Here it comes," she murmured. "Why do I get the feeling there's a lot more to this story?"

Doug laughed and squeezed her tight. "You know me too well. Getting back to what Murdock said," Doug continued. "It seems that his wife's aunt just lost her husband recently and she's moving back home to Kentucky. She needs someone to load up their heavy furniture and help her close up the house and get it ready for sale. They own an old, used car, and she can't drive and doesn't want to learn how. Murdock heard me babbling one day about wanting a car, probably when your folks were here, and he told me about her. He said she might let us have it for next to nothing…." He paused to catch his breath and see what effect this was having on Lydia. She was frowning deeply, he could feel it more than see it, but she said nothing, so he plunged ahead.

"Murdock also said that if I'd go up to Brighton this next weekend, and help this lady close up her house and whatever, that she'd probably let me bring the car back home, and we could pay her a little bit at a time as we could afford it." He paused again, sensing that his wife was on the verge of exploding.

"How in the world does Mr. Murdock know what his wife's aunt will agree to as far as payment goes? She might want cash for all we know, or she might want a horrible amount that we could never afford no matter how long we had to pay on it. This sounds far too risky to me."

"But you're not opposed to me going to Brighton and helping her and finding out about the car?" Doug asked hopefully. "Really, honey, it's about our only chance of getting one and…." He finished lamely, sure that he had ruined his only chance to convince his wife that this might be the deal of a lifetime.

Lydia shook her head in disbelief. "Oh, Doug," she sighed with exasperation. "No, I'm not opposed to your going to help the old woman get moved. It's just that I don't think, even with this raise, that we can afford a car. They cost money to keep them up, don't they? Tires and gasoline and whatever else it takes to make them run. It all costs money … lots of money and we barely have enough to live on as it is without the expense of a car."

"Yes, of course, you're right, honey," Doug said softly, "but think of the convenience a car would make in our lives. Why, you could drive to town and get…"

"Me!" Lydia exploded again. "Not me, buster! Get that out of your head right this minute. I'm never driving any car … ever!"

Doug laughed and hugged her again. "Honey, honey, honey, they're not that complicated. I could teach you to drive in one afternoon. You could watch me several times when I drive to town or church or wherever, and you'd figure it all out right away. You could even practice a little bit at a time, just driving up and down our driveway, and it wouldn't be any time at all that you'd be drivin' all over the place. You'll be wondering what you ever did without one, believe me."

"No Doug. Forget it … absolutely not … not now … not ever! Forget about the driving lessons. I don't want anything to do with driving one of those contraptions. I don't mind riding in one if you don't drive too fast, but honestly, honey, I think they're terribly dangerous. People get killed in those things. Look what happened to Mom and Dad's car and Daddy knows how to drive!"

"People get killed in buggies too," Doug countered lamely.

Having made her case, Lydia left him standing on the porch, went back inside, and flopped down in her chair, quite close to tears.

Doug followed her inside and lit the lamp on the table, not quite sure where he stood in this little dispute. "Then … it's okay if I hike to Brighton this next Saturday morning and help … help this widow woman and … take a look at … at things?" he faltered, searching for just the right words.

Lydia looked up at him in the glow of the lamplight and burst out laughing. "Honestly, Doug, sometimes you act more like a little boy than Aaron does. Why bother asking me at all? You've already made up your mind, haven't you?"

Doug looked at her with a wounded expression on his face, but said nothing.

"When do you think you'll be home?" she asked, ignoring his expression.

He grinned, obviously relieved. "I don't really know. It depends on how much needs to be done to get this woman's house ready … that sort of thing. If she agrees to let us buy the car, then I'll be able to drive it back home." His eyes danced at the thought of it. "Just think, honey, we might own a car of our very own by this time next week."

Lydia smiled up at him, unable to resist his boyish charm. "My little boy … just before Santa slides down the chimney," she said, making a face at him. "That's exactly what you look like right this minute … an excited little boy waiting for his new Christmas bike."

Doug grinned and stooped to kiss her. He grabbed the kitchen lantern off the table, lit it and began whistling a mindless tune. "I'm going down to the buggy barn to clean it up a bit. The woodpile needs restacking, or what there is left of it, and I'm going to straighten everything up in there to make room for our new car … just in case we happen to get it, all right?"

Lydia nodded, resting her head on the back of her chair, her eyes closed in resignation. Only when Doug was out the door and out of hearing range did she allow herself the luxury of weeping; weeping for fear of the unknown, weeping for fear of change, and weeping for the sheer joy of shedding a few tears of exhaustion. She was ready for bed by the time her happy husband came back up to the house, still whistling that mindless tune. Little boys and their toys, she thought. I need to write Mom a nice long letter. She'll understand.

The following weekend, Doug was up before dawn, nervously pacing in the kitchen, waiting for Lydia to finish packing him a basket of food. She looked around the room, trying to think of something else to include in the basket, and finally added a large jug of water and some fruit.

"Honey, I'm only going to be gone for a couple of days. You've got enough food there for at least a full week. I can't carry all that and my clothes too," he protested.

"You need plenty of food and water, Doug. Have you thought about where you'll sleep tonight? Do you suppose she has a barn?" She looked at her husband with genuine concern on her face.

"More than likely," Doug said. "Honey, will you please stop worrying about me! I'll be just fine, I promise. I'll be home before you and the boys even know I'm gone." He scooped her up into his arms and kissed her hard. "I love you so much," he murmured, kissing her forehead and then her nose. "Don't let strangers in the house. Lock the doors at night and keep Ruffy inside after dark, you hear?"

Lydia nodded and promptly burst into tears, her shoulders shaking from the force of her emotion. Doug tightened his hold on her.

"Hey, hey," he consoled, "I'll be back before you know it. Please don't cry, honey."

"But I miss you already," she sobbed, tears streaming down her face. "Please don't take a single minute longer than you absolutely have to."

"Believe me, I won't. I should be in Brighton by noon, and if I get to work right away, hopefully I'll be finished by tomorrow afternoon. Will you and the boys be all right?"

Lydia nodded again, unable to reply. She wiped her eyes and face on her apron and flung her arms around his neck for one last kiss, and then he was gone. She watched him until he was out of sight. He had turned to wave one last time and then disappeared amidst a small stand of trees. The house seemed oddly foreign to her without him in it. She had never been apart from Doug since the day she had said 'I do' to him, and she wasn't real sure that she was going to survive this being alone. She glanced at the clock and decided she'd climb back in bed and maybe get a little more sleep before Ben woke up. She stretched out and sighed, thinking about her husband and how lucky she was to have found him. He was such a good man; good to her and good to their children. Dear Lord, she prayed silently, please watch over Doug and keep him safe, and please, Lord, don't let him buy that stupid car. We don't need one, and please … she drifted off in peaceful slumber.

Benjamin began stirring in his cradle, and within a few seconds, he was crying lustily. Lydia raised her head off the pillow and looked at the clock. She had been in bed exactly seven minutes. She sighed, threw back the quilts, reached down and picked up her starving son. The joys of motherhood, she thought. I wonder just how old and feeble I'll be when I finally get a full night's sleep again. She finally got the baby back to sleep just in time for

Aaron to wake up.

"Where Daddy go?" he asked, looking around the bedroom, his eyes still swollen with sleep. "Where Ruffy go?"

"Ruffy's outside somewhere, and Daddy had to go away for a day or so on business," she said, knowing full well that he wouldn't understand what she was talking about.

"Where Daddy go?" he asked again.

"Never mind where Daddy went. Let's go get you dressed and then get some breakfast," his mother whispered, fearful that she'd soon have both boys to contend with.

She had just finished cleaning up the kitchen when Ruffy let out a mournful howl and then began barking excitedly. She nervously looked out the window, but could see nothing unusual.

"What on earth is wrong with that dog now?" she muttered. "He's gonna wake Ben up if he doesn't shut up." Hurrying to scold the dog, she yanked the back door open and gasped. There, on her doorstep, stood Pastor Jamison and his wife, Bess, dressed in their Sunday best, diligently trying to shield their clothing from Ruffy's exuberant greeting.

"No chance of surprising you with a visit," the pastor said with a grin. "Not with that alarm sounding. Boy, has he ever grown! Last time we were here, he was just a pup."

"Actually, you did surprise me. I didn't hear you until Ruffy started yelping." She invited them into the kitchen and offered them coffee, which they gratefully accepted.

"We thought we'd drop by and see how you were doing," Bess said with a nervous giggle. "We haven't seen much of you at church since the baby was born. How is he anyway?"

"Oh, he's just fine … growing like a weed," she said, pulling her best china out of the hutch. She served the coffee and sat down at the table opposite the preacher and his wife. "We've been meaning to come back to church, but it's been hard to get both boys ready and myself too." Her excuse sounded phony, even as she said it. She glanced up at her guests.

Bess smiled. "We certainly understand that," she said.

"We just thought we'd let you know that you're missed. I'd be glad to help you out with the babies at church, should you need someone to hold one of them," she offered.

"Thanks, I might just take you up on that."

"I was hoping to catch Doug at home this morning," Rodney said, looking around the kitchen. "Is he working on Saturdays nowadays?"

"No, at least not down at the mill. He walked into Brighton early this morning to help a widow woman close up her house and get it ready for sale. She needed someone to load up her furniture and things like that," Lydia explained.

"I see," the pastor said. "That's right neighborly of him."

"Well, I'm afraid he had an ulterior motive," Lydia said. "You see, this woman just recently lost her husband, and it seems that she has this car that she'd like to get rid of, and Doug...."

Both the pastor and his wife burst out laughing. "I see, I see." Rodney said.

Lydia smiled, though she didn't much feel like smiling. "Please pray that he won't get it. I'm afraid of cars. We've made it just fine without one so far and I really don't see the need to have such a thing. They're so dangerous."

"That they are ... that they are," Rodney agreed. "However, Lydia," he paused a moment searching for just the right words. "Times are changing and people have to change with them to keep up. Your husband is a very sensible young man. I'm sure he'll do what's best for his family."

"He'll buy the car, you wait and see," Lydia predicted, making a face. "He's wanted one ever since my folks came for Christmas last year in their shiny, new Ford. He hasn't talked about anything else since then."

"Well," Pastor Rod said, clearing his throat, "the times we live in practically demand an automobile anymore. Everything is so fast-paced. People need to go here and there as quickly as possible. Fact is, Bess and I are working on a deal to buy one ourselves."

Lydia looked surprised. "You too?" she asked, somewhat dismayed.

Bess giggled and nodded her head. "Rod is going to try to teach me to drive so that I can visit some of the church ladies during the week."

"Is Doug going to teach you to drive?" Rodney asked his hostess. "I hear they're pretty easy."

"He wants me to learn, but I'm too nervous, and besides that, there's really no reason for me to drive. Doug would have the car every day at work, and he's the one who stops off at Deacon's Market with my grocery list a couple of times a week. I don't even have to go into town for that, so until the boys start school, I really don't have any reason to drive."

"Well, like I said, things change," Rodney said again with a smile. "You may change your mind if he comes back home with one. You might be surprised."

"Oh, I'd be surprised all right."

CHAPTER 7
A WIDE AWAKE DREAM

Should I take the shortcut through the woods or stick to the road and hope that a car comes by? Doug pondered the question for a few seconds and decided that his chances of getting to Brighton earlier would be better if he took the road. Walking at a brisk pace, he enjoyed the fresh, cool mountain air and the occasional bird that flew overhead or small critter that scurried quickly across the road ahead of him. He thought about the woman he was to meet this morning, Mrs. Vi Wamsley. He had written her name down on a piece of scrap paper when he last talked to Murdock and had then promptly lost his note. He was reasonably sure that was her name. He wondered briefly what the Vi stood for ... Vivian or perhaps Violet or maybe Virginia?

The name of her street conjured up images of scenic places he'd seen in picture books when he was just a kid. Sandalwood Lake Drive. Doug wondered what sandalwood was. He'd never heard of it before. The sun had risen high up over the trees that bordered the road when he finally stopped for a long drink of water. A noisy blue jay scolded him when he sat down in the shade to rest a few moments. Doug watched the bird as it flitted from tree to tree and protested his presence. Probably got a nest close by, he thought as he looked around. He wiped the sweat from his forehead and headed back to the road.

Brighton was only nine miles from Northridge, and Doug knew it wouldn't take more than two and one-half hours to walk, but he found himself hoping for a ride. It was really getting hot. Just before eleven, he strode into the good-sized town. Not a single car had passed him all morning. He stopped and watched the bustle of activity around him for a few minutes. He had been through Brighton several times, but this morning, it looked different to him. He decided he'd save some time, swallow his pride and ask the local barber where Sandalwood Lake Drive was located, but locating the barber proved to be a little harder than he expected. He walked up and down Main Street twice and didn't spot one. Where on earth would a barber be if not on Main Street?

Doug stopped and scratched his head. Glancing down a side street, he happened to see a barber's pole about halfway down the street.

"A-ha! Thar'she blows!" he exclaimed loudly to himself just as two women walked past him. They eyed him suspiciously, exchanged nervous glances, and hurried away, looking back only once to make sure he wasn't following them.

Feeling a bit silly, Doug jammed his hat back on his head and hurried down the street toward the barbershop. A bell tinkled over the door when he opened it. The barber himself was sitting in his own chair reading a newspaper.

"Haircut, mister? Just two bits today." He slid off the high seat and gathered up his paper.

"No, sir, thank you. I just need some directions. Sandalwood Lake Drive ... any idea where that is?"

"About one mile out of town headin' east toward Northridge," the barber said. "There's a sign by the road says...." He thought for a moment, stroking his enormous mustache. "It says something-or-other Hot Springs." He scratched his nearly-bald head and grinned. "Now don't that just beat all?" he said, twisting his newspaper into a tight roll. " I come by there every day, and I can't for the life of me remember what that sign says. Anyway, Sandalwood Lake is right down that road ... you can't miss it."

A few minutes later, Doug was headed back out of town in the direction he'd first come. Mrs. Vi Wamsley lived about a mile out of town by Sandalwood Lake. Well that made sense, he thought. Why else would you call it Sandalwood Lake Drive?

He found the lake easy enough, which looked more like a pond to him. It didn't look nearly big enough to justify calling it a lake in Doug's mind. The house was set well off the road, nestled in a small stand of strange-looking trees. Maybe those are sandalwood trees, he thought. He walked down the long, curved driveway up to the front of the big house. The driveway led to what looked to be a garage in back. He wondered briefly if Mrs. Wamsley's car was housed back there. Mrs. Wamsley herself answered the door.

She was middle-aged, heavyset, and looked very tired. Her salt and pepper hair was pulled tightly into a small chignon at the nape of her neck. "Do come in, Mr. Wheeler," she said, after he had introduced himself. She stepped aside so that he could enter the living room.

"My niece, Carolyn ... ahh, Mrs. Murdock, told me that you might come today. Thank you so much. You can't imagine how much I need your help. Mr. Wamsley, God rest his soul, and I never had any children and frankly, Mr. Wheeler, there's not too many people in this area willing to help a neighbor out anymore. It's a sad day that we're livin' in, don't you think?"

"Yes ma'am, it is, and please call me Doug."

"All right, Doug," she said with a tired smile. "Did T.C. tell you what needs to be done here?"

"Well, ma'am, he said that you needed someone to help load some furniture, and that you wanted to get your house ready for sale."

"That's about it," she said. "I need small things packed into boxes and the bigger items, like the baby grand, the large furniture, and the paintings, will be crated and shipped by a professional mover who will be here sometime next week."

"I see," Doug nodded. "What would you like me to start on?"

"You can start in my husband's library and the study. All of his books need to be packed away. He was a retired judge, you know, and before that, a lawyer."

"Oh yes," Doug said, not knowing how to respond. He looked around the big room and saw several large boxes piled up against the back wall of the library. He rolled up his sleeves and went to work. Two hours later, the library shelves were nearly empty. He glanced around the room for a clock. His stomach told him it was long past noon. He decided he'd see if he could find Mrs. Wamsley, and tell her that he was going to take a break for a few minutes and eat some lunch. He found her in the kitchen talking to a young black woman who was just about Doug's age.

"This is Mavis," Mrs. Wamsley said to Doug. Looking back at the young woman, she added, "this is Mr. Wheeler from Northridge. He came to help me with the packing."

Mavis smiled up at him. "How do you do sir? Can I get you something to eat?"

"Oh, thank you, ma'am, but no … my wife packed me quite a bit to eat in this basket here. This will be fine. She packed enough for a small army," he explained with a grin.

Mavis nodded her head, climbed a small step stool, and went back to work, packing and cleaning shelves in the kitchen that were too high to reach from the floor. "There's lemonade or iced tea in the icebox, Mr. Wheeler," she said over her shoulder. "If you'd care for something to drink…."

"Thank you, miss," Doug said. "I'll be fine." He made his way outside and sat down under a shade tree in the front yard. Wonder where her car is. How should I mention the subject to her? I wonder if Mrs. Murdock told her that I was interested in her car? Wonder if she's willing to sell it and for how much?

These questions whirled around in his head while he munched his sandwich and gulped down his jar of lukewarm lemonade. When he had topped off his meal with an apple, he decided he'd stroll around to the back of the house, and see if there was anything in the garage. He could always tell Mrs. Wamsley that he was looking for more boxes if she caught him. Walking down a brick sidewalk, he crossed through a beautiful rose garden that was well kept and headed toward the large building that he had seen from the driveway. The heavy, solid doors in the front were tightly closed, so he walked around the outside hoping to find a window. There was none. He paused for a moment and then decided the only way to find out what was inside was to open one of those big doors. He looked around the yard and the back of the house. No one was in sight. He yanked hard on the first door. It wouldn't budge. He pulled up on the second one and instantly heard the vicious growling and snarling of what sounded like an enormous dog. He quickly lowered the door and backed away. The dog inside was now thoroughly alarmed and began barking loudly. Doug stood for a minute, not knowing what he should do.

"Sadie, stop that noise right now. Sadie, stop that!" Mrs. Wamsley yelled surprisingly loud, as she hurried down the steps toward the garage. "Sadie, it's all right, girl. Quiet down." She looked questioningly at Doug.

He knew he was turning every color in the rainbow. He cleared his throat. "I'm sorry, ma'am," he said. "I was looking for more boxes and...." He stopped and glanced at her. It sounded like a lie, even to him. He was snooping, and he was sure she knew it.

Mrs. Wamsley smiled up at him and waved his excuse aside. "There's plenty of packing boxes in the house. Let me get a leash on Sadie so she doesn't rush you. She's quite protective, you know."

"Does she bite?" Doug asked a bit apprehensively.

"She might. To tell you the truth, I'm not really sure what she'd do. She was Mr. Wamsley's dog. He just loved her and I'm afraid she's a bit distressed since he passed on ... God rest his soul."

The plump woman huffed and puffed, pulling on the door and motioned for Doug to get up on the veranda until she could quiet the dog. Doug didn't need to be told twice. He hurried to the top step, ready to leap inside the door if the need should arise. Mrs. Wamsley raised the door just over one foot, all the while talking to Sadie. Sadie, a beautiful German Shepherd, bounded out of the garage and sniffed her hand.

"That's a good girl," she praised the dog, patting her shoulder while she clicked the leash to her collar. "What a good girl you are. That's my sweet Sadie. There now."

What happened next, Doug was absolutely sure, would be forever etched in his mind for all time and eternity. The instant Sadie spied him, she let out a roar and bounded for the back steps, dragging Mrs. Wamsley along behind her. Doug zipped through the door, and slammed it just as the huge dog cleared the steps and lunged at the closed door in a frenzied effort to get at him. Doug stared dumbfounded at the enormous head that appeared time and again in the window of the door. The dog repeatedly hurled her body against the door, alternately snarling and barking. Mrs. Wamsley's scolding was swallowed up in the frightening uproar.

Mavis ran from the kitchen, her eyes wide with fright. "Mr. Wheeler, do somethin'," she said, wringing her hands in a tea towel. "Do somethin'."

"What do you want me to do?" Doug nearly yelled in desperation. "What can I do?"

The young woman looked wildly around her. She spotted the huge portrait of Mr. Wamsley leaning up against the wall. "Here," she said, "help me with this picture." She hurried over to the painting.

Doug looked questioningly at her. Why all of a sudden did she need this painting moved? They lugged it over to the door and lifted it up in the window.

"Now, yell, 'Sadie, play dead!' as low and as loud as you can," she advised.

Doug stared at her while she struggled to hold on to her side of the huge portrait.

"Hurry!" she gasped. "I'm 'bout to drop this thing."

Doug cleared his throat and dropped his voice a couple of notches. "Sadie, play dead!" he yelled as loud as he could.

Instantly, the big dog lay down on the top step and whined. They could hear Mrs. Wamsley still reprimanding the dog. "Shame, shame! Mother's so ashamed of you. Bad girl. Come on. Back to the garage for you. Bad girl!"

Doug and Mavis lowered the painting and set it back against the wall. Mavis grinned up at him.

"How on earth did you know that would work?" he asked, completely amazed. "I've never seen anything like that in my life."

Mavis shrugged. "I didn't. Judge used to yell his head off at Sadie, and that's what he'd always yell at her to get her to mind and she'd respond every time." She shrugged again and smiled. "Reckon I'll get back to work."

Doug was standing in the hallway, visibly shaken over the ordeal, when Mrs. Wamsley came back inside. She slammed the door and stared at him for a second or two. "Oh, Mr. Wheeler," she said apologetically. "I'm so sorry about that. There are some people in this world that Sadie doesn't take a shine to, for whatever reason, and I'm afraid you're one of them. Are you all right?"

"Yes ma'am, I'm fine," Doug assured her. "I'm absolutely amazed how well Mavis' plan worked to control Sadie though. That was brilliant."

"Indeed it was ... a work of genius," the woman agreed. She wiped her forehead with her handkerchief and smiled up at him. "Mavis, honey, please fix us all something cold to drink, would you?" she called into the kitchen.

"Yes ma'am, right away."

"Please Mr. Wheeler ... Doug, please have a seat in the living room and rest a bit," she invited.

Doug followed her into the nearly empty living room and found a chair. He sank down into its softness, grateful for the chance to rest a minute and collect his thoughts. "How long have you had Sadie?" he asked, more to make conversation with the woman than out of interest.

"My husband bought her from a breeder when she was just a puppy. We've got papers on her ... she's a purebred, you know. She's nearly seven years old now. I guess in human years that would make her almost forty-nine. Guess she's getting irritable in her old age."

Doug nodded and stretched himself into a more comfortable position. "You'll obviously be taking her with you when you move to ... where was it? Kentucky?"

"That's right and yes, I am taking her with me. She's a lot of company to me now that my dear husband is gone."

"By the way, T.C. told me that you have a car you wanted to sell," Doug blurted out, instantly wishing he'd waited for a more appropriate time to broach the subject.

Mrs. Wamsley sat lost in thought without saying a word for such a long time that Doug decided she hadn't heard him at all. Her eyes were almost closed. He began to feel uneasy and wondered if she was ill. He cleared his throat.

At that moment, Mavis brought in a tray laden with iced glasses of lemonade, and a plate piled high with homemade cookies. "Help yourself, Doug," Mrs. Wamsley said softly, her eyes still half-closed.

He reached for a glass of lemonade and a couple of cookies, wishing that he hadn't mentioned the car at all.

Mrs. Wamsley cleared her throat and stared at the ceiling for a few seconds. "Yes," she said finally. "Mr. Wamsley had a car that I don't need or want. I'll have Emmons take Sadie down to the barn, and you can take a look at it if you like." She closed her eyes again, seemingly lost in thought about something.

"Thank you, ma'am, that'd be real nice. I would like to take a look at it before I leave," Doug said, barely above a whisper. When the old woman opened her eyes again, she looked at Doug and smiled. He gulped down his cookies and drained his cold drink. "Ma'am, I'm nearly finished in the library with the packing and all. Where do you want me to go next?"

"Mercy! You're certainly fast," she said. "I think I'll have you pack up things in the garage, since you'll be out there anyway."

That certainly met with Doug's approval. He was suddenly anxious to finish the library and get out to the garage. Mrs. Wamsley was not in such a hurry. "Are you prepared to spend the night here, Mr. Wheeler?" she asked suddenly.

"Yes, ma'am, if you need me to. I can work all day tomorrow if necessary."

"Excellent!" she said. "You can sleep in the guest house next to Emmons' quarters. He's Mr. Wamsley's handyman, gardener, and part-time chauffeur and I just hate to turn him out after he's been with us for so many years. He's a lovely old man and I wish I could take him to Kentucky with me but of course, I can't. What would people think about such a thing."

It soon became evident to Doug that Mrs. Vi Wamsley was a very lonely woman who desperately wanted someone to converse with or listen to her while she did all the talking. He listened politely, but his thoughts were only on the contents of her garage.

"Well, ma'am," he said, after he had listened to her ramble on and on for about fifteen minutes, "I thank you so much for the cold drink and refreshments, but I'd best be getting back to work." He glanced at her, hoping she'd take the hint.

"Mavis," she called, "ring Emmons and tell him that I would like to have a word with him."

A few minutes later, a stooped, white-haired old man appeared in the doorway, his hat in his hand.

"Oh, Emmons, there you are. Would you please go to the garage and get Sadie, and take her down to the barn? Make sure she's corralled in there. Mr. Wheeler here would like to pack things up in the garage."

The old man nodded his head and quietly disappeared without saying a single word. Doug waited for some sign that the old man had done what was requested of him. He finally got up and strode to the back door. There was no sign of the man or the dog, but the garage door was standing wide open. "Mrs. Wamsley, I think the coast is clear," he said over his shoulder. "I'm going out in the garage."

There was no answer, so he opened the door a crack. All was quiet as he stepped out onto the small porch and looked around, his hand still on the doorknob. He was taking no chances. He gingerly walked down the steps and into the driveway, slowly making his way toward the open garage. He had an uncanny feeling that he was walking into a trap. What if Emmons was still in there with the dog? He took short, cautious steps up to the door, ready for flight if the need should arise. He sighed with relief when he could see to the back of the garage, and it was indeed empty. He caught his breath when he saw the car. It was a beautiful, shiny dark green canvas-topped touring car. It was ornately decorated with brilliant chrome trim that sparkled even in the dim light of the darkened garage. Doug could scarcely breathe.

It was the most beautiful car he'd ever seen. He cautiously entered the garage and almost reverently drank in the beauty of this magnificent machine.

"That's not the car!" Mrs. Wamsley interrupted his thoughts.

"Wha–" Doug whirled around and stared at the woman. He frowned. "What?" he asked, now thoroughly embarrassed. He felt like a little boy again, caught in the act of drooling over something he had no business looking at.

"That's not the car I have for sale," she said. "The one I want to sell is over there." She motioned to an older model black car that was partially hidden by a pile of boxes. Doug peered over her shoulder. An older, hard-topped car, all black and covered with a thick layer of dust, was parked on the other side of the big garage. It was obvious that this car hadn't been driven in quite some time. Doug's mouth went dry. He looked at the car, hoping his disappointment didn't show on his face.

"What year is this one?" he asked.

"Oh my! I was afraid you might ask me something like that. I don't have the slightest idea. All I can tell you is that my husband bought it brand new and he took ever such good care of his automobiles."

"Yes, ma'am, I'm sure he did," Doug agreed, noting that one of the tires was flat. He wiped the side window clean with his handkerchief and peered through the window.

"It's open," she said. "Go ahead and take a look." She yanked on the door handle and invited Doug to have a seat. He noted the beautiful black upholstery. One covered button in the front seat had worked its way loose, but otherwise, it was in perfect condition. The small seat directly behind the driver's seat looked brand new. It just needed a good cleaning.

"How much were you asking for it?" he asked, the blood suddenly pounding in his ears. This was the moment that he'd come here for.

Mrs. Wamsley sighed and looked thoughtful for a few seconds. "I really don't know, Doug. Let me think about it tonight, and I'll let you know before you leave tomorrow. Fair enough?"

"Fair enough!" Doug smiled, though he really wanted to have some concrete answers right now. Oh well, he'd just have to be patient. He sat in the driver's seat and peered out through the small, dusty windshield. A single, rotten-looking wiper blade had torn loose and was hanging down, partially obscuring his view. That could certainly be replaced, he thought. His excitement rose as he examined the older car. Two, small glass-covered dials behind the big steering wheel were shrouded in a thick layer of dust. He wiped one clean with his thumb and stared at the numbers. He began to dream.

Doug somehow got through the rest of the afternoon, packing and repacking, wrapping items in old newspapers, stacking boxes and labeling the largest ones for shipping. He had to admit, he was bone weary by the time supper was served at six thirty that evening. He was ready for bed by eight o'clock and his thoughts turned to Lydia. Wonder how she did today all by herself. He was suddenly, overwhelmingly homesick. Wonder if the boys are all right. The boys! He hadn't had time to think of his family since he'd arrived here. His boys … he smiled just thinking about them. His wonderful family. What would Lydia do tomorrow if he should drive in the driveway with a new car? Would she be happy? What would Aaron think of such a thing? Maybe he was too young yet to think much of anything. He sighed, rolled over on his side and thought about the new car.

Doug heard a rooster crow and opened his eyes. The first faint streaks of daylight were just filtering in through the curtains that decorated the small window of the guest house. Was it Sunday already? He rolled out of bed and searched for his boots. Looked like another beautiful day. He hoped he'd be home by sundown.

"Doug, can you please climb up in the attic and see what's up there for me?" Mrs. Wamsley asked an hour later. "If there's a lot of stuff that needs to be packed, I'll hand you up some boxes. I haven't been up there for ages. There's no telling what all you'll run into. Be careful now," she said as she handed him a lamp.

Doug climbed the steep stairs that led to the stuffy, dark attic. He lit the lamp and looked around. There was indeed a lot to be packed. In fact, he'd never seen so much stuff in all his life. Odds and ends of discarded junk were piled everywhere. Long forgotten pieces of worn, broken furniture were stacked in lopsided heaps. Old books and magazines were piled high at gravity-defying angles. Everything was cloaked in a heavy layer of dust. Thick cobwebs, woven in odd, mosaic patterns reflected the light.

"Send up some boxes," he yelled down to the widow. He busied himself the rest of the morning, packing and labeling boxes and carrying them downstairs to be stacked with the growing pile in the library. When the attic was finally empty, he took a broom and swept it, nearly choking to death on the clouds of dust that he raised.

"Mercy, son, come down out of there before you expire from all that dust."

He handed the broom down to Mrs.Wamsley and then carried a good-sized box nearly full of dirt down to the hallway below. "I need some water," he croaked.

"Mavis," she yelled. "Bring some water, quick. Go out on the back porch, and I'll sweep your clothes off. Goodness me, you're filthy. What will your wife think of me, letting you get this dirty?"

After gulping down the water, Mrs. Wamsley swept the dirt and cobwebs off his back while he beat his legs and chest until he was fairly clean again. He ran his fingers through his hair and mopped his forehead with the sleeve of his shirt.

"You can dump that box of dirt in one of the flower beds, and then I need you to help Emmons load the smaller furniture, and as many of these boxes as you can get on the truck out back," the widow instructed a few minutes later.

Doug soon learned that Emmons was indeed a man of very few words. A simple nod of his head was sometimes the only clue he gave that he understood what was going on. Doug was equally amazed at the strength the old man demonstrated. He was surprisingly agile. He also proved to be an excellent packer. Doug was astonished to see how tightly and perfectly placed the boxes were arranged on the big truck.

"Emmons," he said with an appreciative smile, "you're absolutely amazing." The old man accepted the compliment with a nod of his head and reached down for the next piece of furniture.

It was late afternoon when they had finished loading the truck. All the rooms in the front of the house had that hollow, empty ring to them. Mrs. Wamsley appeared to be very pleased.

"Anything else I can do ma'am?" Doug asked when they had stopped for a break. "You need anything else packed or boxed up?"

"No, young man. You need to be thinking about heading on back home before it gets too dark."

Doug wasn't sure how he should bring up the subject of the car again, but he needn't have worried. Mrs. Wamsley handed him a check for his labor. Doug stared at the amount and then at her signature. Mrs. Rutherford P. Wamsley, she had signed. The check was made out to Douglas Wheeler for the unbelievable amount of one hundred dollars!

Doug's mouth dropped open. He licked his lips and glanced up at her. "Oh, ma'am," he faltered. "I … I can't possibly accept this. This is far too much money. I … I…."

"Nonsense," she interrupted with a snort. "You certainly can accept it and you shall. After all, you earned it … every penny. Now, about the car," she stopped and looked at him for a minute. "I've decided that I need to get exactly one hundred dollars for it. What do you think?" She stood eyeing him with a slight smile on her face. It took Doug a minute or two to comprehend what she was saying. He stared at her and then gulped.

"You mean … you mean this check would pay for the car … in total?"

"That's what I mean!" she said laughing. "Is it a deal?"

Doug gasped and nervously scratched his head. "Oh, boy!" he said breathlessly. He licked his lips. "Oh, Mrs. Wamsley, I never expected … that is … I didn't think … Oh, man … I'm speechless! I'm absolutely overwhelmed!"

"Then we've got ourselves a deal," she said with finality and grabbed the check out of his hand, tearing it in half. "I'll see that Emmons puts some gasoline in it and fixes the tire. Don't ask me how to start the thing. I haven't the foggiest idea."

Doug felt weak. He could scarcely believe his ears. He owned a car! He wanted to hug the old woman and twirl her around the room. He wanted to run through the empty rooms and yell to the top of his lungs. He wanted to do cartwheels. He wanted to sing … to dance … to shout hallelujah to the Lord God above!

Instead, he stood motionless, rooted to the spot, still staring at the woman in front of him.

"Doug," she said, looking curiously at him. "Are you all right?"

He nodded his head and thought for a minute that he might cry, or faint, or something equally undignified. "I just can't believe it!" he finally squeaked. "I absolutely cannot believe it. How do I ever begin to thank you?"

"There's no need to thank me Doug. You earned it … it's yours."

"This is too wonderful for words. My wife … my family … they're all going to be so thrilled. I can't believe this is happening. I can't…." he stammered, at a loss for words.

"It's getting late, young man," she said, giving him a gentle shove toward the door. "Now, get out there and help Emmons get that thing out of my garage … and Doug … drive safely!"

CHAPTER 8
HOMECOMING STORM

Lydia had long since grown weary of pacing. She had nearly worn a hole in the linoleum on the kitchen floor and was tired of hurrying to the window, full of expectation, only to be disappointed again.

"Watch for Daddy," she had told Aaron, who dutifully kept his nose glued to the window, but Doug had not come home.

"Where Daddy?" Aaron asked for the umpteenth time.

"I don't know, sweetheart. I thought he'd be home by now."

She had put Ben to bed early so that she could watch with Aaron. Supper was over and the dishes were finally done. Since the house was stiflingly hot, she decided they'd wait out on the front porch, however, the temperature wasn't much better outside. Ruffy joined them, panting in the late August heat. Lydia sat down in the small swing and fanned herself with an old catalog. Only Aaron seemed not to notice the close heat. He scurried about the yard, finding things that would only interest a two-year-old.

"Look, Mama," he said, handing his mother a small, colorful rock. "Mine."

"Un-huh," his mother said disinterestedly. "A pretty rock."

"Pitty wock," Aaron mimicked.

"Don't put it in your mouth," his mother warned. Her eyes were locked on the dusty road below their house searching for the familiar figure of her husband. Twice she was certain she saw him walking slowly towards the house. Must be the heat, she thought, pressing her palms tightly against her tired eyes. They're playing tricks on me. She was beginning to get worried. Doug had said late afternoon or early evening. It was now dusk and still no sign of him. She swatted at a pesky fly with her catalog and tried to remember exactly what Doug had said to her about his return. She was sure he had said late afternoon or at the latest, early evening. What was keeping him? Did he have to work later than expected, and then walk all the way home from Brighton? Nine miles was a long, long way to walk after two days of hard work. Her anxiety increased with each passing minute. She picked up the worn catalog and began fanning herself again.

Suddenly, Ruffy stood still and listened intently, his keen eyes seeing something in the gathering dusk that she could not see. His nose began twitching, as if he was sorting out scents, trying to determine the unknown.

"What is it, boy? Do you hear something out there? Is it Daddy coming home?" The dog blinked and turned his head to look at her. She reached down and scratched his neck.

"Daddy comin'," Aaron said, clapping his hands together. He jumped down off the small porch, landing on his side. "Ow!" he cried.

Lydia rushed down off the porch and pulled him to his feet. "Aaron, please watch what you're doing, and be a little more careful. You're going to break your neck one of these days." She brushed the dirt from her son's overalls and kissed his sweat-streaked cheek.

Ruffy uttered a low, threatening growl, his body growing tense, his eyes intent on something beyond the fenced-in yard. Lydia listened intently but heard nothing. She watched the big dog. He had heard something, there was absolutely no doubt about that.

"What is it, boy? Huh? What do you hear out there?" She draped her arm over the dog's neck. Ruffy growled again and ran to the edge of the yard. He jumped up on the fence and cocked his head sideways, and began a high-pitched, yipping kind of howl. Lydia stood and strained to see what the dog was hearing. There … a pinpoint of light! It vanished quickly and did not reappear. Her eyes began to ache. Maybe she had just imagined it. Doug hadn't taken a flashlight with him, had he? She couldn't remember seeing one. She watched and waited. There! There it was again, a tiny dim light that seemed to be moving. Her heartbeat quickened. She held her breath for several seconds and waited. Maybe … just maybe it was her husband.

Both Lydia and Aaron jumped when Ruffy started barking in earnest. The little boy hurried to his mother for protection. She knelt beside him and did her best to quiet the dog. "It's all right, boy," she said, rubbing Ruffy's head and ears. The big dog continued to growl, looking resolutely at something out there in the thickening twilight. She turned to walk back up on the porch when she stopped suddenly, her head turned to one side.

"Quiet Ruffy," she said sternly. "I can't hear anything with you making such a racket." What was that noise? It sounded like the faint chug, chug, chug of a motor. She dismissed the idea as highly unlikely, but what else could it be? It was indeed a car approaching their house. She could hear it plainly now in spite of the constant growling and barking. No one else besides some folks by the name of Carson and Mr. Hodgkiss had a car way up here on the mountain, and Mr. Hodgkiss was never out driving his after dark. It had to be Doug, she thought, and that can mean just one thing … he got the car. Despite her eagerness to see him again, she was dismayed to think that he had indeed bought the car. Ruffy began howling and barking loudly and suddenly, in his excitement, jumped the fence and raced down the driveway.

"Ruffy!" she yelled. "Get back here."

"Ruffy, back here!" Aaron repeated.

The dog paid no attention and ran to the end of the driveway, yipping and howling to the top of his lungs. Twin points of light were bobbing up and down as the car maneuvered in and out of chuckholes. Ooo-gaa! Oooo-gaa! Two short blasts from the car's horn announced Doug's arrival back home. Little Aaron rushed to his mother's side, screaming loudly. Ruffy ran circles around the car, barking excitedly.

"Ruffy!" Doug thundered, as he scrambled out of the car. "Cut it out. It's me!" The dog stopped barking, briefly wagged his tail, and then resumed circling the strange car, barking and howling intermittently.

Doug rushed over to his wife and son and hugged them both so tight that he lifted Lydia off her feet. Aaron buried his face in his mother's neck and refused to look at the man who had jumped from this strange machine.

"Hey buddy, it's Daddy!" Doug laughed. He kissed his wife and nudged her toward the driveway and the car. "Ruffy, shut up!" Doug yelled. "Goodnight! He's gonna wake the dead around here." The big, red dog whined and crawled underneath the car.

"Come and look at her, honey," Doug urged. "She's a beauty ... and does it ever handle nicely ... like a dream!" He pulled his wife by her arm up to the side of the car. Aaron still refused to look up from the security of his mother's neck.

"Come on, sweetie pie ... let's go for a quick drive. You're gonna love this car."

"We can't, Doug. Ben's asleep or at least I think he's asleep. Ruffy's made so much noise and then you laid on the horn..."

"Oh, sorry, honey," Doug interrupted. "I didn't know he'd be asleep this early. Come and look at her ... She handles so beautifully. You're gonna love driving her."

Doug is so happy he's delirious, Lydia thought, watching him as he lovingly rubbed the shiny hood with his handkerchief.

Ruffy scrambled out from underneath the car and began sniffing the wheels. "He probably smells Sadie," Doug said.

"Who's Sadie?"

"Sadie is Mrs. Wamsley's dog, a big German Shepherd. She almost ate me alive yesterday. Scared the livin' daylights out of me." He shook his head remembering those terrifying few minutes. "I haven't been that scared … ever! She could have done some serious damage, too." He grinned a boyish grin at Lydia and bent to kiss her again. "Boy, did I ever miss you, young lady," he murmured, kissing her hair, her forehead, her nose....

"Doug!" Lydia warned and stifled a giggle all at the same time. "Aaron's here." She pushed away from him. "How come you're so late? I expected you three or four hours ago," she said rather accusingly. "I was really getting worried about you."

"I know, honey, and I'm sorry. I had no way of letting you know what was going on. Emmons and I had a devil of a time getting this thing started. It's been sitting for quite some time and I guess she just didn't want to get up and go anymore. Emmons tried...."

"Who's Emmons?" Lydia interrupted.

"Emmons is Mrs. Wamsley's handyman and chauffeur. Guess he's been with the family for a long time. Nice old gent. He worked for over an hour trying to get the car running. He'd get it started and then it'd die on him.

"Is this something that you're going to have to do every time you want to drive it?" Lydia asked, trying to keep the sarcasm out of her voice. "Work on it for over an hour?"

"Heavens no!" her husband exclaimed, noting the derisive tone of her voice. "It should run real good now that I've given it a good work out. She can really move when she wants to. Honey, it took me just over twenty minutes to drive from Brighton. Can you imagine that? It took over two and one-half hours to walk there on Saturday. Oh … it's so wonderful. I just love it! Look, Lydia … look at the backseat for the boys."

Lydia followed the beam of Doug's flashlight and took in the neatly upholstered backseat with its rows of covered buttons and layers of thick dust.

"Perfect for the kids," Doug said enthusiastically. "Just needs a little cleaning is all." He drew in a deep breath and exhaled with a blowing sound. "You know something, honey, before cold weather comes, we could take a short trip and maybe drive up north and see your folks. Your mom and dad would love to see the boys, and I know your dad would...." He stopped and glanced at his wife. Her wide smile told him that he'd won her over. She nodded with excitement and grinned, the whiteness of her teeth gleaming, even in the semi-darkness. "Oh, could we, Doug?"

"Sure thing, m' lady," he said with an exaggerated bow. "I'll talk to T.C. or maybe Jack about letting me off for a few days, and we'll take off."

Maybe this car thing wasn't such a bad idea after all. Lydia began formulating some plans right then and there. "Honey, I'm scared to ask, but how much is this thing going to cost us?" Lydia asked rather timidly once they were back inside and Aaron was tucked into bed.

Doug grinned at her, his mouth crammed with fresh apple pie. "Thghat's th bess prrk," he mumbled, crumbs falling into his cupped hands.

"What?" Lydia gasped and then giggled.

Doug swallowed. "I said, 'that's the best part.' We don't owe a single red cent on the car."

Lydia stared at him, her eyes narrowing into a squint. "What? Why not?"

Doug scooped her up and twirled her around in their small kitchen, nearly knocking over a couple of chairs at the table. He set her down and kissed her again and finally related all that had transpired with Mrs. Wamsley that afternoon. "Honey, she is the sweetest lady. I didn't think she was at first, but she really is a dear old soul. You'd love her, I'm sure."

"You mean to tell me that you worked one weekend for a car?" Lydia asked, amazed at the thought.

"That's what I mean to tell you. Isn't that something? She wanted to get rid of this car and she knew I wouldn't just take it so she let me work and *earn it* as she put it. I was flabbergasted and still am. She's quite a lady. I wish you could meet her sometime."

"I'm so proud of you, sweetheart," Lydia said, slipping her arms around her husband's waist. "Are you going to drive to work tomorrow in style?"

"Yeah, if you don't mind. Won't all the guys at the mill be green with envy? There's just a small handful of men who have cars, and they're the ones who have been working at the mill for a long, long time."

"Me firsty," a tiny voice said from the darkened living room. They peered into the room and grinned at their son, who had climbed out of his bed, his sheet dragging on the floor behind him.

"You're firsty?" Doug asked, pulling the small boy into his lap. "Mama, can he have a drink of water this late?"

"Pease, Mama? Drink pease?" Aaron sat in his dad's lap, swinging his legs and looking pleadingly at his mother.

"Yes, of course you can have a drink." His mother kissed the top of his head and gathered him and his sheet up into her arms and carried him to the water pail. "Say goodnight to Daddy," she said as she carried him back to bed and tucked him in.

"We're doing all right honey," Doug whispered in her ear when she returned to the kitchen. "The Lord has certainly blessed us. I have a good job, we have two beautiful little boys who are healthy, we have a nice home and now He's seen fit to bless us with a beautiful car that we don't owe a red cent on. "So much … so very, very much to be thankful for," he murmured.

"I guess I'd better write Mom and let her and Dad know what we're planning," she said excitedly at breakfast the next morning. "They won't believe it."

"Better wait and let me talk to T.C. or Jack first and make sure I can get some time off," Doug said between mouthfuls of toast and coffee. "I certainly should have some time coming. I haven't taken any except for a couple of days when Ben was born, and that was way back in March. I haven't had any time off since then."

Lydia's mind was conjuring up the image of her mother's face when she read the news of their coming. "Mom's going be so excited when she hears about this," she said, her eyes dancing.

"Honey, did you hear a single word I just said?" Doug asked, buttering another slice of toast. "Wait until I talk to the boss before you write...."

"I am!" Lydia said, pinching his earlobe. "I heard you. I'm not writing her until you give me the word."

Doug laughed. "Knowing you, you'll probably have everything packed and waiting at the front door when I get home tonight."

"All right, buster, have your fun," his wife said, trying her best to look hurt. "It just gives me something to look forward to, that's all," she said somewhat defensively.

Doug ignored the tone of her voice and the look on her face. "I'll try to get in to see T.C. or Jack today, but I can't make any promises."

Lydia watched as Doug started the car and waved good-bye as he backed down the driveway. He was right ... the car had started instantly and purred like a contented kitten. She watched him until he was out of sight, a small trail of dust following in his wake. He had looked just like a small boy again ... just before Christmas.

She turned her attention to the unbelievable mound of dirty clothes and diapers piled high on the kitchen floor. From the sound of the kettle on the stove, her water was ready to soak the white things. My poor, old worn scrub board is in for another long workout, she thought as she tossed a handful into the big galvanized tub. Sweat was already dripping from her forehead and running down the sides of her face. She pinned some bothersome loose strands of hair back out of her eyes and bent to the task at hand. She heard snickering. She whirled around and nearly fainted.

There in the doorway of the kitchen stood little Aaron with his five month-old brother in his arms. "Aaron!" she cried, rushing to relieve him of his burden.

"Ben wake," he grunted and grinned up at her.

"Oh honey! Don't ever pick Ben up. He's too heavy for you. You might drop him. How on earth did you lift him out of his crib?"

"Da-da," the baby said as she held him close to her.

"Eat, Mama, me hungwee," Aaron said, and clambered up into his chair at the table. She propped the baby up in his highchair and wedged a blanket around him to hold him upright. She looked at both boys for a few seconds, and wondered if Aaron had pulled the baby out of his crib by his head. Ben seemed to be able to move his head and neck without any trouble and he didn't seem to be in any pain. She watched and worried, but both little boys eagerly ate their breakfast and she finally decided that Ben was none the worse for his ordeal, however his big brother had managed it. A few minutes later, Aaron was busy entertaining Ben by chasing a big fly buzzing around in the window. Ben squealed with delight at the antics of his big brother. She began to relax and forgot about the mound of laundry waiting for her.

Lydia had just pinned the last load on the clothesline when she noticed the darkening thunderheads building overhead. We might be in for it today, she thought. She checked some of the clothes hanging on the line, but they were still too damp to bring in and fold. Hope it holds off for a while longer, she thought, eyeing the clouds with a sense of apprehension.

The storm that broke that afternoon rivaled the one she had gone through the night Aaron was born. The skies simply opened up and emptied their contents with a vengeance. Hailstones the size of small oranges hammered the roof, setting up an unbelievable tumult. Both boys began to scream. Lydia had her hands full trying to comfort them and remain calm herself. Ruffy seemed agitated but otherwise was unaffected by the din. The yard, including her small garden was swept away in a torrent of black, gushing water. Lightning struck close by but thankfully did not strike the house this time. Lydia sat huddled in the middle of the living room with both boys in her lap and Ruffy sitting on her feet. Each time there was a crash of thunder, the boys clung tighter to her and the dog pressed himself harder against her legs. She felt pinned to her chair, unable to move and scarcely able to breathe. She had managed to snatch her laundry in just before the first drops fell. The clothes sat crumpled and crammed in her clothes basket in the kitchen.

When the storm finally abated, she rose to assess the damage. Thankfully, the buggy barn was still standing. Her garden looked as though a train had plowed through the middle of it. There was virtually nothing left. Several fence posts were leaning precariously close to the ground, the rails broken and hanging. Ruts as deep as a foot had been gouged in the driveway. The yard out in front of the house was a tangled mass of small tree limbs, broken boards, and unidentifiable debris. Lydia wondered what the road from Northridge looked like.

"I wonder if your Daddy will be able to make it home tonight with the car," she said aloud, more to herself than to her son.

"Daddy home," Aaron repeated, looking out the front window with his mother.

The familiar sound of water splashing on the floor jerked Lydia's attention away from the scene outside. "Oh no!" she cried, grabbing her mop and bucket. She found Aaron standing under the leak, his hand outstretched, the dirty, brown water splashing in his palm. He blinked as the water dripped off his elbow and puddled around his feet. "Aaron, quit that!" she scolded. "Get your hands out of that water. Let it drip in the bucket. That's what the pail is there for. Keep your hands out of it."

She busied herself with the basket load of clothes, carefully folding the dry things and hanging the damp ones wherever she could find a place. When she had finally finished, she checked on the boys. Both of her sons were seated right next to the bucket of muddy water in the living room, soaked from the waist down. Baby Ben was happily splashing his fat little hands in the water while Ruffy and Aaron were both trying to drink some of it.

"Stop that!" she cried, rushing into the room. "Aaron, don't drink that. It's filthy!" She grabbed Ben up and held him at arm's length. "You're a mess," she said with disgust. "I had you all cleaned up, and now look at you! No wonder Mama has so much laundry to do all the time. Come on, Aaron," she said over her shoulder. "Get in here and get some clean, dry clothes on."

Ben's fussing escalated into screaming as she hauled him into the bedroom. Aaron began to cry. Louder and louder came the protests from both boys, and then Ruffy began to howl. Lydia covered her ears and rushed to the door. "Out you go," she yelled, shoving the excited hound out into the yard. Ben was still screaming when she returned to the bedroom, and Aaron, running a close second to his brother, was hiding under the bed, crying. She could see his feet sticking out.

"Come here to me, boy," she said, dragging him out from under the bed. "Let's get you into some dry clothes." Aaron howled his protests.

"What in tarnation is going on in here?" Doug thundered from the doorway. "I've never in all my life heard such a racket. Aaron, stop it right now, or I'm gonna spank you. Do what your mother says!" Aaron immediately stopped his crying.

Doug picked up his screaming son from his crib. "Hey, hey, hey!" he said loudly in the baby's face. "What's the problem, lil' monkey? Oh brother! He's dripping!"

"I know," his wife replied with a tired, exasperated look on her face. "He's not the only thing dripping around here." She nodded her head toward the living room.

"Yeah," Doug said with a sigh. "I saw the bucket."

"I'll get to Ben as soon as I'm finished with Aaron."

"Here," Doug said, handing the baby to her. "I'll switch with you. You take care of him and I'll change Aaron's clothes. How on earth did they get this wet? Were they out in the storm?"

Lydia filled him in on the details of the afternoon while they wrestled the boys into dry clothing. "By the way," she said, wiping stray hair out of her eyes, "aren't you home kind of early?"

Doug nodded his head as he picked up the soggy clothing from the floor. "Yeah," he said. "Where do you want all this soppin' wet stuff?"

Lydia took the dirty clothes from him and headed back out to the kitchen. Doug followed her, a tiny boy tucked under each of his arms. "When the storm hit this afternoon, T.C. said I could knock off early. I tried to drive home, but the road is washed out so bad, I had to turn around and go back to the mill, park the car there, and walk home. Isn't that terrible? Brand new car and I can't even enjoy it!"

Lydia raised one eyebrow at him. "Sometimes, my darling," she said, with an impish little smile on her face, "feet are better than wheels."

"You think so?" Doug shot back. "Well, Miss Smart Aleck, how would you like to walk when we go see your folks?"

"Oh honey, you got the time off?" she asked hopefully, her eyes sparkling in spite of the tiredness of her face.

"Maybe I did and maybe I didn't," Doug teased.

"Come on, honey, tell me. Did you talk to T.C.? What'd he say? Please, Doug … tell me!"

"Well, Mrs. Wheeler," he said, a wicked little grin playing at the corners of his mouth. He shifted the weight of the boys and cleared his throat. "Do you have your bags packed yet?"

Lydia squealed so loudly, she startled both boys and made them cry again.

CHAPTER 9
RUFFY'S TRIP

Even though Pastor Jamison was delivering one of his finest sermons, it wasn't enough to keep Lydia's mind from wandering. Tomorrow morning, before daybreak, they were leaving on their first vacation. She had washed and ironed clothes, packed and repacked until she was ready to drop. She was mentally checking off items on her 'Things To Do' list. Doug had laughed at her frantic preparations and chided her for worrying about every little detail, but if she didn't worry, who would? She had made arrangements with Max and Georgia's oldest boy, Raymond, to stop by every afternoon after school to feed and water Ruffy. Ruffy loved the Baker kids, and Raymond especially. Check that item off. She had remembered to tell Mr. Lawson, the mailman, to hold their mail for one week. Check that item off. Oh, she thought suddenly, I'd better not forget....

"God will chasten His own and why?" Rodney bellowed from the pulpit. Lydia stared up at him. Was he looking right at her? Her face colored slightly and she lowered her eyes. He must have known I wasn't paying attention, she thought, glancing sideways at Doug. To her utter embarrassment, his eyes were closed, his head nodding forward. She jammed her elbow into his side. His eyes flew open, his face wore a startled, confused look. He sat up in the pew and glanced furtively around him.

Aren't we a great pair? Lydia thought. Here I am planning our vacation, and my husband is sound asleep. Ben was fast asleep in her arms, and Aaron was asleep with his head in her lap. We're all taking a nap this afternoon, no matter what, she thought. Check that item off.

"But the dear Savior loves you, my friend. He died for you. How many friends do you have who would *die* for you?" Rodney asked in a loud voice. "How many?"

"Two!" a tiny voice quickly responded from the back of the church. Ripples of laughter rolled like waves up to the front of the church.

Pastor Rodney removed his glasses and laughed heartily. "Bless your little heart, son," he finally said. "You've got better friends than most of us have ... and you're certainly fortunate to have two of them!"

The entire church enjoyed a few minutes of relaxed hilarity. Much to Lydia's relief, Doug was now fully awake.

"Well," Pastor Rod continued, trying to regain control of his small flock, "out of the mouth of babes."

"Who was that kid?" Doug asked on the way home. "Was that one of Max and Georgia's kids?"

"I don't think so," his wife said. "They were sitting behind us, and I think that child was seated across the aisle from us somewhere toward the back. Wasn't that the cutest thing though?"

Doug laughed again and nodded his head. He had his hands full trying to avoid the deepest ruts and washed out places in the road that hadn't yet been fixed. "Just about the time we get things smoothed out in the road, there'll be another frog strangler, and we'll have to start all over again," he said, gripping the steering wheel tightly.

Lydia clung to Benjamin while Aaron bounced around in the backseat. She began her mental checklist again as Doug expertly maneuvered the car into the buggy barn, now renamed the garage.

"Everybody out," he called, yanking the door open. Ruffy bounded down the driveway, wagging his tail furiously, and happily kissed Aaron in the face as Doug set the little boy down.

"Ruffy, no!" Aaron yelled, wiping his face on his shirtsleeve.

The dog whirled around and promptly licked his face again, nearly knocking him down in the process. As the young family made their way up to the house, Lydia began sifting through all the things that had to be done before tomorrow morning.

Monday morning dawned bright and beautiful. Lydia could hardly contain her excitement as she fed the boys. Doug backed the car up to the house and checked things over one last time before loading all the boxes and bags that Lydia had stuffed their belongings into and stacked by the back door.

"Goodnight, honey," he grunted. "We're only going for a week, not three months. What's in all these bags anyway? We're not gonna have room for the kids."

"The kids are the reason we have to take so much," his wife said defensively. "They need everything under the sun, especially Ben."

The baby heard his name and grinned up at his mother.

"You know I'm talking about you, don't you, you little monkey," she said, spooning another mound of cereal into his open mouth.

"That was the last load, honey," Doug said, wiping his forehead on his sleeve. "I hope there's room for us in the car. Are you about ready with the boys? I want to get on the road before it gets too hot." His wife didn't answer, so he busied himself making sure the dog had water and food. "Hold down the fort, little buddy," he said, scratching the dog's ear. Ruffy seemed to sense the excitement in the air. He whined and trotted behind Doug, never allowing him to get more than a few feet ahead of him.

Lydia changed the baby one last time and made sure Aaron had a few small things to keep him occupied during the trip. She had carefully wrapped sandwiches, fruit and cookies along with a large bottle of water and stuffed them in their small picnic basket. That would take care of dinner. Hopefully, if everything went all right, they should be at Mom and Dad's by sundown.

"All aboard!" Doug yelled as he stuffed the picnic basket into the small space behind the backseat. He helped his wife and son in and slammed the door. Aaron was tucked safely into the backseat with his favorite blanket. The dog, his head sticking above the fence in the front yard, watched their every move.

"Keep the burglars away, Ruffy," Doug yelled. The dog whined and began running up and down the length of the fence. Doug started the car and rolled down the driveway, but as he shifted into low, the car suddenly coughed and backfired, belching a small plume of black smoke from the exhaust.

"What on earth was that?" Lydia asked, a worried expression on her face. "Did something break?"

"Just clearin' her throat," Doug explained. "Nothing to worry about." He glanced in the rearview mirror just in time to see Ruffy leap over the fence and come racing after them. "Go home!" he yelled at the dog. "Go on … get back home."

The dog, however, had no intention of being left behind. He kept pace with the car, even after Doug had picked up a little speed.

"Honey, we can't let him run alongside the car the entire way. What are we gonna do?" Lydia asked with an exasperated look on her face.

Doug slowed the car down and maneuvered around a deep pothole. "Ruffy," he bellowed, "go home!"

The dog paid absolutely no attention whatsoever but crisscrossed behind the car and trotted alongside the passenger door. Lydia bit her lower lip and watched anxiously as Ruffy trotted with relative ease right next to the big front wheel.

"We have to take him back, honey. He can't keep up with us once we get to the pavement. He's apt to get lost if he gets too far from home."

"He can find his way back," Doug assured her. "Don't forget, he's a nose with four legs."

But the big red hound had other plans. Much to Doug's amazement, Ruffy seemed to have grown wings. His long stride carried him, seemingly effortlessly, alongside the car.

Doug finally braked to a stop and opened the door. "You stupid bonehead!" he yelled, stepping down from the car. "What are we gonna do with you?"

Ruffy whined and immediately leaped into the front seat, panting hard.

"Get out of there!" Doug exploded. The dog refused to budge. Doug grabbed him by the neck and pulled hard. Ruffy resisted and began growling.

"Push on him honey," Doug instructed, "an' I'll pull on him. Maybe together we can get him out."

Lydia used her one free hand and pushed while Doug pulled with every ounce of strength he could muster. Ruffy stiffened his legs and growled again, this time more menacingly.

"You stupid, worthless hound!" Doug yelled, his patience having worn thin. "Don't you dare growl at me!"

Ruffy stared straight ahead and seemed to wear a look that said, "Well, take me with you and let's get on with it."

Doug sighed and ran his fingers through his sweat-dampened hair. "Guess he's going with us," he said with resignation. "Get in the backseat, Ruffy. You're sure not ridin' up...."

The hound immediately jumped over the front seat and joined Aaron in the smaller backseat. He sat there looking at Doug as if to say, "Well, are we going or are we just going to sit here all day?"

Doug shook his head in utter disbelief. "If that doesn't beat everything I've ever seen in my entire life! I guess he thinks he's as much a member of this family as any one of us." He shrugged his shoulders, shook his head again, and jumped behind the wheel. "Let's go."

"What about Raymond?" Lydia asked suddenly. "Won't he wonder where Ruffy is?"

"Probably," Doug agreed, "but I don't know how to let him know he's going with us ... unless we turn around and go back up the mountain, and I'm not losing any more time. We've lost enough as it is because of that crazy mutt."

"Look at him!" Lydia said suddenly.

The dog looked at Lydia and then at Doug and then back to Lydia, yawned luxuriously, and barked happily.

"He looks just like he's smiling," she exclaimed.

"And why wouldn't he?" her husband asked with a wry grin. "He won, didn't he?"

It was hard to tell who was sleeping on whom ... whether Ruffy had curled up against Aaron or Aaron had leaned on the dog and fallen asleep. They were actually using one another for a pillow. Aaron had his arm thrown up over the dog's neck.

"You know," Lydia said softly, "for some strange reason, that makes me want to cry. Aren't they sweet together like that?"

Doug glanced over his shoulder and smiled. "Yeah," he agreed, "but you're not going to think so when you see how much hair is sticking to our son. That's when you'll want to cry."

Lydia wrinkled up her nose. "How much farther, Pop?" she asked in a little girl voice.

Doug threw her a withered, sideways glance. "Take a nap, kid," he advised.

Doug drove in silence, his wife, children, and dog all fast asleep. He glanced around the interior of the car appreciatively. He had spent countless hours polishing, scrubbing and spit-shining his marvel machine. He couldn't wait for his father-in-law to see it. Harry would appreciate the fine workmanship that had obviously gone into this great car, a Hudson coupe … a Hudson Super Six, T.C. had told him the first morning he had driven it in to work. All the men had gathered around the car, inspecting and admiring it. Some had looked a little green with envy, Doug had thought.

"A fine machine … and an expensive one too," T.C. had said. "If I didn't already have a good car, I'd try to talk you outta this one."

Doug had polished every crack and crevice, inside and out, right down to the beautiful hardwood spokes of the wheels. He listened to the fine purr of the six-cylinder motor with the appreciation of a conductor listening to a live symphony. How truly blessed he was, he thought, glancing quickly at his wife beside him. Look at how far we've come in just a few short years, and here we are on the road, taking our first vacation in our new car. He smiled at the thought. Our new car! He ran his hands lovingly over the big steering wheel and sighed contentedly. He wondered briefly what his older brother, Carl, and his wife, Peggy, would say if they could see him now. They'd probably be a little jealous, especially Peggy. He could almost see the envious look on her face.

A small head popped up in the backseat. "Me hungwee Daddy," Aaron said suddenly. It was time to stop for dinner.

Harry and Lillian rushed out into the yard when they heard the car driving up their long, narrow driveway. Lydia had her door open before the car rolled to a stop. She flung herself and Benjamin into the arms of her mother. Everyone talked at once.

Harry shook hands with Doug and stood back to admire the car. He shook his head slowly and whistled, a wide grin spreading from ear to ear on his rugged, but still handsome face. "That is one beautiful automobile," he said enthusiastically. "I'll trade you straight across. What year is it, a 1919 or a '20?"

Doug grinned and stretched his tired back muscles. "1920, I think," he replied happily. "Pop, take a look at the interior," he invited, pulling his father-in-law over to the door.

"Out Daddy," Aaron called loudly from the backseat.

"Hey! I guess we'd better let the rest of the family out," Doug said with a chuckle. He opened the door and pulled Aaron out and set him down on the ground just as Ruffy bolted from the car and streaked past them, yipping excitedly.

Lydia's parents looked a little startled at the sudden commotion. "Boy, you weren't kidding. You did bring the entire family, didn't you?" Harry laughed as Ruffy came dashing back through the yard, pausing only briefly to check out an interesting scent in the flower bed up next to the house.

The two men unloaded the car while Lydia and her mother chatted happily about babies in general and specifically how much the two boys had grown.

"Aaron, come and see Nana," Lydia called. "Nana wants to see how big you are now." The little boy wrapped his arms around Doug's legs and refused to get any closer to his grandmother. He shook his head and closed his eyes tight. "He thinks if he can't see you, Mom, then you can't see him either," Lydia explained. "He'll warm up to you in a bit and then you won't be able to get rid of him."

Lillian took Benjamin from her daughter and kissed his little cheeks and hands. "What a handsome big boy you are," she crooned. "Oooohhh! I love these babies," she murmured, squeezing the baby tight. The baby smiled at her, which prompted more kissing and hugging.

Suddenly, Aaron was standing at her feet, holding his arms straight up to his grandmother. "Me kiss, Nana," he said.

Lillian handed the baby back to her daughter and picked Aaron up, kissing his hands, his cheeks and his forehead. "You're Nana's big boy," she said, stopping long enough to get a close up look at her oldest grandson. "My, my, how you've grown."

Lydia walked slowly through the house. Very few things had changed over the years since she had married and moved away. Her mother had left her bedroom exactly as it had been the last time she had seen it … pastel pink with white lace curtains. It seemed smaller than she remembered, but it was plenty big enough for her and Doug and the baby. Aaron would sleep in the guest room with Ruffy. She sat on the edge of the bed and slowly studied the pictures on the walls. The first was her graduation picture and the one next to it was of Lydia and her best friend, Dolores. On the opposite wall, there was a small picture of her and her first date … what was his name? Fred or Frank? Strange that she couldn't remember. At the time, she had thought she was in love forever. She smiled and set Benjamin down on the polished hardwood floor.

She walked over to a tiny picture that was wedged in the frame of a bigger one. It was of her, when she was about six or seven, holding Snickers, her cat, when he was just a kitten. Poor Snickers, he up and disappeared one day and they never saw him again … never knew what had become of him. Lydia remembered crying her eyes out when Daddy's search proved to be fruitless. She vowed never to have another pet … ever! She tucked the tiny picture back into the frame and picked up Benjamin, who had been sitting quietly on the floor, taking in every detail of the small room. "Looking for something to get into, weren't you?" she said, kissing his soft cheek. "Come on, pumpkin, let's go find brother and Nana."

Within five minutes, Aaron and his grandmother were inseparable. He followed her in and out of every room, asking a million questions, and getting into everything within his reach.

The men piled the boxes and bags just inside the front door and hurried back outside to compare engines and tire sizes.

"Cars, cars, cars," Lydia complained to her mother. "That's all Doug has on his mind anymore. Look where he put all our stuff!"

Her mother glanced in the living room at the front door and laughed. "At least he got them in the house. Don't complain too loudly, honey," she said with a wink. "After all, it's because of your new car that you're finally here after all these years."

"Well, that's true," Lydia agreed, "but you'd think he could think of something else to talk about once in a while."

The two women were bustling about the kitchen, setting the table and preparing supper, when suddenly they were startled by a frantic commotion outside. They could hear Ruffy howling about something.

"Ruffy!" Doug yelled. "Get back here, Ruffy."

"Oh, that stupid dog!" she muttered, looking out the dining room window. She explained to her mother how they just had to bring him with them. Suddenly, the car started and backed down the driveway. "Where on earth are they going?" Lydia asked. "We've almost got supper on the table." She and her mother watched as the car disappeared down the long driveway.

"Maybe they're going into town for something … maybe some ice cream that I asked your father to bring home two days ago, or perhaps Doug talked him into going for a short ride. I just wish they had told us how long they're going to be gone. This roast isn't going to stay hot forever." She pulled a sheet of hot biscuits from the oven and covered them with a towel. "Oh well, I guess we'll eat when they're finally finished playing with that new toy of yours."

Lydia made a face and went to see what Aaron was up to. She found him sitting on the big sofa in the living room, a big animal picture book in his lap. He was reading to baby Ben, who was drinking in all the details of each picture.

"Isn't that the most precious sight in this world?" Lillian whispered to her daughter, slipping her arms around her waist.

Mother and daughter watched quietly from the doorway as Aaron continued his explanation of each picture. Ben leaned forward to scratch a picture and drooled on the book. Aaron pushed him back away from the book. "No, Ben!" he cried and wiped the pages on the edge of the sofa cushion.

"Isn't that one of my old books?" Lydia cried suddenly, noticing the front cover. "You've kept it all these years?"

Her mother nodded. "You used to love that book … mother animals and their babies, remember?" She put her arms around her daughter again and held her a few seconds. "Where does the time go, honey?" she asked somewhat wistfully.

"Good question," Lydia agreed. "I can't believe how fast my boys are growing."

Aaron looked up at the two women in the doorway, snapped the book closed and slid down from the couch. "Eat, Mama. Me hungwee."

"That's why he's growing so fast," Lydia's mother said with a laugh. Her daughter rushed over to catch Ben before he toppled from the couch. "Let's get these little boys fed and maybe by the time they're finished, our big boys will be back from their little joy ride," Lillian suggested. They were just putting the food on the table when Doug and Harry returned.

"Ruffy's gone," Doug announced with disgust. "He chased a cottontail through the yard and disappeared. We can't find him anywhere."

"He'll be back," Lydia's dad assured them. "Hounds have an uncanny sense of direction. He's not lost. He'll be fine out there. Don't worry about him."

Funny, Lydia thought. That's almost word for word what Daddy had said to her so many years ago when Snickers had disappeared.

Harry pulled his chair up to the table and glanced around at the worried faces in the room. He hoped against hope that he was right about this. What on earth did he know about hounds anyway? The way his wife was looking at him, he guessed that she was asking herself the same question.

"Where Ruffy go?" Aaron asked after they had asked the blessing on the food.

"He's out chasing bunny rabbits," Doug said simply.

Doug and Lydia kept a wary ear tuned for the familiar sounds of the return of their runaway hound, but Ruffy did not come back.

The next morning, there was still no sign of him.

"Guess I'd better go out looking for him again," Doug said with a worried frown on his face. "The thing that concerns me the most is the fact that he's in unfamiliar country. It's not like he was out roaming around at home."

Lydia nodded, wishing now that they had taken the time to take Ruffy back home and tie him up or something.

"We'll find him. Don't worry," her dad said enthusiastically. "He can't have gone far."

Lydia and her mother played with the boys, went for a walk, and chatted about old times, old neighbors, and old loves. They thoroughly enjoyed the morning, but Lydia couldn't shake the feeling that maybe something terrible had happened to their trusted dog. He had never stayed away this long before. She related the story to her mother about how Ruffy had bravely chased the mountain lion up a tree and couldn't help shedding a few tears.

"He'll be back, honey, you'll see," her mother comforted her.

When Doug and Harry returned just before noon, their faces told the story before they climbed out of the car. No sign of the dog.

Try as she might, Lydia couldn't help the return of her tears. "Where could he be?" she sobbed in her mother's arms.

"Don't fret so, honey," her mother said. "You'll frighten the babies."

"Sweetheart, he'll find his way back here ... just wait and see," her dad tried his hand at consoling her, but he wasn't so sure of that now. "When he gets hungry, he'll show up," he predicted, trying to sound optimistic.

The following morning, Lydia got up early and went outside to check Ruffy's bowl of water and food that she had set out for him just in case, but it was untouched. She sat in the porch swing, listening to the noisy mockingbird's song. "I know this may sound silly to you, Lord, but we can't leave here without knowing what happened to our poor dog. Please, Lord, send him back home or help Doug and Daddy find him, please, Lord," she prayed in a whisper. "Please watch over him and keep him safe. Amen."

The week passed far too quickly, each day a blur of activity, and each day a futile search for the missing dog. All too soon, it was time to head for home. It was with doubly heavy hearts that the young Wheeler family loaded the car and stood in the yard, not wanting to say their final good-byes.

Lillian, her face wet with tears, kissed her grandsons over and over. Lydia clung to her mother, tears streaming down her face.

"Ruffffyyy!" Aaron called in his high, squeaky little voice. "Where Ruffy go?" he asked the adults for the millionth time.

Lydia and her mother stood helplessly beside the car, their arms wrapped around one another, and cried. Even Harry looked quickly away, not wanting his grandson to see the emotion that had sprung up in his own eyes. Doug picked Aaron up and put him in the backseat.

"Where Ruffy?" Aaron asked, with a trace of panic in his voice. "Daddy!" he cried. "No, no!" He tried to force his way back out of the car.

"Stay back there," Doug ordered, trying his best to swallow the lump in his throat that threatened to choke him.

"Daaaddddyyy!" Aaron screamed. "No, Daddy!"

"Come on, Lydia," Doug murmured, "let's go." Tears that had been threatening all morning now found their way to the surface, and Doug angrily brushed them away. "We have to get going."

Lydia hugged her parents one last time and opened the car door. She set the baby down on the front seat and turned to climb up on the seat herself when a streak of red zoomed past the front of the car. The dog skidded to an abrupt halt beside the car and looked up at Doug as if to say, "You surely weren't leaving without me, were you?" Doug stared openmouthed at the animal in front of him.

Lydia ran to her husband's side, her parents right behind her. Little Aaron was still screaming from the backseat, and Benjamin used the steering wheel to pull himself to a standing position and stared out the window at the commotion going on around him.

Ruffy basked in all the loving attention he was receiving. Doug checked him over for signs of injury while Lydia fed him and gave him all the water he could hold. Harry and Lillian washed and doctored his worn, ragged feet and pulled burrs that were attached to his long ears. Aaron showered him with hugs and wet, slobbery kisses. Happy tears were unashamedly shed by the adults, and Aaron and Benjamin, feeling the excitement around them, cried their loudest.

A full hour and a half later, the family was once again loaded up and ready to leave ... this time with the fifth member of the family, who had been given a soft quilt of his own to curl up in. By the time good-byes had been said again and the car rolled slowly down the driveway, he was fast asleep.

CHAPTER 10
LYDIA'S LESSON

"Come on, honey, at least give it a try. I know you'll be good at it, and you just might find that you enjoy it," Doug pleaded, as he followed his wife outside to the clothesline.

"Douglas Wheeler, I'm telling you for the last time, no!" Lydia angrily jammed clothespins down hard on the line and finished hanging out her last load. She turned on her heel, picked up the empty clothes basket, and walked briskly back inside the house with Doug right behind her.

"Honey, lots of women are driving these days and besides, what if one of the kids gets hurt or sick or something like that? Wouldn't it be nice if you could jump in the car and drive them in to see Doc Sorenson?"

"Of course it would," Lydia agreed. "But I hardly think that's going to be possible when you drive the car into work every day."

"Well, then, I'll drive it every other day, or I'll take it on Tuesdays and Thursdays and you can have it the other three. How 'bout that? Wouldn't that work?"

"Oh, Doug, use your head. You're saying that the boys can only get sick or hurt on Mondays, Wednesdays and Fridays. Is that what you're saying?" Lydia asked, her voice dripping with sarcasm. "Because if it is, Doug, you're not making any sense at all."

"Oh for heaven's sake, honey. You're acting just like a child. Why, I'll bet Aaron would be more willing to sit behind the wheel than you are."

Aaron, who was now four years old, perked up his ears at the mention of his name. "Can I, Daddy?" he asked.

"Can you what?" his father asked without taking his eyes off his wife.

"I don't know," Aaron admitted. "Whatever you and Mama are talkin' about."

"Never mind what I'm talking to Mom about." Doug followed Lydia into the bedroom and sat on his side of the bed and watched her as she adeptly folded fresh, clean laundry.

"Lydia, be reasonable. All you have to do is follow my instructions. I'll be right there with you. Just do everything I say, and we'll take it nice and slow. I'll even start the car for you so all you have to learn today is rolling forward in low gear, that's all." He could sense that her reserve was breaking down. She didn't look at him … she didn't smile, but she didn't flat out say no either. Doug charged ahead. "What do you say honey? How about it, huh?"

Lydia sighed and glared at her husband. She shook her head and groaned loudly. "Oh Doug, you make me so angry sometimes. I can't for the life of me figure out why you're so determined that I learn to drive. What if I dent a fender, or hit something and tear a piece off your precious car? What about that? Worse yet, what if I have a bad crash and roll the car on its side? We could all get hurt. Assuming that we survive, are you going to be furious with me for weeks on end for wrecking your pride and joy? What about that, Doug?"

"It's not my pride and joy, honey. Get that straight right now. It's a machine and it's ours, Lydia, yours and mine. And in answer to your first question, no, I'm not going to be mad and yell at you, because I know you won't hit anything. Besides, what's there to hit out there anyway? There's absolutely nothing but a few, small rocks that won't hurt a thing. There aren't any trees right beside the road, and certainly no other cars way up here."

Lydia sighed again and looked straight at her husband. "All right, Doug," she said with resignation, "but only if you promise not to push me too fast, and you'd better not yell at me."

"I promise, sweetheart, I give you my word. Come on, boys. Mama's gonna learn to drive the car today. You want to go for a little ride?"

Both boys jumped up from the living room floor and raced each other to the back door.

"Move, Ben, I was here first," Aaron said, shoving his little two-year-old brother out of the way.

"Me first," Ben protested and promptly swung his tiny fist at his brother.

"Quit it!" Aaron yelled, twisting his brother's arm and shoving him away from the door.

"Both of you stop it right this minute or you can stay in the house," their dad warned. "Come on, Mama, put the laundry down and let's go have a driving lesson. I'll go down to the garage and get the car. I'll even back it up the driveway so you don't have to learn reverse today … how 'bout that?"

Lydia nodded her consent. Why did she always let Doug talk her into such crazy schemes? She was such a weakling when it came to him. He could talk her into absolutely anything, no matter how ridiculous or foolish it seemed to her. What was the matter with her anyway? She and the boys waited until Doug brought the car up from the garage.

"Get in the backseat, boys," Doug said with a wave of his hand. He helped Benjamin climb up on the seat. "Come on, honey. I'll show you the pedals first."

Lydia climbed up into the driver's seat and timidly grabbed the steering wheel.

"Now, first of all, there are three pedals on the floor," he instructed. "Move your feet a minute. The first one over there is the gas pedal. The second one is the brake, and this one here is the clutch. You have to push this third one down in order to change gears. You got that?"

Lydia nodded her head and tightened her grip on the steering wheel. "Doug, I don't know about this," she said nervously. Her stomach began to churn as her apprehension mounted.

"Nonsense, honey. Now, just pay attention. This lever on the floor ... we use that to start the car, but since it's already running, we won't go through that today. Sit down back there in the seat," he said sternly to the two little boys who were standing right behind their mother, watching every move their parents made.

"Now," Doug continued, "keep your foot on the brake and the clutch, then remove your foot from the brake, and ease out on the clutch ... slowly. That's all we're going to do for today, okay? Just learning the pedals, and driving in first gear. Ready?"

Lydia drew a ragged breath and nodded, biting her lower lip. She now had a white-knuckle grip on the wheel.

Doug moved around to the passenger's side and hopped in. "Sit down, boys," he ordered again over his shoulder. "All right, babe, put the car in first gear. Just slide the gearshift forward as far as it'll go. Is your foot on the brake and the clutch?"

"Yes," she squeaked.

He leaned forward to check the position of her feet. "All right, take your foot off the brake and ease up on the clutch," Doug said, grinning at her. "And relax!"

She glanced at her husband. "Now what?" she asked, digging her nails into the palms of her hands.

"Slowly, slowly, let the clutch out and give her a little gas ... just a little."

Lydia followed his instructions, easing her foot off the clutch and giving it some gas. The car lurched forward suddenly, shuddered and died. Terrified, she stared at Doug. "What'd I do wrong?" she asked, her face turning slightly pale.

"I think you eased up on the clutch a bit too fast." He glanced again over his shoulder. "I'm not going to tell you two again," he yelled. "Sit down in the seat."

Both boys clambered up in the seat and glared at one another. "Now I can't see nothin'," Aaron complained, his arms folded across his chest, his lower lip sticking out.

"See nuffin'," Ben repeated, folding his short arms across his chest as well.

"Too bad," their father said as he jumped out of the car. He got the car started again, expertly jammed the gearshift in neutral, and listened a moment while the car idled smoothly. Lydia climbed back into the driver's seat.

"All right, honey, let's try it again," he coaxed. "Get your feet back on the pedals and push the gearshift forward. That's right!" he encouraged, watching her every move. "Now, just ease up on that clutch and give her a little more gas." The car began to roll down the driveway. "Good, good," Doug said approvingly. "What'd I tell you, Mrs. Wheeler? You're drivin'!"

Lydia flashed a quick smile in his direction, not daring to take her eyes off the driveway ahead. Faster and faster the car rolled down the driveway toward the garage.

"Now, honey, don't forget about steering … you're headed toward the garage. Honey, slow it down some and steer … watch where you're going!"

"I am!" Lydia snapped. "Don't yell at me!"

Faster and faster, the car lurched down the driveway. Lydia did her best to steer, but the car seemed to have a mind of its own. She steered toward the left, and then hard toward the right, the car bouncing wildly over small rocks that lined the driveway, and suddenly, the garage loomed right in front of her. Her eyes widened in horror.

"Honey!" Doug yelled. "The brake … hit the brake!"

"I am!" Lydia screamed. "Nothing's happening!"

The car hurtled with lightning speed through the front of the garage.

"Lydia!" Doug bellowed, grabbing at the wheel. "Hit the brake!" There was a deafening explosion as the car plowed through the back of the garage and finally shuddered to a stop.

Large, splintered pieces of siding, two by fours, dirt, and other debris rained down on the terrified family. As the dust began to settle, they stared in stunned silence, hardly daring to breathe. Aaron finally broke the silence inside the car.

"Wow!" he whispered in awe. "That was fun, Mama. Do it again!"

Doug began to laugh and Lydia began to cry. He reached for his wife and held her terrified, shaking body. "It's all right, sweetheart. There, there. We're not hurt … right, boys?"

The wide-eyed children stared first at their father, and then at the wreckage surrounding the car. Benjamin suddenly bent forward and kissed his mother on the neck.

"Not cry, Mama," he said, a worried expression on his face. He patted her neck and shoulders, trying his best to console her.

Doug got out of the car, pulled a few of the broken boards off the roof and the hood, and tried to assess the damage to the garage. The entire back of the garage would have to be rebuilt. He turned his attention to the car. Remarkably, there was one visible scratch to the front chrome bumper of the car. He could see no other damage at all. He helped his family out of the car and back up the driveway to the house.

"Well, Mrs. Wheeler," he said, taking his wife in his arms. "You had your first driving lesson today."

"And my last," his wife said. The look on her face told him he'd better not pursue the subject any further.

"Wash up for dinner," she called a few minutes later to the two boys who were playing just outside the kitchen door.

Doug stood lost in thought, absentmindedly washing his hands at the sink. He reached for the towel and turned to face his wife. "You know, honey, maybe I could build a wider garage and then you…."

"Doug! I don't want to hear another word about my driving. Not another word!"

The screen door banged shut as the boys entered the kitchen. "Mama, that was the most fun thing we've *ever* done," Aaron said enthusiastically. "I wish you would do it again!"

"Me too, Mama," Doug teased, "except I'm fresh out of garages."

He ducked just in time as a large apple flew past his head and hit the far wall.

CHAPTER 11
LAUREY MOUNTAIN SCHOOL

"I still think the old Laurey place would make an excellent school building. Sure, it would take a lot of work, but if we all pitched in...." His voice trailed off as a slight commotion captured the attention of everyone in the room who had gathered to discuss the overcrowded school situation in Northridge.

"There's a skunk at the door," one of the Farley boys said in a hushed tone.

Every neck craned as people tried to get a glimpse of the shiny, black eyes that peered in at them through the screen door. A breathless calm settled over the crowd as they watched the small creature with apprehension. The animal seemed curious about the bright lights and noise and didn't appear to be in any hurry to head for home. Finally, much to everyone's relief, it ambled off into the darkness without incident.

"Whew!" exclaimed Glen Richardson, who seemed to be in charge of the meeting. "That was pretty close! Now, where were we?"

Max Baker, Georgia's husband, wedged his thumbs behind his suspenders and began again. "I was sayin' that we should look into the Laurey place. It's not been used now for years, but it's still in pretty decent shape. It's well off the road, and certainly within walking distance for all our kids up on the mountain."

The room became a hum of murmured voices again as everyone considered this suggestion.

"What about the well? You suppose it's gone dry by now?" Harold Baird asked. "I could look into that for you if you'd like and let you know what I find out."

"I'll tell you what," Glen Richardson said loudly. "Let's appoint several people to gather information for us, and we'll meet again right here next Monday night and see what we've all come up with. Does that sound like a sensible plan?"

Several people nodded, and Glen began writing names down on a large sheet of paper.

"Harold, why don't you go talk to Grandma Laurey and ask her about the property and the well an' all, and see what's involved with that? If we get the property, and it looks good, then Max, you, and Doug talk to Jack Doss about donating some lumber to fix the roof on that old building. I understand it's about done for."

Max and Doug nodded in unison.

"My wife, Evelyn," Glen continued, "still has her teaching certificate. She's going to talk to the school board in town and see what process we need to go through to pull this thing together. I understand from Miss Lender that she's expecting as many as fifty students when school starts this fall, and I don't need to tell any of you that fifty kids in one room is about twenty-five too many. She doesn't know where she's going to put all of them. Something has to be done and soon. We need to gather our information and act fast on this if we're serious about having a school up here on the mountain."

The room became a hubbub of noise once again as people talked to one another about the best plan for attacking this problem.

"Meeting is adjourned," Glen said loudly, "until next Monday night."

"Can you imagine that?" Lydia said on the way home an hour later. "Fifty-some students this fall! Poor Miss Lender is going to need some help, that's for sure. Do you think we have a prayer of getting that old building ready by then?"

Her husband shook his head and shifted gears, easing the car down into a particularly deep rut in the road. "I doubt it," he said. "But I guess it really depends on what shape the old place is in right now, and how many folks are willing to pitch in and do their part to get it ready. The biggest problem before us right now is whether or not Grandma Laurey is willing to sell, and if so, for how much. She may want so much for the place that the school board will say no to the whole thing. We'll just have to wait and see what she says about it. But she might not want to part with the old homestead … even though she owns most of the mountain right now."

Phoebe Laurey, now in her mid-eighties, was sole heir to a vast amount of property in the mountains north of town. Years before, people living on the mountain had given it the name of Laurey Mountain. Most of the mountain folks were either renting property from Grandma or had purchased a few acres from her. Even though she was a kindly old woman, Doug was a little skeptical about the school plans.

"Max and I are gonna stop by the old place on our way home from work tomorrow night and have a look at it. We may have to start all over with our school plans," Doug said, swerving to avoid a good-sized rock in the middle of the road.

"Boy, wouldn't that be wonderful if our kids could go to a school closer to home?" Lydia said, completely ignoring Doug's last remark. "I've always worried about how to get them to and from school if they went to Northridge. Maybe I won't have to worry about that anymore."

"We'd do what everyone else on the mountain has done for years and years I guess," Doug said. "Drive them ourselves or make them walk, which isn't much fun in the wintertime, believe me."

The following evening, Max and Doug bounced over the rutted path – one could hardly call it a road – that led to the Laurey property. In some places, weeds had grown so thick and tall that the original road was completely obliterated. What had once been a beautiful front yard was now overgrown with weeds and brush. The roof of the front veranda was partially caved in, and windows in the front had long since been broken out. A rock chimney gave evidence that either a potbellied stove or a fireplace had once been used to heat the home. Doug noted that the roof sagged dangerously next to the chimney. The two men cautiously stepped up on the porch and looked around. The front door was nailed shut, and someone had scrawled 'No Trespassing' across the door in crude, hand-drawn black letters. Doug poked his head inside a window.

"We can get in this way, Max," he motioned to his friend. Both men climbed through the broken window and stepped into a large room, which probably at one time had served as the living room or parlor. Faded linoleum in a flowered pattern still covered the floor. An old cast iron stove stood erect in one corner, reminiscent of a soldier on duty. The stovepipe was gone, and on closer inspection, they discovered that the roof had leaked around the chimney, and the bottom of the enormous stove had completely rusted out. The walls of the room were painted a drab gray. Thick cobwebs and years of dust blanketed the room. There was a strong, musty odor that reminded Max of his army barracks back during the war. The two men gingerly made their way into a small room that had undoubtedly been a bedroom. The kitchen was small but surprisingly cheery-looking. The floor, where it was obvious that a large wood-burning cook stove had once stood, was caved in. Evidence of field mice was everywhere. Out behind the house was a narrow walkway leading to the well, which was ringed about with loose rocks, the mortar having fallen into decay years before. Quite some distance behind the well was an overturned outhouse with its door hanging by one rusty hinge.

Max removed his hat and scratched his near-bald head. "Well, what do you think?" he asked Doug when they had inspected all the rooms and the grounds outside. "It's really pretty sound-looking for such an old place … that is, except for the roof," he added, looking up toward the chimney.

"Wonder what year this house was built?"

"No tellin'," Doug replied. "Could be close to a hundred years old. You're right about the roof," he added, looking up at the sagging portion next to the chimney. The men walked back inside and looked around again. "We could knock this wall out here," Doug said, motioning to the wall that separated the kitchen from the living room, "and make this one big room and the two smaller rooms could be used for storage or a coat room, don't you think?"

Max nodded his head. "Let's go back outside and take another look at the well," he suggested. "I know Harold said he'd check it out, but it wouldn't hurt to have two opinions on it." The men climbed back out through a small kitchen window, since the back door was nailed shut as well, and walked down the path out to the well and looked around. An old, rusty pump was still intact but appeared to be useless.

"Harold's gonna have to take a look at this," Doug said. "After all, that's his expertise ... but you know what? I think it definitely has possibilities," his skepticism slowly vanishing. "Sure would take a lot of work, but if everyone pitched in, like you said, we could make this happen ... and in relatively short time."

Their excitement grew as they walked around the perimeter of the house, discussing all its good points and what changes needed to be made.

"Assuming Grandma Phoebe deeds the place to the community, our biggest problem is going to be water," Max said, "but if there's still water on the place, I think it would be ideal."

Doug nodded in agreement. "We'll just have to wait and see what Harold finds out from Grandma and see what he thinks about the well and the water situation. If all that works out, then we'll go to Jack and see about the mill donating some lumber. You suppose he'd part with that special order of ash that someone over in Brighton ordered two years ago and never came to pick up? That stuff would make great tables or desks."

"It sure would," Max agreed, "I'd forgotten all about that order. Wonder what ever happened with that? Is it still piled up on the back lot?"

"Last I heard, it was," Doug said. "I haven't had any reason to be on the back lot for such a long time, I don't know if it's still back there or not."

"Guess it wouldn't hurt to ask him about it."

"No," Doug agreed with a grin. "Ye have not because ye ask not. Right?"

"That's right!"

The two men parted company, encouraged by what they saw, and both were eager to do something about it. Doug was brimming over with enthusiasm when he finally arrived home. He followed Lydia around the kitchen sounding her out on his ideas while she cooked supper.

"Boy, you've sure changed your tune," she said, grinning up at him, "but I have to admit that does sound awfully good, honey. I had no idea that place was as big as it sounds. Let's just hope and pray that we get it, and there's plenty of water on the property."

The following Monday night, the crowd at Deacon's Grocery Store was even larger. Everyone in town called the store owner Deacon, though no one knew exactly why. His real name was Byron Smalley, but Deacon seemed to fit him better than Byron. The old man had worked diligently all week long clearing a large area in the back of his grocery store, and he was amazed to see how quickly his storeroom had filled up. The latecomers were forced to stand in the aisles out front in the store itself. Glen Richardson tapped a fork on the side of a glass to get everyone's attention.

"Mighty glad to see the big turn out this week," he said loudly.

"Let's get right down to business and see what we've come up with so far."

"Can't hear you, Glen," someone from out in the store section yelled. "Speak up!"

Glen cleared his throat and called the meeting to order. "First order of business ... Harold ... is Harold Baird here tonight?" He looked over the crowd with a frown on his face.

"No, Glen, he isn't," a small voice said from the back. Nancy, Harold's wife, slowly pushed her way up front. "I'm afraid he's home with a bad throat and fever," she explained.

"Sorry to hear that, Nan. Did he get a chance to go see Grandma Laurey?" Glen inquired, squinting at the tired-looking woman who was still trying to make her way up front.

Nan Baird nodded her head. "He sure did, Glen," she said with a wide smile. "I'm happy to report that Grandma said she'd be happy to sell the old homestead to the community for such a worthy cause."

Wild cheering, clapping and whistling rose to a crescendo to the point that Glen had to bang on the heavy glass several times to regain order. "I think I can speak for all of us when I say that is extremely good news," he said with a grin. "The question now is how much is she asking for it?"

"One dollar!" Nan yelled with a short, excited laugh.

"One dollar?" Glen gasped.

The entire company of people stood in rapt silence for about ten seconds, and then wild cheering, clapping, and hoots of joy erupted again and spilled out into the street. Nan Baird finally worked her way up front and handed Glen a yellowed piece of paper.

"This is the deed to the property, water rights included," she said. "Grandma Laurey signed it over to the town of Northridge with the stipulation that it become a school … and here's the Bill of Sale."

"I'm beginning to think this is something we should have looked into years ago," Glen yelled when he could find his voice again. The wild, joyous celebration in the store rivaled the one that took place the day the war ended a few years before. "My wife, Evelyn…." he yelled, paused a moment, hoping for a lull in the din, and started again. "My wife talked to the school board and she now has the floor," he yelled, trying desperately to gain control of the crowd again. "Honey, come on up here."

Mrs. Richardson stepped up in front of the crowd and cleared her throat as her husband hammered loudly on the table with a broken handle from an old coffee grinder.

"Well, friends and neighbors," she began, "the school board in Northridge is only too happy to help us with the task at hand. I spoke with the Superintendent of Schools…"

Wild cheering erupted once again, and Mrs. Richardson smiled and waited a few moments before continuing. "As I was saying, I spoke to the Superintendent last Thursday, and he has assured me that they'll be available to help us every step of the way. We will still be governed by their rules and regulations, and it's my understanding that the school schedule and the curriculum will be the same for our school as other schools in this area. They've been very concerned about the growth in the student body over the last few years and knew something drastic was needed soon to cut classes down to size. They will see to it that money is allocated throughout the year for supplies needed for a new school up on the mountain. However, he did say that they are most appreciative of any and all volunteer help in preparation of the building, the grounds, the road to the property and other projects."

A loud murmur rose in the large room with everyone volunteering at once to help out. Glen finally put his finger and thumb in his mouth and whistled shrilly for attention. "Let's have a sign up sheet on the table here, and each of you can write in the time and date when you might be available, and what your expertise is. Max, I'm gonna put you in charge of that if you don't mind. Can you kind of coordinate all of that for us?"

Max shrugged his shoulders and then laughed. "I'll sure try," he said, slightly embarrassed.

"He can do it!" Georgia yelled above the din.

Max shoved and pushed his way up front to the table.

And so, the Laurey Mountain School was formed that night. Excitement and morale was high in the small community in the weeks that followed. Work began in earnest the first Saturday in May 1928. Neighbors helped neighbors, fathers and sons worked together, and mothers and daughters worked side by side, painting, cleaning, and pulling weeds. Older women, who had long since raised a family, helped out by bringing dishes of hot food to the tired workers. A real sense of pride and accomplishment pervaded the entire township of Northridge. Max and Doug had talked to their boss, Jack Doss, about donating lumber for the project.

"Sure," Jack had readily agreed. "Just make sure that it's secondary stock. I'm afraid I can't donate grade A lumber, but you can take what you need of the other."

Doug grinned at Max and thumped Jack on the shoulder. "What about that special order of ash that was never picked up?" he asked. "Is that still piled up out back?"

Jack thought for a minute. "To tell you the truth, I had forgotten all about that, but if it's still out there, and you guys can use it, it's yours."

"We figured it'd make good tables, or maybe a few desks, or something like that," Max explained.

The Northridge Saw Mill and Lumber Supply, with the slogan of 'You see 'em ... We saw 'em,' was only one of many businesses that wholeheartedly supported the project and donated to the worthy cause. Northridge Water Works donated a new pump, and work began on drilling a new well. The Casey Brothers Smelting Company contributed a beautiful cast iron stove to be delivered as soon as the roof was repaired. The School Board met several times with Mrs. Richardson, who had agreed to serve as teacher for the 1928-29 school year. She would be in charge of twenty-two to twenty-five students to start with, and she immediately began planning her schedule and collecting supplies. Boxes and boxes of books, paper, crayons, pencils, paints, chalk, and the like began arriving on a daily basis at the Richardson home, filling their small storeroom to overflowing. Evelyn began to wonder where on earth she'd put one more box if something else should arrive.

Work on the building and grounds progressed smoothly the first few weeks of summer. The first casualty occurred on a sweltering afternoon in July. Max and his son Raymond were on the roof rebuilding rafters that had rotted away several years before. The old roofing and rafters had been removed and chopped up into manageable pieces for firewood to be used in the stove during the cold, winter months. Standing on a precarious perch high above the ground, Raymond waited for his father and Doug to finish nailing the last rafter into place. Two neighborhood boys, Raymond's age, were passing up four-by-eight roof sheathing to be nailed down to the new rafters when a small commotion took place down in the yard below. Abby, Harold and Nan Baird's sixteen year-old daughter, arrived in a buggy with her mother and alighted with a huge picnic basket laden with cold chicken, fruit, biscuits and beans.

"Come an' get it," she called loudly, lugging the heavy basket into the shade of the house. "Hi Ray!" she called, looking up and smiling at Raymond Baker.

Raymond squinted into the sunlight and waved back just as a stack of sheathing was shoved toward him. The impact to his shins was just enough to send him tumbling over the edge. With a cry of alarm, he disappeared from view.

Max stared in horror at the empty spot where just a moment before his son had been waiting for the roofing. He rushed as quickly as he could, precariously balancing his feet on the edge of each rafter, until he reached the ladder and stared fearfully down at the crumpled form of his son below. "Raymond!" he cried, throwing his hammer down. He clambered down the ladder in record time and rushed to his son's side.

Abby had watched in horror as Raymond's lanky body hit the ground, and she had rushed to help him. The boy's head was cradled in her lap as she bent over him. "Raymond, oh Raymond," she cried in genuine alarm.

Other workers had gathered around, all peering at the helpless form of the boy on the ground.

"Raymond!" Max yelled again. He could see no sign of injury, but that didn't mean his son wasn't hurt badly. He bent down close to Raymond's face, searching for signs of breathing.

"Abby," Raymond whispered softly, searching the sea of faces above him.

"It's Dad, son," Max said. "Are you hurt bad?"

"Uh-huh," his son slowly nodded his head. "What happened?"

"You fell off the roof, son. Be still and don't make a move. We'll get you to the doctor," Max said, his voice shaking.

Doug ran up to his friend's side, his face sweating profusely in the hot sun. "How bad is he?" he asked.

"I don't know," Max said, his white face showing the fear he felt inside. "We need to get him to town … to Doc Sorenson right away."

"Let's make a stretcher and carry him on some of these boards," one of the men suggested. Several men and boys quickly nailed together a pallet wide enough to carry the injured boy. They lifted Raymond up on the makeshift stretcher and loaded him on the bed of a small flatbed logging truck that Doug had used to deliver a load of lumber earlier that morning.

Raymond groaned loudly as they gently slid the stretcher in the bed of the truck. Doug clambered aboard and started the truck while Max and Glen Richardson jumped in the back and guarded the injured boy. The truck lurched down the bumpy road, a rooster tail of dust spiraling out from behind it.

Several people stood in a quiet group, huddled together in the shade of the old house and prayed for Raymond's safety and protection. All work stopped that afternoon. It was finally decided that it was too hot to work in the sun, so everyone adjourned inside the old building to await news from town.

"Well, son, you're a mighty lucky lad," Doc Sorenson said, as he finished up his lengthy examination a couple of hours later. "One sprained ankle, when you could easily have broken your neck, or back, or both … is not too bad a deal. You're a mighty fortunate young man." He wrapped the ankle tightly and found a pair of wooden crutches for the boy. "Use these," he said, "and I'd advise you to stay off that ankle. Sprains are worse than breaks. They take much longer to heal, especially if you try walkin' on 'em before they're fully healed. Have your Ma get some ice, keep your foot elevated, and put ice on it as much as you can. That'll keep it from swelling so much. You should be good as new in a few weeks. And I'm giving you something for pain." He stopped for a minute and looked at the boy in front of him. "I don't advise taking this stuff unless you absolutely have to. If you have any trouble, or the pain becomes unbearable, come back and see me. And another thing … stay off of roofs!"

Raymond grinned at the doctor and tried out his crutches.

"Bring those back once you don't need 'em anymore," the doctor added, watching his patient over the top of his glasses.

Max, Doug, Glen and Raymond rode in silence back to the schoolhouse, eager to share their good news. Raymond was elated to see that Abby had stayed to learn the outcome of his accident.

"Boy!" she exclaimed when she saw him hobbling towards her on crutches. "You're a sight for sore eyes. I was scared to death you had broken your neck or something."

To his absolute horror, Raymond found himself blushing bright red. He hoped that Abby would think him just badly sunburned. The women all fussed over Raymond that afternoon, each knowing the perfect remedy for a sprain. Raymond basked in the flurry of attention that was lavished on him, but his thoughts and eyes were for Abby only.

CHAPTER 12
GEORGIA TO THE RESCUE

The last few notes of the sweet old hymn were lost to the congregation as the heavy hymnal slid down from the music stand and crashed on top of Mrs. Crenshaw's hands. The garish blast that emanated from the old organ startled everyone in the church sanctuary. The poor elderly woman's face turned a pretty pink as she glanced first at the pastor and then over the congregation.

"Sorry," she said softly and held up the culprit book.

"That's quite all right, Mrs. Crenshaw," Pastor Rodney said with a smile. "Perhaps the devil doesn't appreciate your playing, but we certainly do."

At that very instant, the head usher caught his toe on the corner of the large rug that ran just inside the vestibule door, and the offering plate he was holding crashed to the floor, coins rolling in every direction. Several people toward the back of the church rushed to help the embarrassed usher to his feet. Children scrambled from their pews to collect as much of the runaway change as they could find.

"My goodness!" Rodney exclaimed. "This seems to be the Sunday for mishaps. I'm a little reticent to mention that next Sunday is our baptismal service. Those of you who are scheduled to be baptized next Lord's Day need to be here a bit earlier than usual." He paused for a moment and looked pensively over his flock.

"That reminds me of a true story," he said and began to chuckle as though enjoying a private joke. "I guess it would do no harm to tell this." He looked questioningly at his wife who smiled and nodded her head. He paused again and shuffled the papers on the pulpit as if trying to decide whether or not he should continue. He cleared his throat.

"Several years ago, when I was in Bible College and seminary, I had a very dear friend, Brother Don Tippel. He was a fine young man with a real heart for the ministry. After we graduated, brother Don was called to a small church down south, and I remember how excited he was at the prospect of finally filling a pulpit. Several weeks after we had gone our separate ways, he wrote to me and told me all about his very first baptismal service. Being new to the pulpit, he was understandably nervous about this upcoming service. You see, brother Don was a very small man, probably didn't weigh much more than 120 pounds. The baptistry in his church was extremely small, and since his first candidate was a very large woman, he decided that he'd conduct his first service down at the river. Apparently there was a good-sized river that ran just below the church. At any rate, I remember Don writing that he sure didn't want to run the risk of getting sister Margaret stuck in the baptistry pool." Pastor Rod paused again for a moment, his eyes sparkling and a wide smile spreading across his face as he recalled Don's descriptive letter.

"Well, to make a long story short," he continued, "sister Margaret was all for this plan and decided that she'd buy a new dress for the special occasion. She found just what she was looking for ... a brightly colored ... I believe he said it was a bright pink print dress that was loosefitting. Well, sir, come the following Sunday morning, the entire congregation gathered on the banks of the river to witness this momentous occasion. Sister Margaret entered the river and stood next to brother Don. He thought that he ought to mention something about that new dress, so he said to her, 'Sister Margaret, don't you look lovely this morning. Is that a new dress you're wearing?' 'Why, yes it is pastor,' she replied. 'I got it especially for today.' 'Well,' says brother Don, 'it's a mighty pretty dress too.' With that, he lowered her into the water. To his absolute shock and horror, he suddenly lost his grip on her and she began to thrash around and knocked his glasses off into the water." Rodney stopped and looked around as the congregation began chuckling.

"Wait a minute, wait a minute ... there's more," he said, chuckling himself.

"Sister Margaret began to float downstream. My dear friend Don, frantically grabbed at her and caught only a piece of that bright, pink dress. That's the only thing he can see at this point as his glasses are at the bottom of the river. Well, you guessed it. Don heard a horrible ripping sound."

The room exploded into laughter. Rodney reached into his back pocket and pulled his neatly folded handkerchief out and wiped his eyes. He held up a finger to quiet the group.

"To brother Don's immense surprise and embarrassment, the dress was dangling in his hand while his baptismal candidate was floating downstream on a surprisingly strong current, dressed only in her slip. He told me that at that very moment, he fervently prayed the Lord would strike him dead, right there in the water." Rodney waited a moment for the laughter to die down.

"With the torn dress in his hands, he made a frantic effort to catch up with her, plowing through waist-high water. His entire congregation was dumbfounded by what is transpiring before them. By some miracle of miracles, the big woman got hung up on some trusses of a bridge that crossed the river some ways downstream. She was just pulling herself up out of the water when poor little Don, still plowing through the water, arrived on the scene, still holding on to her ruined dress. Don said he seriously considered ducking under the current and swimming out into the Gulf, into eternity."

Pastor Rod stopped for a moment and enjoyed a loud belly laugh himself. "Poor Donald," he said, wiping his eyes. "I can just see him to this day, holding that bright pink dress above his head. But … instead of drowning himself, he handed the dress back to the woman who snatched it out of his hands, and yelled as loud as she could, 'Preacher, I would have gladly given you my new dress if I'd known you wanted it that bad. You certainly didn't have to try and drown me for it!'"

It took a full five minutes before Rodney could gain control of his flock.

"Now you understand why, with all the mishaps that have happened here this morning, I'm a little reluctant to mention a baptismal service."

There were a few more minutes of joyous laughter inside the small church before quiet would reign again. Lydia noticed that even Ina Potts had enjoyed the story. She had removed her glasses and was wiping her eyes with a lace hankie.

"Well, praise the Lord!" Rodney cried. "It does the soul good to laugh once in a while. Incidentally, Pastor Don Tippel is still faithfully serving the Lord … as a missionary in New Guinea … and nowhere near any water!"

Once again, the congregation broke up in unrestrained mirth, and it was some time later that Rodney finally began his sermon. Somehow, they got through the service without further mishap or interruption.

"What was so funny at church?" Aaron asked, when they had arrived back home. "I saw some people laughin' and then cryin'."

"No one was crying, Aaron. Everyone was laughing at what Pastor Rodney was saying," Doug explained, noting the deep frown on his son's face. "Someday, you'll understand."

Aaron stared at his parents as they recalled parts of the story and began laughing again. He looked at his little brother, shrugged his shoulders, and nudged Benjamin outside to play.

"Hold it right there, you two," Lydia said loudly as she turned them from the door. "Not before you change your clothes. You know better than to go out to play in your Sunday clothes."

Both boys groaned as their mother herded them toward their bedroom. "Stop arguing and fussing. You know the rules," she said sternly. "And don't go running off somewhere. Dinner will be ready in just a few minutes."

"Honey, have you been baptized?" Doug asked suddenly, while helping his wife set the table.

"I was afraid you'd ask me that," she replied. "No, I haven't. I've always intended to be, but never got around to it," she admitted rather sheepishly.

"Well, now is the perfect time to go ahead with that. Didn't Rodney say he had six candidates next Sunday? You might as well be number seven... that is unless you're afraid Rodney will drop you," he teased with a big grin.

Lydia made a face at him and shook her head. "I don't think this is the best time for that," she murmured.

"And why not, may I ask?"

"Because," she stopped and glanced outside to make sure the boys were out of hearing range. "Because, Mr. Wheeler, you're going to be a daddy again," she said in a near whisper.

Doug's smile faded. He stared openmouthed at his wife. "Honey!" he gasped. "Why on earth didn't you tell me sooner? I've had you workin' like a beaver on the schoolhouse. Oh sweetheart, why didn't you say something?"

"I wanted to wait until the perfect time to tell you. Besides, I feel just fine, and I'm perfectly capable of working right alongside the rest of you out there. I wanted to do my part at the school. After all, our boys are going to be going there...." She paused and looked up at her husband.

Doug shook his head in disbelief. "I just wish you had told me sooner. When's the baby due?" he asked, pushing her hair aside and kissing her moist neck.

"February sometime, as near as I can figure." She pushed Doug away with her elbow. "Stop that, honey," she laughed. "I'm burning the potatoes."

"Well, young lady, I don't want you out at the school site anymore, do you hear? You stay at home and take care of yourself. Have you been to see Doc Sorenson yet?"

Lydia shook her head. "How could I, silly? You have the car every day, and I'm not about to ask someone else to take me in to see him. I don't want everyone in the neighborhood knowing our business, so I haven't said a word to a soul. You're the first to know."

"As well I should be!" Doug said, sneaking a bite of the frying potatoes. "One day next week," he said, gulping down the hot mouthful, "I'm coming home early from work. We'll get Georgia, or maybe Barbara Ann, to watch the boys for us, and I'll take you in to see the doctor myself. I want to make sure you and the baby are all right."

"Fine by me," his wife said with a sigh. "Guess I'll have to let Georgia know the truth, won't I?"

"I reckon so, ma'am," Doug said in a silly voice and wrapped his arms around his wife.

"Dinner's ready," she murmured. "Call your sons in to wash up, will you?"

Doug turned her around to face him and lifted her chin. "You've made me a very happy man, m' lady," he said with an exaggerated bow. "I'm at your beck and call."

Lydia rolled her eyes. "Okay, Shakespeare, call your sons in to wash up."

"Well, I declare!" Georgia exclaimed a few days later. "Why didn't you tell me sooner?" she scolded.

"You sound exactly like my husband," Lydia said with a laugh.

"Well," Georgia said defensively. "You should have told us sooner. You shouldn't have been down there at the school scraping paint and scrubbing and all. Girl, didn't your mama ever tell you that you're in a delicate condition, and that you shouldn't be workin' like a farm hand?"

Lydia laughed heartily. "I guess she did," she admitted. "At least to some degree."

"Why didn't you listen to her then? I've a good mind to turn you over my knee."

"I'd like to see that!" Lydia laughed. "Seriously, Georgia, Doug and I wondered if we could impose on you to watch the boys for us for an hour or so one day next week. Doug insists on taking me to the doctor himself and...."

"Of course you can. Don't be silly ... and you're not imposing," Georgia interrupted. "Anytime you want to go to town without the kids, bring them by. They'll have a great time playing with Peter. I'll bet you both want a girl this time, right?"

Lydia smiled. "We'll take whatever we get, but yes, it would be nice to have a daughter. We can't decide whether to call her Rebecca or Rachel. What do you think?"

"I like Rebecca myself, but what if *she* is another he?"

"Well," Lydia said, "if she turns out to be another he, his name will be Michael James, and we're giving him to you!"

"That's what you think!" Georgia exclaimed. "I like the name, but not the idea. I have enough of my own, thank you very much."

"I love the name Rebecca Louise... after Doug's mother, or Rachel Anne after my mother. My mother's real name is Lily Anne, but over the years, she shortened it to Lillian. Got tired of writing both names, I guess."

"Nice names," Georgia said appreciatively. "You bring the boys over anytime. In fact, Peter has nearly driven me crazy wanting to come over here and play with Aaron. Would you mind if I sent him over one afternoon with a note telling you what time to send him back over the hill?"

"Heavens no!" Lydia said. "My boys would love to have him come to play. They fight with one another, so maybe with a third boy here they'll get along a little better."

"Well then, you send the boys over to my house some afternoon too. Do you think Aaron can find his way back home from our place?"

"Oh, I'm sure he could. He's been back and forth with me at least a thousand times," Lydia said. "He could probably find his way back home in his sleep."

At that very moment, the screen door was yanked open and Benjamin rushed into the kitchen, streams of perspiration pouring down his little browned face.

"What's the matter?" Lydia asked, somewhat alarmed by his sudden appearance.

"Mama," he exclaimed breathlessly, "Aaron and Peter are up in dat tree down dere," he pointed toward the garage. "Dere stuck too."

"What big tree?" Lydia asked, frowning at him. "And they're stuck?"

"Yep!" he replied. "Come on, Mama, dere stuck," he said, pulling on his mother's arm.

Lydia looked at Georgia, alarm written on her face. Georgia shook her head and laughed. "Boys will be boys!" she said. "Let's go see what this is all about." She pushed her chair back away from the table and picked Benjamin up. "You're sure not climbing any tree to rescue any monkeys," she said, glancing at Lydia. "I've climbed 'em before and I can climb 'em one more time. Benjamin, show me which tree they're in, would you, sweetie?"

Benjamin was only too happy to oblige. "Down dere," he said, pointing to the far border of the Wheeler property.

"Way down there by the road?" Georgia asked.

"Yep!" Benjamin replied with certainty.

Georgia set him down, and the two women followed him down to the big elm tree next to the road. The two boys were nowhere in sight.

"Honey, are you sure they're up in this tree?" Georgia asked skeptically, when she saw how high up the first branches were.

"Uh-huh!" Benjamin nodded. "Dere stuck, way high up."

"Peter Thomas!" Georgia yelled. "Are you up in this tree?"

There was no answer. Lydia tried. "Aaron, where are you?" she yelled. She waited for an answer but heard nothing more than the sighing of the wind through the branches of the tree.

"Peter … Aaron!" Georgia bellowed her loudest. "Where are you?"

"Mama … we're stuck," came the faint reply from on high.

Georgia gazed up through the thick foliage. "They're up there all right," she said, turning to look at Lydia, "but I sure don't see them. "Peter, are you hurt? Is Aaron hurt?" she asked loudly.

"No, we're just stuck," Peter said, now much louder.

"Are you afraid to come down or are you really stuck?" Georgia asked. There was no answer. She looked at Lydia and shook her head. "They're scared," she said. "How in the world did they make that first branch, that's what I'd like to know," she said, looking up at the tree. "That's way over my head. How on earth did *they* do it?"

"Part monkey, I guess," Lydia said. "Shall I go get a ladder?"

"No, ma'am, you shall not!" Georgia said sternly. "I'll go get the ladder. Is it in the garage? Does Doug have any rope?"

Lydia nodded her head to both questions. "I'm not sure where the rope is, but it's probably up there too. He has a lot of stuff like that hanging on the wall. I'll go with you and find the rope, and you get the ladder."

Georgia nodded her head. "Stay right where you are, Peter," she yelled. "Don't either of you boys try to climb back down. I'm getting a ladder and I'll be up to get you, all right?"

"Okay," came the feeble reply.

The two women, along with Benjamin, walked back up to the garage and found the needed items. Back at the tree, Georgia leaned the ladder up against the base and wedged it tightly against the first branch high above her head.

"Wish me luck," she said over her shoulder and began her ascent. "Sit tight!" she yelled upward. "I'm coming up to get you."

Grabbing the lowest branch, she hoisted herself up until she was straddling it. Even then, the ground looked a long way down to her. She pulled herself to the next highest branch and waited a few seconds, trying to catch her breath. Looking up, she realized she had a long way yet to go. She still could not see either boy. Branch by branch, Georgia slowly worked her way upward until finally she could see one small leg dangling down from a branch still high above her. She stopped again to rest, puffing from the exertion.

"Do you see them yet?" Lydia yelled up to her.

"Yeah, I can see one leg. I'm nearly there," she yelled back, her words coming in short raspy gasps.

She slowly, painfully, branch by branch, worked her way ever closer to the dangling leg. Finally, she was within a few feet of the boys. Peter was below Aaron. The branches were becoming much more spindly and smaller, and she breathed a quick prayer, asking the Lord to keep the tree together under her weight.

"Ma!" Peter cried out, reaching his arm toward her. She could see the fear on his face.

"Now, Peter, listen to me," she instructed. "Grab my arm and hang on. I'm gonna take you down part way, and when you feel you can make it down by yourself, I'm coming back up for Aaron. Do you understand me?"

Peter nodded his understanding and reached for his mother's arm. He grabbed her hand and swung his body unexpectedly, forcing her outstretched arm to bear his full body weight.

"Oh!" she cried, and bit her tongue to keep from yelling. She pulled him quickly to her and lowered him to a branch just beneath her feet. She moved her wrist and elbow to make sure they weren't broken. Beads of sweat forming on her forehead began to trickle down the sides of her face, into her eyes. She wiped her face with the side of her arm.

"Stay right there, Peter. Don't move. Let me get Aaron down this far, and then we can all go down together." She pulled on the branch above her head and hoisted her body up another couple of feet. Aaron was straight ahead in front of her, his eyes filled with terror. His body was visibly shaking.

"Aaron," she said quietly. "Now listen carefully to me. Give me your hand and I'll –"

She was interrupted midsentence by a blur of activity. Aaron dove straight for her through the branches. With a frantic cry, she lunged for him and caught him by his overall suspenders, stretching the muscles in her left arm to the breaking point. Yanking hard on him, she was able to pull him close to her own body just in time to recover her footing. The little boy was shaking violently and wrapped his arms tightly around her neck. She tried to look down to see where Peter was but couldn't bend her neck far enough.

"Peter," she called in a slightly strangled voice. "Are you right below me where I told you to stay?"

"Yeah, Ma … are you gonna whip me?"

"Listen to me, Peter," his mother said, ignoring his question.

"Georgia? Georgia, where are you? Do you have the boys yet?" Lydia yelled up, interrupting her train of thought.

"Yeah, Lydia, I'm up here with the boys," she yelled back. "They're both just fine." She hoped her voice was convincing. "All right, Peter," she continued, "can you work your way back down through the branches?"

There was no answer.

"Peter?" Nothing. Georgia adjusted Aaron's weight and pulled one of his arms from the strangle hold he had on her neck and looked down. Her son was nowhere in sight.

"Peter!" she screamed. "Where are you? Are you all right?"

"Here he comes!" Lydia yelled loudly. "He's nearly down on the ground. I'll help him down the ladder."

Georgia suddenly felt like weeping. Her body began to sag under the extreme pressure of precariously balancing her own weight, plus the dead weight of Aaron, who was hanging on for dear life.

"Aaron, do you think you could grab my waist?"

"No!" he cried. "Don't let me go!" He tightened his grip around her neck.

"Aggghh!" she cried. "You're chokin' me." She tried to pry the little boy's arms free, but he frantically fought her and began to scream.

"Georgia!" Lydia shrieked. "What's the matter? Oh, God help us!" Little Benjamin grabbed his mother's skirt and began to wail.

"Lydia!" Georgia yelled. "We're fine. Aaron's just scared, that's all. We're coming down. Peter?" Georgia yelled, trying to make herself heard above the screaming in her ear. "Are you down yet?"

"He's down on the ground, right here with me and Ben," Lydia said loudly.

"Aaron, stop making so much noise," she scolded. "You're not in any danger now. I've got you, so hush now."

Aaron stopped his crying but continued his death grip around the woman's neck. Georgia was certain that both her arms were now broken beyond repair. She could see blood oozing from a bad scrape on her right arm, and the fingers on her left hand were swollen and turning blue. She wiggled them just to make sure they weren't broken. Must have happened when I caught Aaron, she thought. She breathed another quick prayer and started her descent again.

"No! Don't move!" Aaron cried, panic-stricken.

"You're all right now," Georgia said. "I'm not going to drop you, I promise. Lydia? Can you hear me?"

"Yes."

"You still have the rope?"

"Yes, I've got it right here. Benjamin, stop your noise. I can't hear Aunt Georgia," she scolded.

"Give it to Peter and have him climb back up to me, would you?"

There was no reply from below, so Georgia had to assume that Lydia was giving Peter instructions. She waited for what seemed an eternity before she finally heard her son huffing and puffing as he tugged the heavy rope up to his mother.

"Peter, can you hear me, honey? Do you have the rope with you?"

"Uh-huh," came the gasped reply.

She reached as far below her as her arm would extend and touched the coil of horsehair rope. She pulled on it and looped it around her arm. "Thank you, Peter. Take your time, but go back down and stay with Aunt Lydia. Be careful, honey."

"I will," came the squeaky reply.

"Aaron, listen to me. I'm not going to let you fall."

The little boy nodded his head but stared wide-eyed at the rope.

"And I'm not going to hang you either," she said, reading his mind. "I'm gonna tie one end to your waist and lower you down to your Mama. You're gonna have to be a big, brave boy ... as brave as Peter has been. Do you understand?"

Again, the little boy nodded his head.

"All right then, just trust me, and you'll be down on the ground with your mother and brother in just a minute or two." Georgia fumbled with the rope, her swollen fingers hampering her work, but finally she had a double knot tied around Aaron's small waist.

"Now," she instructed, "when I pry you loose ... *if* I can pry you loose, you can hang onto the rope above your head, and I'll feed you down through the branches. Do you understand?"

Aaron started visibly shaking again but nodded his head.

"Peter, are you down yet?"

"Yes, Georgia, he's down here with me. He's fine," Lydia answered. "Are you and Aaron all right up there?"

"Be down in just a minute," Georgia yelled back. "Here we go, Aaron. Are you ready?"

Before he could answer, she yanked his arms from around her neck. He screamed and frantically tried to grab her again. She swung him down below her, slowly feeding the rope over the large branch above her head. She glanced down at the struggling form that was thrashing wildly about below her. She tried to calm him, but his terrified screaming drowned out her efforts. After what seemed an eternity, she saw Lydia's arms reach up to grab Aaron and she felt the rope go slack. She gathered up the excess and let it drop down out of the tree.

"Now, smartie pants, make sure you can get yourself down without breaking your own neck, *if* it isn't broken already," she said quietly to herself as she started down. Lydia reached her arms out to help Georgia down off the ladder and then enfolded her in a bear hug. The two women clung to one another for a few moments, mustering what little bit of strength they had left. Georgia turned and hugged her son, lifting him off his feet. "I'm so proud of you, Petey," she said, kissing his dirty little face. "You were such a great help."

"Georgia, what on this earth would I ever do without you?" Lydia said, her eyes filling with tears.

"Learn to be a monkey, or at least climb like one," Georgia said with a grin, hiding her swollen hand down at her side.

CHAPTER 13
THE DEDICATION

"Mama, can I go to school this year?" Aaron asked his mother one hot and sultry August afternoon. "Peter says he's goin' and I wanna go with him," he added, still scraping the large icing bowl Lydia had given to him.

She glanced at him and smiled. She finished swirling the last drop of frosting on the beautiful cake she had baked for the school dedication ceremony that evening.

"Sorry, honey," she said, licking the frosting off her knife. "You're not quite old enough to go yet, and neither is Peter. You just turned five, and you have to be six years old before you can start school. Just be patient, son ... it will be here soon enough."

"But how come it takes so long?" Aaron asked in an irritated voice. "I've been waitin' for years an' years an' years!"

His mother tipped her head back and laughed heartily. "You'll change your tune as soon as you're in school. You've got years and years to go after you start school, so don't be in such a rush to get there."

"I'm goin' to school too," Benjamin said, swinging his feet while he licked his spoon.

"You're not goin' with me," Aaron said hotly. "You're too little to go when I start. You hafta stay home with Mama."

"I am too goin' to school, huh, Mama?" Benjamin's eyes were blazing. "I can go when you go, so there!"

"No, you can't. You're not goin' with me an' Peter, because they don't let babies in school, so there!" retorted his big brother.

"I'm not a baby, and I am so goin' to school, an' don't call me a baby!" Benjamin yelled, threatening to throw his spoon at Aaron.

"Hey, hey, hey! Now that's enough from both of you," their mother said wearily. "Hurry up and finish your treat, because you both have to have a bath tonight."

"What's tonight?" Aaron asked.

"We're going to the dedication of the new school tonight. Isn't that wonderful? And just in time for school to open next week. I can't wait to see how the old place has changed."

"What's dad ... dadcashun?" Benjamin asked, the spoon crammed sideways in his mouth.

"Dedication is a ceremony we go through when we want to set apart something very special ... in this case, it's our new school," his mother explained.

"You're so dumb, Ben," Aaron said. "I know what that means and you don't. You're a dumbbell!"

"Aaron!" Lydia gasped. "That's quite enough out of you. You apologize to your little brother right now!"

"Sorry, stupid," Aaron said and started laughing.

Lydia snatched the razor strop from off the nail on the wall by the back door. Aaron jumped from his chair, sending the bowl and spoon crashing to the floor. For some strange reason, the big bowl remained intact.

"You pick that up this instant and then you apologize the right way to your brother, or you're not going to be able to sit down for a week," his mother yelled.

Aaron picked up the bowl and spoon and set them back on the table. "Sorry," he muttered, glaring at his brother.

"What on earth has gotten into you, Aaron?"

"Nothin'," he said. "I just wanna go to school."

His mother carried the bowl and spoons over to the sink and replaced the strop back on the nail. "You'll be going soon enough as it is. I don't want to hear that kind of talk in this house ever again. Do you understand me, young man?"

Aaron nodded his head and hurried through the living room.

"Don't run off anywhere either," his mother said loudly. "As soon as I can heat some water, I want both of you to get ready for a bath."

There was a collective groan as both boys disappeared into their small bedroom. Lydia wiped her forehead with the corner of her apron and put a large kettle of water on the stove to heat. She brought her galvanized tub inside and set it on the floor. The tub itself was so hot from hanging on the wall outside in the sun, she decided she'd better add quite a bit of cold water first.

"Come on Ben, you're first," she called when the kettle of water began to sing on the back burner.

"Ha, ha, you hafta go first," taunted Aaron.

Ben shrugged his shoulder and hurried out into the hot kitchen, struggling out of his overalls. Lydia made quick work of scrubbing her youngest, hair and all. "Aaron," she called. "You're next. Come on." She added a bit more hot water to the tub and sent Ben back to the bedroom to summon his brother. She groaned loudly when she heard the fighting begin.

"That's it!" she said, hurrying over to retrieve the razor strop. "I've had just about enough of this!" She burst into the boys' room and pulled Aaron off the bed.

"Get out there, right now!" she demanded as she swung the strop against his backside.

"Ow!" he cried as he dashed through the living room. "I'm goin', Mama … as fast as I can."

"You'd better hurry and you'd better do a good job," she warned, "or believe me, you're going to feel this again!" She waved the strop over his head.

Aaron leaped into the tub, sloshing water over the side. He watched as the water pooled on the kitchen floor around the tub. His mother noticed it too.

"Aaron, can't you be a little more careful? Look at the mess you've made."

"Sorry, Mama," he said. "I'm scrubbin' … see? I'm scrubbin' hard … the way you like me to." He demonstrated by lifting his leg out of the water and dragging his washcloth over it.

Finally, the baths were over and the kitchen cleaned up … just in time to start supper. She arched her aching back and tried to think of something cool and simple to put with yesterday's leftover meatloaf.

A short time later, after supper was over, Lydia washed the meal off her son's faces and got them dressed for the evening's festivities.

Doug whistled in amazement at the transformation. "Don't you two look snazzy! Go sit down in the living room and try to stay clean while Mom and I get ready. And…." he added, looking back at them over his shoulder, "I don't want to hear any fighting or wrestling in here, do you both understand?"

The boys answered in unison and settled themselves in the living room, quietly arguing over who got to sit in Dad's chair and who got to turn the pages of the book they were going to look at.

"What'd I just tell you two?" Doug growled, his head sticking out of the slightly open bedroom door. "I'm not going to warn you again." He closed the door and sighed. "Honey, I don't know how you put up with it day after day. It would drive me crazy in nothing flat."

Lydia turned her attention away from the mirror and laughed. "It's strange, but some days they're as good as can be, and others … well, other days are like today when they argue about everything and one or both is crying all the time. There are days when I feel like running away from home, believe me!"

"I don't doubt it a bit," Doug said sympathetically. "We're going to have to lay down the law around here. Which tie looks the best with these pants?" He held up two of his best ties and presented them to her.

"Either one goes with your pants." She shrugged and turned back to her hair brushing. "Oh!" she gasped suddenly.

Doug whirled around and stared at her. "What is it, honey? Are you all right?"

She nodded and continued to scrutinize herself in the small mirror on the dresser. "I think I just found a gray hair!" she said, pulling on one stubborn hair that insisted on sticking straight up.

Doug laughed and kissed the back of her neck. "I love you even if you do have one white hair, Mrs. Wheeler," he said with a boyish grin.

Lydia wrinkled up her nose, grinned back at him and swirled her hair up on top of her head and fixed it there with her small combs. "It's just too hot to wear this mop down tonight," she said as she slipped into her dress. "Where are the boys?"

"They're sitting in the living room, staying clean," he said. "At least they'd better be if they know what's good for them."

"Ha!" his wife said. "You want to bet?" She opened the bedroom door and peeked out. To her utter amazement, she found the boys sitting side by side in the living room, looking at the wild animal book that Grandma Wheeler had sent them for Christmas last year. Aaron was explaining to Benjamin how a giraffe bends his head down in order to get a drink of water from a pond.

Lydia quietly closed the door and turned to glare at her husband. "That is so aggravating!" she complained, watching Doug as he struggled into a clean pair of socks.

"What is?" he asked, glancing up at her. "Are they into something they shouldn't be?"

"No!" his wife exploded. "They're sitting out there like two little angels reading a book."

"Well, what in the world is wrong with that, woman?"

"Nothing. It's just that if *I* had told them to sit down and stay clean, they'd be outside in the yard by now, rolling in the dirt with Ruffy."

"Sorry, honey," Doug said, shrugging his shoulders. "What can I say? I just happen to have two very obedient children and you don't!"

"*Your* sons sure weren't very obedient this afternoon. I finally had to spank Aaron." She smoothed her hands down over her dress and looked at her image in the mirror. "Oh, just look at me! I look terrible tonight and I'm getting so fat!"

"You look absolutely beautiful, sweetheart." Doug pulled her into his arms. "Prettiest woman on the mountain and she's all mine."

Cars, buggies and wagons were parked at odd angles and in snarled knots all the way around the new school building. Lydia, her eyes roaming the outside of the old building, was astounded at the seemingly miraculous transformation. The long porch in front had been torn down, and in its place a wide sidewalk with two wide steps had been built to grace the double front doors. She caught her breath as she stepped inside the large room filled with people. Gone was the old, faded wallpaper. The walls were now painted a pale yellow with gleaming white trim around the blackboard and windows. Long tables had been set up toward the back of the large room to hold homemade pies of every kind and description, several cakes, and large platters overflowing with a dozen kind of cookies. Cold drinks were also being served along with coffee for the adults. Lydia set her cake down along with the rest and looked appreciatively around her. The entire front of the room was filled with long desks, each capable of holding two students. The teacher's desk, at the front of the room, rested on a five-inch raised platform. Great stacks of books were piled high over in one corner. Two large maps, one of the world and the other of the United States, decorated one wall. A brand new wood-burning stove was nestled in the back corner of the bright room. The old linoleum had been removed to reveal a beautiful hardwood floor that had been painstakingly refinished to a soft, glowing sheen. Lydia could not believe she was in the same place. This room looked nothing like the old Laurey homestead.

Someone began ringing the large bell that was housed in the short steeple at the front of the building, and within a few minutes, the large crowd inside had nearly doubled to the point that there was standing room only. Lydia was grateful when Doug found an empty seat and pushed her down into it. Glen Richardson, along with his wife, stood up front behind the big desk and waited until everyone who wanted to sit had found a chair.

"Friends and neighbors," Glen yelled. "Everyone please find a seat. There's a couple over here to my right."

When the room had quieted some, Glen cleared his throat and began. "Mr. Eric Peterson, the Superintendent of Schools, is here with us tonight, and he's going to lead us in pledging allegiance to the flag. Mr. Peterson."

The room thundered with loud applause as the short, stocky man huffed and puffed his way up to the platform, grabbed the American flag, and held it high.

When the pledge was finished, Mr. Peterson adjusted his glasses and looked over the crowd.

"This is a momentous occasion," he said with a slight smile. "Never in my thirty-two years of working in the school system have I ever witnessed such enthusiasm and such sacrifice as I have seen over the last three months since this project was started."

Wild applause and whistling erupted, interrupting his speech. The short little man tried twice more to continue but finally gave up and went back to his seat. Glen Richardson banged on the teacher's desk in an effort to restore order. He held up his hands and grinned at the boisterous crowd.

"Special thanks," Glen yelled and stopped. "Special thanks go to each and every one of you who contributed to this effort."

The applause was thunderous. Benjamin and Aaron stared wide-eyed at their parents and covered their ears with their hands.

"We have a few commemorative plaques that we'd like to hand out to the local businesses who so generously donated time, material, and money to this project. But first and foremost, we'd like to present a plaque that states our undying thanks to Grandma Phoebe Laurey for her generous donation of the building and grounds. Grandma Phoebe, come on up here."

The old woman made her way up front with the help of Deacon and Harold Baird amidst wild cheering and applause.

"Grandma, this plaque says,

'To Phoebe Laurey
Our Undying Gratitude
For Your Generosity
We Thank You'
Laurey Mountain School
August 26, 1928"

Glen handed the shiny plaque to the old woman, who held it as high over her head as she could manage and blew a kiss to the crowd, who were instantly on their feet, clapping, cheering, and whistling. Several other plaques were handed out before Glen was finished. The dedication ceremony was finally concluded with a rousing verse of 'America the Beautiful' and Pastor Rodney Jamison closed with a prayer of benediction. The huge room instantly became a hubbub of voices as people began visiting with one another and making their way back to the refreshment tables. All in all, it was a most gratifying evening for the entire community.

Laurey Mountain School officially opened its doors the following Monday morning to accept twenty-nine students, even though there was still a little more finish work to be done around the grounds. Only one real argument had developed during the renovation process when there was a difference of opinion as to what color the building should be painted … red or brown. In the end, it was decided that white would be the best choice to everyone's satisfaction.

Aside from a few smashed thumbs and split fingers, remarkably, only one major casualty occurred during the entire three months of remodeling and construction, that being Raymond Baker's rapid exit from the roof in early May.

CHAPTER 14
A SECRET IN NEWTON

"Georgia, you absolutely amaze me," Lydia exclaimed with admiration. "Somehow it seems fitting that you'd be the first woman on the mountain to learn to drive."

Georgia beamed at her friend's praise. "I am rather proud of it now that you mention it," she said. "I have to admit though, at first I was pretty nervous, but it's really quite simple."

When Max had learned that Doug and Lydia had a car, he had pestered Georgia until finally, several weeks later, she had given in to his persistent badgering, and they had purchased one of their own.

"Now the kids want to learn to drive … especially Raymond," Georgia said, rolling her eyes. "Max is scared to death that Raymond will wrap it around a tree somewhere. It's probably a blessing in disguise that he sprained his ankle so bad … he can't work the clutch pedal … at least for a while."

Lydia laughed. "Can't say as I blame you for being worried. That car of ours is nearly impossible to drive. I don't know how Doug remembers everything that needs to be done just to keep it on the road. It's beyond me!"

"Me too!" Grandma Baker interrupted as she joined the two younger women in the Bakers' living room. "Those contraptions are dangerous. Give me a horse an' buggy any day. I can't for the life of me figure out why everyone is in such a hurry these days."

Georgia threw her head back and enjoyed a hearty laugh. "Times are changing. Lydia, this is Max's mother, who has come to live with us, and Mother, this is my dearest friend, Lydia Wheeler."

The women exchanged greetings and almost instantly liked one another.

"I agree, Mrs. Baker," Lydia said to the older woman. "It's a hurry, hurry, rush, rush world we live in today."

"Ma, can we go to the back pasture?" Peter asked suddenly. "Me an' Aaron wanna check the gopher traps out there. Maybe we got a gopher by now."

Georgia looked questioningly at her guest. "It's all right with me if it's all right with Aaron's mother," she said.

Aaron rushed up to his mother with a pleading look on his face. "Can we go, Mama, please?" he begged. "We never get to go way out in the back pasture. It's so much fun, please, Mama. I'll be real careful, I promise, and I won't step in anything."

Lydia looked at her freckle-faced son standing in front of her and sighed. "Put your jacket on first and don't go too far down there. We have to be getting back home before too long … and no tree climbing!"

The two boys instantly disappeared, leaving little Benjamin behind. He ran through the living room and tried to unlatch the heavy front door but was unable to open it. "I'm goin' too," he grunted, struggling with the latch.

"No, Benjamin," his mother said. "You can't go with them this time. Maybe next time."

"Mama!" he cried. He threw himself across her lap and began to cry. "Mama," he protested loudly. "I wanna go too."

Grandma Baker jumped up and rushed into the kitchen. "Come here, young man," she called loudly. "I have something very special just for you."

Benjamin dried his tears with the back of his hand and disappeared into the kitchen. A moment later, he returned to the living room, all smiles.

"Look, Mama!" he said happily, waving a freshly baked gingerbread man cookie at her.

"Well, what do you say, Benjamin?"

"Thank you," he whispered, suddenly shy again. He quietly ate his cookie and went back to the wooden blocks he'd been playing with before.

"Well, girl," Georgia said with a tug on Lydia's arm as she sat down next to her. "How's baby Rebecca these days?" She reached over and patted Lydia's swollen tummy. "Kickin' up a storm in there, huh?"

"Boy, you've sure got that right," Lydia agreed. "She's a strong little stinker … and so active. I don't remember the boys being this active. You still think this one's a girl?"

"Sure do," Georgia replied. "No doubt about it. That reminds me," she said suddenly, jumping up from the couch, "I have a little white dress that I've saved all these years for somebody special. I'll be right back." She disappeared with a swish of her skirt into the back bedroom.

"Here it is!" she exclaimed loudly, a few minutes later. She returned with a small white dress, trimmed in tiny yellow ribbons and a faded lace collar. Lydia held it up in front of her and squealed with delight.

"Oh Georgia, it's absolutely precious. You're giving this to me for Rebecca?"

"Sure," Georgia said with a smile. "My girls sure can't wear it anymore." She chuckled at her own little joke. "Remember this little dress, Mother?"

she asked her mother-in-law. "I made it for Barbara Ann when she was about a year old, and then Cindy wore it for a while too."

"I think I'm the one who added those ribbons on it, didn't I?" the older woman asked.

"Could be," Georgia replied. "At any rate, it's going to be Rebecca's dress now."

"Oh Georgia, I don't know what I'd do without you," Lydia said, hugging the little dress close to her. "I wonder just how many times I've said that over the years I've known you."

"Oh pooh!" Georgia scoffed, waving her friend's compliment aside. "I say the very same thing about you. If I can ever get the car away from you know who … would you like to go to Newton with me some Saturday and do a little shopping?"

"Could we?" Lydia squealed. "Oh, Georgia, that'd be so much fun. I don't have very much saved for the baby but I'd sure love to go window shopping."

"Good," Georgia said. "Let's do it soon, before it gets bitter cold. Max and Doug can take care of the kids for us, and Mother, you're welcome to come too if you'd like."

"I just might do that," the old woman agreed. "That is, if you'd drive real slow. I could get a little early Christmas shopping done, couldn't I?"

"Georgia, do you think you could drive in the busy city?" Lydia asked suddenly.

"I don't know," Georgia admitted, "but there's only one way to find out."

The three women enjoyed planning their trip to the big city until it was time for Lydia and the boys to go home.

"Now don't forget, Lydia," Georgia reminded her at the front door. "Talk to Doug about our trip as soon as possible."

"Believe me, I won't forget," Lydia said, her eyes sparkling. "He's probably not going to like the idea of watching the boys very much, but it will be good for him."

"It'll be good for us too," Georgia said as she waved good-bye.

Lydia couldn't wait for Doug to come home that night. She watched and waited and finally saw the headlights of their car as Doug wound his way up the road towards their home.

"Daddy's home," Aaron announced, just as Doug parked the car in the garage.

Lydia's excitement mounted while she waited for him to get to the house. The instant he opened the door, she made her announcement. "Hi honey … guess where I'm going?" Without waiting for him to answer, she blurted out her plans. Doug looked positively shocked at first and then worried.

"I don't know, honey, if that's such a good idea. What does Max say about it?"

"Well, actually, Georgia hasn't talked to him about it yet, but I'm sure he'll say yes." Her eyes danced as she watched Doug's face for signs of approval.

Doug scratched his head. "Who's gonna take care of the kids?" he asked, eyeing her suspiciously.

"Georgia and I thought that you and Max could handle them one Saturday while we're gone. They can do without you down at the school project for one Saturday."

"Is that right? I'll bet good old Max has something to say about that." Doug slammed his lunch pail down on the table. "What made you decide to do this all of a sudden anyway … and how are you going to get there?"

"Georgia knows how to drive, and she's going to take me and Max's mother," Lydia said rather defensively, her excitement turning to near anger.

"Georgia's driving?" Doug exploded. "All the way to Newton? Do you have any idea how far that is? That's a good-sized city, honey. She can't drive in city traffic. I'd even be a little worried about driving in Newton myself."

Lydia's heart suddenly felt like stone. Her shoulders slumped forward as she dejectedly plopped down into one of the kitchen chairs. She sat looking at the pattern of her worn tablecloth for a few moments, her anger rising with each passing minute. Suddenly her head snapped up, and she stood to her feet so fast, she nearly knocked her chair over. "I don't care what you say!" she said loudly … too loudly.

Doug turned and stared at her, his lips parted as if he was about to say something.

"Georgia and I never get to go anywhere together. You and Max go off hunting and fishing and traipsing all over the countryside, and we never say a word to you about it. We just let you go. It's not going to kill either one of you to stay with the kids for one day … in fact, it will do you good. You'll get just a little taste of what we go through every single day of our lives."

She paused and drew a ragged breath. She started to say more … a lot more, but she glanced at her husband who was standing at the kitchen sink looking out the window, his jaw muscles working furiously. He turned and faced her, his stance screaming that he was ready to do battle.

"Georgia … drivin' all the way to Newton … I just don't know about this at all. I'll have to see what Max thinks about it, but I can tell you right now that I don't like it. I don't like it one little bit." He paused and rubbed his tired eyes. "Let me talk to Max and see what he has to say about it."

"I *know* what he'll say," Lydia said more sarcastically than she intended. "It's only because he won't want his wife driving his precious car."

"That's crazy and you know it," Doug said, his anger rising. "How long has she been driving anyway? Two months? Three months?"

Lydia shrugged her shoulder, walked briskly into the bedroom and slammed the door. Men! she thought to herself, too angry to cry. They always have everything their way … their cars … their house … their jobs … their everything! Georgia's probably going through the very same thing with Max.

Doug's surly look, as he watched his wife climb in Max and Georgia's used Model T Ford the following Saturday morning clearly revealed how he felt about the subject.

"Don't worry, Doug," Georgia yelled. "I'll bring her back in one piece."

"I sincerely hope and pray so, Georgia," he said as politely as he could. "Say bye to your mother, boys," he added.

"Bye, Mama," Aaron called, waving his hand at the car and squinting in the early morning sunlight.

Benjamin began to cry. "I wanna go too," he cried.

Doug grabbed him and lifted him up on his shoulders. Lydia waved to them until they were no longer in sight. She then turned to Georgia and Grandma Baker and giggled excitedly. "Do you believe this? We're actually going to Newton on a shopping trip. It took me forever to get to sleep last night for thinking about today. Ohhh-weeee! We're going to have fun!"

The two older women laughed and agreed.

"How on earth did you manage to talk Max into it anyway?"

Georgia looked at her curiously. "I didn't talk him into anything. I merely told him that Mother and I were going to pick you up on Saturday morning to go shopping in Newton for the day. You know what his comment was?"

"I can only imagine!" Lydia said with a nervous laugh.

"He said, 'Oh?' and that was it, wasn't it, Mother?"

"That's about it, all right," Max's mother replied. "When he was a little boy, I would never have figured him to be a man of so few words. He jabbered nonstop for years!"

"Well, Doug had plenty to say. I guess he made up for your husband's lack of comment. He's worried about three women being alone on the road, and about me being nearly six months along, and about you driving too fast, and what if the car breaks down, and on and on and on. He sounded like an old mother hen."

"If I know men, I'll bet he was most worried about being left alone with two small boys all day," Mother Baker said with a snort. "Let's face it, girls

… men don't have the foggiest notion how to take care of little ones. They don't know what women have to go through all day long."

"Isn't that the truth!" Georgia exclaimed as she expertly shifted gears.

"Wow, Georgia! I'm impressed," Lydia said enthusiastically, watching her friend as she shifted through all the gears as though she'd been driving for years. "How'd you learn all that so fast?"

"Now don't go too fast, Georgia," Mother Baker warned from the backseat. "I want to go to heaven, but not today, thank you."

"I'm taking it nice and slow, Mother. Let's just pray that we don't run into much traffic. I haven't driven in a city with lots of cars goin' every which a way. I hope I don't get nervous and hit something."

"So do we!" Lydia cried, grinning first at Georgia and then back at Grandma, who was bouncing around in the seat behind her.

The trio rode in relative silence for a few miles, each with her own thoughts. Lydia finally broke the silence. "I robbed the little tin can that I've been saving money in for the baby," she admitted with a guilty shrug of her shoulders. "Isn't that awful?"

"No," Georgia replied. "Maybe you'll find something for the baby that you just can't do without, and then you'll be glad you have the money with you."

Lydia smiled again. She and Georgia had like minds. Maybe that's why they were such close friends … more like kindred spirits.

"Look at that!" Georgia exclaimed suddenly. "We're only five miles from Newton! Boy, it didn't take us long to get here, did it?"

They began to meet more and more traffic on the narrow road. Sandwiched in between cars, they would meet an occasional farmer headed back from town driving his horse-drawn carriage or buckboard.

"Interesting, isn't it?" Georgia commented.

"What's that?" Lydia asked.

"The fact that you don't see very many buggies or wagons anymore. Just about everyone in the big city has a car these days. People are in such a hurry nowadays."

Suddenly, without realizing it, they were in the big city. Cars and people crowded every street. Georgia looked a little bewildered as she slowed the car down, trying desperately to see in all directions at once.

"Help me keep an eye out for cars and don't let me run over anybody," she said, biting her lower lip.

"We'll do our best, dear," her mother-in-law said, leaning forward in her seat so that she could see the town a little better. "By the way, where are we going first?"

"Look out, Georgia!" Lydia screamed suddenly. Cars from every possible direction seemed to be headed straight for them.

Georgia's eyes widened with alarm. She yanked hard on the wheel to avoid a sure collision with a man in a big touring car. He honked his horn and shook his fist at her as he roared past them.

"Georgia! We're on a one-way street!" Mother Baker shrieked suddenly from the backseat. "I just saw a small sign back there with the arrow pointing the other way. Oh, Lord, have mercy! Georgia, turn around! We're goin' the wrong way!"

Georgia gripped the wheel and turned sharply. The front wheels of the Ford jumped the curb with a horrible grinding thud. The car careened wildly down the sidewalk through a crowd of early morning shoppers. Georgia jammed her foot down hard on the brake pedal, nearly throwing herself and Lydia through the windshield. The Ford shuddered, coughed and died, a mere few inches from a stout-looking lamppost on the corner. People screamed and ran for cover. Mothers grabbed their children, dragging them out of harm's way. Men shook their heads and obviously cursed the woman at the wheel.

"Oh, dear God!" Georgia gasped, looking straight ahead. "Are you both all right?" she asked fearfully without looking at either of her passengers.

Lydia nodded her head and looked around her. Mother Baker's hat had fallen from her head and lay crumpled on the floor beneath her feet. She retrieved it and was trying to straighten it out when the constable arrived on the scene.

"Stand back, folks, stand back," he yelled in a loud, authoritative voice. "Show's over, folks," he said to the crowd that had gathered around the car. He peered at the women inside and slowly shook his head.

"Ladies," he said, tipping his cap with his nightstick. "This your automobile, ma'am?" he asked Georgia, who was white-faced and visibly trembling.

"Yes, your honor … I … I mean yes, sir," she stammered.

"And let me guess … this is your first time driving in the city, right?" he asked, tapping his nightstick in the palm of his free hand.

Georgia nodded and glanced quickly at Lydia. The officer followed her glance and noted Lydia's advanced condition. He raised one eyebrow at her.

"Ma'am, are you all right?"

"Yes, sir, I'm just fine," she answered meekly.

The officer sighed loudly and turned his attention back to Georgia. "Here in the city, ma'am, we drive our automobiles on the streets and leave the sidewalks for our pedestrians. Do you think you could manage to get this car off the sidewalk and park it somewhere safely on the street without jeopardizing the lives of innocent people?"

Georgia's face flushed beet red. There was also an instant spark of fire in her eyes. "I most certainly can, sir!" she snapped and promptly started the car again.

"All right, folks, that's it. Give this lady plenty of room. Get back out of the way ... all of you," the constable ordered, waving both hands at the crowd around the car.

Georgia pushed the clutch pedal halfway down, eased the car in reverse and backed away from the lamppost. She then shoved the gearshift into low, and bounced down off the sidewalk and back into the street. A few people clapped and cheered as she drove around the corner and parked the car against the curb.

"Why on this bloody earth do they have one-way streets?" she exploded in a fury that Lydia had never seen before. She started to answer her friend when Georgia burst into tears. "Max would kill me a hundred times over if he'd seen what just happened back there," she sobbed. "You both have to swear on your very lives that you'll never, ever breathe a word of this to a living soul ... ever!" She blew her nose and cried even harder.

Lydia reached over and patted her shoulder. "You don't have to worry about me ever saying a word about this. Doug would never let me out of his sight again if he knew about it. It's all right, Georgia. We're all fine and no one got hurt. We can be thankful for that."

"For two cents, I'd go back and pop that arrogant smart aleck right in the nose!" Grandma Baker said, her lips drawn in a thin line. "He sure thought he was something, didn't he? Out there strutting around like a proud peacock, wavin' that stupid stick around in the air like he was gonna hit somebody." She shoved her rumpled hat down hard on her head and grabbed her pocketbook. "Come on, girls," she said. "There's a drugstore with a soda fountain across the street. Let's go get something cold to drink ... my treat. When we're through with that, let's go shopping and forget about this mess."

Georgia dried her eyes and sniffed. Lydia handed her another hankie and they grabbed their purses.

"Can you imagine the look on the boys' faces if they had witnessed that fine how-do-you-do back there?" Georgia said with a hint of a grin as they enjoyed their ice cream sodas.

Lydia rolled her eyes. "Thank God they weren't with us."

"Oh look!" the elder Mrs. Baker exclaimed suddenly. "There's a mercantile down the street. When we're finished here, let's go over and see what they have that we absolutely cannot live without."

A few minutes later, the three women were happily chattering while they shopped in McCormick's Mercantile. Grandma Baker was trying on new hats, Georgia was drooling over some new fabric that had just come in, and Lydia had found the prettiest narrow pink ribbon that she'd ever seen. She had to have at least half a yard to decorate the little white dress that Georgia had given her. She could replace the faded yellow ribbon with this pink and give the dress new life. She also found a new pair of shoes for Aaron; he had quickly outgrown his old ones. She found small, inexpensive toy trucks for each boy, and a package of cotton diapers for the new baby. Oh, for just a little more money, she thought wistfully.

The incident earlier that morning was soon forgotten as the trio priced and examined nearly every item in the big store. Lydia spied some large red and white suckers for a penny a piece at the front counter and bought one for each of her boys. Grandma bought several skeins of yarn and Georgia loaded herself down with several bolts of brightly colored yard goods to make school clothes for her girls.

"I've got my work cut out for me," she said with a gasp as she dropped the heavy load down on the counter. "Looks like Mother does too," she added, noting all the yarn the older woman had chosen. "You should see what that woman can make with a skein of yarn. She's absolutely fantastic."

The tired trio headed for home in early afternoon, happy as clams with their outing and their fine purchases. Georgia had to admit that she was certainly more at ease when they were once again on the narrow, dirt road headed back to Northridge.

"Give me the good old country any day," Grandma said. "I'd rather walk than put up with all that traffic and hustle and bustle. Reminds me of a bunch of ants walkin' all over each other."

"Swear on a stack of Bibles that neither of you will ever breathe a single word about what happened this morning," Georgia said when they were nearing home. "No matter how mad we may get at one another from time to time."

"What happened this morning?" Lydia asked in feigned surprise, rolling her eyes at her friend. "I don't remember a single thing except a delicious ice cream soda and shopping, shopping, shopping."

"My lips are sealed," Grandma said, making the motion of buttoning her mouth. "What Max and Doug don't know won't ever hurt them. It'll be *our* little secret!"

CHAPTER 15
A CHRISTMAS SURPRISE

"They came!" Doug whispered excitedly in his wife's ear. "They finally got here! I've got them hidden in the back of the car." He chuckled to himself, his eyes dancing with excitement. Lydia smiled at her husband. She loved that innocent, childlike look he sometimes got on his face when he was extremely happy or excited about something, and at that very moment, he was both.

"Boy, that was close. They just made it in time," she commented as she stirred the hash they were having for supper.

"As soon as the coast is clear, I'll go down to the garage and see about putting them together."

"You mean they're in pieces?" his wife asked, a surprised look on her face.

Doug nodded his head and tasted the hash in the big skillet. For several weeks, they had been saving Doug's raise in pay each week for the boys' Christmas. Lydia had ordered a tricycle for Benjamin and a small, two-wheeler bicycle for Aaron. She had been worried for the past week that they wouldn't arrive in time for Christmas, which was now just a couple of days away. The instant supper was over, Doug, unable to wait another second, jammed his arms into his heavy coat, grabbed the kitchen lantern, and headed toward the back door.

"Where you goin', Daddy?" Benjamin wanted to know. "Can I come with ya?"

"No, not tonight, son. I'm going down to the garage to work on something. You boys stay here and keep your mother company, and keep the fire going. Tomorrow, we'll go look for a perfect Christmas tree, I promise."

Both boys squealed with delight. Hunting for the perfect tree with Daddy was nearly as much fun as decorating it and then finding what Santa had left for them on Christmas morning. Doug lit the lantern and disappeared outside, loudly whistling his own version of *Joy to the World* and *O, Come All Ye Faithful*. He could hardly contain his excitement as he hurried down to the garage, Ruffy close at his side.

"You gonna help me, boy?" he asked when they reached the garage. "At least you can't tell the boys what you've seen down here." He lifted the surprisingly heavy boxes out of the back of the car and began the task of putting the smallest one together first. He stood back an hour later and admired the shiny, red tricycle. He grinned when he imagined the look on little Ben's face when he woke up Christmas morning.

"Now for the big one," he said to Ruffy, who looked up at him with tired eyes and yawned. Two hours later, both bikes were finally assembled. Now, he thought, where to hide them so that the boys won't find them before Christmas morning? He looked around the small building. The car took up most of the available space, but maybe if he rearranged some of the overflow odds and ends that he had stored overhead in a makeshift attic, he could find room enough for the bikes. He climbed the short wooden ladder that was hanging on the wall, and getting down on his hands and knees, he crawled to the tiny space that served as a storage loft. He added that to the plans when he had replaced the back of the garage after Lydia had tried to drive straight through it. He smiled, recalling the morning of her one and only driving lesson. He piled several boxes of junk and two old tires out of the way and hoisted the bikes up over his head, cramming them as far back against the wall as they'd go. He stacked the boxes back out in front of the bikes, and discovered that there was now absolutely no room for the two old tires. Oh well, he thought, no harm in them sitting outside behind the garage. He rolled them out and leaned them up against the back wall of the garage.

"That's done," he said with satisfaction. "Come on, Ruffy, let's go thaw out before bed."

The house was warm and quiet. Doug pulled his boots off in the kitchen, and sank down in the nearest chair to thaw his frozen feet. Ruffy curled up behind the cook stove and within a few seconds, he was snoring loudly.

"Did you get 'em done?" Lydia murmured sleepily when Doug crawled in bed a few minutes later.

"Yep!" he said happily as he turned down the wick of the lamp. "This is gonna be a great Christmas, honey … I can't wait."

A light snow began falling sometime during the night, and by morning, there was close to six inches on the ground. Both boys were delighted with the transformation of the front yard and immediately began making plans to make a snowman.

"Before you make too many plans, you boys need to bring in the wood," their mother reminded them.

Aaron frowned. "We brought in a lot yesterday," he said. "Where'd all that go?"

"Where indeed!" his mother said. "How do you think we stayed so nice and warm in the house yesterday?"

"We put our coats on?" Benjamin suggested.

His big brother rolled his eyes and pointed to the fireplace. "All that wood is ashes now. Mama, can't we bring the wood in later?" he asked hopefully. "We wanna make a big snowman."

His mother shook her head. "Work gets done first around here, remember? When your work is finished, then you can play. And don't forget," she added with a twinkle in her eyes, "Santa is coming late tonight, and you want to be on your best behavior."

"Oh yeah!" Aaron said, a wide grin spreading on his face. "Just one more day and then it's Christmas!"

Benjamin stared up at his older brother, his eyes full of anticipation. "I want a bicycle," he said.

"Me too!" Aaron agreed enthusiastically.

"Well then, you'd better mind me and Daddy, and bring in lots of wood," Lydia said.

The boys needed no further prodding. They finished their breakfast in record time, donned their boots, coats, knitted hats and mittens. Lydia made sure their coats were properly buttoned up under their chins and sent them out.

"You do a good job and no fighting," she warned. She watched them somewhat wistfully as they headed down toward the garage. Oh, to be a small child again, she thought. Christmas was so much fun when I was five or six. Her thoughts tumbled back to the Christmas when she received the beautiful doll from Granny. She remembered how heartbroken she was when she came home from school one afternoon, a few weeks after Christmas, to find that Snickers had shredded the doll's hair and dress and disfigured the left side of her beautiful face. Her thoughts were jerked back to the present as she watched the boys running to the garage.

"Where you goin', Daddy?" Aaron asked, his cheeks rosy from the cold air.

"I'm going to town with Mom's grocery list. When I get back from the store, we'll go tree hunting."

"Yippee!" Benjamin said happily, throwing a handful of snow up in the air over his head.

The boys found their wagon and began loading it with wood. The haul back up the driveway in six inches of snow was harder work than either of them had suspected. After the second load, they decided they'd brought in enough, abandoned their wagon on the back porch, and eagerly started to work on their snowman.

Lydia was busy putting the finishing touches on her mincemeat pie when she realized that the kindling box beside the cook stove was nearly empty. She hurried to the back porch to gather an armload and noticed the empty wagon on the porch. She couldn't see the boys but could hear them giggling together as they worked side by side, rolling an enormous snowball. She listened to the happy sounds for a minute and decided to let them play. After all, she reasoned, it is Christmas Eve. She collected the wood and hurried back inside. The snow continued to fall, big fluffy flakes, transforming the world into a soft, magical play land. She watched the boys from the kitchen window and noticed that Ruffy was enjoying this as much as they were. He bounded through the small drifts, nose buried deep, sniffing out some interesting scent covered by a blanket of white. Suddenly, she heard another sound, the sound of their car coming back up the driveway. Doug was back already? She watched him as he parked the car back inside the garage. Now what? she wondered, as she watched him walk back up the driveway ... without her groceries.

Stomping his feet at the back door, he stuck his head in and grinned at her. "Sorry, honey," he said. "The snow is too deep on the road. I was afraid I'd get stuck, so I turned around down by the school and came back home. Do you want me to walk to town and get everything on your list?"

Lydia sighed and brushed a lock of hair out of her eyes with her free hand. "No, I don't think I need anything that bad," she said. "I'll make do with what we've got. Don't worry about it."

Her husband blew a kiss in her direction. "I'm gonna play with the boys," he said with a grin and slammed the door.

Lydia smiled. "You're still one of them, Doug." She wiped the steamy kitchen window clear and watched him scooping up handfuls of snow and flinging it into the air. The boys squealed and chased after him as fast as they could run. Ruffy joined in the mayhem and barked excitedly as he dashed around the trio in ever widening circles.

"Come on, boys," Doug yelled. "I've got a surprise for you." He started running towards the garage. The boys shrieked with glee and raced after him.

What on earth is he up to now? Lydia wondered. He's surely not going to give the boys their bikes early. She watched as the three of them disappeared behind the garage. A few minutes later, Doug reappeared, rope in hand, pulling the boys on one of the old tires. He pulled them up the long driveway, turned around in front of the kitchen window, and ran back down. About halfway down, Benjamin slid off and rolled on his back in the snow. Doug and Aaron collapsed in a pile in front of the garage, both laughing. She watched the fun for a few more minutes when she suddenly realized she could smell something burning. Whirling around, she saw smoke curling up around the door of her oven. She grabbed her potholders and yanked on the door of the oven. Her beautiful pie was scorched nearly beyond recognition.

"Oh no!" she cried in despair and grabbed the blackened dish from the oven. She rushed to open the back door to allow the smoke to escape. "Well, there goes our Christmas pie," she muttered. "Thank goodness we're not having company this year."

"Something's burning!" Doug exclaimed a few minutes later when the three of them came tromping into the warm kitchen. "Did you burn something?" he asked innocently.

"What's burnin'?" Aaron asked, gulping down a glass of ice cold milk.

"Our Christmas pie, that's what," Lydia said with disgust. "I got busy watching you three having so much fun outside that I forgot to keep an eye on my pie. I'm going to have to think of something else for Christmas dessert, I guess."

"Mama, we're gonna go find a Christmas tree," Ben announced, his eyes dancing.

"First, you're going to get out of those wet clothes and get some hot food inside of you," his mother said. "Come on, kids, let's get you both into some dry clothes."

After the noon meal was finished, and the boys were warm and dry, they eagerly joined Doug back outside and watched as he retied the rope securely to the old tire, and strapped a large board on top.

"What's that for, Daddy?" Aaron asked, as Doug finished securing the board.

"Well, come here and I'll show you. Sit down there and hang on. Come on, Ruffy, let's go!" The boys scrambled aboard their makeshift sled with Ruffy running first to Doug and then back to the boys, pausing only momentarily to yip excitedly.

"Bye, Mama!" the boys yelled.

"Here, Aaron, hang onto the hatchet, and be careful not to cut yourself. Hold it out away from you," Doug instructed, handing a small ax to his son. Aaron grabbed it and pointed the blade away from his body. Doug pulled gently on the homemade toboggan and they were off. With loud squeals of delight, they disappeared down the road amidst millions of swirling snowflakes.

Lydia drew a shawl around her shoulders and grabbed the wagon handle. Somebody around here had to make sure they had enough wood brought in for the night. She walked slowly down to the garage, remembering that first winter they'd lived here, and she had run into that nasty wolverine. Doug had been right, of course; getting Ruffy had been a good thing. They hadn't seen any wild animals around their place since he had treed the big cat. She loaded up the wagon and slowly made her way back up to the house. A couple more trips and she'd be done. She was exhausted by the time she had finished her chore. Instead of baking another pie, she decided she'd curl up and take a much-deserved nap.

She had just dozed off when she heard the Christmas tree expedition return. They had a tall, beautifully shaped fir tied down to the sled. Both boys looked exhausted, soaked, and nearly frozen. "Hurry up, boys!" she yelled from the open back door. "Get in here and thaw out."

"Go on in the house and get warmed up," Doug said with a wave of his hand. "I'll make a stand for our tree, and after supper tonight, we'll all decorate it and sing Christmas carols."

The boys hurried inside, both trying to talk at the same time. "We saw a fox, Mama!" Benjamin said, his eyes wide with wonder. "He was scared of us and Ruffy chased him."

"Did Ruffy catch him?" Lydia asked as she helped him out of his wet overalls.

"No, he couldn't...."

"Mama, did you see our tree?" Aaron interrupted. "It's the most beautifullest tree that me an' Daddy ever found," he said proudly.

"I found it too," Benjamin said, his story about the fox forgotten for the time being. "I helped Daddy put it on our big sled, and he's gonna take us for a ride again. It's so much fun! Mama, you can ride with us if you want to! Even if ya fall off, you don't get hurt!"

"Thank you, pumpkin, but I think Mama will pass on that for right now."

"We get to decorate the tree tonight, Mama! Daddy said we could. Can we make some popcorn to put on it?" Aaron asked, his eyes dancing. "Remember, like we did last time when it was Christmas? That was so much fun. Can we, Mama?"

"We'll see," his mother replied.

The tree was up and decorated. Lydia had to agree with her son when he said this was the prettiest one they'd ever had. She stood back and admired the homemade decorations of popcorn, colorful paper chains, crocheted snowflakes, and tiny angels that she and her mother had made over the years. The boys sat in quiet wonder and gazed at the tree when it was finished.

"Wow!" Ben said appreciatively. "I love Christmas!" His smile suddenly changed to a frown. "I hope Santa Claus can find our house. The snow might cover us up. What if he can't find it?"

"He can find it," Aaron assured him. "He knows right where it is, doesn't he, Mama?"

"I suppose he does," Lydia agreed.

Benjamin looked seriously at his brother for a minute, the frown deepening on his face. "I sure hope he knows that I want a bike."

"He does," Aaron said matter of fact. "He knows that I want one too."

Doug threw a big log into the fireplace and called the boys over to the circle of lamplight. "Sit down here, boys, and listen while Mama reads the Christmas story to us."

Lydia opened the big family Bible to the book of Luke, chapter two. The boys sat cross-legged on the floor in front of the snapping, crackling fire and listened attentively.

"Did Jesus get a new bicycle for his Christmas when he was a little boy?" Benjamin asked when she had finished.

"No, honey, they didn't have bicycles way back then. I guess Jesus had to walk everywhere he went."

"Poor little Jesus," Benjamin sympathized. "I would let him ride mine if he lived by us. Really, I would!"

"Stupid!" Aaron snorted. "Jesus lived a long time ago … at least a hundred years ago, an' besides, you don't even *have* a bicycle for him to ride."

"Aaron, your brother is not stupid, and I think that's very sweet of him to want to share his bike with Jesus," Lydia said, pulling her youngest son up into her lap.

"Another thing, Aaron," Daddy said with a smile, "Jesus lived one thousand nine hundred years ago. That's a long, long time ago, isn't it?"

"Wow!" both boys said in unison.

"That's way more than I can count," Aaron admitted.

"Speaking of time," Doug said, glancing at the clock, "it sure looks like it's about time two little boys I know were fast asleep in their beds."

Both boys jumped up and, in their haste, ran into each other.

Aaron shoved Benjamin aside, dashed into the cold bedroom, and leaped into the bed. Shivering, he dove underneath the heavy quilts before his brother had even made it to the door. "Ha ha ha … I'm nearly asleep and Santa is gonna bring me my present first," he taunted.

Benjamin jumped up on his side and struggled with the heavy quilts until his mother came to his rescue and tucked him in. She kissed both boys goodnight, and reminded them to say their prayers before going to sleep.

But sleep was a long time in coming. The boys began to whisper excitedly under the quilts, and it wasn't long before they were giggling.

"Santa Claus won't come to anyone's house if he hears whispering and giggling," Doug warned them. "That's about enough now. Go to sleep."

He and Lydia waited for what seemed an eternity, and finally, all was quiet, and Doug felt it was safe enough to go get the bikes.

Lydia hung the boy's stockings above the fireplace which were filled with hard candy, an orange, nuts, and a yo-yo for each of them, and then rearranged some of the decorations on the tree. She could hardly wait to see their little faces in the morning when they saw their gifts. She arranged the wrapped gifts that Grandma and Grandpa Begg had sent to all of them and was just retrieving out of hiding the package that Grandma Wheeler had mailed when Doug came back with the bikes, his hands nearly frozen to the frames.

He stomped his feet at the back door and brushed the snow off his back and out of his hair. "Man alive!" he exclaimed in an excited whisper. "We must have well over a foot out there!"

Lydia helped him out of his coat, grabbed a rag, and wiped the melting snow from both bikes.

"Let's stick them way up under the tree," Doug whispered, "so they won't see them the minute they come out in the morning." He pushed and shoved each bike as far back as he could reach, nearly toppling the tree with the effort.

"Honey!" Lydia giggled. "Be careful. You just about knocked it over."

Doug added another log to the dying embers and admired the tree one more time in the dim light from the fire. "Sure is pretty," he whispered. He put his arm around his wife, and the exhausted young couple headed for bed. They had just settled themselves in the crisp, cold sheets, and dozed off when they heard a loud shriek.

"Bikes! We got bikes, Ben! Two of 'em! Bikes!"

Doug leaped out of bed and dashed into the living room, followed by his sleepy wife. Aaron and Benjamin stood in the glow of the firelight, wildly waving their arms and jumping up and down.

"Just look at all the presents we got!" Aaron exclaimed. "He came, Ben ... he really came! Santa's been here!"

Benjamin was ecstatic as he peered underneath the tree in the dim light. He squealed and jumped around in a circle. "I got a bike ... I got a bike!" he chanted happily. "Oooo, thank you, Santa Claus! I love you, Santa! I love my bike!"

In their exuberant jubilation, the boys hugged one another and danced arm in arm beside the tree. "We got bikes," they sang together. "We got bikes!"

"Merry Christmas, sweetheart!" Doug laughed and hugged his wife. "How about some coffee?"

She yawned and grinned up at him. "Sounds good, Santa. Thanks ... I could use a cup!"

CHAPTER 16
BABY MAKES FIVE

Rebecca Joy Wheeler was born late in the evening of February 12, 1929.

Doug was drying the supper dishes for Lydia, and she was reading the boys a bedtime story, when she suddenly stopped short and gasped. "Doug," she called in a somewhat strangled voice. "Better go get Doc Sorenson."

"What's wrong, Mama?" Aaron asked, looking up into his mother's face with concern. "Are ya sick?"

"No, honey, I'm not sick."

Doug tossed the dish towel aside and hurried into the living room. "Come on, boys," he said, and ushered them into their bedroom, closing the door behind him. He explained to them that he had to go get the doctor to see about getting them a new baby brother or sister.

"A new baby?" Aaron frowned at his father. "Why do we need a new baby? How come we're getting' a new baby, Daddy?"

"No more questions," Doug said sternly. "Aaron," he said, looking very seriously at his son, "I need you to keep an eye on Ben for Mama while I'm gone. Mama's going to lie down for a while, and you and Ben need to get ready for bed. Do you understand me?"

Aaron ignored his father's question and stared wide-eyed at him. "Is Mama gonna be okay?" he asked in a worried voice.

"Yes, Mama's going to be just fine. Aaron, did you hear what I just said? You and Ben get ready for bed. No horsing around tonight. Mama and I need your help, and you're in charge, Aaron. Do you understand me?" He looked skeptically at his oldest son.

Aaron nodded his head and glanced at his brother.

"And don't forget to say your prayers," Doug reminded them as he headed back into the living room. "I'll see you both in the morning."

Benjamin watched as his father helped his mother into their bedroom and closed the door. He looked quizzically at his brother. "What happened?" he asked, nervously turning the storybook in his hands.

"Nothin' happened. Daddy's goin' to get the doctor so he can bring us a new baby, that's all. You heard Daddy … get ready for bed."

"A new baby?" Benjamin stared at his big brother for an explanation, and when one didn't come right away, he began frowning. "How come we're gettin' a new baby?"

"How should I know?" Aaron shrugged his shoulders. "I guess 'cause we wanted one, or maybe 'cause Mama and Daddy ordered one ... I don't know."

Both boys struggled into their pajamas and tiptoed to the closed door of their parents' bedroom. They stood in the semi-darkness listening, their ears pressed against the door. Hearing nothing at all, Aaron gently tried the doorknob. The door swung back on its hinges and their mother lifted her head off the pillow and smiled at them.

"Come and give me a kiss goodnight," she said softly. Both boys bounded up on the bed.

"How come you're in bed, Mama?" Benjamin asked, as he bent to kiss her goodnight.

"Just tired, sweetie," his mother said with a long sigh that ended in a slight groan.

"Where's Daddy?" Aaron asked, glancing around the darkened room.

"He went into town to see about getting the doctor," Lydia explained when she could talk again. "He'll be back pretty soon, and I want both of you to be in bed fast asleep, you hear?"

The boys nodded, kissed her again and scrambled down from the big bed.

"Don't forget to say your prayers," she reminded them as they backed out the door.

"We won't," Aaron promised.

"Is Mama sick?" Benjamin asked his brother when they were back in their own room.

"Naw, I don't think so. She looks pretty fine to me," he said, pulling the quilts up around his chin. "You hear my prayers, and then I'll hear yours," he suggested as Benjamin dove under the covers beside him.

"Rebecca Joy," the doctor repeated, as he filled out the blanks on the birth certificate and signed it, later that night. "Nice name for a little girl. He yawned extravagantly, handed the document to Doug, and collected his bag and overcoat. "You'll need to take that to the courthouse to have it recorded," he reminded Doug.

Doug nodded and rubbed his tired eyes. "Thanks so much again, Doc," he said as he walked the old man to the back door.

The doctor stopped in the doorway and looked thoughtful for just a few seconds. Turning to Doug, he added, "Mother and baby are doing just fine.

You know where to reach me if you need anything more." He jammed his hat on his head and was gone.

Doug felt as if he'd been awake for at least a week. He checked on the boys and then crawled into bed beside his wife. She moaned softly and flashed him a very tired smile.

"We finally got our little girl. She's beautiful, isn't she?"

"Just like her mother," Doug whispered, and kissed his wife lightly on her forehead.

They peered over the side of the bed at the tiny, sleeping baby in the cradle.

"I'll bet you looked just like that when you were born," Lydia whispered. "Just look at all that dark hair!"

"I called Mother while I was in town. She'll be here on the last train tomorrow afternoon. I'll go over and see if Georgia can stay with you while I go get Mom," Doug said softly. He turned and looked at his wife when she didn't respond. She was fast asleep.

Tired as he was, Doug found it very difficult to relax and find sleep for himself. He had a daughter! Two sons and a daughter! Who would have ever thought that Doug Wheeler could be so fortunate? Thank you, Lord, for such a beautiful family, he prayed.

"Rebecca Joy?" Georgia said the following morning. "I thought you were going to name her Rebecca Louise."

"We were," Lydia admitted, with a tired smile, "but when she was born, she brought us so much instant joy that we decided, on the spur of the moment, to name her Joy … Rebecca Joy."

"She certainly is a beautiful baby," Georgia said, looking down at the tiny infant in her arms. "Just look at all that hair! My stars … I believe she has enough to braid right now." She smoothed the baby's thick hair back away from the tiny, perfect face. "What a perfect little doll," she murmured, and placed a light kiss on the soft, little cheek.

The boys grinned at her description of their little sister. "She's not a doll," Aaron scoffed. "She's a real live baby."

"An' she cries … loud," Benjamin added.

"Yeah, it sounds like a cat when she cries."

Both boys giggled over that description.

"Are you boys gonna help your Grandma when she gets here?" Georgia asked. "She's gonna need all the help you both can give her, like getting in the wood, and drying the dishes, and taking the garbage out … stuff like that."

They both nodded eagerly. “I’m in charge of things … Daddy said so,” Aaron said proudly.

“I can’t do any dishes … Mama said I might break ‘em,” Benjamin explained.

“Well, maybe so,” Georgia agreed with a laugh, “but you can be a great help by helping Aaron bring in the wood, and by helping to make your bed, and things like that, right?”

The little boy nodded his head. “Yeah, and I’m gonna read a good story to my new baby,” he added, and ran into his room to find the perfect book to read.

Lydia and Georgia snickered. “Isn’t that the sweetest thing in the world?” Georgia asked in a whisper.

Not wanting to be left out of the praise, Aaron said, “I’m gonna help Grandma the most ‘cause I’m the biggest. And you know what? Next year, I’m goin’ to school and Ben can’t go.”

“Is that right?” Georgia asked in an amazed voice. She winked at Lydia. “You and Peter! Going to school together next year! My, my! Aren’t you two something? Just growing up right before our eyes, aren’t you?”

Aaron nodded his head and skipped out to the kitchen, and then back to her chair. “If you need anything, you just holler for me, all right?” he said to Georgia, his face dead serious.

“I certainly shall,” Georgia agreed. “Thank you, Aaron.”

Aaron puffed out his chest and slowly headed toward the back door. “See ya later … I got work to do … wood an’ all.”

Georgia and Lydia held their mirth until he was well out of hearing range.

“You can sure be proud of your boys,” Georgia said after they enjoyed a good laugh. “They’re both pretty special kids.”

“Am I special too, Aunt Georgia?” Benjamin asked, his arms loaded down with his favorite books.

“You most definitely are,” Georgia said, lightly pinching his still chubby cheeks. “You most definitely are. Very special!”

Doug arrived early in the evening with Grandma Wheeler. Tired as she was, she saw to it that supper was on the table and the boys in bed by eight. “Little ones need their sleep,” she said with an air of authority. “Douglas, may I hold my new granddaughter? You’ve had the pleasure all evening long, and I’d like to say I got to hold her at least once before I have to go back home.”

Doug laughed and handed the baby to his mother.

“She looks just like you, son,” she said a few minutes later. “You had lots of dark hair like that, and her nose … that’s your nose if ever I saw it! Look at that perfect little rosebud mouth! She's absolutely beautiful. She's Grandma's precious little darling."

Doug beamed at his mother's glowing words. "I'm pretty proud of her myself," he said. "In fact, I'm proud of every member of my family." He stood over the rocking chair behind his mother and gazed lovingly down at his tiny newborn daughter. "She is beautiful, isn't she?"

"Of course she is! All my grandchildren are beautiful," his mother exclaimed rather indignantly.

"Mom, you'd think your grandchildren were beautiful even if they looked like toads run over by a train," Doug teased.

"Well, they don't look like toads, and they really are beautiful. Speaking of beautiful, I need my beauty rest and I'm wondering where on earth I'm going to sleep?"

"Oh, sorry, Mom … I almost forgot. We have a cot stored down in the garage. I meant to go down right after supper and get it but I forgot. I'll run down right now and get it. Just give me five minutes and I'll have a bed fixed up for you that's fit for a queen."

His mother rolled her eyes. "That'll be the day!"

A half-hour later, she eyed the narrow, lumpy bed that he had hastily made up for her in a corner of the living room.

"Hrumph!" she snorted. "Only a backward, heathenistic mass of crazed lunatics would offer their queen something that looked like that!"

"We offer only the very best for our queen," Doug teased with an impish grin.

"Hrumph!" Louise Wheeler said again. "If I'm still among the living by morning, pull me out of this wondrous chamber of slumber, and I'll get your breakfast for you … that is providing I can still move."

Despite the lack of comfortable accommodations, Louise Wheeler slept soundly and was up before the rest of the family the next morning.

Doug stumbled sleepily out into the kitchen, drawn by the mouthwatering aroma of frying bacon and fresh, ground coffee. "Hi Grandma," he murmured, pouring himself a large cup of coffee. "How'd you sleep last night?"

"I've had better nights," his mother said, "but all in all, not too bad. You look like you should have stayed in bed this morning. Didn't you sleep well?"

Doug yawned and shook his head. "Baby kept squeaking and making little noises that woke me up. Guess I'll have to get used to having a baby in the room again." He yawned again and gulped his coffee. "It's been nearly four years since we've had a new baby … Benjamin will be four next month."

"Mm-mm," his mother responded rather absentmindedly. "How do you want your eggs?"

The bumps and ripples of having a new baby in the house began to smooth out under the supervision of Grandma Wheeler. The boys had the utmost respect for her and jumped at her every command. Lydia was amazed to see such immediate obedience to her orders.

"Grandma, what else do you want me to do?" she heard Aaron ask. "Do you have some more work for me?"

"Is that *my* son I hear talking? I'd give anything to have him ask me that just once in a while," she complained to her mother-in-law when the boys had gone outside to play.

"You have to be firm and show them who's boss," Mother Wheeler advised. "Otherwise, they'll try to take over. Now," she said, rising from her chair, "let's get some of these dirty clothes washed." She rubbed and scrubbed and rinsed clothes until her hands were nearly raw. Then, donning her coat, she headed outside to pin the dripping clothes, along with a dozen, brand new, white diapers on the line, which promptly froze in the crisp, early morning February air.

"You touch these clothes, dog ... you're as good as dead," she said to Ruffy as she hurried back inside to thaw out.

"It looks strange to see baby things on the line again after so many years," Lydia commented at noon as they sat down to eat. "You forget how tiny babies are when they start out in life."

"Grandma, me an' Ben found a new trail that we can ride our bikes on," Aaron said after she had asked the blessing.

"Oh? You boys be very careful and watch out for snakes," she replied. "That's the last thing we need is for one of you to come home all snake bitten!"

"Snakes!" Aaron exclaimed with a laugh. "Grandma, it's too cold for snakes." He and Benjamin snickered.

"Don't you laugh at me," Grandma scolded. "Winter snakes ... that's what I'm talking about. Isn't there such a thing as winter snakes?" She left the question hanging over the table.

Aaron looked at his mother and then at Benjamin and shrugged his shoulders.

Benjamin took a large bite from his sandwich. "Do winter snakes take bites this big?" he asked his grandmother, holding up his sandwich.

"How on earth would I know?" his grandmother replied. "All I'm saying is that you boys be careful, and be on the lookout for snakes, and other horrible creatures out in the forest that bite or sting. Your mother and I have enough to do without having to worry about things like that."

The boys finished their lunch and headed for the door. "Bye, Mama an' Grandma," they said in unison as they buttoned up their coats. As soon as the door was closed, Lydia heard them hissing and spitting at one another, and giggling as they mounted their bicycles.

"Winter snakes, here we come!" Aaron shouted as he rode down the driveway. Benjamin, pedaling with all his might, was right behind his brother. Lydia smiled and watched them until they were out of sight. Winter snakes, indeed!

Saturday came all too soon, and Doug, along with the boys, packed Grandma into the car for the long drive back to Newton and the train station.

"Mother, how I can I ever thank you for all you've done?" Lydia said, hugging her mother-in-law. "I'm going to miss you."

"My pleasure," Louise Wheeler said, giving Lydia one of her rare smiles. "Take good care of my precious little angel." She hugged her daughter-in-law and kissed the baby one more time.

"Come on, Mother," Doug urged. "We're gonna miss your train if we don't hurry. Be back later this afternoon, honey," he added, kissing his wife. "Go take a nap."

The train depot was a beehive of activity. People stood in small groups both inside the station and outside on the platform despite a brisk, cold wind that had started blowing.

"Brrrr! Feels like snow tonight," Doug commented. "Are you going to be warm enough, Mother?"

"Of course, silly. I'll be on the train most of the night."

The boys watched with mounting excitement as the big train pulled into the station, the noise of the steam, the shrill whistle and the brakes nearly deafening them. Grandma kissed each of them good-bye and hugged her son.

"Douglas," she said, when the noise had abated, "buy your wife a washing machine."

"I wish I could, Mother, but as you well know, we don't have electricity on the mountain yet."

"That's no excuse, Douglas. They've had gas-powered machines out for years now. Get that poor girl one before her hands fall off. You boys behave yourselves and help your mother," she said, as she stepped up on the train. "No fighting, you hear? And don't forget to say your prayers at night."

The two little boys stared as Grandma disappeared inside the train amidst other passengers.

"All aboard!" the conductor yelled loudly as the train began to slowly move down the track. Grandma Wheeler was gone.

The boys were unusually quiet on the trip back home, and within a few minutes, Benjamin was fast asleep. Aaron finally broke the silence as they left Northridge and began the ascent up the winding mountain road toward home. "Daddy, is there such a thing as winter snakes?" he asked, leaning forward in the backseat.

"Winter snakes? Not that I know of. Who told you such a thing?"

"Grandma did," he said. "She told us to be careful riding our bikes, and watch out for winter snakes."

Doug laughed heartily. "All grandmas are worried about things like that, I guess. Grandma just wanted you to be careful when you're out riding."

They rode in silence a few minutes longer when Doug suddenly exploded in laughter. "Winter snakes indeed! You boys better watch out for those dreadful winter snakes." He was still laughing as he parked the car in the garage. "Poor old Grandma," he said, rolling his eyes. "I wonder where she comes up with some of these things."

"Who's here?" Aaron asked suddenly, noticing the maroon roadster parked close to the house.

"Looks like Pastor Jamison and his wife," Doug said as he strode up the driveway to the back door. Ruffy bounded out to meet them, and he stopped to stroke the dog's head. "I'll bet Mama didn't have a chance for a nap after all."

Ruffy turned his attention to the boys, licking each of them in his ususal exuberant greeting.

"Cut it out, Ruffy!" Ben exclaimed, wiping his face on the sleeve of his jacket.

"Congratulations Doug!" Pastor Rodney said as he rose from his chair, shaking hands with the younger man. "She's a mighty beautiful child."

"Thank you, Pastor," Doug beamed.

"What do you boys think of your new sister?" Bess Jamison asked as the boys made a beeline for their bedroom.

"We like her, I guess," Aaron answered, shrugging his shoulders.

"She sure cries a lot," Benjamin added, making a face.

The pastor and his wife laughed at his imitation. "Spoken like true brothers," Rod said.

The boys disappeared into their room and closed the door.

"See you and the boys in church tomorrow?" the Pastor asked Doug.

Doug nodded and glanced at his wife. "I doubt Lydia will be able to make it though. It's kind of early to have the baby out and all."

"Oh, I should say!" Bess exclaimed. "Too cold for a tiny baby."

"Thank you so very, very much for the beautiful sweater and booties," Lydia said as their guests rose to leave. "We'll certainly put those to good use."

Several friends and neighbors made their way to the Wheeler house, bearing food, gifts, and words of encouragement over the next several days. Ina Potts even braved another go-round with Ruffy. This time however, whether it was because of the dog, or the fact that it was so cold ... Lydia couldn't decide which ... Ina arrived with her friend, Mr. Hodgkiss ... in his car.

"Why, Miss Potts, how nice to see you again," Lydia exclaimed when she answered the door. "And Mr. Hodgkiss, please come in."

Russell Hodgkiss quickly removed his hat and stood just inside the door, obviously very uncomfortable. Ina, however, headed straight for the rocking chair in the living room, plopped herself down, and began chattering about the unbearable cold weather.

"Please, Mr. Hodgkiss, have a seat. Would you both care for some coffee?" Lydia asked them, hoping they'd turn her down. Neither of them responded, so Lydia decided not to mention it again. Ina babbled on, scarcely noticing her companion as he quietly seated himself in Doug's chair.

"Well, what do you think of our new president?" she asked, looking at Lydia over her glasses.

"I ... I ... I'm afraid I haven't had much time to follow political things in Washington," Lydia confessed. "I'm afraid I don't know very much about our president."

"He's a very frugal young man, and that's exactly what we need in this country. Yes sir, President Hoover's gonna do all right," she predicted.

"I certainly hope so," Lydia said with a smile.

"Well, I see you've had the baby," Ina said, suddenly switching topics of conversation. "What'd you get this time?"

"We have a little girl," Lydia said, "born on the twelfth."

"And what did you name her?" Ina asked.

"Rebecca Joy."

Ina nodded her head. "That's a sensible name. Certainly is a lot more sensible than Ina. I don't for the life of me know what my mother was thinking of when she named me. Ina Irene ... isn't that a horrible name? My classmates used to call me I'ma Pott which they quickly changed to I'ma chamber pot ... just to make me miserable."

"Kids can sure be mean, can't they?" Lydia said in a sympathizing voice.

Russell Hodgkiss nodded his head and smiled.

"I should say they can!" Ina exploded. "One of those mean Thompson boys used to dangle my long braid down inside the inkwell on his desk. My hair was dyed permanent blue-black on the ends for many years."

To the surprise of both women, Russell burst out laughing at this piece of history.

"Oh, you just hush up over there," Ina said, her eyes blazing. "It was really quite horrible at the time. Those Thompson boys deserve the hottest part of Hades for what they put me through. Why, one day, they even dropped a live mouse in my lap. I nearly tore my desk apart getting away from that one."

Russell slapped his knee and exploded in unrestrained laughter. Ina glared at him with disgust. "Go ahead … laugh your fool head off," she muttered. "You'll get your reward one of these days … right along with those Thompson boys."

At that moment, the baby began to stir and cry in the bedroom beyond the living room.

"Now look what you've done, you old fool. Woke the poor little baby up. I declare, Russell, you're worse than the Thompson boys at times!"

"Sorry ma'am," the old man wheezed as Lydia made her way into the bedroom.

"It was time for her to be awake anyway," she said, as she carried the baby back into the living room. "Would you like to hold her, Miss Ina?" she asked.

"Oh, my heavens no!" she said, grabbing up her purse. "I'd drop her right on her head. Here's a little something for the baby," she said, retrieving a small package from her purse. "It's not much, but maybe she'll get some use out of it one of these days before long."

"Why, Ina, bless your sweet heart!" Lydia exclaimed as she accepted the tiny gift. She settled Rebecca in her lap and fumbled with the wrapping, finally uncovering a small, silver spoon.

"Oh, Ina, it's beautiful. Thank you so much."

"'Tis nothing," Ina said, for once, at a loss for words, her face turning slightly pink. "Come on," she said to her companion, "we'd best be on our way."

Lydia rose with her company and walked slowly to the back door.

"Where are the boys and that awful dog of yours?" Ina asked suddenly. "It's sure quiet around here today."

"They're over at the Bakers' house playing with Peter Baker," Lydia explained. "Georgia Baker has been a godsend to me since Rebecca was born. I don't know what I'd do without her. We're really blessed with wonderful neighbors."

"That we are … that we are," Ina agreed.

"You have a beautiful daughter, and I apologize again for wakin' her up," Russell murmured as he hurried out the door.

"No need for apology," Lydia assured him. "Please come back again any time that you and Miss Ina are in the neighborhood." She closed the door tightly against a blast of cold air and hugged the baby tightly to her chest.

"Time to feed Mama's hungry girl," she said.

Poor Ina, she thought a few minutes later. No wonder she was so disagreeable from time to time. Poor I'ma chamber pot!

CHAPTER 17
IN THE DOGHOUSE

"Honey, you need to get out more. Come on, a trip to town will do you a world of good," Doug looked pleadingly at his wife. "You haven't been out of the house since Rebecca was born. Come on, honey ... you'll feel better."

Lydia sighed and gave him one of her long, level stares. "Doug, I'm a hideous mess. Look at me! I haven't been able to do anything with my hair for weeks now, and I've had the same outfit on for the past three days ... and now you want me to go shopping with you?"

"Go fix yourself up. I'll watch the kids. Here, give me Becca, and I'll keep an eye on the boys. Hurry! Go comb your hair and whatever." He lifted six-week-old Rebecca out of his wife's arms and waved Lydia toward the bedroom when he suddenly realized that the baby was sopping wet.

"Uggghh!" he muttered. "You're a mess, baby Bec." He followed his wife into the bedroom and handed the baby back to her.

Lydia looked at him quizzically. "I thought you were going to take care of her," she said, her frown deepening.

"She's soaked," he said defensively. "I'll go clean up the kitchen and get the boys ready, okay?" Without waiting for an answer he hurried back into the kitchen, grabbed a few dishes off the table, and set them in the sink. I'll wash 'em later, he thought. "Aaron!" he yelled. "You and Ben get in here and get cleaned up. We're going to town."

The two boys scurried into the house, eager to go anywhere, but especially to town. "Daddy, can I spend my big money that Grandma and Nana sent me?" Benjamin asked, his eyes dancing.

"Grandma sent you some big money? When?"

"For my happy birthday. Grandma Wheeler sent me a letter with a big money in it, and then Nana and Grandpa sent me some more. Can I take it to town and buy something?"

Doug looked down at his son and laughed. "I guess you can, Ben ... it's your money, but I doubt that Deacon has much in his store that would interest you."

Benjamin didn't hear another word. He rushed off to his bedroom to retrieve his fortune.

"Get back out here," Doug yelled. "We need to scrub about a pound of that dirt off your face. Aaron … you too."

Both boys came back into the kitchen, and Doug did his best to wash some of the yard off their faces. It was at that moment, while he was scrubbing them, he noticed for the first time that they both had freckles.

"Hey! Where'd you get those?" he teased. "I thought that was dirt and tried to wash 'em off your nose, but they won't come off."

Benjamin giggled and wriggled his arm free of his Dad's grasp. Aaron rolled his eyes. "Daddy, you know that's not dirt. Me and Ben have had those for years an' years. Peter said his Grandma told him that it came from the angels when they make cinnamon cookies. Some of the cinnamon falls off the cookies, and it falls all the way down here and lands on our noses. Is that true?"

"Well," Doug laughed, "that sounds a bit farfetched to me. Personally, I think it's nutmeg!"

"Oh, Daddy!" Aaron exclaimed. "You're a nutmeg!"

"Look at my big money, Daddy," Ben said proudly, producing several big coins from his pocket.

"Wow!" Daddy exclaimed. "What are you going to buy with all that money? Maybe a new house for all of us to live in, and a couple of new cars?"

"I don't think I have that much," Benjamin answered seriously. "I'm gonna buy something big for me, and maybe something little for Aaron, and something real tiny for Becca, and maybe something for you and Mama. I'll probably be out of money by then."

"I would imagine so," Doug agreed. "All right, boys, let's see about your hair. Go get me the big comb."

Benjamin disappeared into the bedroom, and Doug finished cleaning off the table.

"Can't have the comb, Daddy," Benjamin said a minute later. "Mama's usin' it right now, and she said it would be a month of Sundays before she was through with it. What does that mean?"

"It means she's going to need it for a long, long time. Well, let's just wet your hair down and get it out of your eyes." Doug did his best with water and his fingers, and to his surprise, the boys didn't look half-bad when he was finished.

"We're ready!" he yelled to his wife. "Come on, boys, let's go get the car."

The three Wheeler men grabbed their coats and headed down to the garage. Doug backed the car up to the house and let it idle smoothly while he waited for Lydia.

"What on earth is keeping your mother?" he wondered out loud a few minutes later. "Did she decide to take a bath or something? Aaron, run in and see what's keeping her."

"Maybe she's takin' a nap," Benjamin suggested. He stood up and jingled the coins in his overalls pocket just to make sure they were still there.

Aaron came running out of the house a few seconds later and squeezed into the seat behind Doug. "Mama said if you can't wait a minute for her to get ready, then just go without her."

"If we can't *wait* just a minute!" Doug exploded. "We've waited so long now, I can't remember what we're even going for. The store's gonna be closed before we get to town at the rate she's moving. We'll probably run out of gas to boot if we sit here in the driveway much longer."

"You want me to go tell her that for ya, Daddy?" Aaron asked.

"No, that's all right, son. I value my life a little more than that. I'd sooner wrestle a wildcat."

Lydia finally slammed the back door and hurried to the car, baby Rebecca tightly bundled in a big blanket in her arms. Doug whistled when he saw her. She had changed her dress and shoes and had done something magical with her hair, which was piled up on top of her head.

"You look beautiful, honey," he said, winking at her.

"Daddy said you were a rested wildcat, Mama," Benjamin blurted out.

"Oh, he did, did he?" She glared at her husband who was staring straight ahead as he jammed the gearshift into low and drove down the driveway.

"He did not!" Aaron said, momentarily jumping to Daddy's defense. "He said he would rather fight a bobcat … or something like that."

"You're both wrong," Doug shot over his shoulder. "I never said anything like that at all."

"Uh-huh! Likely story," Lydia said scornfully, glaring at him again.

Deacon greeted the family with his usual, "Hi ya, folks … be with ya in a minute," when they entered the store. The boys raced to the candy aisle and began drooling over the enormous selection of hard candies, chocolates, and licorice that he kept stored in large glass containers on the countertop as well as inside the case.

Lydia handed Rebecca to Doug and mumbled as she walked past him. "You'd better hold her. This wildcat has sharpened her claws." She fumbled in her coat pocket for the long list of things they needed and handed it to Deacon while she went to inspect what little fresh produce he had in the store. An inviting fire was snapping and popping in the huge potbellied stove in the center of the store. Lydia glanced at the large wooden barrel of pickles that sat next to the small meat case in the back corner of the store and wondered if she should indulge and take a few back home. It had been a long time since she'd tasted a fresh pickle. The bell over the door tinkled again as another customer entered the store.

"Hi ya, folks, be right with ya," Deacon called loudly, without looking up to see who had come in. Lydia carefully picked through the bananas and apples that the old man had on display. Some were nearly to the point of spoiling. She wrinkled up her nose at one very soft apple and decided on a few oranges instead.

"Oh, my gracious, sakes alive, she's absolutely beautiful, Doug," she heard a woman's voice say. Lydia looked through the rows of canned goods, and to her dismay, there stood Jack Doss' wife, Rosalyn, talking with Doug. Rosalyn always reminded Lydia of a perfect rose garden, neat and trim, with every hair in place. She had a beautiful, flawless complexion ... one that made Lydia feel like an old, worn out hag. She had never seen Rosalyn dress in anything plain. Everything the woman owned had flowers on it, and today was certainly no exception. Lydia could see a small portion of the beautiful flowered dress at the front of the open woolen coat with fur trim she was wearing. She wished now that she had spent a little more time getting herself ready. She felt ugly, fat, and old. She was acutely aware of her faded dress, the run down heels on her old shoes and her shabby, worn coat with one button missing.

"Hi there, Lydia!" Rosalyn sang out with her perfectly melodious voice. "Don't you look lovely? And after just having a baby too! I don't know how you do it, dear."

"Hello, Rosalyn," Lydia said, forcing herself to smile at the woman. Rosalyn smiled back, displaying a perfect set of sparkling, white teeth. Lydia felt even uglier standing next to her when she caught a whiff of Rosalyn's expensive perfume, which made her feel slightly heady. She wondered if it had the same effect on Doug.

"I was just telling Doug I don't think I've ever seen a prettier baby in my life." She smiled broadly at Lydia again. "She's just an absolute doll!"

"Thank you," Lydia said, suddenly feeling ashamed of herself for her unwarranted thoughts and feelings about this woman.

"My, my, my!" Rosalyn exclaimed. "Just look how your boys have grown." She watched the two boys as they studied the confections behind the counter. "Seems like just yesterday my own kids were about that age. They sure grow up fast, don't they?"

"How old are your kids now?" Doug asked, more to make conversation, than out of curiosity.

"Jeremy's thirteen and Christina's our big sophomore in high school this year. She's fifteen, soon to be sixteen."

"Good night!" Doug exclaimed. "When I first met Jack, he used to talk about them a lot, and I think they were something like five and seven. It's downright scary how fast time flies."

"Mm-mm," Rosalyn nodded, and flashed those perfect teeth again. "I should say it is," she murmured. "Well, I won't keep you. I'm sure you're as frantically busy as I am. It was so nice to see you both again ... and congratulations on that beautiful baby." With a wave of her hand, she disappeared toward the back of the store.

Doug's eyes followed her for a moment before he turned and looked again at his wife. He gulped and hugged Rebecca close to him.

"Can I help with our list, honey?" he asked feebly.

Lydia shook her head. "Deacon's filling it right now," she said in a rather sad tone. She walked over to the boys and stood, looking down at the candy counter. Doug sighed, wondering why on earth he seemed to be in the doghouse when he hadn't done a single thing, except compliment his wife and talk to his boss' wife for a few minutes. He stood, watching his family for a few seconds when a thought struck him. *His wife was tired!* That was it! He could plainly see that. *'Buy your wife a washing machine,'* his mother had said, *'before her hands fall off!'* That's not a bad idea, he thought. I'll look into that the first of next week. Maybe Sears and Roebuck has something in their latest catalog that we could afford. He ambled over to the counter and began drooling over the enticing sweets on display there.

"Benjamin," Aaron was saying, "buy chocolates. They're a lot better than hard candy. Look at those over there. I bet you could buy lots of those."

Benjamin pressed his nose up against the glass and carefully studied each confection behind the case.

"How much do these cost?" he asked, staring at the pile of chocolate covered cherries.

"I don't know," Aaron admitted. "You'll have to ask Mama or Daddy. I can't read those big numbers."

"There you are, folks. I think I got everything on your list. Incidentally, the soup is on sale this week, five cans for fifty-nine cents." Deacon smiled at the young couple as he placed four large boxes filled with groceries up on the countertop. "What else can I get for you today?"

"I think that'll about do it," Lydia smiled at him. "Ben has a little birthday money that is burning a hole in his pocket." She smiled and glanced at her sons.

Deacon laughed. "I'll be right with you, boys," he promised. He added up the list and handed the total to Doug who fished in his pocket for the right bills. When the grocery bill had been paid, he turned his attention to his younger customers who were having a terrible time deciding which treat to buy.

"Well, young fellas, what's it gonna be today?"

Doug handed the baby back to Lydia and took the boxes out to the car.

"I think I'd better supervise this little transaction," their mother said to the old man behind the counter. "Benjamin would be happy to purchase every single piece you've got in the store."

Deacon laughed and wiped his hands on his big white apron. He grabbed a small brown paper bag, and stood ready to fill the order. In the end, Lydia allowed the purchase of five cents worth of ribbon candy, and another five cents worth of chocolates. The boys were ecstatic and rushed out to the car to show Daddy. Lydia, following a few seconds later, was coming down the steps when a sudden gust of icy, cold wind whistled around the corner of the old building, billowing her skirt out in front of her, and obscuring her view of the bottom step. She misjudged the distance and suddenly lost her balance. She pitched backwards and sat down hard on the step above, her left hip and elbow taking most of the impact.

"Oh!" she cried, tightening her grip on the baby in her arms. To her absolute dismay, Rosalyn chose that very instant to come waltzing daintily out of the store.

"Oh my dear!" Rosalyn cried, tossing her bags aside on the top step. "Are you hurt?" She rushed down the steps and tried to help Lydia to her feet.

"I ... I don't think so," Lydia stammered, struggling to regain her composure.

Doug finally looked up and stared in confusion at the two women. He rushed from the car. "What on earth happened?" he gasped, squatting down beside his wife. Before either woman could answer, he had pulled his wife back on her feet.

"I slipped," Lydia murmured softly.

"Are you all right, honey?" he asked, fear registering on his face. "Did you hurt anything?"

"No," Lydia answered simply. But I wish I'd killed myself, she thought glumly to herself.

Rosalyn retrieved her groceries and with a wave of a gloved hand hurried to her own car.

It figures she'd know how to drive one, Lydia thought dismally as she allowed Doug to help her into their own car. She glanced down at Rebecca, who, amazingly, had remained sound asleep throughout the ordeal. Thank goodness she wasn't hurt, she thought. The ride home was silent. The boys had their mouths too full of sweets to make much noise, and Doug was trying desperately to understand his wife's moodiness. He stole furtive glances at her from time to time.

Lydia stared straight ahead, her mind a turmoil of shame, self-doubt, and embarrassment. Pastor Rodney once said that the Lord chastens His own, she thought. That's what I get for thinking such ugly thoughts about Rosalyn. After all, the woman has never done a single thing to me. She's only trying to be friendly. What on earth is wrong with me anyway? Why do I feel so inferior when I get around her? Is it because they have so much more than we do? Their lives seem to be so perfect. Rosalyn was so perfect. That was it! Rosalyn didn't have a single flaw that Lydia could see. She was absolutely perfect. She had everything any woman could ever ask for … a beautiful home, a great husband who obviously adored her, two wonderful children, a beautiful car, and scads of beautiful clothes, even if they were all flowers. Lydia Wheeler! she scolded herself silently. You're jealous! It's a sin to be envious and covet what other people have.

"You sure you're all right?" Doug interrupted her thoughts.

Lydia nodded her head, the tears suddenly very close to the surface. "I'm fine. Just tired, I guess."

"Tell you what, sweetheart," Doug said, placing his hand on her knee. "When we get home, I'll put the groceries away, and then I'll make supper for us tonight. You just put your feet up and take it easy. How does that sound?"

The tears that had been threatening all afternoon suddenly flooded her eyes and coursed down her cheeks before she could stop them. She searched in every pocket for a hankie. Finding none, she mopped up her face with the sleeve of her coat and nodded her thanks to her husband. He grinned back at her, patted her knee, and promptly hit the largest pothole in the winding road up to their house. The boys bounced wildly in the backseat, squashing candy in the process.

"Here, Mama, I saved this one for you," Benjamin said, shoving a flattened piece of chocolate at his mother.

"What about dear old Dad? Does he get some chocolate too?" Doug asked, quickly swerving to avoid another hole in the road.

"Nope! Sorry, Daddy, they're all gone," Benjamin mumbled, his mouth full.

"Do you mean to tell me you boys ate all that candy?" Lydia asked, whirling around in her seat to stare at her sons. "Give me those bags, right now!" she demanded. She was astounded when Benjamin handed her two empty bags. "You won't eat a bite of supper," she scolded. "And you'll probably both be sick as a dog tonight."

Much to her surprise, however, both boys ate a hearty meal and never complained of stomachaches at all.

"They have cast iron stomachs like their Pa," Doug said with a laugh. "I used to be able to eat a mountain of garbage without any problem. Just ask Mother. I nearly cleaned her out of house and home a few years ago." He suddenly scooped his wife up into his arms and kissed her tenderly.

"I love you, honey," he said. "Who needs chocolates anyway? You're all the sweets I'll ever need."

"I love you too," Lydia whispered, tears threatening to surface once again.

Doug buried his face in her sweet-smelling hair and sighed, hoping against hope that whatever he had done was forgiven, and he was out of the doghouse.

CHAPTER 18
SPRING WITHOUT LIFE

The days of April and May were glorious. The weather was picture-perfect and Lydia, wearied after a long, wet winter, was as eager as the boys were to get outside. She hurried through her morning chores inside the house each day to leave plenty of time in the afternoon to work outside and enjoy the balmy weather. Her garden was going to be bigger and better than ever before, she had told Doug just a few nights ago. She glanced at Rebecca, who was propped up in her cradle so that she could see her mother and brothers. Just a couple of weeks before, she had started smiling at all of them. Lydia smiled, remembering that special moment. What a precious addition she was to their family. The boys seemed to love and enjoy her as much as she and Doug did.

"Becca!" she called loudly. "Baby Becca!"

The baby listened intently and seemed to be looking for her but soon lost interest and stared instead at her own little fist. Lydia went back to work with her spading, one shovelful at a time. It was backbreaking labor, but she loved every minute of it. The boys were busy in the driveway building roads for their little homemade cars and trucks.

"Benjamin!" Aaron yelled suddenly. "Stop it! You just messed up all my roads! You can't cross my roads with your own dumb roads."

Benjamin stood up and looked behind him, scratching his head. "Then why can't we use the same roads?" he asked.

"Why indeed?" their mother echoed as she rested on the handle of her shovel for a minute.

"Mama, he doesn't know how to make a good road, and he keeps crossing my roads and messing them up," Aaron complained.

"Then why don't you make the roads, Aaron, and let Benjamin make little buildings with some of those blocks of wood that Daddy sawed up?"

That met with the approval of both boys, and peace reigned once again. Lydia was about halfway through her spading when Georgia and Peter arrived for an early afternoon visit. Aaron and Peter decided that exploring the woods around the house was far more interesting, and the two of them ran off, leaving Benjamin on his own. He soon lost interest in house building and went in search of his mother. He found the two women engaged in conversation over some crumb cake and a glass of cold milk.

"Where's Peter and Aaron?" Georgia asked, putting her arm around the little boy.

Benjamin shrugged his shoulder. "I don't know. They took off for the woods a while ago."

"They didn't invite you to come along?"

Benjamin shook his head. "Nope," he said simply. "Mama, can I have somethin' to eat?"

Lydia cut him a small piece of the crumb cake she had made for dessert. "Would you like some milk with that, honey?" she asked, ruffling his hair.

He nodded his head and sat cross-legged on the kitchen floor next to the cradle and watched his baby sister.

"Mama!" he cried suddenly. "She wants some of my cake. Look at her! She's reachin' for a piece."

The women laughed as the baby extended her tiny hand, and straightened her short fingers out toward Benjamin.

"Aww!" Benjamin said and reached over to kiss her. "Sorry Becca," he said, "but you can't have any cake yet. You have to grow some teeth." He demonstrated by opening his mouth and pointing to a row of straight, white teeth.

The baby nodded her head as if she understood every word.

"She knows what I'm sayin'," the little boy cried. "Did you see that, Mama?" He grinned up at his mother and Georgia. "She's smart," he added, rocking the cradle back and forth. He played with her for a few minutes longer until she lost interest, and drifted off to sleep.

"She sure is a good baby," Georgia commented. "I wouldn't mind having one more if I could be assured of having one that good."

Lydia raised an eyebrow and grinned at her friend. "Believe me, she has her moments. Sometimes, especially during the night, I'd gladly give her to you. But you're right … all in all, she's a real good baby. I've certainly been blessed. All three of my kids have been good babies."

"Was I a good one?" Benjamin asked. "Was I the best?"

"You were one of the very best," his mother said with a smile. "But you didn't stay a baby for very long. It seems like you were born one day and the next, you were up walking around and talking."

"Isn't that the truth?" Georgia agreed. "I still can't get over the fact that my baby is going to start school this fall. It seems just yesterday, he and Aaron were crawling around on the floor together, and now here they are, big school boys."

Lydia nodded. "I keep trying to save a little out of each week's pay to set aside for some school clothes for Aaron, and every time I manage to save a dollar, it seems like something comes up, and we desperately need it elsewhere."

"You said a mouthful there, girl," Georgia said. "I can remember back when Raymond, or maybe it was one of the girls, started school, I had managed to put a little aside for their clothes, when Max came home from work with an abscessed tooth that was killing him. It took every single penny I'd scraped together, and then some, to get him fixed up." She laughed and shook her head. "That's life, I guess. I sometimes wonder how on earth we ever made it back then when the kids were real little. Poor little Peter, I'm afraid he's gonna be decked out in hand-me-downs when school starts this fall. Thank goodness he's not particular about his clothes ... yet. The one thing I am going to have to get him is a new pair of shoes. He completely destroyed the last pair we got him. There's hardly anything left of them ... just a tongue and the laces." She tipped her head back and laughed heartily.

Lydia smiled and sipped her glass of milk. "Aaron needs new shoes too," she said. "I don't...."

"Can I have some new shoes too, Mama?" Benjamin interrupted her, wiping his milk mustache with his dirty hand.

"I don't know, son, we'll see."

"If I can get away one of these days before long ... and I can get the car away from Max, would you like to go into Newton again with me and Mother?" Georgia asked. "The girls have been badgering me to make them some new dresses for church and school, and we sure don't have the yard goods supply here that they have in the big city. Maybe we could find the boys some shoes at the same time and kill two birds with one stone."

"Sure," Lydia instantly agreed. "That'd be fun. I'd love to go if I can get Doug to watch the kids again for me."

Benjamin had been sitting, quietly listening to the conversation, when he suddenly stood and faced his mother. "You're gonna kill some birds?" he asked, his brown eyes wide with disbelief.

"No, Mr. Big Ears, we're not going to kill any birds," his mother said with a laugh. "That's just a saying, Ben. When we say we're going to kill two birds with one stone, it simply means that we're going to accomplish two tasks at the same time. Do you understand?"

Benjamin nodded his head, but the frown deepened on his forehead. He studied the two women in front of him.

"He hasn't the slightest idea what you're talking about," Georgia said with a chuckle.

Aaron and Peter suddenly charged into the kitchen, covered with dirt, and starving.

"Go wash your face and hands, and I'll fix you both a snack," Lydia said.

"Mama and Aunt Georgia are gonna go kill some birds," Benjamin announced loudly.

"How come?" Peter asked. "Don't you like birds, Ma? I thought you said you liked birds."

"Oh brother!" Georgia cried. "Of course I like birds. I wouldn't harm a single feather on a bird. You know that!"

"How come Ben said you were gonna kill some then?"

"Never mind! Hurry up with your snack. We've got to get home … I need to start supper pretty soon," Georgia said, glancing at the clock.

Lydia groaned. "Me too," she said with a grimace. "What are you having tonight?"

"Chicken," Georgia said. "I need to get home … and *kill* one of our chickens for supper tonight!"

The two women laughed so hard they woke Rebecca up from her nap. The boys gulped down their milk and escaped back outside.

"I think our moms are batty sometimes," Peter admitted as they listened to the uproarious laughter inside.

"Yeah, me too," Aaron agreed.

Benjamin cast a worried glance at the screen door. "They're really gonna throw some rocks at the birds, and kill two of 'em. I heard 'em say that."

Aaron shook his head in disgust. "I'll bet Daddy would really be mad at Mama if he knew that."

Peter nodded in agreement. "My Dad said he'd thrash the daylights out of Ray an' me if he ever caught us shootin' at birds. I wonder if he'll thrash the daylights outta Ma if he finds out what she's plannin' on doin'."

"Probably so," Aaron said, wiping the crumbs from his dirt- streaked face. "Wonder why they think it's so funny?"

Peter shrugged his shoulders and frowned. "A long time ago, my ma used to be a girl, and I think girls are touched in the head sometimes," he said thoughtfully. "Maybe she's still a bit touched."

"Hold down the fort, girl, and keep the faith," Georgia called loudly as she stepped out the back door. "Come on, youngin', let's get ourselves back home."

The boys waved good-bye as Peter and his mother strode quickly down the driveway and disappeared through the trees at the crest of the hill. The baby was crying lustily when the boys went back inside the house.

"Rock her, would you?" their mother asked as she cleared the drinking glasses from the table. She pulled leftovers from the icebox, noting that the ice was nearly melted. She needed to tell Doug to bring home another block of ice tomorrow night.

"Mama, can I hold her?" Aaron interrupted her train of thought.

"What?"

"Can I hold Becca? I promise I won't drop her, and I'll be real careful ... please?"

"Go sit in Daddy's big chair, and I'll put her in your lap."

"I'm gonna hold her too," Benjamin said, running with Aaron into the living room. Both boys jumped up into the overstuffed chair, their arms outstretched.

Lydia placed the baby in Aaron's arms and folded Benjamin's arms over her tiny legs. "Hold her tight, now," she instructed. "She can get real squirmy."

The boys held their precious cargo tightly and grinned up at their mother. "How's this?" Aaron asked.

His mother nodded. "I'll feed her as soon as I have supper going."

The boys took turns talking to their little sister, and within a couple of minutes, she had stopped crying and was listening to them.

"She likes us, Aaron," Benjamin said, planting a kiss on the bottom of her foot. "Look at her little toes," he said, counting them one by one.

Aaron placed her tiny hand inside his own. "Look how big my hand is next to hers," he said. The baby smiled a crooked smile at him, and Aaron leaned forward and kissed her soft, velvety cheek.

Supper was finally over, the dishes were done, and the baby was bathed, fed, and ready for sleep. Lydia tucked her into the cradle and flopped down, exhausted, into her big chair next to Doug's. The minute she sat down, both boys pounced on her, each of them holding his favorite book.

"Read to us, Mama, please," Benjamin pleaded, looking up at her with his big, chocolate brown eyes.

"I'm first!" Aaron said, shoving his book at his mother. "Read mine first."

Doug had carried the living room lamp over to a small table in the corner and was working on a jigsaw puzzle. "Let your mother rest a minute," he said.

"That's all right, honey. I love reading to them. Go get me the kitchen lamp, Aaron, and be careful with it. I just filled it this afternoon."

Aaron ran into the kitchen for the lamp while Benjamin snuggled up into his mother's lap and held up his book for her to read. She kissed the top of his head and squeezed him tight.

"Guess you're first tonight," she said.

"That's not fair!" Aaron complained. "I said I was first. Come on Ben. Move over. That's not...."

"Aaron!" Daddy growled. "That's just about enough out of you."

Aaron scrambled up beside his brother while their mother lit the lamp and turned the wick down. Just as she opened the first book, baby Rebecca began to fuss, which quickly escalated into frantic wailing.

"Baby Becca wants to hear the stories too," Benjamin said, halfway sliding down from the chair. "Can we go get her?"

"No, leave her alone. She'll be all right. She needs to cry herself to sleep once in a while," their mother said. Benjamin wriggled back up beside his mother as she began to read. By the time she had finished the story, Rebecca was quiet and had fallen asleep.

"Now time for my story," Aaron said, opening his book to the first page.

When both books had been read, Lydia tucked the boys into bed and listened to their prayers.

"God bless Daddy and Mama and Aaron and baby Becca and Ruffy an' me too," Benjamin said. "How was that, Mama?"

Lydia smiled at him and squeezed his hand.

"God bless Daddy and Mama and Ben and Becca an' Ruffy and me an' Peter," was Aaron's prayer.

Lydia kissed them both and carried the lamp back out into the living room.

"Good night, Daddy," they called together.

"Night, boys," Doug said absentmindedly.

Lydia collapsed back into her chair and had just settled herself when the boys' bedroom door creaked open and Benjamin stuck his head out.

"What is it, Benjamin?" she asked wearily.

"Mama," he said rather sheepishly, "you aren't really gonna kill those birds, are you?"

"Oh, for heaven's sake, Ben! Of course I'm not going to kill any birds. I thought I had explained that to you."

"Why are you going to kill some birds?" Doug asked. "Are they eating your seeds out in the garden again?"

Lydia sighed loudly. "No, honey. I'm not going to kill any birds anywhere. Georgia and I were talking today, and she said we could kill two birds with one stone, and Benjamin thought we were really going to kill some birds. He's been worried about it ever since."

"Well, I don't blame him," Doug said in a teasing voice. "Poor little defenseless birds. What chance do they have against old deadeye here?"

"Douglas Wheeler!" Lydia exploded. "Don't you dare encourage these boys. You know perfectly well that I'm not going to kill any birds … ever!"

Doug delighted in teasing his wife and enjoyed a hearty laugh at her expense. "Back to bed, Benjamin," he finally said when the fun was over. "Your mother is not going to kill any birds, so you can quit worrying about it."

Lydia carried the dimly lit lamp into the bedroom and turned down the bed. She tucked Rebecca in tight and got herself ready for bed. Easing her tired body down into the cool sheets, she stretched luxuriously and yawned.

"Lord, please watch over all my fam…." She didn't even hear Doug when he joined her a few minutes later.

She awoke some time during the night, her heart pounding wildly. She gasped and sat straight up in bed. She had been dreaming … slaughtering birds … all kinds of birds! She shuddered and wiped her clammy hands on the quilt, remembering that she had had her hands around the neck of some strange bird, choking the life out of it. The bird's eyes would bulge when she put pressure around its neck. She shivered at the thought and slipped out of bed to check on the baby. She was sleeping peacefully. Lydia crawled back into bed and tried not to think about birds anymore. Wouldn't Georgia get a laugh out of her dream? She drifted back to sleep … this time uninterrupted by dreams.

She awoke when Doug struggled out of bed the next morning, yanking the quilt and sheet off the bed onto the floor when he got up.

"Sorry, honey," he mumbled.

Lydia grabbed her housecoat and slipped her cold feet into her crocheted slippers. She tiptoed out of the bedroom and headed to the kitchen to start a fire in the cook stove. Soon, a nice blaze was crackling and popping, and within minutes, the aroma of fresh ground coffee permeated the cool morning air. She was buttering a slice of toast when Doug appeared, clean-shaven and fully dressed.

"Did I scare you last night when I popped up in bed?" she asked, while pouring him a cup of coffee.

"No. What'd you pop up for?"

"I had a terrible nightmare that I was strangling birds right and left, all over the place. It seemed so real. I remember seeing that last bird's eyes bulging out when I tried to strangle him." She shuddered again at the thought.

Doug laughed. "Not hard to tell what you were thinking about last night before bed."

"Looks like another beautiful day," Lydia commented a few minutes later, looking out the kitchen window. "I can't wait to get back in the garden. I'm almost finished with the spading and then I can start planting." She poured herself a cup of coffee and sat sipping it, her mind filling row after spaded row with tiny seeds.

The boys' bedroom door creaked open and Benjamin appeared at the table. "I'm starvin," he announced, rubbing his eyes.

Lydia pulled him into her lap and kissed the top of his ear. "How about a scrambled egg and a piece of toast?"

Benjamin nodded his head and yawned.

"Becca is sure sleeping this morning," Lydia commented as she lifted Benjamin off her lap and into his own chair. "She's usually raising the rafters by now if I haven't fed her."

"Want me to go wake her up for ya?" Benjamin asked in a sleepy voice.

"That's all right, honey. I'll go get her while you eat your breakfast."

Before she could finish fixing Benjamin's breakfast, Aaron stumbled from the bedroom. "I smell somethin' good," he murmured, and plopped down in his chair at the table.

"Just followed your nose out here, huh?" Doug asked, tousling his hair.

Aaron ignored the question and gulped down his glass of milk.

Lydia added another egg to the frying pan and buttered more toast. "More coffee, honey?" she asked, coffeepot in hand.

"Thanks," Doug murmured, handing her his empty cup.

"By the way, Doug, I need another block of ice. This one's nearly gone."

"Sure doesn't last long, does it? Better write it down for me...."

Lydia interrupted him by handing him a list of things she needed from Deacon's store.

"I thought you said you needed ice." Doug's eyes ran down the list. "A lot more here than just ice."

"I know," she murmured, handing the boys their breakfast.

She gulped down a swallow of lukewarm coffee and hurried into the bedroom to check on Rebecca.

"Becca ... dumpling ... it's time to wake up," she said softly. The baby didn't stir. Lydia looked down at her daughter, and her heart skipped a beat. "Rebecca!" she said, louder this time. She leaned forward and touched the baby's cheek. It was cold and hard ... very hard!

"Rebecca!" Lydia screamed. "Oh God! Oh God! No! Noooo!" An unearthly-sounding scream was torn from her throat just before her world faded into blackness.

"She's coming around now," Doc Sorenson said gravely. "I think she'll be all right."

Lydia's eyelids fluttered briefly. She felt sick. What was the matter with her? She raised her hand up to her face. Her head hurt … bad. Had she fallen and hit her head? Why was she in bed? "Ohhh!" she moaned. "Doug…."

"I'm right here, sweetheart. I'm right here."

She could feel Doug's rough, warm hand on her arm and then on her forehead. "What happened?" she mumbled, unable to collect her thoughts.

Doug looked helplessly at the doctor who stood on the other side of the bed. Doc Sorenson nodded to Doug and held up his hand.

"I'll try to explain this to her," he murmured softly. "Lydia, dear, can you hear me?" he asked as he sat down on the edge of the bed. He grabbed Lydia's free hand and held it in his own. He cleared his throat and began to pat her hand. "Can you hear me, dear?" he asked again.

Lydia nodded her head and rubbed her eyes. "What's the matter with me, Doc?" she asked feebly.

"You're going to be fine dear. You fell and struck your head on the bedpost but that's not…." He stopped and cleared his throat again. "That's not what I need to talk to you about." He glanced nervously up at Doug, who was standing right behind him.

"Maybe you'd better tell her after all," he said, rising from the bed and wiping his forehead on his clean handkerchief. "I'll go talk to your boys."

Doug nodded his head, bit his lower lip and cleared his throat.

"Honey," he whispered hoarsely. "Honey, I have some very bad news to…."

"Becca! Where's my baby?" Lydia asked, her voice rising. "What's wrong with my baby?" She tried to rise to a sitting position, but both Doug and the doctor pushed her back down into the pillow.

Doug swallowed hard and coughed softly. He brushed Lydia's hair back from her forehead. "Darling," he began again, the baby…." His voice trailed off.

Lydia arched her back and screamed. "Noooooo! No, Doug … she's not … no, Doug, please don't tell me she's…."

Doug sat down hard on the bed, tears coursing down his face. He pulled his wife into his arms and held her, sobbing into her neck and hair.

"She can't be, Doug … she can't be," she sobbed. "Not our baby, oh Doug, please tell me she's not … Oh God … this can't be happening."

Doctor Sorenson turned his face to the wall, reluctant to witness this heartbreaking scene. There was absolutely nothing he could do or say at this point to help these young people. He slipped quietly out of the bedroom and decided that his service could best be put to use by talking to the two little boys who were huddled together in their own room. He knocked on the door and opened it a crack.

"Is my Mama hurt real bad?" Aaron asked fearfully, his white face stained with tears.

"No, boys, your mother is going to be just fine. She fainted, that's all. She's got a little bump on her head, but she's going to be all right."

"Why is she crying so much then?" Aaron asked, his eyes showing the fear that he obviously felt inside.

"That's what I need to talk to you both about," the doctor said. "Sometime during the night, the angels came and took your little sister home to heaven."

"You mean...." Aaron stopped, his eyes widening as the impact of this statement began to penetrate his understanding. He stared first at the doctor, and then at his brother.

The doctor nodded his head. "Your little sister is dead," he said as gently as he knew how.

Benjamin started sobbing, dove back under the covers, and covered his head with the quilt. Aaron sat, stunned into silence, his lower lip trembling.

Doctor Sorenson squatted down beside the little boy and put his hand on Aaron's shoulder. "Listen to me, son," he said softly. "Your parents ... especially your mother, are going to need some help here today. Tell your dad when he comes out, that I've gone over the hill to the Bakers' house to see if Mrs. Baker can come and sit with your mother today. Can you remember that?"

Aaron blinked and nodded his head.

"I'll be back in just a few minutes to take care of some details here. Tell your dad that I'll be right back."

Aaron swallowed hard and nodded again. "Yes, sir," he said, barely above a whisper.

The doctor quietly closed the door, and a moment later, Aaron heard his car start in the driveway.

"Ben," he whispered. "Come here, Ben." He pulled the covers away from his little brother and crawled in beside him. Benjamin rolled over, looked at Aaron, and both boys began sobbing. "Our ... poor little ... baby," Aaron sobbed, when he could talk again. "We didn't even know the angels were here last night. Poor baby...." His voice trailed off.

The door opened and Doug walked in. His eyes were red rimmed and swollen. He sat down on the edge of the bed and without a word pulled both boys into his lap. The three of them clung to one another until Aaron remembered the doctor's message.

"Daddy," he whimpered. "The doctor said he'd be right back. He's gone to get Aunt Georgia."

Doug nodded his head and blew his nose. He drew in a deep, ragged breath. "We have to be strong, boys … for Mama. She's taking this really hard."

"Is she going to be all right?" Aaron asked, his voice shaking.

"Mama," Benjamin said, his arms outstretched toward the door.

"Not just yet, Ben," Doug said holding his son tight. "Mama's resting right now. She hurt her head when she fell, so she needs to sleep, but she's going to be all right," he added, noting the fearful look on both little faces in front of him. "We've got to be strong," he said softly, wondering how on earth he could possibly be strong enough to get his family through this.

"Why, Daddy?" Aaron asked plaintively. "Why did the angels take our baby?"

Doug shook his head. If only he had an answer to that.

"Doug! Doug!" It was Georgia's frantic voice. Before he could rise from the boys' bed, the door was opened, and Georgia burst into the room, her face a mixture of grief and shock. "Oh my poor babies," she cried, cradling the boys in her arms.

Benjamin and Aaron began to cry again.

"There, there, sssshhh," Georgia soothed. "Aunt Georgia's here now, and we'll get through this somehow."

"Did … di … did you know that the angels took our ba … by?" Aaron stammered between wrenching sobs.

In answer, Georgia simply nodded her head and tightened her hold on them.

Doug, unable to speak, stood and squeezed Georgia's hand. She rocked the boys gently for a few seconds, unable to think of much else to do that might help them. "How's she taking this?" she asked in a whisper, looking at Doug.

Doug shook his head. "In shock," he managed to mumble. Tears coursed down his face again in spite of his efforts to keep them at bay. "Sh … she's sleeping right now."

"Dear God," Georgia moaned, "Bless her sweet little heart. I can't begin to imagine what she's going through." The tears that she had held back now rushed to the surface and spilled down her face unchecked.

"Georgia," Doug croaked, when he was somewhat composed, "could you please stay with the boys for a bit? I need to go over some things with the doctor, and then get back to Lydia."

"That's what I'm here for," Georgia said. "You go do the things you need to do and don't worry … I'll watch over them." She hugged both boys. "And Doug," she said, just as he was walking out the door, "Max is going to let Jack Doss know what has happened, so you needn't worry about work right now."

Doug nodded his thanks but said nothing and closed the door.

The doctor was filling out some papers at the kitchen table. On the chair beside him sat a good-sized basket that Doug guessed contained the body of his baby daughter. He sucked in his breath when he saw it.

The doctor glanced up at him. "I need your signature here on the death certificate," he said, while still scribbling something.

"What did she die from?" Doug asked, nearly choking on the lump that was reforming in his throat.

The doctor shook his head. "I only wish I knew," he said.

"Medical science has no answer for this type of thing. A seemingly healthy child just seems to simply quit breathing as far as we can tell. They all die in their sleep, apparently without any struggle at all."

Doug stared down at the tiny, wrapped bundle in the basket. How could this have happened to them? And so suddenly, without any warning at all? And why … why … why? That was the hardest one to answer, because there was no answer. His eyes were drawn back to the form the doctor had filled out. Under cause of death, he had written acute asphyxiation, etiology unknown. Doug didn't understand the terms completely but signed where the doctor indicated and handed the form back to him.

"I just don't understand it. She was so healthy, so perfect. Such a good baby. It doesn't make any sense at all." He rubbed the back of his neck, and wished that the huge knot there would dissolve.

Suddenly, Lydia was standing there beside him. He whirled around and stared at her. "Honey, you shouldn't be out of bed!"

"Where's my baby?" she asked, in a surprisingly strong voice. She completely ignored the doctor and Doug. "I want to hold my baby one last time."

"Honey, I … I'm not sure … I'm not sure that's a…." Doug faltered, trying to turn his wife back toward the bedroom.

The doctor stood up. "Doug, that's perfectly fine and perfectly normal. She can hold her baby all she wants." He pulled out a kitchen chair for Lydia to sit in, but she turned and stumbled back into the living room.

"I want to rock her one last time," she said evenly.

Doug looked nervously at the doctor, a question written on his face. The doctor nodded his head and lifted the tiny bundle out of the basket and handed it to Doug. "Go stay with her," he murmured.

Doug placed the bundle in his wife's arms and knelt down beside the rocking chair. Lydia slowly unwrapped the body, so that the baby's face was showing and began to rock, ever so slowly, her tears falling on the folds of the blanket. She held the motionless body close to her own and rocked, savoring the sweet preciousness of her child, her only daughter.

"Lydia ... honey," Doug said softly a few minutes later. "The doctor needs to know if you have a special dress you want the baby dressed in."

Lydia answered him without taking her eyes off the familiar little face nestled in her arms. "The little white dress that Georgia gave me for Rebecca ... the one I added the pink ribbons to. It's in the top dresser drawer." Her voice sounded hollow and flat.

Doug went into the bedroom to find the dress. He found it along with many other articles of dress for Rebecca. I should do something with these right now, he thought, but what? Where would I put them that Lydia wouldn't find them sooner or later? He closed the drawer and returned to the living room, unable to decide what to do. "Is this the one?" he asked, holding up the white dress.

His wife nodded her head. "Get her white booties too. I don't want her feet to be cold. And Doug ... get the new white blanket that your mother sent her ... the one with the satin trim. It's in the second drawer."

Doug found the articles of clothing and took them along with the blanket into the kitchen and handed them to the doctor. Doug turned to go back into the living room and nearly collided with Georgia and the boys coming out of the bedroom. When Benjamin and Aaron saw their mother, they both began to cry. Lydia held out a free arm to them and they rushed to her side.

"Our poor ba ... by," Benjamin wailed.

Doug's shoulders began to shake as his grief poured over him. Seeing his family in such pain was almost unbearable. He lowered his face into his hands and wept openly. Georgia slipped her arms around him and held him close for a few minutes. Even the doctor jerked his dampened handkerchief from his pocket and blew his nose again.

When the tide of emotion had ebbed, Lydia kissed the precious little face one more time and slowly covered the body again. She rose from the rocking chair, walked slowly back into the kitchen, and placed her baby into the doctor's arms. The doctor watched her retreating back with growing concern. She allowed herself to be led back into her bedroom, and only after the door was shut tight were her cries of unbearable anguish and grief heard throughout the house.

CHAPTER 19
LIFE WITHOUT LIFE

Word of the tragic event that occurred in the Wheeler household the night of May 19, 1929, spread quickly through the small community of Northridge. A steady stream of friends, neighbors, and acquaintances flowed in and out of the house, all bearing food, flowers, money, their sympathies, and shared stories of their own heartaches in similar losses. Lydia bore the stress with quiet dignity until the day of the funeral, the day her parents arrived. She had seen to the needs of her boys, making sure they were washed and their clothes were ready for the service that was to be held at the church at one o'clock. Aaron and Benjamin were quiet, nearly forgotten in the flood of activity around them until Grandma and Grandpa Begg arrived. Grandma took them into her arms and held them, trying her best to erase the sorrow that had touched their young lives.

Doug watched his wife with growing anxiety. She was becoming increasingly quiet and withdrawn. She ate very little and slept even less. Her ashen face looked strangely blank, somehow detached from reality. He worried about her strength giving out completely. He finally pulled his mother-in-law aside and asked for her opinion and help.

"She seems to have pushed this terrible thing to the back of her mind. I don't think she's really dealing with it at all," he confided to Lillian. "I can't help but worry about her. She doesn't want to talk about it either."

"Well, Doug, just give her some time. She's suffered a terrible blow. It's especially hard on mothers when they lose a child, but I really think she'll come around. She's weathered some pretty tough times in her life and she's always come out on top. She'll be okay."

"I wish I could be that optimistic, Mom," he said. "If only she'd start eating something. She's already lost quite a bit of weight."

Lillian patted his hand. "I know," she said. "I'll be with her for a few days and I'll do my best to get her to eat something."

Louise Wheeler arrived shortly after Lydia's parents. Doug's older brother Carl and his wife Peggy had brought Louise with them, all the way from southern New Hampshire.

"We would have been here sooner, but Mother couldn't remember how to get to your place. She told me when we started out that she knew exactly how to find you, but we sure got lost on her directions." He shook his head and looked sorrowfully at his brother. "Sure sorry to hear about your baby, Doug," he added, giving him a bear hug.

Louise Wheeler, her face a picture of weariness, promptly burst into tears when she walked into the house. Doug was surprised at his mother's display of emotion but decided that it must be due to her exhaustion. "I cannot believe it!" she kept saying. "I simply cannot believe it! She was so healthy ... so alive!"

"I know, Mother ... it's hard for us to believe too."

Lydia dug out the only black dress she owned, a long-sleeved woolen dress that was much too warm to wear the end of May, but she'd have to make it do. Her mother helped her with her hair, twisting it into a small knot that would be covered with a small, black hat.

"I'm glad you thought to bring an extra hat, Mom. I don't even own a hat, much less a black one," she admitted. She arranged the soft black veil that was attached to the top of the hat, smoothing out the creases down over the narrow brim with her fingers, then suddenly, without saying a word, yanked it off her head and tossed it on the bed.

"It's all right, honey," her mother said, picking up the hat. "You don't have to wear one if you'd rather not. Darling, I want you to try and eat something before we go to the church," she added. "I've made some soup for Doug and the boys, and there's plenty for you."

"I'm not hungry," Lydia murmured.

"I know you're not, honey, but you need a little something to keep up your strength. Come on ... do it for me, please, honey. Before you get dressed, go eat a bite of something."

She led her daughter out of the bedroom into the kitchen, which was crammed with people, all talking in hushed tones. Lydia looked around her in a daze. Mother Wheeler, along with Carl, Peggy, and their two children, sat at the table. Doug, her dad, and the boys stood up against the counter next to the sink. Pastor Rod and Bess had come to pray for the family, and Georgia was just coming in the back door, her arms laden with various sized dishes and bowls of food. Lydia slowly looked around her kitchen at the familiar faces. She wanted to run, to scream, to empty out her small home of all these well-meaning people, to turn back the hands of time, but instead, she said barely above a whisper, "Thank you all for coming."

"She needs to eat a little something," her mother explained, "if we could have a place at the table."

Several chairs were pulled back as everyone vacated the dining area.

Pastor Rod stepped forward and placed his hands on Lydia's shoulders as she sat down at the table. "I'd like to say a brief word of prayer for this family if I may, and my wife and I will be on our way," he said with a quick smile. He bowed his head and cleared his throat, leaving his hands where they rested.

"Oh blessed Father, we ask that You be a special blessing of comfort and peace to this dear family right now … right this minute. Bring healing to this young couple whose wounds are so open and raw, whose hurt is so evident and tangible. We ask that You strengthen them as only You can. We give You the praise and the glory and ask this in the name of our blessed Savior. Amen."

Silence enveloped the small crowd for a few seconds following Rodney's prayer.

"Thank you Rod," Doug finally murmured. "Appreciate you coming all the way up here."

Rodney squeezed Lydia's shoulders, shook hands with Doug, and made his way back outside. Bess stooped and whispered something in Lydia's ear to which Lydia responded with a nod of her head. Louise Wheeler blew her nose as Carl and Peggy ushered all the children into the living room.

Lydia had a nearly overwhelming desire to jump up and scream; scream until she could not utter another sound. Instead, she forced a few spoonfuls of hideous-tasting soup down. She felt sick … deathly sick. She looked at her mother who seemed to be constantly hovering over her. She wished that she'd just go sit down somewhere and leave her alone. Why didn't they all go away and just leave her be? She pushed the bowl away and made her way back through the crowded living room into the sanctuary of her bedroom to get ready for what lay ahead.

One by one, the cars pulled out of the driveway. Doug, Lydia and the boys climbed into their own car. Lydia's arms felt empty … as dead and empty as she felt inside without her baby. She pulled the veil down close to her face and checked her purse again for the stack of hankies that she'd crammed in there earlier. Aaron and Benjamin sat quietly in the backseat, their eyes a mirror of the turmoil, fear, and confusion they felt.

Doug drove in complete silence all the way to the small church in Northridge. He was surprised at the number of vehicles parked around the church building. Where are they going to put everyone, he wondered, but he said nothing.

Inside, the church seemed darker than usual. Different sized vases held flowers of every imaginable color and variety. Lydia had never seen so many flowers. The air seemed nearly suffocating with the pungent odor of roses, mums, lilies, daisies and peonies. Mrs. Crenshaw looked up briefly from her music as they entered the church and made their way down front. The entire family gathered quietly around the small white casket, and gazed at the tiny, perfect body that was wrapped in a snowy, white blanket. Her head rested on a small, satin pillow. Someone had made an attempt to comb her dark hair. The white dress, though much too large for her, had been expertly tucked underneath her body, and it added to the overall appearance of a small angel, a small, sleeping angel.

Peggy began to sob uncontrollably and Carl pulled her away from the casket to the back of the church. Aaron looked at the small form before him, but Benjamin was suddenly afraid to look and instead began to cry. Grandma Begg rushed to his side and lifted him up into her arms. She quickly carried him to the back of the church.

Doug put his arm around his wife and when he felt her tremble, he gently guided her to a seat in the front row and sat down beside her. The organ music swelled as more and more people arrived and took seats behind them. Lydia decided at that very moment that she wasn't going to make it through this nightmare. I'm going to die, she thought. I hope I do. I can't bear this pain any longer. She fixed her eyes on the little face, memorizing every detail … one that was so familiar to her yet now looked strangely foreign. She studied the delicate pattern of the tiny lace collar on the white dress. How ironic … how cruelly ironic, that she had thought she was giving the little white dress new life by adding those pink ribbons. Now, just months later, this same dress played a key role in this scene, this unspeakable death scene. The beautiful white dress would never have a new life now. It would soon be gone … lost to her sight … just as her precious child was gone, lost to her. Lydia felt hysteria rising to the surface. She's not gone, she said to herself. My baby's not dead. She's asleep. She's just asleep. This can't be happening. Oh God, why? Why? Why? She wanted to jump up and scream again, scream until her voice was gone … and then run … run for hundreds of miles to get away from this horrible scene, this hideous nightmare. Run from all these people who looked on her with pity in their eyes and said things like 'what a shame' and 'that's too bad' or 'I'm so sorry.' She shuddered and thought for a minute that she was going to vomit. She pulled a hankie from her purse and held it to her mouth, fighting the nausea.

Pastor Rodney was suddenly behind the pulpit, looking over the packed church. A hush settled over the congregation. Doug grabbed Lydia's hand, as much to give himself strength as to help her.

"On behalf of the Wheeler family, I thank each of you who have come today to pay tribute to this precious little one that God has seen fit to recall into His own presence." He cleared his throat. "Why something like this happens is completely beyond our comprehension, and we're left with a helpless but not hopeless feeling. We're helpless, but not hopeless," he said again, stressing the point. He bowed his head in prayer again and prayed for wisdom, strength, and for special healing to those whose lives this little one had touched.

Mrs. Crenshaw played an introduction, and her granddaughter, Elizabeth, rose to sing, her sweet voice filling the church.

Safe in the arms of Je-sus, Safe on His gen-tle breast,
There by His love o'er-shaded, Sweetly my soul shall rest.
Hark 'tis the voice of an-gels, Borne in a song to me
O-ver the fields of glo-ry, O-ver the jas-per sea....
Safe in the arms of Je-sus, Safe on his gen-tle breast,
There by His love o'er-shaded, Sweetly my soul shall rest.

Lydia suddenly slid forward in her chair, her body slumping downward, and she would have fallen to the floor had not Doug snatched at the back of her dress and pulled her back into an upright position. Her eyes fluttered briefly and then filled with tears as a tidal wave of grief engulfed her, and she began to weep uncontrollably. Doug pulled her limp body up against his own and held her there until she regained some control.

Elizabeth Crenshaw glanced quickly at her grandmother and then at Pastor Rodney and decided one verse was enough. She closed her hymnal and took her seat. Rodney stepped up to the pulpit again. He waited for a moment until Mrs. Crenshaw had finished playing the last stanza of the song.

"Rebecca Joy Wheeler," he said in a loud voice, "born February 12th ... went home to be with the Lord May 19th. She was just 96 days old, scarcely three months old. She brought great joy to her family those brief three months...."

Sounds of crying and snuffing filled the church as people reached for their handkerchiefs.

Lydia, some days later, could not recall another single word that Rodney had uttered that afternoon. The only thing she could remember was the lid of that tiny box closing down on her child. She would never, ever forget that. As long as there was life in her own body, she would remember the last sight she had of Rebecca. Her only thought at that very moment was that her baby would suffocate with the lid down.

Rebecca was buried in the small cemetery right behind the church. Lydia wanted to fall in on top of the casket as they lowered it into the small hole. She wanted to feel the dirt being shoveled in on top of her. She wanted to smother this insidious pain that plagued her night and day.

One by one, people left, promising to write, promising to remember them all in prayer, promising ... promising ... promising. Finally, her mother and dad also bid her good-bye. Rather than sadness, she felt a strange sense of relief to see them go. She wanted to be alone, really alone, and she was secretly happy when Doug finally decided that it was time he went back to work. She sat at her kitchen table and watched the boys as they used the rows of her now-abandoned garden for their new roads. Her mother had washed and then packed up all the baby things she could find and stuffed them into the cradle and had given it to Doug to store down in the garage. Lydia had been angry, really angry with her mother when she realized what she had done. She couldn't hold back the flow of harsh words that seemed to boil out of her innermost depths.

"How could you?" she had nearly screamed at her mother. "You had no right, Mother!" She saw her mother's confusion and hurt, and though she knew she should apologize, she felt powerless to do so. She had embarrassed Doug, hurt her mother deeply, and angered her father. It was soon after that episode that her parents thought it best to leave. She hadn't argued with them. She stared now at the pile of dirty clothes heaped on the floor. No more baby things to wash, she thought miserably. No more diapers. No more anything. She felt numb, unable to feel much of anything, other than this dull ache in her heart. At night, her dreams played cruel tricks on her, twisting the facts around, and waking her on more than one occasion in a pool of sweat, her heart beating wildly. By day, she was aware of only the pain that seemed as physical as it was emotional. Doug, on the other hand, seemed his old self again, able to laugh and play with the boys again. Lydia looked again at the pile of clothes and burst into tears. I don't want to scrub clothes, she thought. I don't want to do anything, ever again. I just want to hold my baby and love her again. She sat, unable to stand, unable to focus her attention on anything but what she was feeling inside. Why, Lord? Why? Wasn't I a good mother? Didn't I love her enough? Did I love her too much? Was she too hot that night? Was she too cold? Did that big blanket suffocate her? I should have checked on her that night. Her mind went back to that last night. She remembered reading to the boys and hearing Rebecca's loud wailing. 'She wants to hear the stories too,' Benjamin had said. Lydia remembered telling him to let her cry … she needs to cry herself to sleep, she had said. Oh God, how I wish I had held her that one last time, and rocked her to sleep. If only I had held her that one last time … if only I could hold her again and hear her crying. If I could only touch her one more time and hold her close to me. If I could just see her one more time and hear those sweet little noises she always made when she was full … like a little pig, grunting after a big meal. Lydia's loud sobbing brought both boys running into the house.

"Mama!" Benjamin cried with a frantic look on his face. "What's a matter?"

Aaron put his hand on her arm and pulled it down away from her eyes. "Please don't cry, Mama," he pleaded, his own eyes filling with tears. "Don't cry, Mama."

Lydia wrapped her arms around both boys and cried uncontrollably a few seconds longer. "I'm all right," she finally managed to say. "I'll be all right in a few minutes."

"Are you cryin' 'cause you got so many dirty clothes to scrub?" Benjamin asked, looking around at the piles on the floor.

"No, honey," his mother said, and smiled in spite of the pain she was feeling. "Mama is just remembering baby Becca, and that makes me sad," she said, hugging them both tight. After assuring them that she was all right, she sent them back outside to play. She forced herself to get up and heat some water. Before she could soak the first load of Doug's work clothes, a maroon car pulled into the driveway. Ruffy jumped up and started barking loudly.

Oh no, Lydia thought, when she looked out the window. Pastor Rodney and Bess were getting out of the car and trying to fend off Ruffy's welcome.

Lydia tried to dry her eyes on her apron hem and smoothed her hair as best she could. What did they want with her? Why didn't people just leave her alone to grieve in peace?

Rodney stopped to talk with the boys for a few minutes as Bess made her way to the back door. Lydia opened the screen door and tried her best to smile.

"Hi, Bess," she murmured.

The pastor's wife slipped her arm around Lydia's waist and hugged her. "We're not staying but a minute," she said, eyeing the obvious work that needed to be done. "We just wanted to drop by and see how you were doing."

Lydia shrugged. "All right, I guess. Please sit down." She cleared the boys' books and a few toys from the living room chairs and offered the woman a seat. "Would you care for anything to drink?" she asked.

"No thank you, dear. We can't stay long."

Rodney joined them and sat down with a thump. "Boy, it's getting hot early today," he said with a tired smile. "Lydia, how are you doing? Are you...." His voice trailed off as his eyes adjusted to the darkened living room, and he could see the young woman seated across from him a little better. He noted the red, swollen eyes and the hollow cheeks. He frowned. "Pretty rough, isn't it? You're having a pretty hard time, huh?" His voice was low and full of compassion.

Lydia nodded her head and burst into tears again. "I can't seem to ss ... sstop," she stammered. "I can't think of anything else but her. I've tried and tried, but I can't seem to get...." She gave up talking and buried her face in her apron.

"We understand perfectly, my dear," Rodney said. "That's a natural part of the grieving process. Did you know that tears are a perfectly natural part of healing?"

Lydia didn't respond but gave herself over completely to the despair she felt inside.

"I know exactly what you're going through," Bess said. "Believe me, I know how you feel and where you are right now in the grieving process."

Lydia's head came up and she stared at the older couple. "How could you know? How could you *possibly* know how I feel?" she asked, a little more harshly than she had intended.

Instead of answering her, Bess began to fumble in her big purse for something. Lydia watched her for a few seconds, suddenly concerned that she had greatly offended the woman. Bess finally found what she was looking for, and drew out a small, leather-covered book that was held closed on one side by a small snap. She unsnapped it and handed it to Lydia. Lydia mopped up her tears enough to see what the pastor's wife had given her. Neatly framed in the worn leather case, was an old, faded photograph of a young couple with a small boy. The couple, she realized with a start, were obviously Rodney and Bess. A much younger, much thinner Bess was holding in her lap a small dark-haired boy. Rodney had not changed that much. He sported a mustache back then but otherwise looked pretty much the same. She looked questioningly at Bess.

Bess nodded her head and smiled. "That's right," she said, even though Lydia hadn't said a word. "That's Rod and me and our little Timothy, when he was two."

"Timothy?" Lydia barely breathed the name.

Bess leaned forward in her chair and looked into Lydia's teary eyes. She sighed and nodded her head. "Timothy was our son," she explained.

"Your son? He *was* your son?" Lydia asked in a whisper. "What happened to him?"

"While Rodney was still in seminary, Timothy was born. He was our pride and joy. He was so precious." Her face began to glow as she remembered the past. "Anyway, to make a long story short, we went on a July 4th picnic with the youth group from our church. Rod and I were chaperons for thirty-some young people. We loaded up a huge wagon with hay and took off for the mountains, up to a lake in the pines. We had a big picnic and had planned on having fireworks that night." She sighed, her pensive gaze staring at nothing for a moment as she remembered the details. "That evening, I was busy with all the food stuff and Rod was busy setting up games for the kids to play. I guess the young people thought I was watching Tim and I assumed that some of the girls in the group were watching him. They all adored Timmy and had asked my permission to watch him while we played horseshoes that afternoon. I thought they were keeping an eye on him and as it turned out, no one was. We missed him about six o'clock that evening."

Her eyes began to fill with tears as the memories flooded back. She covered her mouth with her hand and shook her head. Rodney reached over and squeezed his wife's arm. He finished the story for her.

"We made a frantic search for him all through the night. That was without a doubt the longest and most horrifying night of our lives. We finally found him the next morning. He had drowned in the lake, not far from where our picnic table was set up."

"Dear God!" Lydia gasped. "I'm so terribly sorry. I never knew … I'm so sorry."

Bess patted her hand and smiled at her through her tears. "Not many people do know about Tim. It was a long, long time before I could even talk about it. He would have been nineteen this past spring had he lived," she added. "To make matters worse, we could never have any more children, so all we had left was memories."

Lydia's tears coursed down her face. "I'm so sss … sorry," she sobbed. She looked again at the faded photograph.

"So you see, my dear, I do indeed know exactly what you're going through. I'm well acquainted with grief. I know right where you are in the process of denial, grief, sorrow and anger. You have to work through all those emotions."

"How did you ever get through it?" Lydia asked when she could talk again.

"I very nearly didn't," Bess confessed. "I almost destroyed Rod's ministry, and I really took a nose dive, didn't I, honey? I hated everything and everybody. In fact, when I look back on it now, I can see that I very nearly destroyed my marriage and lost everyone who is dear to me. Rodney blamed me and I blamed him for quite a while after Tim's death." She stopped and glanced at her husband. "We fought to the point that we nearly went our separate ways. It was just terrible." Bess rose to her feet and sat down next to her husband in the overstuffed chair. She looked up at him and smiled, linking her arm around his. "Thank God, the senior pastor of our church took the time to counsel us and show us from God's Word where we were both wrong. If he hadn't intervened, we probably would not be here today."

Rodney nodded his head in agreement. "That's for sure."

"I can't imagine you two ever fighting ... over anything. You seem so loving and so right for one another," Lydia said.

Bess laughed. "It hasn't always been that way, believe me!"

"Lydia, that's why we stopped by this morning," Rodney said, leaning forward in his chair and looking past his wife. "We know from experience that the road ahead of you and Doug is going to be a rough one ... very rough. We'd like to offer our help in any way that we can. If you ever need us, please don't hesitate to call on us."

"I'd even be happy to come and see you all by myself, woman-to-woman," Bess offered. "I can assure you that you're going to have periods of depression, doubt, anger and guilt over the next few months, sometimes to the point that you might think you're losing your mind. I went through every one of those feelings and they're all perfectly normal, so if you ever want to talk about it...." She left the invitation open and gestured with her hands, making it clear to Lydia that she had a friend who did indeed understand.

Lydia lowered her eyes and stared at the braided rag run on the floor, shame and guilt sweeping over her. It had never occurred to her that anyone else in the world had suffered a loss as great as her own.

"Thank you so much, " she said. "Thank you both so much." She glanced at Bess and received a warm smile.

"I still to this day," Bess confessed, "wonder what Timmy would look like now, and what sort of young man he would have become. I can't help it. I guess it's the mother in me. I think part of us never does fully let go of our children, even though we know they are safe in God's care."

Lydia nodded and began twisting a loose thread on the hem of her apron. "I'm sure you're right," she said. "I wake up in the middle of the night thinking I've heard Rebecca crying. A couple of times, I've even gotten out of bed and reached for my robe when I realize...." She dropped her hands in her lap, unable to say in words what her heart knew to be true.

"Like I mentioned the other day at the funeral service," Rodney said, "we feel helpless in times like these, but certainly not hopeless. If you truly love the Lord and you're one of His own, you're given the promise that you'll be reunited with loved ones who have gone on ahead. I know without a shadow of a doubt that Bess and I will be with Tim again one of these days … and what a glorious day that will be."

Bess' eyes twinkled at the thought. "I can't wait to hold him in my arms again," she said.

"Will he still be a little boy?" Lydia asked.

"I believe he will be," Rodney said. "You see, in God's realm, time ceases to exist. The angels are ageless, as is God Himself, and so I'm convinced that little ones who precede us in death will be the same age they were when they left us. We're told in Scripture that we will know as we are known, and I believe we'll recognize our loved ones the instant we see them again."

Lydia sat lost in thought for a few seconds when Pastor Rod suddenly jumped up from his chair. "Come on Bessie," he said, pulling his wife out of the chair. "We were only going to stay a minute, and we've been here nearly an hour. Do let us know, Lydia, if we can help you and Doug in any way at all."

"Oh, I almost forgot," Bess said, digging again in her purse. "I jotted down a verse that I remember helped me when I was where you are right now." She handed a small piece of paper to Lydia. "Read it and ask the Lord to help you apply it." She squeezed Lydia's hand tight.

Lydia rose and thanked them both as she accepted the slip of paper from Bess. After they had gone, she realized that she had enjoyed their visit after all, which was something of a surprise to her. She unfolded the paper and read what Bess had written in neat, even script.

> *"The Lord is nigh unto them that are of a broken heart and saveth such as be of a contrite spirit. Many are the afflictions of the righteous; but the Lord delivereth him out of them all." Psalms 35:16*

She folded the paper and tucked it into her apron pocket, and headed back to the kitchen. While she scrubbed clothes on the scrub board, she thought about Bess, and what she had obviously been through. To lose a two-year-old child by drowning … their only child. And Bess had said they could never have any more. How had they survived? How had they ever overcome such agonizing sorrow? How could Bess talk about it now and keep smiling? She decided she definitely wanted to talk to her one of these days before long … when she felt a little better.

Sweat trickled down her back, soaking her dress. She twisted the excess water out of the heavy overalls and threw them in her wicker basket.

It was going to be a scorcher today. She wiped her forehead with her apron and smoothed her hair back out of her eyes. She heard her boys laughing about something as she stepped outside and headed to the clothesline. She dropped the heavy basket on the ground and wondered with a stab of envy if she'd ever be able to laugh again in her life. How truly blessed children are, she thought. They didn't have a care in this world. How quickly their wounds are healed. How quickly their sorrows melt away, and life becomes a joy once again. Oh, to be a child again, protected from the hurts of this life. She thought of Rebecca, who would never have this chance to enjoy life, who would never experience any of the ups and downs, the twists and turns of life. Rebecca, who would never see her first birthday, or enjoy a Christmas, who would never go to school, never go out on a date, never marry, or raise a family of her own.... To her utter disgust, she realized that tears were cascading down her face again, making her nose run. I wonder if I'll ever stop crying ... .if this pain in my heart will ever die so that I can heal. How was it possible to reach the place that Rodney and Bess had reached when her entire body ached to hold her child one more time. Lord, help me, she prayed silently while she pinned another pair of overalls on the line. I need you ... I've got to have your help ... right now.

CHAPTER 20
WOES COME IN THREES

Summer bore down on the residents of Northridge in relentless waves of heat and humidity. Day after day, clouds would build over the mountains, lightning would flash, thunder would rumble, and the wind would blow ... all to no avail. The varied complaints about the weather soon fell on deaf ears as obviously no one was capable of doing much about it. The Tuesday afternoon before Aaron's sixth birthday, Doug had stopped off at Deacon's Grocery to pick up the few things on a list that Lydia had given him that morning. He handed the list to Deacon and joined the other few patrons who were standing on the front porch, fanning themselves. He nodded a greeting to a couple of older ladies who were standing in the shade, waving a folded newspaper in a desperate attempt to move the air around them and cool their faces.

"Ain't you off work kinda early today?" a man's voice asked him when he had stepped out onto the veranda. Doug turned and faced Harold Baird, who was seated on the railing of the porch, his long legs draped over the railing, a tall glass of lemonade in one hand and a hand-rolled cigarette in the other.

"Harold," Doug said in greeting. "How are you doin'?"

"Burnin' up like everybody else," he replied, lighting his cigarette and exhaling slowly. He gulped the last of his cold drink and ran his thumb over the condensation that had beaded up on the outside of the glass. "Old Jack close the mill early today?"

"Yeah," Doug said. "Some of the guys were getting sick this afternoon. If it doesn't let up pretty soon, we're liable to have some serious consequences."

"Ain't it the truth," Harold agreed, taking another long drag on his cigarette before tossing it over the railing into the dirt parking lot around the store. "I can't remember it ever being this hot and sticky without a drop of relief."

The small group on the porch watched as a car pulled up to the store and parked in the shade of a big elm out front. Steam rose in billowing clouds from the overheated radiator as it lurched to a stop. A stranger got out and went around to open the door for his passenger. Grandma Phoebe Laurey gathered her ponderous skirt about her and slowly disembarked from the hot car.

"Afternoon, Grandma," Harold Baird said, shooing a pesky fly away from his face.

"Phoebe, how nice to see you," one of the ladies murmured. "How are you doing, my dear?"

The old woman seemed not to hear any of the greetings directed her way. She laboriously climbed the steps up to the porch and stood for a moment to catch her breath. Doug smiled and held the screen door open for her and she disappeared inside without so much as a single word to anyone, the young stranger right behind her.

"Who was that kid with her?" Harold asked no one in particular.

Doug shook his head. "Don't know. Never seen him before."

"She was acting mighty peculiar," one of the women commented. "I wonder if she's all right."

"Well, you know Phoebe," the other woman said, frantically fanning herself with the newspaper. "She's hard of hearing and all. She probably didn't hear us when we...." She was interrupted midsentence by a loud thud, followed by a tremendous crash of something inside the store.

Harold nearly collided with Doug as the two men scrambled for the front door. They found Deacon at the back of the store bending over Phoebe Laurey, who was laying on the wood floor, face up, amidst an odd assortment of can goods. Her eyes were wide open, and other than seeming to be a bit dazed, she appeared to be uninjured.

"Grandma!" Deacon cried in a frantic voice. "Are you hurt? Can you hear me? Don't try to speak. Just stay calm, dear, and I'll get you a glass of water." The middle-aged man glanced up at the small porch crowd who had gathered around the old woman and shrugged his shoulders. "I didn't see it happen, but I think maybe she just got too hot."

Harold knelt down beside the old woman. She fixed her eyes on his face and began moving her lips again. "She's tryin' to say something," he said to Doug, his face pinched with concern. "Grandma, don't try to talk right now. You've fallen, and until we can get Doc Sorenson over here to check on you, we don't want you to move."

Phoebe Laurey seemed not to comprehend what he was trying to say. She continued to stare at Harold and move her lips in an effort to speak.

"Where's that kid she came in with?" Harold asked suddenly, looking around the group.

"Why, he left," one of the women said. "Didn't you see him leave just after Phoebe fell? He rushed back outside just as we were coming in. Wonder who he is. I've never seen him before and I'm pretty sure she has no family around here."

The two men stared wordlessly at one another. Deacon hurried back with the glass of water and handed it to one of the ladies standing beside the fallen woman. "See if you can cool her down a bit. I'm gonna run down to Doc Sorenson's and see if he'll come back and check her out," he said in a rush as he tore his apron off and threw it behind the counter. "Be right back ... you fellas keep an eye on things for me?"

"Sure thing, Deacon," Harold said. He and Doug backed out of the way and allowed the two elderly ladies to do their best for their fallen friend.

Doug sighed. "It's probably the heat," he said. "Some of the guys at the mill were acting rather strange today too. Just too stinkin' hot for some folks."

"Phoebe!" one of the women screamed suddenly.

The two men whirled around in time to witness Phoebe Laurey's last breath. She died with her eyes wide open, her mouth sagging with her final desperate attempt to speak.

"Phoebe!" the woman gasped, shaking her shoulder. "Phoebe! Oh dear God, she's dying!" She rose and nearly stumbled over Doug who was standing right behind her. "She's dying, I tell you, she's dying!" she cried, a note of hysteria in her voice. "Do something!"

"Mrs. Martin, please come over here and sit down. Over here, dear. The doctor will be here soon." Harold Baird guided the distraught woman to a chair beside the old potbellied stove, which was now covered with jars of delectable preserves that Deacon had displayed for sale. The bell over the door tinkled as the doctor and a red-faced Deacon rushed to the back of the store. The doctor tossed his bag down beside the body and placed his fingers on the side of Phoebe's neck. He leaned forward, listening intently for breath sounds, then gently closed her eyelids and rose slowly to his feet, shaking his head. "Sorry, folks, there's not a thing I can do," he said. "I'm afraid I'm too late. She's gone."

"Dear God in heaven!" the second woman said. "She never made a sound. Never said a single word."

"You suppose it was the heat or maybe her heart?" Deacon asked, suddenly very shaken by the ordeal. "I'm positive she didn't slip on anything here in the store. She went down without a sound. Never even uttered a cry. The first thing I know, she's down on the floor with all the cans rolling around beside her. I looked up just in time to see that young fella racing outta here for all he was worth."

The doctor fixed a steely gaze on Deacon's face. "What young fellow are you talking about?" he asked.

"Miss Phoebe came in with some stranger. Never seen him before today. A young fellow."

Doug and Harold nodded. "We saw him too, Doc. None of us outside on the porch had ever seen him before. He didn't say a word to any of us, but then ... neither did Phoebe. We all thought Miss Phoebe was acting rather peculiar," Doug admitted.

"That's right, Doc," Mrs. Martin said, rising from her chair. "Phoebe never hesitates to stop and visit with me and Sarah, but today, she just ignored us. Mighty strange if you ask me."

"Doc, what do you think she died from?" Harold asked. "Could it be the heat?"

"I'll have to examine the body before I know for sure, but offhand, I'd say she most likely had a stroke," he said, staring down at the still form on the floor. "Can you fellows stick around and help me with the body? I'm going back to my office for the car, and I'll bring a stretcher with me."

Harold and Doug nodded their consent, both shocked and unnerved by this tragic turn of events.

"I *thought* she was acting mighty strange when she arrived here. Remember, Sarah, I told you I thought she was acting funny," Mrs. Martin commented to her friend.

"Little did we know she'd never leave this store. Bless her old heart," the woman named Sarah said. "Little did *she* know she'd never leave the store."

"Do either of you ladies know if Miss Phoebe had any kinfolk living around here?" Doug asked.

The women thought for a moment and finally both shook their heads. "I've never heard her say a word about any," Mrs. Martin said. "Do you suppose that young fellow was a long lost nephew or cousin or someone like that?"

"I doubt it," Harold said, lighting another cigarette. "I've known Phoebe all my life and I've never heard her even mention a relative before. She's the last of the Laurey family as far as I know. Seems to me she had one cousin who moved away or died, but that's been years and years ago."

"I wonder what she was trying to tell us," Doug said, more to himself that to the others in the stifling room.

Harold shook his head and blew smoke out the screen door at the front of the old store. He made a sucking noise through his teeth. "She acted like it was real important too. Poor old thing. Nan is sure gonna be upset when she hears about this."

Doctor Sorenson backed his long, black car up to the front steps of the store. People gathered in the street, curiously watching as the old doctor drew a stretcher from behind the seat.

"Somebody must have passed out in this heat," one interested passerby said.

"If we don't get some rain pretty soon, we're all gonna be passing out," Mr. Lawson, the mailman said, wiping his forehead for the ninetieth time that afternoon.

Doctor Sorenson made his way back up the steps, struggling with the cumbersome stretcher. Doug held the door open, and with the help of Deacon, the four men easily lifted Phoebe Laurey up on the heavy litter.

"Well sir," the doctor said, wiping his forehead with his handkerchief, "that's two woes down ... just one more to go."

Deacon frowned and glanced at Doug and Harold.

"What are you talkin' about, Doc? Harold asked. "Two woes down, what's that supposed to mean?"

"You've never heard the saying that woes come in threes?" the doctor asked, surprise written on his tired, wrinkled face.

"Can't say as I have," Harold admitted.

The old man twisted his lips into what some people might have considered a smile. "There's a saying goes like this," he explained.

"Double troubles, have we none.
Single trouble, makes just one.
All our troubles, as you'll see,
Come to us in groups of three."

The men exchanged quick glances, frowning at one another.

"I'm afraid I've never heard that before either," Doug said. "That's a new one on me."

"Laugh if you want to," the doctor shot back, somewhat irritated, when he noted their skeptical looks. "If you'll just stop a minute and think about this, you'll see that it makes perfect sense and it's true. First one was your little baby, Doug, taken suddenly in May, and now Grandma Phoebe is suddenly gone from us in July. You mark my words, before summer's end, we're gonna lose another one. I've seen it happen time and time again. If your first woe is a death, then you'll have two more in rapid succession. If the first trouble is...." he stopped and scratched his chin, "let's say a bad accident, then pretty quick, you'll be plagued by two more. And by the way … just in case you guys think the heat's gotten to me … I didn't make that up. I believe it's in the good book somewhere about the three woes. Ask Jamison next time you see him." With that, he spread a sheet over the dead woman and indicated that he was ready to move the body to his car.

The three men glanced at one another with raised eyebrows. Woes coming in threes. That sure didn't sound very hopeful. The four men carried the body out to the car, struggling down the steps, the sweat pouring off their faces.

"Just hope I'm not next," Harold grunted as he slid the stretcher into the back of the doctor's big car.

"Can a couple of you ride down to my office with me and help me unload?" he asked suddenly.

Doug and Harold volunteered as a swarm of people headed straight for Deacon's store to pummel the poor man with a myriad of questions.

"Looks like Deacon has his work cut out for him," the doctor observed as he slid behind the wheel.

Deacon hurried back into his store, the crowd pressing in around him.

"Poor Deac," Doug said. "I hope he finds the time to fill Lydia's order, otherwise, I just might be the final woe when I get home tonight." He suddenly realized how late it was getting and how very tired he had become. He and Harold walked back over to the store when they had finished helping the doctor.

"Sure is peculiar, ain't it?" Harold said, as they climbed the steps together. "About that strange kid an' all."

Doug had to admit that he found it all a bit strange as well. "Wonder how Grandma Phoebe intended to get back home since her ride disappeared."

"Maybe she figured one of us would take her on home," Harold sighed heavily. "Who knows.... I guess it doesn't matter now what she was figurin' on. Wo–" he stopped suddenly and ran his thumbs under his suspenders and grinned. "I durn near said woe is me! Reckon I'll be careful about saying that from now on."

"You didn't take Doc seriously, did you?" Doug asked, teasing his friend.

"No," Harold said, chuckling. "But, all the same, next time I see old Jamison, I'm gonna see what he thinks about that. It sure can't hurt, can it?"

Doug shrugged his shoulders and laughed. "What do I know, Harold? I'm too hot to think about anything but getting home. Guess I'd better see if Deacon has those groceries ready."

Deacon had indeed filled both Doug and Harold's orders and had the groceries waiting on the countertop when the men entered the store. "Put it on your tab, boys?" he asked, pulling a pencil down from behind his ear.

"Yeah, thanks, Deacon. I'll settle up with you later," Doug said, grabbing his box and heading toward the door.

He sat lost in thought on the drive home. Three woes, huh? He'd have to ask Lydia if she'd ever heard of that. It would appear as if the doctor firmly believed it. Funny, Doug thought, how a medical man with so much book knowledge could be a little superstitious on the side. He thought about Phoebe Laurey's life. Apparently she had grown up in the area when it was settled back in the mid-1800s. I wonder what will become of all her property? She has no heirs that anyone is aware of. Does everything go to the state? He shifted down into low and eased the car down into a deep rut in the road. Lightning flashed across the sky in the distance, but Doug barely noticed it. Wonder if the doctor was right … about trouble coming in threes? If that *was* true, who would be the third? He'd have to remember to ask Rodney about it the next time he talked with him.

He parked the car in the garage and reached for the box of groceries on the seat beside him. Ruffy's nose was immediately thrust through the open car window.

"Hi there, boy," Doug said, scratching the dog's head. "Did you keep all the dangerous critters at bay?" Ruffy answered him by furiously licking his hand and whining. "Come on, boy, let's go see what Mama's cooked up for supper," he said, slamming the car door. "She's cooking something wonderful!" he said, sniffing the air appreciatively.

Lydia looked as tired as he felt when he entered the kitchen.

"Daddy, Daddy!" Benjamin cried, throwing his arms around Doug's legs. "Hi, Daddy!"

Doug set the groceries down and picked up his son. "Still got those freckles, I see," he said with a laugh. "Hi honey. Something sure smells good."

Lydia nodded and swatted at a persistent fly that seemed intent on sampling their supper. "Better get washed up. Supper's almost ready. Ben, you and Aaron go wash your hands for supper."

Doug decided he'd wait until after supper to tell her about Phoebe. No sense ruining their meal.

Lydia was changing. It didn't take an expert to figure that out. Doug had watched her from a distance and didn't like what he was seeing. She rarely looked at him anymore. She spoke to him only when he spoke to her first. She never smiled and was always on the verge of tears. Doug felt as though he was walking on thin ice all the time. He had tried to be patient … that had been Doc Sorenson's advice. "Give her some time," he had said. "She'll come around." But when? How long was this grieving process supposed to last? Doug could see no progress in that direction at all. In fact, she seemed to be more and more withdrawn lately. It had been a full two months and she seemed no better today than she was the day they found Rebecca. He was worried … worried and frustrated. He carried Ruffy's food out and plopped it in his bowl. Maybe if I tell her about Phoebe, she'll realize that death happens to other people too. Maybe that will give her something or someone else to think about for a while. He cleared his throat and charged back inside, picked up the linen dishtowel, and began drying the dishes for her.

"We had a bit of excitement at Deacon's store today while I was there," he began, glancing sideways at her.

"Oh?"

Doug paused and when it became evident that "oh" was all the response she was going to give, he plunged ahead. "You remember Phoebe Laurey?"

Lydia nodded her head and continued scrubbing the big skillet in the dishpan.

"Well, the poor old thing toppled over and died this afternoon, right there in Deacon's store … right by the big stove."

"It's this terrible heat. We're all going to die if we don't get some relief pretty soon," she said in a flat voice without looking at him.

"Doc said he thought she might have had a stroke. I felt so bad … her lying there on the floor, looking up at us, and we couldn't do a single thing to help her."

"What do you want from me, Doug?" his wife snapped suddenly. "At least she had a long, full life." She dissolved into tears, snatched her apron off, and rushed from the room, slamming the bedroom door behind her.

The muscles in Doug's jaw worked furiously as he briefly considered smashing every single dish he had just dried. What under the sun was wrong with her anymore? He couldn't seem to get through to her, no matter what he said or did. Nothing pleased her anymore. He couldn't even have a sensible conversation with her. What was he going to do? Both boys were staring wide-eyed at the closed bedroom door. Neither said a word. Doug sighed and threw the dishtowel over the rack to dry.

"Come on, guys … it's time for bed."

"Can Mama read us a bedtime story, Daddy?" Benjamin asked in a hushed voice.

"Not tonight, son. Mama's not feeling very well. Don't forget to say your prayers tonight."

"Should we pray that Jesus makes Mama feel better?" Aaron wanted to know.

"Absolutely … most definitely!" Doug said.

"Can you read to us, Daddy?" Benjamin persisted.

"Not tonight Ben. It's getting late. Maybe tomorrow night I can read you a story. You hurry up and get in bed."

With the boys finally in bed, Doug slumped wearily down in his chair and fanned his sweat-streaked face with a newspaper. He leaned his head back and tried to think. He wondered if Georgia had been over for a visit recently. Lydia never mentioned her anymore. Maybe he should go over and see Georgia himself and get her advice. A big moth began fluttering around the lamp beside him. I'm going to ask Rodney's advice too, he thought. Maybe he and Bess could pay her another visit. She had seemed somewhat better after their last visit. He sighed and watched the moth flitting wildly around the light, pausing only momentarily to rest on the table. He rose and sought relief from the heat outside. The clouds, which were so numerous in the afternoon, had all dissipated, leaving the night sky studded with millions of stars shining down on him. He walked slowly down the driveway, Ruffy following close behind. He tilted his head back and stared up into the vastness of space. Who is man, God, that you are mindful of him? Doug remembered the verse from last week's Sunday school lesson. Who am I, Lord, that you are mindful of me? I am nothing, yet you created me, know me intimately, and love me. I am so unworthy, Lord … so unworthy. I've made a complete mess of things. Doug sank to his knees, right there in the driveway. Keeping his eyes fixed on a group of bright stars overhead, he poured out his heart to the Lord. "I need you, Lord … desperately need you," he said, his body suddenly shaking with the surge of emotion as his anguish was released. "Oh God!" he cried, "please help me to help her. I don't know what to do anymore. Please give me wisdom. I'm losing her, Lord, and it's killing me. I love her with all my heart, but I can't seem to reach her. Tell me what to do, please, Lord," he sobbed. The grief that he had held in check for the past two months suddenly rose to the surface and threatened to engulf him right where he knelt. He wept openly for several minutes, the pent up grief seeming to come in waves that shook his entire body.

"Forgive me, Lord, where I have failed. Help me to be the kind of husband, father and neighbor that I should be."

Ruffy seemed to understand his master's agony and pressed his warm body up against Doug's for reassurance. Doug rose to his feet and blew his nose. Looking up, he added, "Please give me strength, guidance, and wisdom. Thank you, Lord. Amen."

Doug Wheeler walked slowly back into his home a few minutes later, a much stronger man.

CHAPTER 21
A UNIQUE BIRTHDAY

Aaron George Wheeler was six years old the day of Phoebe Laurey's funeral. A hot, dry wind had begun to blow early in the day. Men and women alike clung to their hats as they made their way into the crowded church in Northridge. The temperature inside the church was stifling. Fans of all sizes, colors and patterns were frantically busy, waving the uncomfortable air around in every pew in the small sanctuary. They looked somewhat like fluttering butterflies to Mrs. Crenshaw, who sat at the organ with streams of perspiration coursing down her plump, lined face.

Lydia, unable to force herself into the hideously hot black dress, was dressed in a simple, lightweight cotton dress with a small white collar. She did, however, wear the same black hat that she had worn two months before. She sat several pews back with her boys, staring down at her rough, dry hands through the soft folds of the black veil. Doug was seated on the front row, serving as a pallbearer along with Glen Richardson, Max Baker, Harold Baird, T.C. Murdock, and an older man she didn't know. Poor Aaron, she thought, stealing a sideways glance at him. Instead of birthday cake, he has to suffer through a funeral for someone he never really knew. Both boys seated beside her looked as though they were melting right before her eyes. She moved her fan over in front of them and waved it for a few seconds. They looked up at her and grinned, grateful for the brief respite from the crushing heat in the packed building.

"On behalf of Phoebe Eileen Laurey," Rodney began, as the organ music faded away, "I want to thank each of you who have attended this service today. Because of the extreme heat, we'll keep this service as short as possible. I'm sure Grandma Phoebe would forgive us."

Thunder suddenly rumbled in the distance. An excited murmur rippled through the crowd as Rodney opened his Bible.

The ceremony was strikingly similar to the one he had conducted for Rebecca; the pain and shock of that day descended once again on Lydia, opening anew the wounds that she was trying so desperately to heal. She always came right back to that unanswerable question of why? She looked at the back of her husband's head, which was lowered as if he too was studying his hands. She loved him with all of her heart, but she didn't understand him. And it was painfully obvious that he didn't understand her either. She knew he fully expected her to be over this by now. She could see it in his eyes, in his face. He couldn't understand her constant tears, couldn't understand why the least little thing reminded her of Rebecca. She vigorously fanned her face, hoping to keep the tears at bay that were threatening once again. She tried to listen to Rod and focus her attention on the kind, old woman who had left this world suddenly … at least she had a full life. The thought crept in, undermining her reserve not to think about it anymore. *My precious baby didn't get the chance for a full life.* Her arms ached to hold her just once more, to feel her soft warmth, to smell that precious newborn smell, and the scent of milk on her breath.… The hot tears coursed down her face and dripped down on her hands.

Thunder rumbled again, this time much closer. The congregation's attention was diverted momentarily as gusts of hot wind picked up layers of soft earth in the parking lot and swirled them past the windows. Rodney paused and listened to the increasing wind.

"Folks," he said suddenly, interrupting his funeral sermon, "maybe we're going to be blessed with a little rain."

Excitement rose once again, the fans fluttering with increased agitation. The windows began to rattle as the intensity of the wind increased.

"If any of you have car windows rolled down, please feel free to take care of that.…" Rodney's voice trailed off as about half the congregation stood on its feet and hurried to the front door. Before the men and boys could return, the storm was upon them. It seemed to Lydia that this storm rivaled the one six years ago to the day … the day Aaron was born. The funeral service was completely forgotten, even by Pastor Rodney, as people rushed to the windows trying to get a glimpse of what was happening outside. Some who were caught outside decided to wait it out in their cars. Within a few brief seconds, the parking lot, along with the cars and their occupants, were completely obliterated from the view of those left inside the church. Rain, driven by high gale force winds smashed into the side of the building, threatening to break the glass in the small windows. Hailstones bounced wildly, creating a thunderous roar on the roof overhead. Aaron and Benjamin rushed up to the first window they could find and stood spellbound along with other children and watched the fury of the storm. Lightning struck close by, followed immediately by a loud crash of thunder.

"That one might have hit the steeple," T.C. Murdock shouted to Doug.

Everyone in the church instinctively ducked as another brilliant flash lit up the inside of the building with an ethereal light, with the thunder vibrating the foundation. Older children squealed with excitement, younger ones began to cry. Mothers and their babies sat huddled in a tight knot in the middle of the sanctuary. Grown men ran from window to window, chattering excitedly. Lydia watched the chaos around her and suddenly thought of her mother. Mom was right … men are just little boys in big pants. She watched Doug, grinning happily as he bent down and lifted Benjamin up into his arms. He bent low and said something to Aaron who grinned up at him. A warm hand suddenly clasped her shoulder. She turned to see Georgia smiling down at her. Georgia leaned forward and scooped her up in a bear hug. Lydia removed her hat and fanned her tearstained face.

"Isn't this something?" Georgia shouted above the din of the storm. She sat down with a heavy thump. "We're sure not going to bury Grandma today," she said loudly. "That hole they dug this morning is probably running over with water about now."

Lydia hadn't thought of that. "I wonder if we're going to be able to get home," she said, leaning close to her friend's ear. A worried frown crossed her face.

Georgia shrugged her shoulders. "Who knows? We might not be able to get back up the mountain. You know what weather like this does to our road. Might have to spend the night right here."

Lydia's shoulders sagged as the thought of spending the night in the church settled upon her. Spend the night with all these people … one of them dead … and on Aaron's birthday too.

"I sure hope not," she said gravely. "We really need to get home. Today is Aaron's birthday and we were going to have cake and…." Her hand flew to her mouth as another bolt of lightning cracked nearby, increasing the intensity of the rain. Thunder nearly deafened them. Someone's baby toward the back of the church began screaming. Bess joined Lydia and Georgia, her face a mixture of excitement and fear.

"I'm not sure I wanted *this* much rain!" she yelled, trying to make herself heard over the tremendous level of noise. "This is too much!"

Georgia and Lydia nodded their agreement.

"We were just wondering if we'd be able to get back home," Georgia said. "I'm afraid our road may be washed out again." Georgia suddenly slapped her forehead and stared at the two women seated beside her. "I just remembered something … I left my wash hanging out on the clothesline. It's probably blowing around somewhere in Brighton by now."

Bess laughed and Lydia smiled.

"I have a birthday cake sitting on my kitchen table that needs my attention," Lydia said. "Today is Aaron's sixth birthday. I need to get home and get some icing on it," she said, a doubtful look on her face.

"What a shame … to be six years old today and have to spend it stuck inside a church at someone's funeral," Bess said sympathetically.

The storm finally began to subside and one by one, the few who had been trapped inside their cars ran through the lake that a few minutes before had been the parking lot. They stomped their sodden boots at the door and made their way back inside, all chattering, as much from the dramatic drop in temperature as from the excitement of the storm itself.

"Folks, there's no way we can drive out of the parking lot in our cars," T.C. announced, shaking his head. "Water has cut a four foot gully right across the driveway, and in some places, it's deeper than that. Washed all the gravel out that we hauled in there a couple of years ago. We're not drivin' out of here tonight … that's for sure."

"Can't we fill it in?" Harold asked. "We could all gather up our shovels and…." His voice trailed off as T.C. shook his head.

"Not unless you divert that wall of water coming through there," he said. "All that runoff from the mountain is emptying into that one main ditch out front. It's probably gonna get worse instead of better tonight. We can still walk out of here but we won't be able to drive out for at least a day or so."

"Folks … let me have your attention," Rodney yelled from the pulpit. "Quiet down, please. Listen up. We've got quite a dilemma here. We obviously can't lay to rest our dear sister Phoebe. We'll have to conclude her service," he stopped and thought for a minute, "maybe on Sunday. We'll try to let everyone know. Our immediate problem right now is the fact that most of you Laurey Mountain people are looking at spending the night here in town."

A loud, collective groan was heard over the crowded church.

"Mr. Lawson just told me he got caught up on the mountain, trying to deliver your mail and he was forced to walk out. He says the road is terribly washed out, and there's a tree down across the road about a hundred yards from the school entrance. Please do not try to get back home today. He says it's quite dangerous. Water is running dangerously high in several low spots."

Another loud murmur of voices interrupted the pastor as residents of the mountain voiced their dismay and concern.

"Listen up, people!" Rodney yelled again. He licked his lips and waited for the room to quiet. "I guess the best way to handle this is for as many of you town folk who have room for some neighbors to please open your hearts and your homes. The rest of you mountain people will have to stay overnight here in the church." Rodney held up both hands as objections were being raised. "We have Sunday schoolrooms, three good-sized rooms that can handle a couple families each. Any of you town folk who have extra bedding and the like, please bring what you can back to the church. Deacon, can we count on you for supplies and food stuff from your store?"

"You bet, pastor," Deacon replied. "Come on, Mother," he said to Esther Smalley. "Let's go see what we can scrounge up for these folks."

"Wait a minute! Wait just a minute please," Rodney yelled once again. "I need about six or eight strong-armed men to carry sister Phoebe back to Doc Sorenson's office. We can't take her in the hearse, so if some of you fellows will just gather around up front here...."

Several men pushed their way through the crowd and Rodney stared in surprised when he suddenly had thirteen men volunteering to carry the casket. Others headed out of the church to gather supplies at home. Georgia and Lydia decided they'd better check out the sleeping arrangements and went to investigate the schoolrooms attached to the side of the building.

"Our families can use this big one," Georgia said, "unless you're bothered by snoring. Max can literally raise the roof. Let's hope it doesn't rain anymore tonight or we might all get soaked." She laughed at her own little joke and was warmed at the sound of Lydia's laughter as well.

"Max tells me that I snore just as loud, if not louder than he does, so I hope we don't keep you up all night."

"We'll be just fine," Lydia said.

The two women were interrupted by a loud commotion out in the sanctuary. Some of the men and older boys were moving several pews out of the way to make room for tables that were being moved out of the adjoining Sunday schoolrooms. They watched in awe as the room was transformed into a large dining room, complete with tablecloths and napkins. As if by magic, food began to appear. A large bowl of potato salad, a home-smoked ham, cold chicken, a large pot of baked beans, a couple of watermelons, and several loaves of home baked bread covered the tables.

"Would you look at that?" Georgia exclaimed. "We're sure not going to go hungry tonight."

The women organized the food on three of the tables while the men set up folding chairs. Each time the front door of the church opened, someone else entered, laden down with more food or bedding. By five thirty that afternoon, there was enough food and bedding to comfortably care for a small army. Rodney was moved to tears at the outpouring of love that was shown that afternoon. When all had gathered and quieted down, he cleared his throat and swallowed hard.

"Our blessed Father," he prayed, his voice shaking with emotion, "how thankful we are today for the rain." Several amens were heard throughout the room. "And how thankful we are," he continued, "for each other, for the outpouring of love and sacrifice that has been so graciously shown here today. We set this day aside, not one of mourning the passing of Sister Phoebe but one of celebrating her life. We thank you, oh God, for supplying all our needs according to Your riches. Bless this food to us and bless our fellowship together as we partake. In Christ's blessed name we pray, Amen."

The room resounded with a hearty amen from both men and women and instantly became a loud hum as chairs were dragged up to the tables and food was passed around.

When everyone had eaten their fill, a hush fell over the crowd.

Esther Smalley emerged from one of the small rooms toward the back of the church. She carried a large cake, complete with lit candles, and set it down in front of Aaron Wheeler. Everyone joined in the singing of happy birthday. Aaron looked embarrassed and happy all at the same time. He leaned far over the cake and blew. All six candles were extinguished. The crowd applauded noisily.

"Wait a minute … wait a minute!" Esther said, holding up her hands. "There's more. What would a birthday be without presents?" She handed Aaron two small packages that had been hastily wrapped in tissue paper. He stared at the bundles and then at his mother.

"Go ahead," Lydia said, smiling at her son. "You can open them."

He nervously opened the smallest one and discovered he had a brand new yo-yo. "Oh boy!" he cried and quickly tore the paper off the remaining package. His eyes widened as he beheld a toy fire truck, complete with a little fireman who sat up on the front seat.

"Wow!" he breathed. He turned the truck over in his hand and glanced up at the people crowded around him. "Wow!" he said again.

"I think he means thank you," Doug said, laughing.

"What do you say, Aaron?"

"Thank you!" he cried enthusiastically.

The room was instantly a buzz of laughter and voices. Children of all ages came to inspect the new toys while the women whisked the cake away to be cut and served. Aaron was obviously enjoying all this attention that had been lavished on him.

"Esther, thank you so, so much," Lydia said a few minutes later. She put her arms around the older woman and hugged her tight.

Esther, who was easily embarrassed, tried to shrug off Lydia's appreciation. "T'was nothing," she said. "The yo-yo came right out of the store and the little truck … well, believe it or not, that was one of our own boys' toys when he was little."

"Really?" Lydia exclaimed. "It looks brand new. You've sure made one little boy happy tonight, and I thank you from the bottom of my heart."

"T'was nothing … really," Esther said again.

After the food had been put away, the women tackled the job of setting up cots and making pallet beds on the floor while the men formulated a plan for repairing road damage.

"Max, you and Doug can take a group up on the mountain with you tomorrow and saw up the tree that's across the road," T.C. said. "I'll talk to Jack about lending a couple of crosscut saws to you for the job."

Max nodded his thanks. "We'll split it up and haul it down to the schoolhouse for the stove this winter."

"Hard to think about having a fire in a stove tonight, isn't it?" Doug said. "Even though it's cooler now, it's still muggy."

By ten o'clock that night, a small army of volunteers had been divided up into groups, each with specific orders to repair a certain section of the road and do whatever was necessary to get the mountain folks back home.

Lydia tucked Aaron and Benjamin into a makeshift bed right beside a larger one for her and Doug.

"Mama," Aaron said, his eyes bright with excitement, "this was the very best birthday I ever had in my whole life."

"Was it, honey?" she asked, brushing his hair back off his forehead. "It was really special, wasn't it?"

He nodded happily, his new fire truck tucked underneath his arm.

"I wish today was *my* birthday," Benjamin said. "You're lucky, Aaron."

"You had a nice birthday just a few months back, young man," his mother reminded him. She kissed them both and reminded them to say their prayers.

"Mama," Aaron said suddenly, "do you s'pose Ruffy's okay? Is it all right to pray for him?"

"Of course it's all right," Lydia said. "And I'm sure Ruffy's just fine. He probably crawled under something and stayed nice and dry. We'll see him tomorrow. He'll be okay."

"God bless Daddy, an' Mama, an' Aaron an' his new fire truck.… I wish I had a new fire truck … an' God bless Ruffy. Please don't let Ruffy get wet, okay, Jesus? Amen," Benjamin prayed, his eyes tightly shut. Lydia had to smile at the sincerity of his prayer. Oh, to be a child again, she thought wistfully to herself.

Extra sheets had been draped across long stretches of clothesline to give each family as much privacy as possible. It was late when the last lamp had been extinguished. Lydia rolled on her side and whispered goodnight to Doug. Much to her surprise, the makeshift bed was nearly as comfortable as her own bed at home. Doug squeezed her hand and kissed her nose. She closed her eyes and tried to pray. She had just drifted off when she was abruptly jerked wide-awake by a horrible sound … an entire roomful of snoring. Georgia wasn't kidding, she thought, folding her pillow down over her ear. A few minutes later, Doug joined in, adding to the cadence and rhythm of their noisy sleep.

"Thank you, Lord," Lydia prayed in a whisper, "for such good friends … even if they do bring down the rafters."

CHAPTER 22
AARON'S BIG DAY

Aaron's excitement knew no bounds, which made Benjamin all the more envious with each passing day.

"It's not fair," Benjamin had complained to his mother on numerous occasions. "I want to go too."

Lydia tried her best to be patient with him, but she was rapidly growing tired of the constant whining and complaining.

"How come Aaron gets new stuff and I don't?" he asked in a whiny voice one Saturday afternoon in early September.

"What does Aaron get that's new and you don't?" his mother asked, trying to keep her irritation out of her voice.

"Stuff to wear. He has new shoes and I don't. An' he got some new pants and shirts and I don't got some," he complained.

"I don't *get*, you mean," his mother corrected.

Benjamin frowned at her. "That's what I said … I don't get some new clothes. An' he gets to go to the barbershop, and get a spensive haircut and I don't get one."

"The word is expensive, Benjamin," Lydia corrected again. "You mean expensive."

"Yeah, a spensive haircut … like Daddy's."

"I'm telling you for the last time, Benjamin," Lydia said, keeping her voice as even as her patience would allow her. "Aaron has to have new clothes to start school. You'll get new clothes and new shoes when you start. Just be patient. And Daddy took him in just this once to get a real haircut. When you start school, Daddy will take you in for one too, I promise."

"But why can't I go to scho–"

"Benjamin!" his mother said sharply. "We've been through this a hundred times now, and I don't want to hear any more about it. Do you understand me?" She clipped the handle back on her iron and began ironing one of Aaron's new shirts. Steam rose up in her face as the hot iron sizzled, drying the dampened shirt.

Benjamin sat at the table, silently watching her, his lower lip turned down in a pout. "Will you iron my new shirts too when I get 'em?" he asked, his eyes following the smooth strokes of the iron. "An' will you iron my new pants too?"

Lydia tried to hide a smile. "Of course, I'll iron your clothes," she said. "Don't be silly. I iron things for you right now, don't I?"

Benjamin put his head down on an outstretched arm that was flung out across the table. He idly swung his foot and watched his mother. "How many more days 'til I can go to school too?" he asked. His foot stopped swinging while he waited for her to answer.

"I have no idea. You've got close to two more years before you can go, but that doesn't mean you can't visit school from time to time."

"I can?" he cried, his head coming up off the table. "Can I go with Aaron on the first day?"

"No, you cannot!" his mother said firmly. "Have you gotten in your share of the wood yet?"

"No," Benjamin admitted. "I'm waitin' for Aaron to help me, but he's in town, having fun with Daddy." The lower lip protruded once more.

"I think I see that green-eyed monster again, don't I?"

Benjamin jumped up from the table and made ferocious, growling sounds as he made his way outside. "Watch out, Ruffy, I'm gonna bite you," he yelled to the dog who lay panting in the shade of the huge willow tree next to the driveway. Ruffy raised one eyebrow at him and closed his eyes again, sighing contentedly.

"Benjamin," his mother called. "Don't run off anywhere. As soon as Daddy and Aaron get back, we're going to have dinner." She placed her flat iron back on the stove to reheat it. If she hurried, maybe she could finish this ironing before they returned. She looked at all the new things hanging on coat hangers. It had taken all she'd been able to save the past few months to outfit Aaron for school. How they would ever manage with two boys in school was more than she could imagine right now.

She pulled her new hankie, a gift from Bess Jamison, out of the basket of clothes and pressed it, remembering the recent visit she'd had with Bess. They had talked about this very thing, how much everything cost now days, and how little money was left over out of each week's pay. Bess had dropped by unexpectedly, which in itself was not surprising, but what was surprising, was the fact that Rodney was not with her. Bess had learned to drive their car and had ventured out on her own to do a little visiting, she had said. At first, Lydia was dismayed to see their pastor's wife on her doorstep, but as soon as she invited Bess in and they had settled themselves in the living room, she began to relax and realized that she really enjoyed this woman's company.

Bess understood her like no other person on this earth … not even her own mother.

"How long was it … or how many months went by before you … what I mean is.…" Lydia searched for just the right words.

"You mean, how long did I grieve for my little Tim? How many months did I carry that almost unbearable ache in my heart?" Bess finished for her.

"That's exactly what I mean," Lydia said, grateful that Bess understood what she was trying to say.

"It takes a long, long time, I'm afraid." She sighed and straightened the hem of her skirt. "If I remember rightly, it was several months before that horrible ache began to subside. Seems to me that just about the time I felt I could live again, we were facing the first anniversary of his death, and that brought back the pain and I was right back where I started. But let me tell you something that may help you Lydia. I know for a fact that God's Word can help, because it certainly helped me. And of course, with each passing day, you heal just a tiny, wee part of that hurt."

Lydia nodded in agreement. "I know what you're saying. It will soon be four months for me and I'm beginning to feel that too, but I'd still like to know why though," she confessed. "If I could *only* understand why, I think it would help me a lot and maybe help me start to heal."

"You may never know why, dear," Bess said. "I think several years went by before Rod and I actually knew why Timmy was taken from us."

"You mean you *know*?" Lydia asked, leaning forward in her chair and staring at the woman across from her.

"Yes, we're pretty sure we know why now. Rod and I were both so busy … busy with the church and the young people, busy with this and busy with that … just busy, busy, busy. God couldn't get our attention, we were so busy all the time. We feel that He finally took back our little Tim to draw us closer to Him, so that we'd rely totally and completely on Him. Another thing that I thought about … not too terribly long ago, is the fact that we serve a very jealous God." She noted the look of surprise on the younger woman's face. "It's true, Lydia. God wants our complete love and devotion, and I think it's actually possible to love our children more than we do Him."

"But doesn't He give us children to be loved and nurtured?" Lydia asked, somewhat surprised. "I always assumed that He loves us so much and He gives our children to us.…" She stopped midsentence and stared at the pastor's wife.

"Of course, He loves us and gives us children to love and cherish, but at the same time, we're told in Scripture that we are to love Him first, then our spouse, and lastly, our children. If we get that order mixed up, who knows …

that's a distinct possibility as to why He took my little Tim back." She sighed loudly and stared down at the floor for a few seconds. "We had no one," she continued, "to turn to after we lost Tim, but eventually, through several months of praying and repenting, we were drawn closer to the Lord. Rodney and I came very, very close to divorcing because of Tim's death, but the Lord got a hold of us through our pastor and really dealt with us. You know, Lydia, I have to confess, there was a time that I felt the Lord was picking on us, and I can remember one incident when I blurted out that I thought God was cruel ... not loving, but downright cruel." She shuddered and shook her head. "I can't imagine saying that now. I had a lot of repenting to do, believe me. When I look back on those days now, I know the direction we were headed in was not what He wanted. So ... He stepped in and changed that direction, and our lives have been blessed ever since. I couldn't see that at the time, but years later, it has become crystal clear to both Rod and me."

"Do you think maybe the Lord was trying to tell me and Doug something?" Lydia asked, a hint of fear in her eyes.

"Certainly, that could be one reason. Another one may be that somewhere down the road, He may lead you to another young couple who are grieving over their loss, and He'll use you to come alongside them and help them in their hour of need. That's how He uses us."

"I would have been willing to help someone like that anyway. He didn't have to take my baby to prove it," Lydia said defensively.

"Awwww, but *now* you have personal experience ... not only with your head, but also with your heart. You know firsthand what it is to lose a child, and God will use you if you'll let Him."

Before she rose to leave, Bess dug in her purse for a small package, which she handed to Lydia. "A little something that I made especially for you," she said with a smile. "Each time you use it ... and you *will* use it ... read the verse in the corner. I hope it helps." She placed her arm around Lydia's shoulders and offered a brief prayer for Lydia's understanding, comfort, and healing.

Lydia unwrapped the small, soft package and found a lace-trimmed hankie neatly folded inside. She read the verse that was embroidered in tiny stitches with dark blue thread.

"Trust in the Lord with all thine heart;
and lean not unto thine own understanding.
In all thy ways acknowledge Him
And He shall direct thy paths." Pr. 3:5,6

She read the verse and then read it again. Bess smiled at her and left her with this last word of advice.

"Lydia, don't try to figure out the Lord's business. Just give your pain, doubt, and confusion to Him, and trust Him to work all this out. He knows what He's doing. Lean on Him, and above all, trust Him," she said and then was gone.

Lydia now stared at the hankie, her hand trembling and her eyes filling with tears. Oh Bess, she thought, if only I knew how to give this pain and doubt to the Lord, but I don't. She folded the new hankie so that the verse in the corner was showing. She read it again and said, "Lord, I want to trust You with all my heart. Please show me how to do that, and how I can have the kind of peace that Bess has."

"Who are you talkin' to, Mama?" Benjamin asked, his nose pressed against the screen door.

"I'm talking to Jesus," she said simply.

"Oh," Benjamin said. "Tell Him I said hi. Does He have a dog at His house?"

Lydia laughed. The sound seemed strange to her, and she suddenly realized that it had been a long time since she'd heard herself laugh. "And Lord, help me to laugh again," she added.

Two shirts for Doug, a dress for her, and a couple of small things for the boys, and she'd be done. A few minutes later, Ruffy's excited barking told her that Doug and Aaron were home. Oh well, she'd finish after dinner. She pulled her ironing board out of the way and stirred the soup that was simmering on the back burner of the stove. Aaron burst through the door first, talking nonstop about town, his haircut, and how much better the road was now that the repairs were finally finished. Lydia was amazed at how grownup he looked with his neatly shaped, tapered haircut.

"You're such a handsome boy," she said, admiring the back of his head. "The little girls in class are going to love you."

Aaron turned around and glanced up at her, an embarrassed grin on his face. "Feel my hair," he said suddenly. "It feels funny … like a porcupine." He ran his hand up the back of his head.

"Lemme feel it too. I wanna feel a porkypine," Benjamin said, rushing up to his brother.

"So the road's finally finished?" Lydia asked Doug as he plopped a big bag of groceries down on the counter.

"Yeah, and what a difference! You remember that bad spot just below the school where the water had washed out the road … right down to bedrock? It's smooth as silk now … almost like pavement."

It had taken nearly a month of hard labor to finish the road repairs, so extensive was the damage from the storm in July. Doug had done his share, working most evenings and every Saturday. A new culvert had been added just above the school in an effort to divert the water under the road rather than allowing it to run over the road, carrying with it all the topsoil. The men had worked long, hard hours getting that thing in place. Doug had come home night after night, filthy and bone weary. Rocks had been piled on either side of it to keep it from rocking, and then it was buried, one shovel full at a time. Lydia was glad the job was complete now that school was about to start. She had been concerned about Aaron and other small children passing the men and equipment on their way to school each day. Now that worry was behind her.

Doug was elated that he could finally drive the car into town again. He had been forced to walk, as did everyone on the mountain until the repairs were completed.

Monday morning dawned bright, clear, and crisp with a definite feeling of fall in the air. Aaron dressed in his favorite new outfit and his new boots. He gulped down his breakfast and didn't have to be told once to brush his teeth. He was ready to go by seven o'clock.

"What's taking so long?" he asked impatiently, looking at the big clock on the wall.

"It's not time to go yet," Doug said, laughing. "Next week, we won't be able to drag you out of bed."

Lydia carefully packed a big lunch for him and set the sack by the back door. "Come here, Aaron," she called. "I want to comb your hair." She and Ben were going to walk with him this morning so that she could take care of the registration formalities. Ben was nearly as excited as Aaron when the three of them left the house a little while later. Ruffy howled his protests at being left behind and nearly uprooted the tree he was tied to.

"Poor Ruffy, he wants to go to school with all of us," Benjamin commented, as they walked down the driveway.

"Tomorrow morning, Aaron will be walking all by himself," Lydia said, hoping that Benjamin understood her comment, though as far as she could tell, it fell on deaf ears. She watched her sons as they skipped down the road ahead of her. Their pace slowed considerably, she noticed, as they neared the school. Children of all ages milled around the school grounds. Some of the smaller kids were standing in line waiting their turn at one of the three swings. The merry-go-round was loaded down to the point that Lydia doubted it would move an inch.

"Can I go swing?" Benjamin asked excitedly.

"You'll have to wait in line to swing," his mother said. "Maybe later, Ben. You'd better stay with me and Aaron this morning." She opened the door and stepped inside. The large room was crowded with parents standing in small groups, visiting with one another, all clutching a handful of forms. Mrs. Richardson was nearly obscured from view by the stacks of books piled high on her desk. Those who had finished the paperwork had formed a ragged line, waiting patiently with their children to see the teacher.

"Hey, Mama, there's Peter up there!" Aaron said suddenly, pointing toward the front of the line. "Hi, Peter!" he yelled.

"Ssshhh!" Lydia scolded, holding her finger to her lips. "Honey, you can't just yell things out when you're in the classroom. You're going to have to learn to be quiet when you're inside."

Peter waved his greeting, and Georgia, grinning from ear to ear, waved her handful of forms at them.

Lydia found the forms she needed and sat down at an empty table at the back of the room, flanked on either side by her sons. Brother, she thought, scanning the forms. They need to know everything under the sun about us. It took her a good twenty minutes to complete the paperwork and sign everything. She and the boys finally got in line when she was sure she had completed the registration. Georgia and Peter were no longer in sight.

"Where'd they go?" Aaron asked, craning his neck to see the front of the line. "Did they go home?"

"They're probably finished with all of this," Lydia suggested. "Peter's probably waiting outside for you."

A little girl began to scream at the front door as her mother tried to leave. She pulled her child away from her skirt and tried to talk to her. With arms outstretched, the little girl began to sob uncontrollably. Mrs. Richardson rushed over to see if she could help and spoke briefly with the mother, who reluctantly disappeared through the open door. Mrs. Richardson had her hands full as the little girl became nearly hysterical, her arms flailing wildly as she fought the teacher off in a desperate attempt to escape outside.

"What's wrong with her?" Aaron asked anxiously, watching the scene at the door from behind his mother's skirt.

"Is she gonna get a whippin'?" Benjamin asked fearfully. He backed up a step or two.

"Poor little thing," Lydia said sympathetically. "She's absolutely terrified. Probably never been away...." She dropped that thought as the door flew open again and the little girl's mother reappeared, hands on her hips, looking extremely exasperated. She said something to Mrs. Richardson and then pulled the child outside.

"Betcha she's gonna get the belt," Benjamin predicted gravely. "How come she's so scared?"

"She's probably never been away from her mother before," Lydia explained. "Poor little thing."

A frightened hush fell over the children waiting in line with their parents. Benjamin stood a little closer to his mother, his eyes wide with apprehension. Mrs. Richardson came back to her desk and apologized for the delay. "Guess we have to expect that sort of thing from time to time," she said with an apologetic smile. "Now, who's next?"

Lydia and the boys slowly inched their way forward to the front of the room. She wished that she had foreseen this and had come a bit earlier. Georgia was most likely back home by now. She sighed and shifted her weight to her other leg. She looked around the big room, studying all the improvements. One would never guess that this had, at one time, been someone's home. She tried to imagine Grandma Phoebe living here years ago. The room, which she assumed had once been the living room, was now an open, spacious, brightly-lit room, full of newly finished desks lined up like so many soldiers. Large windows that opened out to the playground filled one side of the room. The other side was decorated with large maps with bookshelves at the far end. Coat hooks lined the wall just beneath the maps. Up front, behind Mrs. Richardson's desk, was a long blackboard with the alphabet printed in large, neat letters centered near the top. Aaron suddenly spied a box of crayons on each of the desks.

"Do I get one of these?" he asked his mother, pointing to the boxes of crayons. "Is this where I'm gonna sit?"

"I don't know, son, you'll just have to wait and see where Mrs. Richardson places you," she said. She looked around her. Everything had a new smell to it. Her eyes slowly wandered over the remarkable transformation. Phoebe Laurey would have been thrilled to see this today, she thought. She tried to imagine Grandma Phoebe as a little girl playing quietly by the stove with perhaps a homemade doll in this very room.

After what seemed to be hours, it was finally their turn. Mrs. Richardson took the registration forms from Lydia and quickly scanned them. She smiled down at Aaron.

"Welcome to Laurey Mountain School, Aaron," she said. "Your desk will be ... let's see," she thought for a moment, consulting her chart, "the first one in the third row. If you'll just have a seat, we're about ready to start class." She glanced at the clock on the wall and smiled at Lydia. "These all look fine, Mrs. Wheeler," she said, indicating the sheaf of papers in her hand.

"Good to see you again. Next!" she called loudly, and suddenly it was time to leave Aaron. Lydia walked him to his desk and handed his lunch to him. When she leaned down to kiss him good-bye, Aaron shied away, holding her at arm's length, obviously embarrassed by her actions.

"Oh, I see," she said, standing erect again. "Well, I'll just say good-bye then."

They left him there, standing by his desk, looking like he might cry. Lydia grabbed Benjamin's hand and walked briskly to the door. Benjamin, much to her surprise, was more than willing to go. She turned to wave to Aaron, a lump growing in her throat, but he was not looking at them. He was now seated at his desk, his attention drawn to a group of noisy, older children over in the corner. She and Benjamin made their way back outside. The line for the swings was even longer now, and though Benjamin watched the children with interest, he did not ask again if he could join them.

"Poor little Aaron," Lydia murmured suddenly. "I hate leaving him in there with all...."

"Can we go back and get him?" Benjamin interrupted. He stopped in the school yard, and pulled on her hand. "Let's go get him, Mama."

Lydia laughed. "We can't go back and get him. He has to stay. He's in school now and it's the law. He has to go to school. He'll be all right, you'll see." She and Benjamin slowly walked back home, stopping only once to watch a gray squirrel busily gathering acorns. About halfway home, they heard the clanging of the school bell. School was officially in session.

Lydia hoped that she was right ... that Aaron would be all right. He had looked like he was going to cry when she left. Maybe she should have stayed a little longer just to make sure he was going to be okay. Maybe Benjamin was right. Maybe they should have gone back and gotten him. He might be crying hysterically by now. Oh, Lydia Wheeler! Stop it! she scolded herself. What's the matter with you? Aaron would be just fine. Mrs. Richardson would see to that ... maybe. But then, she had so *many* children to look after. What if some bully stole his lunch, or what if some of the bigger boys teased him, or hit him? What if ... oh, stop it! She shook her head angrily and tried to shrug off her fears. What's the matter with me anyway? Aaron's not a baby anymore. Better get used to it right now. Benjamin would be in school too before she knew it. Then I'll be all alone, she thought dismally.

Ruffy met them at the end of their driveway, bringing with him evidence of what had transpired at home while they were gone. He was overjoyed to see them again and barked excitedly, dragging the frayed rope behind him.

"Bad dog! How on earth did you break that rope?" she scolded.

"Bad dog, Ruffy," Benjamin said and then giggled as the dog licked him in the face. "I told ya he wanted to go with us, Mama. He would love to go to school, wouldn't ya, boy?" Benjamin ran up the driveway with Ruffy bounding ahead of him, dragging the rope behind him.

The long morning dragged by. Even with all the washing Lydia had to do, she couldn't keep her mind off of Aaron. Were the other kids behaving? Was someone picking on him? She kept watching the driveway and the road below the house for the familiar figure of her oldest son. She hoped every day wouldn't be this hard. She was a nervous wreck. Why hadn't she thought to ask Mrs. Richardson what time classes would be dismissed? She pinned her last load of clean clothes on the line and decided she and Benjamin would eat an early lunch. She began to relax while they ate until Benjamin said, "I hope Aaron doesn't fall off that big merry-go-round. He better hold on tight, huh, Mama."

"He'll hang on tight," she said, wishing he hadn't mentioned that. What if Aaron did fall off? Would Mrs. Richardson know about it? Would she know what to do for him if he was hurt bad? By early afternoon, she had conjured up in her mind a most horrible picture … a picture of Aaron limping down the road, his arm in a sling, his shirt nearly torn from his body, his nose bleeding, one eye swollen shut, and his belly growling from near starvation because a huge bully had stolen his lunch. When she actually did see him walking toward home, her first impulse was to run down the road to meet him and scoop him up into her arms.

"Benjamin," she called excitedly. "Here comes Aaron! Look! Down the road … here he comes!"

Ruffy spied Aaron and darted down the long driveway, barking happily with Benjamin right behind him. Aaron ran all the way from the main road to the house, his wide grin telling the whole story. "Mama!" he shouted. "It was fun! I love school!"

"Did ya hang on tight to the merry-go-round?" Benjamin wanted to know.

"No, I didn't even get a chance to ride it yet. Mama, I'm starved. What's to eat?"

"What did you do today? Did you learn how to spell your name or learn the alphabet? Did you eat all your lunch?" Lydia bombarded him with questions, as anxious as Benjamin to hear all the details. She handed both boys a glass of milk and some homebaked cookies.

Aaron frowned. "We didn't learn any of that stuff," he said, his mouth full of cookies. "All we did is color today, and Mama, guess what?" he added excitedly.

"What?"

"We even get our own box of paints to paint pictures with! Can you *believe* that? Mrs. Richardson told us today that we get our own paints … soon as they get here. They haven't come in yet, but she said maybe tomorrow. I've never had my own crayons before and paints too! I can't wait to see my very own paints!" He whirled excitedly in the middle of the kitchen, nearly spilling his milk.

"Sit down while you drink that. Your own crayons and paints too. How exciting!"

"I want some too," Benjamin said. "Mama, I want some paints too."

Aaron frowned at his little brother. "You'll just have to wait 'til you're big enough to go to school, and then you'll get yours." He stopped momentarily to gulp down the last of his milk. "An' guess what else, Mama? We get our very own workbook to put numbers and things in. Mrs. Richardson passed those out today, and I got one. It's in my desk right now. I could show you if we walked back down to the school. You wanna go see it?"

"Yeah, let's go!" Benjamin cried.

"Hold on, you two," Lydia said. "We can't go back to the school today … it's closed for the day. Once school is over, they lock it up for the day. It won't be open again until tomorrow morning."

"Then I'll show you tomorrow morning, all right, Mama?"

Lydia shook her head. "Sorry, honey. Mothers are not allowed at school after the first day. I only got to come this morning to get you registered. I won't be going with you anymore."

"Oh," Aaron said, obviously disappointed. "But I wanted to show you all my new stuff."

"I can come and see your workbook," Benjamin said happily, as he danced a little jig beside his brother. "Mama said I could visit school."

"I'm sure you'll be bringing your papers home pretty soon and then we'll all get to see your work. Don't worry."

Aaron grinned at her and wiped his milk mustache off on his sleeve.

"Did that little screaming girl ever come back?" Lydia asked suddenly. "I felt so sorry for her."

Aaron shook his head. "I guess her mama took her home 'cause I didn't see her again, but there was a different kid there who started bawlin'. Mrs. Richardson had to take that kid outside and she was gone for a long time."

"Poor little kids," Lydia murmured. "The first day of school is so traumatic for them. I remember how scared I was, but I don't think I ever threw a fit like that." She sat lost in thought for a few seconds, remembering her first day at school.

"Did you cry when we left?" Benjamin asked, interrupting her thoughts.

"No!" Aaron said indignantly. "I'm not a baby!"

"Can I go visit tomorrow, Mama?" Benjamin asked hopefully. "Please? I want to see Aaron's workbook and his paints an' stuff."

Lydia shook her head. "No, Benjamin. I'm afraid not. Mrs. Richardson has her hands full enough right now just managing the kids who have to be there without worrying about little brothers who are visiting. But," she added, noticing the look on his face, "you can go one of these days before long … I promise."

"Probably not for a long, long time," he pouted.

His mother ignored him. "Aaron, did you see Peter?"

"Yeah. We ate our lunches together and watched the guys playin' baseball after lunch. It was so much fun!"

"So, you think school's pretty great, huh?"

"Yeah!" Aaron said with a wide grin. "I'm just sorry that I didn't start a long time ago!"

CHAPTER 23
BLACK TUESDAY

Ina Potts stood shivering on the porch of Deacon's grocery store. She pulled her woolen coat up around her throat, even though the late afternoon sun had warmed the front porch to a comfortable 68 degrees. She watched both sides of the street for Mr. Hodgkiss' car. "Where *is* that man?" she fumed under her breath. "I'm gonna wring his scrawny neck when I do see him."

"Afternoon, Ina," Nan Baird called pleasantly to the older woman. "Are you waiting on a ride?" she asked, noticing the box of groceries sitting on a low chair on the veranda.

"He'll be here," was Ina's curt answer. She paced back and forth, scarcely noticing other familiar faces that came and went. I'm gonna give that man a huge piece of my mind, she decided. The very idea of leaving a lady stranded in front of a grocery store when he promised he'd be right back. He'll wish that he'd hurried up a bit. She sat down beside her box and craned her long, thin neck in the direction of Maple Street.

Russell Hodgkiss had gone to the blacksmith's shop to see about getting the tines of his pitchfork sharpened. He had dropped Miss Ina off at Deacon's store for a few groceries she needed with the promise of returning a few minutes later. Now, nearly an hour had passed and there was no sign of him. Ina was left stranded and fuming.

"How do, Miss Potts?" Mr. Lawson said, tipping his small cap in her direction.

Ina glared at the man. "I've certainly been better," she muttered. "I'm freezing."

"Maybe you could wait inside the store?" the mailman asked, holding the door open for her. "It's got to be a little warmer inside."

"And miss my ride?" Ina asked, raising one eyebrow. "Not hardly!"

"Suit yourself," Mr. Lawson replied, allowing the screen door to bang a little harder behind him than he normally would have.

"Hrumph!" Ina grunted. "Men!" She stood and resumed her pacing across the length of the long porch. I'm gonna skin Russell alive if he *ever* does get here. What on earth could be keeping the man? Her heart suddenly skipped a beat. I hope he hasn't been hurt, or gotten sick, or something. What if his heart gave out all of a sudden, or what if he suddenly had a severe stroke like poor old Phoebe Laurey? She began to mull these horrifying thoughts over in her mind when the familiar chug, chug, chug of Russell's car reached her ears.

He pulled into the parking lot and hurried around to open the passenger door for her.

"Sorry I'm a bit late," he hollered, grinning up at her. "Where's your groceries?"

If ever a legendary dragon in the folklore of old could spew fire from his mouth, he found his match in Ina Potts that Tuesday afternoon. She glared at the old man without saying a word, grabbed up her box of groceries, stomped down the steps, and flung her body into the front seat. She yanked the door out of Russell's hand and slammed it closed on the tail of her coat. He started to say something to her about it but thought better of it.

Brother! Russell thought, walking around to the driver's side. I knew she would be upset … but like this? He started the car and backed out of the parking lot. Ina riveted her eyes on the road, her head held high.

Might as well get the chewing up and spitting out over with, the old man thought with a weary sigh. "Sorry to be a little late," he ventured timidly. "Time just got…."

"Sorry!" Ina nearly shrieked, interrupting his apology. "Sorry doesn't even come *close* to it, buster! Sorry indeed!" She paused for a moment while Russell rolled down his window and spit. "Sorry is what you are all right … and that's a filthy habit … positively disgusting!" she sputtered.

"What is?" he asked, completely mystified.

"Hawking out the window like that. It's filthy and it's vulgar."

"I wasn't hawking out the window," he said defensively. "I was merely spitting … and how else is a man supposed to get rid of … of…."

"Never mind!" she snapped. "You're just plain nasty, Mr. Hodgkiss … absolutely vulgar! Not a drop of decency in your entire body!"

To her complete amazement, Russell reached over, squeezed her knee, and chuckled.

"You're cute, Ina, did you know that? You're so cute when you get hoppin' mad like that."

Ina Potts was completely caught off guard with his reaction. She had expected a little fight … but this?

Russell glanced sideways at his passenger who sat straight as an arrow, balancing her box of groceries on her bony lap. He chuckled again and shook his head. "You can't fool me, Ina. You're put out with me, and that's for certain, but your bark is definitely worse than your bite."

"Well, we'll just see about that! I've never bitten you yet, you flea-bitten old codger, you! Not that I'd ever *want* to bite...."

Russell's hearty laugh was contagious. Ina couldn't hold back for long, and soon a tiny smile was tweaking the corners of her mouth. "You make me sick!" she said in feigned anger.

"I make myself sick too ... sometimes," he admitted. "Really, Ina, I am truly sorry for keeping you waiting so long. Please forgive me."

Ina sat up even straighter and looked out her window for a few seconds before answering. "I'll think about it," she sniffed.

They rode in silence for the duration of the trip home. When he pulled into Ina's driveway, she turned and looked at him. "Would you like to have a homecooked meal tonight, Russell?" Before he could answer, she added, "Just make sure you change that filthy shirt before you come. Dinner is at six thirty sharp. And don't you dare be late!" she warned, grabbing her box and opening the door.

"Forevermore!" she shrieked, when she stepped out of his car. "Just look what your filthy car did to my good coat!" She slammed the door, glared at him, and yelled something further, which he didn't catch. She set her box of groceries down and began furiously brushing the dirt from her coat.

It was just as well, he thought, as he backed out of her driveway. Probably chewing me up about something else. He whistled a little tune as he headed home. Glancing in his rearview mirror, he grinned at himself.

"Not bad, old boy," he murmured. "You've got a date for tonight!"

Lydia checked her pot roast that had been slowly cooking all afternoon. The house smelled wonderful, making her hungry for the first time in several weeks.

"Mama, what's two minus one?" Aaron asked, laboring over his arithmetic problems at the kitchen table.

Lydia set two apples out on the table. "If I take one away, what do you have left?" she asked.

He stared at the single apple for a second or two and then grinned up at her. He finished the rest of his problems in record time without asking any further questions.

Ruffy announced Doug's arrival home by racing down the driveway yipping and howling intermittently. Doug, however, broke his usual routine of jumping from the car, scratching Ruffy's ear, and throwing a stick for him to chase while he walked up to the house. Lydia's brow knit into a worried frown as she watched him from the kitchen window. He completely ignored the dog and walked slowly, with his head down, as if meditating on something extremely important. Lydia wondered briefly if he was sick or hurt.

He opened the back door and stood looking at her, his dark eyes smoldering in his rather pale face.

"What is it?" Lydia asked quickly. "Are you all right?"

He shook his head. "Yes, and no," he answered. He heaved an enormous sigh and sank down into the nearest chair at the table.

"What's the matter, honey?" Lydia asked, suddenly very nervous. "Did you lose your job?"

Doug shook his head. "You boys get outside and get some wood in," he ordered.

"But Daddy, I'm…."

"Now!"

Both boys scrambled to the back door and disappeared outside.

"Okay, honey, you're scaring me. What on earth has happened?" Lydia cried. She swallowed hard, searching for answers on her husband's face.

Doug shook his head, rubbed his eyes and sighed again. "We got word just a little while ago that the Stock Market crashed today," he said, staring straight at her.

"What is that? I … I don't understand what you're talking about," Lydia said, her eyes full of fear. "What is the Stock Market?"

"That's what keeps our country's economy booming. The bottom fell out of the market today. Investors have just lost thousands and thousands of dollars … maybe millions."

"But … what does that have to do with us?" Lydia asked. "We certainly can't invest anything. How are we going to be affected by this?"

"They might have to shut down the mill, and I'd be out of work. We don't know yet how bad it is. No one fully understands how this is going to trickle down to us poor, working folks."

"How did this happen? Didn't anyone see this coming?" his wife asked, completely perplexed.

"I really don't know if anyone saw it coming or not," Doug admitted, "but it's pretty devastating all the same. T.C. thinks that we've just produced so much stuff in this country that there's now a huge surplus, and no one is buying anything. We've over-produced goods and products, and there's no market for the excess." He looked at his wife and shook his head. "I really don't understand the enormity of it myself, but I do know that our president and his cabinet are very upset. Some people are blaming President Hoover … said the entire thing was his fault, but I find that hard to believe. Anything this big is never just one person's fault."

He placed his hands over his wife's trembling ones and looked deep into her eyes. "I promise you, honey, that if I should lose my job, I'll do my dead level best to keep us going here. We might have some real rough water ahead, but we'll make it ... even if I have to leave town to find work. You understand?"

Lydia nodded, her frown increasing. "It makes no sense to me at all. How could something like this have happened? Aren't there people in our government who are supposed to watch for things like this?"

"I have no idea," Doug admitted. "I just wanted you to know that we may have to tighten our belt a little here and there, or maybe a lot. No one knows for sure how this is going to effect the country."

Aaron stuck his head in the back door. "Daddy," he called, "Mr. Baker is here."

Doug rose to greet his friend and neighbor. "Come on in, Max. I didn't hear you drive up."

Max entered the warm kitchen and removed his sawdust-covered hat. "Lydia," he said in a greeting. Turning to Doug, he said, "I left my car down below your garage and walked up. I'm just on my way home, and thought I'd better stop off and let you know the latest."

"Please sit down, Max," Lydia invited.

Max shook his head and remained standing. "Thanks," he said. "I'm only stayin' a minute."

"What's the latest?" Doug asked, noting the pallor of his friend's face.

"It's Jack," he said simply. He swallowed hard. "He's dead!"

Doug stared at him, his mouth dropping slightly open. "What?" he gasped. "Jack Doss? Dead? What do you mean, he's dead? He can't be dead! What on earth are you talking about, Max?"

Max inhaled deeply, pursed his lips into a thin line, and looked over Doug's shoulder to the yard outside. He shook his head, ran his hand down over his face, and exhaled slowly.

"He's gone, Doug. Sheriff said self-inflicted gunshot wound to the head."

"*Oh, dear God!*" Doug gasped again. "Why ... wha ... what on earth happened? He was fine when I left ... a bit shaken, but we all were. I ... I can't believe this! Why? Why would he *do* such a thing?"

Max shook his head in disbelief. "Nobody knows. None of us can shed any light on it. T.C. is nearly crazy with what's happened. He told me that Jack's office was a mess ... papers scattered everywhere. Nothing was where it should be. He said it looked like the office had been ransacked. And he's the one who had to let Jack's wife know." He shook his head again, his eyes mirroring the shock and horror he was feeling inside.

Lydia closed her eyes tight and shook her head.

"That poor woman … and the *children!* I can't imagine getting that kind of news. I wonder how she's doing?" She bit her lower lip in an effort to keep it from trembling.

"Not good, from what I understand," Max said.

"Jack … dead! I absolutely cannot believe it!" Doug cried. "This can't be real! Max, why would he do such a thing? I just don't … should we go back down to the mill? Does T.C. need any us back down there to help out?"

"No," Max answered simply. "The sheriff ran us all out of there as it was. Said he didn't want us touchin' a single thing. T.C. told us to go on home … said he'd handle what needed to be done. I guess we're going to have a meeting in the morning so I thought I'd better prepare you."

"When did it happen?" Doug asked. "Must have been right after I left?"

Max nodded his head. "Yeah, I guess about ten to fifteen minutes after a bunch of you guys left. We were wonderin' if it had anything to do with the Stock Market crashing and all. We heard that several wealthy people … business men and such, up in Washington are doin' the same thing."

"Maybe so, but Jack didn't have money to invest, did he?" Doug asked skeptically.

"Beats me," Max admitted. "Seems to me he lived pretty well, but what in the world do I know?"

Doug shook his head. "It doesn't make any sense. He was such a nice guy … one of my *best* friends. If he was in any trouble, you'd think he would have confided in one of us, wouldn't you?"

"Yeah, you'd think so," Max agreed, twirling his hat in his hand.

Lydia sat, stunned into silence, watching the sawdust fall from Max's hat onto her clean floor.

"Daddy," Aaron interrupted at the back door again. "Mr. Baird is here."

Harold Baird entered the kitchen, his face haggard and pale, even behind a week's worth of stubble. "You guys heard the news?" he asked quietly.

Both Max and Doug nodded their heads.

"It's terrible, isn't it?" Doug asked. "What on earth possessed him to do such a thing?"

"Must have had some troubles on his mind that none of us knew anything about," Harold said. "Poor devil. Sure is a shock."

"Did the sheriff have any ideas? Did he say *anything*?" Doug asked, his mind reeling.

"If he did, he sure didn't share it with us. He just told us to get on home."

"I heard that there was another woman in his life," Harold ventured. "You guys ever hear about that?"

"No, and I don't believe that about Jack. We're probably gonna hear all kinds of stories out there before this thing dies down," Max said. "But as far as I know, he was devoted to his wife and kids."

"You know ... this might be Doc's third woe," Harold said, on his way out the door. "Remember what he said about woes coming in threes when Grandma Laurey died? Maybe the old man's got something there after all. See you fellas in the morning," he added, and closed the door behind him.

"Three woes?" Max said, looking questioningly at Doug. "What was that all about?"

Doug explained to him about Doc Sorenson's theory of woes coming in threes. "Doc said it was mentioned in the Bible and I meant to ask Rod about it, but I forgot to."

"Never heard of such a thing," Max said, jamming his now clean hat back on his head. "I'd better get on home. Georgia's gonna be worried about me. See ya in the morning."

Doug and Lydia sat in stunned silence for a few minutes after the men left. Lydia stared at the sawdust scattered all over the floor and rose to get her broom. While she was sweeping it into a pile, the boys each brought in an armload of wood and let it fall into the box, making an even bigger mess.

"What happened?" Aaron asked. "What's wrong?" He glanced at his parents when neither of them offered an explanation and, sensing that something was seriously wrong, hurried to his bedroom, Benjamin close behind him.

Lydia pulled the roast from the oven and set the heavy pan on top of the stove. Her appetite was gone, but what did it matter, she thought. She had lost her appetite while Rosalyn Doss had lost her husband. The world simply did not make sense anymore.

On Friday, November 1, 1929, the shocked and stunned community of Northridge prepared for yet another funeral.

Lydia held up the woolen, black dress she had worn to Rebecca's funeral just five months before, and decided that it was cool enough this time to wear it comfortably. She rubbed a tiny smudge out of the skirt and turned her attention to her boys' clothes. Aaron had plenty to wear, but poor little Benjamin was just getting by with Aaron's hand-me-downs. She decided he could wear his Sunday outfit for the funeral.

Doug sat in the living room, polishing his shoes. His usually sunny disposition had taken on a somber tone the past few days. If anyone at the mill knew anything, they weren't sharing information with the rest of the crew. In fact, it seemed as if there had been an unspoken order not to discuss what had happened. Doug and Max, along with others, had been called into the office Thursday morning, and asked to serve as pallbearers the following day.

T.C. Murdock had been asked by the family to say a few words in addition to Rodney's message.

Lydia hated the thought of yet another funeral. She couldn't imagine the pain and suffering that Rosalyn was experiencing. Her heart ached for the woman. Three funerals in the space of five months was too many, she decided. Maybe Doc was right about the three woes. She dressed quickly and brushed her hair.

"Aaron ... Benjamin, come out here and let me comb your hair," she yelled from the kitchen a few minutes later. Both boys scrambled to be first, but calmed down when their mother gave them one of her stop-it-right-now looks.

The young family rode in silence to the church, that was already overflowing with cars and people.

"You got an extra handkerchief?" Doug asked in a whisper as they got out of the car. "I forgot one."

Lydia handed him one of her hankies without lace and tucked the rest back inside her purse. "Come on, boys," she said, reluctantly ushering them towards the open door. She could already hear strains of soft organ music as they made their way up the steps to the door. Poor Mrs. Crenshaw, she thought, as they entered the quiet, darkened sanctuary. She's sure been kept busy lately ... far too busy.

Doug joined the rest of the men who had gathered in a small knot next to the doctor's long car, which served as a hearse.

"You guys hear anything else about all this?" he asked quietly.

"Not a single word," Harold answered. "Nan heard that his wife is taking it pretty hard," he added, crushing out his cigarette with his recently shined boot.

"I wouldn't doubt it," Max said. "Who wouldn't? Heck, we're all in shock and takin' it pretty hard if you ask me."

"We're about ready to start, gentlemen," Rodney said, shaking his arm into his suit coat as he walked briskly towards them. "I'm going to need you fellows to enter through the side door and sit up front across the aisle from the family. When the service is over, you'll be the last ones out ... with the casket, okay?"

The group nodded and followed Rodney to the side entrance.

Lydia found three seats near the back of the church and gratefully sank down into hers. The music, the flowers, the smell, and even the hush over the crowd, all brought painful and vivid memories flooding back to her. She could barely see up to the front of the church where the casket was, but she noticed that it was closed, draped with flowers of every imaginable hue. As her eyes became accustomed to the darkness of the church, she found Rosalyn, supported by her two children and Carolyn Murdock, all seated on the front row. People she didn't recognize were seated there as well, and Lydia decided they must be either Rosalyn's family, or perhaps some of Jack's family. The stance of grief in the way Rosalyn was sitting, with her head down and her shoulders slumped forward was all too familiar to her. Rosalyn's beautiful face was shrouded by a heavy, black veil.

The pallbearers entered the church along with Rodney and settled themselves while Mrs. Crenshaw played the final notes of *Abide With Me*.

Rodney rose, smoothed the front of his jacket, and set his Bible on the pulpit. Looking over the packed church, and then at the bereaved family, he began his sermon.

"This is a sad day … a very sad day. John Taylor Doss, known to most of us simply as Jack, was my friend. He was a good friend to all of you here today. We have truly suffered a great loss, and it is with a very heavy heart that we find ourselves here today to pay tribute to this fine man … a man of integrity, wisdom, and compassion. All of you, I dare say, could get up here and share stories as to how this man has touched your life in some way. Jack Doss was only forty-three years old. He left a lovely wife, Rosalyn, and two lovely teenage children, Jeremy and Christina, and our love and prayers are with this family today."

Folks in every pew reached for their handkerchiefs.

"This past week," Rodney continued, "our nation was seized by an unprecedented calamity with the collapse of our economy. Though we don't fully understand these things, we know that our God does, and He'll see us through this hour of economic tragedy. Though we don't understand the untimely parting of this dear brother, God does, and He'll see us through this as well. We need to pray for our nation and the leaders of our nation, and we need to pray for this dear family who have suffered the greatest loss. Mr. Murdock, if you'll please come now to offer the eulogy."

T.C. walked first over to Rosalyn, bent forward to hug her and the children, and then mounted the steps up to the pulpit.

He cleared his throat nervously and allowed his eyes to sweep over the congregation. "Rodney said it so well, folks … this is indeed a sad day. I have lost my … vvv … my very best…." His voice broke and he paused for a moment, trying desperately to control his emotions. Several people began to cry openly. "My very best friend," he finally managed to mumble. He paused again, gaining a little more composure. "Jack was the first man I met in Northridge when Carolyn and I moved here in 1920. He gave me my first job ... at the sawmill. He was like a brother to me. Our families have shared holidays together, our kids grew up together, and Jack made me foreman at the mill about seven years ago. I lo ... ved him like a brother." Tears flooded his eyes and he paused a moment to wipe them away with his handkerchief. "I don't ever remember him saying a bad thing about anyone ... *ever*. He was a good man, always willing to lend a helping hand to anyone who was down and out. We're all in shock." He shook his head. "If there's a special place in heaven where this old world's best folks go, that's where Jack is right now, smiling down on all of us." He hurried to his seat and buried his face in his handkerchief.

Rodney stood behind the pulpit again and opened his Bible, and read from I Corinthians chapter 15. He cleared his throat and read with a loud, clear voice.

"O death, where is thy sting? O grave, where is thy victory? The sting of death is sin; and the strength of sin is the law. But ... thanks be to God, which giveth us the victory through our Lord Jesus Christ."

People all over the church were grabbing handkerchiefs and dabbing their eyes. Mrs. Crenshaw began playing a beautiful tune that Lydia didn't recognize.

Rodney ended the service by quoting Psalm 46:1. "God is our refuge and strength, a very present help in trouble."

As the organ music swelled, everyone seated behind the family rose to pay their respect to Rosalyn and her children. Lydia didn't relish the idea of facing her, because she didn't really know what to say. However, she reasoned, she couldn't turn the other way and run out of the church, so she made her way slowly down to the front of the church along with everyone else. When it was finally her turn to hug the widow and murmur her condolences, she promptly burst into tears.

Rosalyn hugged her and murmured, "I know the feeling well, my dear. Thank you for coming today."

Lydia mumbled something inaudible and ushered her boys outside, wishing that she had said or done anything but cry in front of Rosalyn.

The graveside ceremony behind the church was short and to the point. Rodney prayed for the family again and ended the service as a cold rain began to fall.

CHAPTER 24
A LIFE UNVEILED

Doug slammed his lunch pail down and looked around the sparse office of the Northridge Lumber and Sawmill. The place looked deserted. He knew no one would be in Jack's private office. That had been locked up since last Tuesday afternoon when the unspeakable tragedy had taken place. He glanced briefly at the padlock that had been placed at Jack's door. It was still there ... still guarding the secrets that lay beyond those walls.

Doug scratched his head and went back outside. Even the mill, which was usually a beehive of activity and noise, was quiet this morning. He walked down past the lumberyard and into the work shed where he labored every weekday along with Max and several other men. The place was empty. What was going on around here? He began to feel rather uneasy when suddenly someone whistled shrilly at him. He looked up and saw one of the mill's new recruits motioning to him. He hurried across the yard and joined the young man. Doug glanced at his name badge and stuck out his hand.

"Morning, Gary," he said, reading the young fellow's name. "Where is everyone this morning?"

"Mr. Murdock called an emergency meeting this morning. Guess we didn't get the word out to quite everyone in time." He motioned over his shoulder to the largest shed at the mill. "We're just about to start," he added, leading the way to the building.

"I thought the meeting was scheduled for tomorrow," Doug said as they neared the shed.

"I guess it was, but Mr. Murdock said we were going to have this emergency meeting this morning, and he asked me to watch the grounds and make sure everyone made it over here," Gary said, holding the door open for Doug.

The room was buzzing with low voices as the men waited patiently to see what this was all about. Doug looked around for T.C. but couldn't find him. He saw Max and worked his way through the small crowd over to his friend.

"So T.C. called a special meeting this morning, huh?"

Max nodded his head. "That's what I'm told. I just heard about it a few minutes ago when I got here."

"Wonder what it's about."

Max shook his head slowly. "Your guess is as good as mine. Weren't we supposed to have a meeting tomorrow?

"That's what I thought too, but maybe they decided to move it up a day," Doug replied.

A stir at the front of the room captured everyone's attention as Sheriff Melburn entered the room, glanced up quickly at the group of assembled men, and then turned to see if T.C. Murdock had followed him out of the adjacent office.

T.C. stood directly behind the sheriff, looking pale and drawn, as though he hadn't slept in a week. "Is everyone here?" he asked quietly.

The men turned, looked at one another, and nodded their heads, whispering in hushed tones.

"All right then," T.C. said, with a slight shake of his head. "Might as well get started here." He glanced nervously at the sheriff, who was looking up into the bare rafters of the room.

"Thank you all for coming this morning. I realize that most of you were told that the meeting was to be tomorrow, but due to some unusual circumstances, we've decided to have it this morning. I'm glad to see that everyone made it." He cleared his throat and briefly glanced at the sheaf of papers he held in his hands. He hesitated, as though agonizing over what he had to say to his men. "This past week has been one of the hardest that I personally have ever experienced." He exhaled slowly. "We have suffered a terrible loss here at the mill, and I'm doing my best to keep all of you informed of … of–" He dropped the sentence and allowed his eyes to roam over the familiar faces before him. "Sheriff Melburn has agreed to attend this meeting to answer any questions that may come up."

He looked again at the papers in his hands and rubbed his eyes. He sighed heavily and cleared his throat. "In the course of one week's investigation, it has been discovered that…." He paused and ran his fingers through his hair. "Boy, this is hard," he muttered, more to himself than to his men. "It has been discovered, unfortunately … that our friend Jack Doss was involved in some things that he shouldn't have been."

All eyes were locked on T.C. Murdock's haggard face. It was deathly quiet in the room. No one moved. No one hardly dared to breathe.

"It is with great distress and grief," T.C. continued, "that I must inform all of you that Jack Doss took, without our knowledge, a great deal of the mill's profits and invested them primarily in the Stock Market … for his own gain. It has been discovered by careful and painstaking investigation that some thirty-five to forty thousand dollars have simply disappeared over the past six to eight years. The newspapers in Brighton and Newton have both run the story, which will be out either tomorrow or the day after. I wanted you … the employees of the sawmill, and you … his friends, to know about this from us … rather than reading about it in the papers."

An audible collective gasp ricocheted around the room. Men stared dumbfounded at their foreman, and at one another, unable to grasp the enormity of what was being revealed to them.

"We now understand why Jack chose to end his own life last Tuesday afternoon," T.C. continued. "Records have been discovered that indicate he invested heavily in the Stock Market, and subsequently lost everything. Bear in mind that this took several years to juggle the books and conceal what was being done with the money. The bottom line, gentlemen, is that…." T.C. stopped, looked down at his hands, his eyes shining with unshed tears, and his voice quivering with emotion. "The whole of it," he continued, "is that the mill … is broke. There is no money in the bank like we thought. We're flat busted." He shook his head, backed up a step or two, and dug frantically in his back pocket for his handkerchief.

The men were shocked into absolute silence. Sheriff Melburn finally broke the silence by asking if anyone had any questions.

"Yeah," one fellow near the front said. "What's gonna happen to our jobs?"

"It depends on the market," T.C. said, pocketing his handkerchief. "Whether or not we can stay afloat depends totally on the demand for wood and wood products in the next few months. If the experts in Washington are right, we might be headed into a nationwide recession or worse yet, a total collapse of our economy. If that happens, then I doubt very much if we'll be here by this time next year."

Doug and Max stared at one another. How could this have happened? Jack was such a decent sort of fellow. How could he have led a double life so convincingly … without his closest friends having even an inkling about it?

"Sheriff, is anything being done to help Jack's family?" a man known only as Slim asked.

"That I don't know," the sheriff admitted. "What we can tell you is that all of his assets are at this time frozen. That means that everything he owned outright is being held as possible security until this mess here at the mill is sorted out. An attorney from Brighton is looking into that aspect of it right now. I don't know at this time if Mr. Doss had made provision for his family or not."

"If there are no further questions," T.C. said, "I need to make one more announcement. The mill is closed for the duration of this week. The Sheriff needs access to the office, and I feel that it's best if we're closed for the next couple of days to allow him room to do his job. Plan to be back to work on Monday morning. We'll do our best to have pay for all of you at that time. Meeting is adjourned."

Instead of a buzz of voices, quiet prevailed, and the men filed outside, each with his own thoughts.

Doug and Max retrieved their lunches from the office and headed to the parking lot to their cars.

"Makes no sense, does it?" Max said, as they reached the cars. Doug set his lunch on the seat and leaned his back up against the car door.

"You could knock me over with a feather right about now," he admitted. "I would have sworn on a stack of Bibles that Jack was as honest as the day is long."

"Yep," Max agreed. "I was just thinkin' back on all the times Jack helped me personally over the last few years. When things would get a little tight, or when the wife was sick, and he knew about it, he'd slip me a twenty. That's the kind of guy he was." He shook his head and spit on the ground.

"Or at least, that's the kind of guy we *thought* he was," Doug commented. "Makes you realize that we really don't know folks as well as we think we do."

"Ain't it the truth!" Max said. "I sure thought I knew Jack. Guess I didn't, and neither did anybody else. Wonder if his wife knew anything?"

"Probably not," Doug said. "No one else did, so why should she? Boy, that's got to be rough on her and the kids."

"Yeah," Max agreed. "I wonder if she'll end up losin' the house."

"It's a definite possibility, I guess. I'd sure hate to see her and the kids turned out of their own home." He shook his head again, trying desperately to make some sense of this horrible news.

"Hope we don't end up losin' our jobs over this," Max said with a little irritation in his voice.

"We might lose them since the Stock Market bottomed out, but I doubt that Jack's pilfering will have much to do with our jobs," Doug said reasonably. "Have you thought about what you might do if you lose your job here?" he asked his friend.

Max shook his head slowly. "Can't say that I have," he admitted. "Never thought much about it one way or the other. Guess I'd better start."

"The world has gone absolutely crazy in the last month or so, hasn't it? Look how our lives and the lives of our families have been directly influenced by what's happened just this past week," Doug said, standing on the running board of his car. "Makes me wonder what tomorrow's going to bring."

"Don't even think about it," Max advised. "Things are probably gonna get worse before they get better again."

"Don't know how that would be possible," Doug said, climbing in behind the wheel. "If you hear anything more, drop by the house and let me know and I'll do the same."

Max nodded his head, tossed his lunch in through the open car window and followed Doug out of the parking lot.

Doug realized that he was grinding his teeth on the drive home. How on earth was he going to explain all of this to Lydia? Lydia, who seemed to be making such progress lately toward healing … and now this. She was very upset about Jack's death … how would she take this news? Doug decided the best way to handle it was to first pray about it. He prayed fervently, first for Jack's widow and his children, and then for his own family and their future, and especially his fragile wife. By the time he drove in the driveway, he felt ready to share what he knew.

Ruffy and Benjamin met him in the middle of the driveway. Doug scooped his son up into his arms and hoisted him up on his shoulders, making Benjamin squeal with delight, and Ruffy ran beside him, yipping happily at seeing his master so early in the day.

Lydia was busy making up the beds when Doug appeared in the doorway. She stared up at him for a minute with a startled expression on her face. "What's wrong?" she asked anxiously. "Are you sick?"

"Heart sick," Doug answered. He put Benjamin down and told him to go out and play.

"I wanna play with you, Daddy," Benjamin said. "Come on." He pulled on Doug's arm.

"Not now, son. I need to talk to Mama. Go on outside. I'll be out later."

Benjamin disappeared into the kitchen, and Doug pulled his wife into his arms, burying his face in her hair.

"What is it?" she murmured, knowing that something was terribly wrong. "Why are you home so early?"

"We had a special meeting this morning," Doug said. "Come on out in the living room and sit down, and I'll tell you all about it."

Lydia sat in stunned silence while her husband divulged all that he had learned an hour before. He finished with, "We need to pray hard and ask God to watch over us and keep us in the weeks to come, and we need to remember Rosalyn and her children."

"Where was God when all this was happening?" Lydia demanded suddenly. "Where was God when Jack needed Him? Where is He now that Rosalyn is in such despair? I don't understand any of this, Doug. Where is God right now while our community is falling apart? We pray and nothing … nothing happens … except something terrible. We prayed, and our precious Rebecca died. We prayed, and Grandma Phoebe died right in front of everyone. We prayed, and Jack killed himself. And we're praying now, and poor Rosalyn can't even get over the tragic death of her husband before she finds out he was a crook! We're praying, and she's probably going to lose her house and everything she owns. What about all that, Doug? Answer me that!"

Doug shook his head and rose to his feet, unable to answer his wife's sudden outburst. He had foolishly thought just a few minutes before that she was getting better, but now … now he could see something was festering inside her … ready to boil over at any moment. He walked outside without saying a word to her.

Doug Wheeler needed help. He didn't know what to say anymore, to anyone, least of all his own wife.

"Daddy, can you play with me now?" Benjamin ran up and pulled on his arm. "Please, Daddy?"

"Not now, son. Daddy has to go back into town. I'll be back in just a little while. You keep an eye on Mama for me, will you?"

"But Daddy, I thought you said you'd play with me an' Ruffy. Daddy … wait … you said…."

Benjamin stared at the retreating back of his father until he disappeared inside the garage, backed the car out, and drove down the road toward town.

"Come on, Ruffy," he said sadly, turning back toward the house, his arm around the dog's neck. "Daddy must be mad 'bout something. Come on, boy. I'll play with you."

CHAPTER 25
THE CLEANSING

The shock waves that reverberated over the community of Northridge following the sudden death of Jack Doss were nothing compared to the trauma caused by the screaming headlines of the local newspapers from Brighton and Newton.

After reading the paper on his lunch break, Doug felt sick. The paper was depressing enough with all the devastating economic news, but the article about their troubles at the mill really turned his stomach.

"Look at this," he said to Max, who was seated beside him, enjoying a piece of his wife's homemade apple pie.

Max scanned the headline and shook his head sorrowfully.

"Embezzler Takes Own Life" was emblazoned across the top of the page in bold type.

"Wouldn't you think they'd have a little more respect for his widow and children than to print something like that?"

"Yeah, but I guess respect doesn't sell papers. Scandal is what sells, and something like this is big news."

Doug nodded his agreement. "It's a sad, sick world we live in this day and age." He sighed, folded the paper up and tucked it under his arm.

Max combed the pie crust crumbs out of his mustache with his fingers, and shook his head, a sad expression on his face.

"Have you heard anything about our jobs … how long we'll have 'em?" he asked, a note of apprehension in his voice.

"Not a word," Doug said. "But that's something I've been meaning to talk to you about. What do you think about the idea of you and me going into the wood cutting business if the mill closes?"

Max didn't answer right away, but sat quietly, allowing the idea to formulate in his mind. "Not a bad idea," he finally responded. "I'll give it some thought."

"Just an idea," Doug said. "People still need wood to burn no matter what the rest of the job market looks like. We won't get rich at it, but at least we won't starve either."

Max nodded in agreement. "Something to think about all right," he said. "Right now, we'd better get back to makin' lumber."

Lydia had the entire morning to herself. Benjamin had begged, pleaded, and pestered her to allow him to visit school to the point that she was sure she was losing her mind. A note sent home from Mrs. Richardson gave her the outlet she so desperately needed. On Friday, the note said, school would be dismissed at noon due to a school board meeting. All children would be dismissed at that time.

Lydia decided that Friday would be a good day to allow Benjamin the desires of his heart. She called him in out of the yard Thursday afternoon after Aaron had come home from school.

"Benjamin, how would you like to go to school with Aaron tomorrow?" she asked, a twinkle in her eyes.

Benjamin's big brown eyes widened with excitement. "Woohooo!" he howled. "Oh, yes, yes, yes! Thank you, Mama, thank you!" He hugged her legs tightly and then ran to his bedroom. "I'm gonna go get ready right now!"

"Hold on a minute," his mother laughed. "You've got plenty of time to get ready. Right now, I want you and Aaron to bring in the wood and change Ruffy's water and feed him."

Benjamin's face fell into a frown. "But Mama, I need to get ready. I sure don't wanna be late!"

Aaron rolled his eyes. "You're not gonna be late, dummy," he said scornfully. "We have to go to bed tonight first."

"Aaron's right, Benjamin," Lydia said. "And Aaron, your brother is *not* a dummy, and I don't want you calling him names anymore. Now ... both of you please go do as you're told."

Benjamin fairly flew out the door and raced over to Ruffy, giving him a bear hug. "I'm goin' to school tomorrow, Ruffy!" he exclaimed. "Maybe next time, you can come too!"

The dog jumped up, feeling something exciting in the air, and raced down to the garage with the boys, happily yipping while they loaded the wagon with wood.

Now, the house was finally quiet. Benjamin had nearly driven them all crazy in his frenzy to get ready, but at last, peace and quiet prevailed. Lydia could do as she pleased this morning. She celebrated by having a luxurious peaceful daydream at the kitchen table with her third cup of coffee. Then she decided it would be a good time to make a list of things she needed to do before Thanksgiving. Her parents were coming again for the holiday, and she wanted everything to be perfect. She made another list of the groceries she would need in order to prepare the meal. She sat lost in thought when Ruffy suddenly started barking. She could tell from his bark that something unusual was happening outside.

Oh, no! she thought. Now what? She looked out the kitchen window and watched with dismay, if not anger, as a dark green car pulled into the driveway. Who on earth was that?

"Ruffy!" Lydia yelled. "Get back here, right now!" The dog reluctantly obeyed, ambled back to the house, and flopped down beside his doghouse under the now, nearly bare willow.

Lydia stood in the doorway, shading her eyes against the early morning sun, and was stunned to see Rosalyn Doss emerge from the car. She quickly smoothed her flyaway hair and snatched her worn apron off, tossing it in the corner on top of her rag bag.

She glanced quickly around the kitchen and living room and noted with dismay how cluttered the rooms were with the boys' books and toys.

"Rosalyn!" she called, holding the door open. "What a pleasant surprise!"

"I hope you don't mind me dropping in unannounced," the woman apologized. Her expensive perfume permeated the kitchen as she entered, making Lydia feel like a rag doll again.

Lydia was suddenly very uneasy in the presence of this woman. What on earth was she coming to see her about?

"You'll have to excuse my house," she mumbled. I'll bet there's never a single thing out of place in *her* house, she thought.

She took Rosalyn's beautiful black coat with the fur trim and carefully placed it over the back of a chair. "Please, come on in the living room and sit down. Would you like a cup of coffee?"

"I'd love one," Rosalyn said, flashing her a bright smile.

Lydia hurried back into the kitchen, grabbed her best china cups and poured the coffee. How on earth could this woman, who had suffered so much the past two weeks, be so happy? With shaking hands, Lydia served the coffee, added more wood to the fire, and then sat down across from her guest.

"I hope I'm not keeping you from anything," Rosalyn said, glancing around the room. "Are both your boys in school?"

Lydia shook her head and swallowed a sip of coffee. "No, Benjamin is just visiting school today. They're on a half-day schedule today, and he's been begging to go to school with his brother, so I decided today was a good day for that. I was just sitting at the table when you came, making out a list of things I needed from Deacon for Thanksgiving dinner." The instant it was out of her mouth, Lydia could have died. Why did I *have* to say that? "I'm sorry, Rosalyn, I shouldn't have said that," she said with embarrassment.

"Why not?" Rosalyn asked. "Everyone needs to prepare for Thanksgiving dinner. My goodness, there's nothing wrong with that, and there's certainly no need to apologize." She flashed another one of those perfect smiles at Lydia.

"My folks are coming for a few days, more to see the boys, I'm sure, and it'll be so nice to have them again," Lydia said, feeling that she must explain herself in some way.

"That's so nice," Rosalyn said. "It's wonderful to have family close enough that you can be with them for the holidays. That's what makes the holidays so much fun."

"How … how are your children doing?" Lydia asked hesitantly.

Rosalyn sighed and dropped her hands in her lap. "Not too well, I'm afraid. This has really been hard on them. And that brings me to the real reason why I came this morning. I came to thank you for being such a good friend to me. I've always enjoyed talking with you when we'd meet in town at the store, or at church. I cherish those times and I … well, I really came to say goodbye to those who are really special to me."

Lydia couldn't help but stare at the woman. She was *special* to Rosalyn? She gulped a mouthful of hot coffee and set her cup down with a clatter in the saucer. "Good-bye?" was all she could manage to say.

Rosalyn nodded her head. "Yes, I'm afraid that the children and I are being forced to move, and perhaps it is for the best. Everything must go … the house, the cars, and the furniture. We're allowed to keep our clothes and personal effects, but that's about it." She smiled a sad smile. "My children are my biggest concern right now though. They're the ones who are suffering the most. They've really had a hard go of it since their father died." She sighed again, and for the first time, Lydia saw the stress and grief in her eyes.

"I'm so terribly sorry," she said softly. "Where will you go?"

Rosalyn thought for a minute, as if trying to decide whether or not to answer the question. A rather resigned looking smile crossed her face. "I have a dear aunt and uncle near Newton who have invited the children and me to share their home until I can get on my feet. I'll have to find a job, which won't be easy at my age, but there again, maybe it's for the best. Christina and Jeremy aren't looking forward to starting another school, but I've told them that they shouldn't fight change. Sometimes change can be a good thing."

"I suppose that's true, but I understand how they feel," Lydia said, feeling terribly shallow and immature next to this woman. "May I ask you something, Rosalyn?" she asked suddenly.

"By all means … anything you want."

"How do you keep smiling in the face of all you've been through the past two or three weeks?"

In answer, Rosalyn smiled. "I have to admit, Lydia, it hasn't been easy. I was devastated to learn of Jack's death, and then to find out with the rest of the town what he had been up to all these years. I must admit that my pride took a real beating, and I would have folded completely had I not known the Lord … personally. He makes all the difference. Without Him, I'd be dead."

Lydia nodded her understanding but said nothing.

"How are you doing, Lydia?" Rosalyn asked, turning the question back on her hostess. "Are things getting a little easier for you? You know," she continued, without waiting for Lydia to answer, "I've prayed for you every single day since your baby died."

"You have?" Lydia asked, astonished. "Why … thank you."

"It's been a real privilege," Rosalyn said. "I can't imagine what it must be like to lose one of your children, and my heart nearly broke for you and Doug when I heard of your loss. So I decided since there was nothing I could do to help make things better for you, that I'd lift you up in prayer every day, and that's what I've done, and I'll continue to do so." She smiled again.

To Lydia's dismay, she realized her face was wet with silent tears. She pressed her eyes tightly with her palms and laughed nervously. "I don't think I'll ever quit crying," she admitted. "The pain is better, but it's still there."

"Of course it is," Rosalyn agreed. "Pain like that doesn't evaporate overnight. I just wondered how you were getting along, that's all. And don't ever be ashamed of your tears. In fact, I think God gave us tears as a cleansing agent. We need to remember that Jesus wept when He was grieved, and if it was all right for Him, it's all right for us."

Lydia nodded her head. "I'm doing much better, thank you," she said. "And I'm going to start praying for you every day too. I should have been all along."

"Thank you so much. I need prayer. This has really been a terrible blow to me. I … I loved my husband very much. Well…." she said suddenly, jumping up from her chair, "I've taken up enough of your time and I must be on my way. Please do look me up if you're ever in Newton. My aunt and uncle are Ted and Emma Jean Hoff. Aunt Emma Jean is my mother's sister," she said by way of explanation. "She's a wonderful lady, and I love her dearly. Take care of yourself, Lydia, keep praying, and keep looking up. Our dear Lord knows all about suffering. Remember that!"

Rosalyn collected her coat, hugged Lydia, and was gone. Lydia stood in the middle of her kitchen feeling shame, guilt, and humility all at the same time. Here's a woman, she thought, who has suffered a far greater loss than I have … and she's smiling. She obviously loved her husband, and it must hurt terribly to see her children in such unspeakable pain … her entire life is upside down and she's smiling. Keep looking up and praying, she had said. Our Lord knows all about suffering. I haven't been praying on a regular basis for anyone, and she's been praying for *me* every day!

Guilt crashed down on her, right where she stood, and she felt she could no longer stand under the weight of such crushing shame. Right there in her kitchen, Lydia Wheeler sank to her knees and poured her heart out to the Lord, asking His forgiveness for her unbelief, for her shameful behavior, and for her lack of faith.

"Give me strength, Lord, and a peace about losing my baby. And Lord," she continued, "I pray for Rosalyn. Forgive my jealously of her. Help her, Lord, as she's forced to move away from all that's familiar to her. Help her and her children in the days to come. Help her to heal from the terrible blow of losing Jack. Thank you, Lord, for loving me even when I wasn't lovable. Amen."

Later on, Lydia couldn't recall how long she stayed on her knees, but that's where Aaron and Benjamin found her when they came home from school. Her eyes were red-rimmed and swollen and she was so stiff, they had to help her to her feet.

"Mama, are you all right?" Aaron had cried in alarm.

"Yes, son, I've never been better," she replied, hugging both boys tightly to herself. "Mama's never been better," she repeated, smiling at them through her tears. She blew her nose, tied her apron around her waist, and whispered a prayer of thanksgiving.

Lydia Wheeler was finally beginning to heal.

~~~
~~~